M000297130

IN AXMINSTER
WORKHOUSE

Holiday Standalones

The Christmas Knife

Hot Chocolate Kisses

The Little Matchboy

Standalone

The Duke of Hand to Heart

IN AXMINSTER WORKHOUSE

A Gay M/M Historical Romance

JACKIE NORTH

Jackie North

MM Romance Author

This book is dedicated to...

Oliver and Jack
--My Dickensian OTP

N.J. Nidiffer
--Forever remembered

And to all those orphans out there
--You know who you are

"Heaven knows we need never be ashamed of our tears, for they are rain upon the blinding dust of earth, overlying our hard hearts. I was better after I had cried, than before—more sorry, more aware of my own ingratitude, more gentle."
--*GREAT EXPECTATIONS BY* CHARLES DICKENS

"The sea is the graveyard of the Chateau d'If."
--*THE COUNT OF MONTE CRISTO BY ALEXANDRE DUMAS*

CONTENTS

1. It Was The Worst Of Times   1
2. Wherein Is Shown The Constancy Of Workhouses   17
3. Becoming Acquainted With Stones and Bones   35
4. Comprising Further Particulars Of Axminster Workhouse   49
5. Temptation Beneath Rainy Skies   59
6. Relates The Interview In Master Pickering's Office   73
7. Oliver Continues Refractory   93
8. In Which They Pick Oakum   105
9. When Afternoon Grows Black And Deep   119
10. Becoming Acquainted With A Workhouse Kitchen   131
11. Senseless Wrath, Senseless Cruelty   145
12. Diversions In The Dark, Or Distracting Oliver From The Truth   159
13. Saying Yes But Not Saying Why   167
14. An Afternoon To Regret   189
15. Considerations Made Over Workhouse Gruel   197
16. The Battle In The Dining Hall   213
17. After Being Rescued From Refractory   233
18. Containing Revelations Of The Darkest Sort   253
19. When The Bough Breaks   267
20. In Which Bargains Made Become Revealed   283
21. Crossing The River Styx   291
22. Oliver's Orders Must Be Followed   299
23. Traveling On Horseback With Jack   317
24. Taking Milk At Sunset   333
25. The Ring Of Bells   353
26. Becoming Posh Gentlemen   397
27. The Swan In Winterbourne   417

28. Jack Is Cared For   437
29. Supper At The Swan And What Happened After   449
30. Destination: Hale   475

Jackie's Newsletter   481
Author's Notes About the Story   483
A Letter From Jackie   485
About the Author   487

❧ I ☙

IT WAS THE WORST OF TIMES

The road to Axminster rose and fell, and the cart went with it, as though it was on the crest of a wave. As the cart passed through a gathering of trees, Oliver saw a faraway steeple amidst the shatters of rain, and heard the dull clang of a church bell. The odor of the town, of animals and manure, of cooking and of coal fires, became apparent long before the appearance of cottages and sheds and houses. The town seemed to rise on the hillside in a brick-speckled blanket, and as the cart clattered down a lane shouldered by trees and garden walls, Oliver tried to catch his breath.

The rain was stopping as they turned with the curve of the road, and went down a narrow lane, where the cart stopped in front of a gate. One of the constables got down to unlatch the gate, and as the cart pulled through, for a moment, Oliver could only stare, for he'd never seen a workhouse so new. The stones of the square walls were pale gray, rather than being drenched in coal dust. The caps on the tops of the walls were a paler gray, almost white, and the spikes that lined the walls were painted bright blue, and stood out against the hazy, rain-speckled sky. All of the windows looked like wide-open eyes bound with brown trim.

As the cart pulled up in front of a large double door with new brass hinges, one of the constables jumped out and knocked for the porter. He came and unlocked Oliver's and Jack's leg cuffs from the brackets in the floor of the cart, and it was then Oliver realized they were meant to get down from the cart and go into the workhouse.

This he could not do.

The brown door to the workhouse opened and out stepped the porter, a dapper man in a dove gray coat, with a hat that had a brass tag upon which the word *Porter* was stamped.

"Did you bring the rain with you, gentlemen?" asked the porter.

"Never you mind your jocularity," said the constable in the cart. He tied the reins to the peg by the brake and jumped out to stand next to his companion. "These two are accused of theft, only our magistrate is on circuit, so we need you to keep them until the next quarter session in June."

"Will they be trouble?" The porter looked at Oliver and then at Jack.

"I reckon they will," said the constable, who had knocked on the door. "That one has already swung at me with his fist more than once."

It seemed obvious to Oliver that while the constable meant Oliver, the porter was looking at Jack. The porter came over to the cart and dragged Jack out by his shirt collar. He called for someone through the open doorway, and gave Jack a shake.

"You'll be minding your manners, or I'll have something to say about it."

Then he turned to Oliver.

"And you'll be getting out; now, mind me."

But Oliver couldn't move. All he could hear was the pounding in his ears, as though he'd brought the roar of the ocean with him. The salt scent was missing, though, and in its place was a stench from long ago. The slippery mud on stones beneath a workhouse pump. The slice of Mr. Bumble's cane as he shoved Oliver's head beneath the ice-cold water until his whole body was soaked and turning blue. The hours of black air in the dark room, the separation from anybody he knew. And the inevitable scouring of his whole body with stinging lye soap before he was returned to the oakum-picking room.

There was an oakum-picking room inside of this place. Harsh brushes and lye soap. Food that wasn't fit to feed a pig. A dark room. All nightmares he thought he'd left behind long ago now hove to before him, a giant, gray-stoned beast set to devour him.

If he went through that door, he would never come out.

"Nolly."

Jack's voice.

Oliver flicked his eyes that way, and saw the edge of Jack's face, which was blanked out all too quickly as someone grabbed Oliver and pulled him out of the cart. He could barely find his footing, could not seem to focus on the voice that was speaking to him. It was a cross voice, and it wanted something from him. Something Oliver had no idea how to give him.

He felt the blow to the head and held his breath as he was dragged across the threshold. In the hallway, voices clanged and footsteps echoed, and he had to scramble or be trampled.

The voices stopped, and the footsteps, and Jack was suddenly beside him, pressing close so they were shoulder to shoulder. He caught Jack's scent, the sweet oil from his hair, the almost-faded funk of tavern smoke and beer. Half closing his eyes, he took a breath and tried to focus.

The porter was right there, knocking on a broad, polished door.

"You're lucky Master Pickering is in today, or I'd have a job of it doing the paperwork on you."

"Enter," said a voice from beyond the door.

The porter turned the brass knob and swung it open to reveal an office with a highly polished floor, and a sense of strict orderliness about the bookshelves and on the desktop. Behind the desk sat an older man, well groomed in his spectacles and beard, and wearing a fine dark suit.

"Good day, Master Pickering," said the porter to the man behind the desk.

"Good day, Porter. What do you have there? Have they been processed?"

"I would sir, only these two are to be held for the quarter session in June, so they need your signature."

"Very well; I'll call for you when they are ready for the rest of their processing. By the way, did you see Workmaster Chalenheim?"

"He was just here, sir. Shall I send for him?"

"No, never mind. These two look older than sixteen, so I'll probably put them in with the men."

"Very good, sir."

The porter nodded, tipped his hat, and left the room, closing the broad door behind him.

The room was so very ordinary, with nothing remarkable about it, save that the sight of it had Oliver's thighs quivering to hold him upright. He and Jack were both still in wrist cuffs, and every time they shifted, the cuffs clinked and the chains between them rattled. And still the Master wrote on in his day book, something that so absorbed him that he did not even raise his head to acknowledge there were two young men in his office.

Finally, he tapped his pen, wiped it on the blotter on his desk, and laid the pen in the tray. He raised his head and took off his glasses to look at them.

"To be kept for quarter sessions, I see," he said. "I'm Master Pickering, and I'll be getting the official report soon enough for the details, so you might as well tell me whether or not you're going to be any trouble while you're here."

Oliver did not quite know what to say, as trouble seemed to follow him wherever he went. But in spite of that, he knew he had to speak up, for if the Master sent to London for any information attached to their names, he might receive information about Oliver for which he was completely unprepared. As well, an ex-convict such as Jack would surely be sent back to Australia, even for the theft of a few books.

Oliver was about to speak when he heard Jack take a breath.

"No, sir," said Jack. "It was all a misunderstandin' anyhow."

"Did I ask you for an explanation? No, I did not. Now, give me your names and I'll write them in the book."

Oliver cautioned a look at Jack; surely Jack knew that any sass and attitude would be harshly dealt with? Or maybe, since this wasn't a convict prison on a faraway shore, Jack might think the workhouse a gentle place. At the very least, they couldn't give false names; the constable's report from Mrs. Heyland would have proven them wrong almost immediately.

"Oliver Twist, sir," said Oliver. His voice came out thin and reedy, as though he were again nine and standing before the board at the Hardingstone Workhouse.

He wanted to nudge Jack to do the same, but that sort of motion would only attract the Master's attention, and in the wrong way. So he tipped his head at Jack, and then at the Master, who was busy writing down Oliver's name in the day book. With raised eyebrows, Jack nodded.

"Jack Dawkins, sir," Jack said, with the slightest bit of mockery that Oliver hoped that only he could hear.

When the Master finished writing, he tapped his pen and looked up.

"You are to be kept at this workhouse until the quarter sessions, which are less than two months hence. Though you are not here on charity, you will follow all the rules of this workhouse, and do anything instructed of you without question, is that clear?"

"Yes, sir," said Oliver.

Jack's mouth was moving in time with the words, but Olivier realized that there was no sound coming out. He needed to talk to Jack, to tell him that this was no jolly game, where they would have even the slightest chance of coming out on top. The front door to the workhouse was locked and only the porter had the key; there was no way out.

~

IT WAS BEYOND JACK TO UNDERSTAND WHY NOLLY LOOKED AS though he would rather take an arrow to his heart than follow the porter out of the office and down the hallway. Or why he'd always given workhouses a wide berth whenever Jack would follow him through the streets of London. They were just buildings, and far less severe than any jail Jack had ever been in, to wit, Newgate.

He didn't reckon the *Bertha May* had counted as a jail, for all there was no way to leave her when she was at sea. And Port Jackson, while it had been a jail, had been warm, at least, and there had been no walls. In particular, since this was just a workhouse, it would probably prove terribly easy to break out of.

But he couldn't tell any of this to Nolly, not while they were being led down a passage and Nolly refused to catch his eye. Though Jack did try, Nolly kept his head lowered, his eyes about two feet in front of him.

He acted like nobody was near, not even Jack. But they were not alone, for beyond the passage, where wooden floors turned into stone, Jack could hear people walking, marching, almost, and the smell of boiled food. A shout, something banging.

The porter turned into a room that looked wide enough to house several people, should they be inclined to sleep on the stone benches that lined the wall, or in one of the two metal tubs in the middle of the room. There were wooden shelves stacked high with clothes, all dark brown and gray, rolls of stockings. Folded jackets.

The porter stopped next to one of the tables.

"Mr. Bassler will be coming, and you're not to give him any trouble, do you hear? We have a refractory room, same as every other workhouse."

Since Nolly didn't say anything, Jack wouldn't either, although he imagined the proper thing to do would be to say *yes, sir,* and *no, sir,* the way Nolly always did. All smooth and polite, the way proper folk lied to each other when they pretended the manners didn't cover something more vicious and hateful.

Jack barely had time to look at the lock on the door, only to note that it was sturdy and new, before Mr. Bassler arrived, bidding a silent goodbye to the porter as he left.

Mr. Bassler was balding, with dark strings of hair across his pate, and wore rolled-up sleeves beneath a long, dun-colored apron over his hefty belly. He carried a wooden box with a handle on it.

The box contained items that, at first, Jack couldn't figure out what they were for. Then the door opened again, and two men dressed like Mr. Bassler came in carrying large buckets of not-quite steaming water, and then Jack knew.

"Say there, gents," said Jack, backing up. "I'm sure my friend an' I here can handle a bath on our own. So what d'you say? We'll have a wash an' let you know when we're done so you c'n show us to our rooms."

Without a pause, Mr. Bassler put down his wooden box, strode over to Jack, and slapped him across the face. It wasn't a hard blow, more of the type to be a warning, and indeed Mr. Bassler opened his mouth to state that warning, the one Jack would be sure to attend to, now that one side of his face was quite warm. Only Nolly charged into action, lunging at Jack's abuser, his teeth bared, and Jack knew that things were going to become violent quite quickly.

"You're not to touch him," said Nolly, low and fierce, his chin jutted, standing between Jack and Mr. Bassler, as if the world was his to save and Jack his to rescue. As if they weren't behind several locked doors with no way out, for even if Nolly could get Mr. Bassler to stand down, there was no guarantee that someone else might not take objection to Nolly's flash-paper temper.

Before Jack could open his mouth to tender some advice

about their untenable situation, one of the water bearers put down the bucket and grabbed Nolly from behind, a headlock Jack had seen Bill Sikes perform once or twice, hundreds of times, actually, pinning Nolly to him so tightly that even though Nolly kicked and squirmed, he was held fast.

"He only just—" began Jack, but Mr. Bassler held up his hand.

"Be quiet, you," he said to Jack. He pointed at Nolly. "You're not here on *charity*, need I remind you. You're being held till you can be tried and convicted for theft. And that means you need to follow the rules, and there are consequences for breaking them. Do you understand?"

Jack almost held his breath, for everybody in the room could see how it might go one way or the other. Only Nolly was blind to this, was fighting against the traces that Jack couldn't even see. Nolly kicked backwards into the water bearer's shin, who let go of Nolly with a curse, but the other man, taller and stronger than the first, took Nolly up, as if he were no more troublesome than a package.

Mr. Bassler shook his head. "You've a way with keeping things calm, Workmaster Chalenheim, and I thank you for it."

"'Tis no matter," said Chalenheim with a nod, accepting the thanks, tightening his arm around Nolly's neck. "I live to serve."

Mr. Bassler turned to Jack. "Your mate here thinks to be making trouble; am I to expect the same from you?"

"No," said Jack. "Why no, *indeed*. Why would I do that? Why would I even think it?"

"You've got a saucy mouth on you," said Workmaster Chalenheim. "But what can you expect from a city boy."

As to how Chalenheim was able to figure out that Jack was not a country boy, Jack could not determine, for the workmaster seemed to be only looking at Mr. Bassler, waiting for his next orders.

"I believe I can take it from here," said Mr. Bassler. "But you'll be on hand, won't you, Workmaster, if I need you?"

"Yes, indeed," said Chalenheim. Giving Nolly a shake, he bent his head so his mouth was directly upon Nolly's ear. "You'll behave, now won't you, lad? You'd better, for I've got other duties to tend to this evening, lest you trouble Mr. Bassler, and I need to return to this room. I won't, will I?"

When Nolly didn't answer, preferring to snarl and tug on Chalenheim's arm, making Jack's eyebrows rise, Chalenheim twitched, pulling Nolly's head back till he could hardly be getting any air. "Will I?" asked Chalenheim.

"Mister," said Jack. "Say, mister, will you stop? He can't breathe—"

He was about to stride forward to do some rescuing of his own, when Chalenheim let Nolly go and, ignoring Nolly's gasps for air, poured the water from the two of the buckets into one of the tubs. When this was done, he and the other man walked out of the room with the buckets, closing the door behind them. Leaving them with Mr. Bassler who, by himself, might not appear to be much of a threat. Still, he evidently had some muscle at his beck and call, and was powerful enough that Jack did not want to test him again.

Besides, there were other ways, there *had* to be, to find a way through the workhouse and to the outside. The only trick was finding the right door and the right key. Which they could do if only Nolly would stop glaring and fighting it. Whatever would happen would happen, and if they could just slip beneath it—

"I'll be cutting your hair first," said Mr. Bassler, as he pulled a chair away from the wall and into the center of the room. "Checking for head lice, and then you'll be having a wash, and I'll check for body lice. Then you're to go into the men's ward, where you'll be assigned a bed. In the morning, you'll be assigned duties. Any deviation from that plan, and I'll be calling someone with a more able arm than mine to remind you of your situation. So." Mr. Bassler leaned down to pull shears out of the wooden box; he snipped them and pointed at the chair alongside one of the tubs. "Any questions?"

"No," said Jack, leaving off any attempt at being polite by saying *yes, sir.* "No questions, I have no questions. As I am sure No—" But then he stopped. He didn't want them using his pet name for Nolly. "Oliver's got no questions neither, do you, Oliver."

In a moment, Nolly was going to strike out again; he held his jaw taut as he looked at Mr. Bassler, at the room, at the closed door, beyond which could be heard a great number of sounds Jack couldn't identify. But though Nolly looked as though he could identify them, he shook his head, and stood there, shivering. Jack wanted to give him a kind word, any kind word, to soothe him, to let him know that they'd be out of the workhouse's reach just as soon as Jack could arrange it, and he would, quick as might be.

"You first, then," said Mr. Bassler as he pointed his shears at Jack.

Jack shrugged. A haircut was nothing to him, and the bath wouldn't be either. He would show Nolly how it was done, how to act like it didn't matter, how to go along to get along so that those in charge would lose their wary watch upon them and they would be able to make an escape. It was always easier to make a show of being obedient without actually *being* obedient, a talent that Nolly did not seem to possess. But Jack did.

As he sat in the chair, he jerked his chin at Nolly to keep his spirits up, to let him know that Jack was here, and all would be well. But Nolly looked away, and ground his teeth as Mr. Bassler, with hard, poking fingers, positioned Jack's head, scrubbing his fingers through Jack's hair to search for lice. Then he tipped Jack's head where he wanted it and began to cut Jack's hair.

The shears were sharp, snip-snipping around his ears, sending dark locks to fall on his lap, on the stone floor. At one point, the shears came too close to his scalp, and Jack jerked back and felt a warm tickle slide down behind his ear.

When Mr. Bassler was finished, he pushed Jack to a standing position, and Jack ran his hands over his head. The hair was short, and probably sticking out in a comical way, but it would grow back, so he could bear it till then, till it was long enough for Nolly to run his fingers through it, like he did, sometimes.

"You now," said Mr. Bassler, pointing at Nolly with the shears, which still had some of Jack's dark hair sticking to it. "Do not make me call Workmaster Chalenheim in here, for he does not like to be disturbed during his evening duties."

For a moment, it looked as though Nolly was going to refuse, and Jack would have to witness him being abused all over again.

"Oliver," he said.

He thought to say more, but when Nolly looked at him, there was such a dark hate in his eyes, not for Jack, but for their situation, that Jack couldn't bear to speak words of advice about being obedient, let alone words of encouragement. The most he could do was to give his head a little shake that Nolly should stand down, that now was not the time. Later there would be time, and opportunity. And freedom.

He was surprised when Nolly gave him a small nod and sat in the chair and let Mr. Bassler prod his head and turn it this way and that, looking for head lice. Not finding any, apparently, he began to cut Nolly's hair in an untidy way, close in the back, the forelock, golden and lovely, sheared off too short upon his forehead, giving him the look, if you couldn't see his eyes, of an imbecile. But, Jack supposed, that was the point. Anybody finding him would no doubt question why such a fellow was at large and would be at pains to return him to the nearest workhouse. This workhouse.

"You," said Mr. Bassler. "Take off them clothes and get into the tub."

Jack didn't hesitate, truly hadn't even considered it, but Mr. Bassler gave him a feint with the shears, leaning over Nolly's head, and there was a good moment when Jack was sure that Nolly would grab those shears and slice through Mr. Bassler's neck with them. So Jack hurried and scrambled to undo his laces, and tear off his jacket and trousers, and his shirt and the scrap of his undergarment, till he was standing naked upon the stones and shivering harder than he could bear to have anybody see.

"Get in, soak all over, even your head, then stand up. Do it now."

Jack did it, concentrating on his task rather than the expression on Nolly's face, which indicated he would do someone great harm, and quite soon, if he could manage it. Jack needed to get through this and get Nolly through it, so that nobody got hurt, and so when they escaped from the workhouse, which they would, no one would be after them for murder. *Again.*

He stepped into the cold tin tub, which was somehow mounted into the floor, and sank to the bottom of it. The barely warm water wasn't terribly deep, but he dipped his head back and got himself wet all over. Then he scrambled to his feet, dripping, the water only coming up not even as far as his knees.

Mr. Bassler grabbed a brush and some soap from his wooden box, and, dipping both in the tub at Jack's ankles, began to scrub his bare skin. The tub felt icy beneath his feet, and the water was cool across his ankles. The soap stung, biting into places where the skin was thin, and the brush added to this, almost burning where the rash was along his left side, his left leg.

"What's this, then?" asked Mr. Bassler, giving the rash a good, strong swipe with the brush.

"Don't know, mister," said Jack. He hissed through his teeth as Mr. Bassler took another dab at the rash. "It goes away, come spring," he said. This was a lie, as he'd gotten the rash aboard the ship that had brought him back to England, from the disinfectant lye being applied too liberally before he'd been released. But that explanation would involve including details about why and how he'd been returned to England, and why he'd been deported in the first place, information Jack wanted to keep to himself just now. Forever if he could, especially with Nolly sitting in the chair, glaring, watching. "'Tis just a rash."

Mr. Bassler finished the scrub, using the brush a great deal too liberally in places where Jack considered that he oughtn't to have, between his legs, the inside of his thighs, where such a hard brush had no place being. Then, satisfied, Mr. Bassler took up a bucket of water that completely lacked the rising steam that would indicate that it was the least bit warm. It was cold as Mr. Bassler poured it over Jack, rinsing his hair, his shoulders, which at least got the soap off him, though the rash was still stinging and would itch later, Jack knew.

"Get out, you," said Mr. Bassler. "There're clothes for your size over there, on the shelf. Get dressed; use your own boots, but leave your clothes. They'll be sanitized and ticketed."

Jack could not have moved faster if he tried, for he wanted to be out of range when Nolly was called upon to repeat Jack's obedient behavior. He pulled down a pair of trousers that looked as though they might fit, and the rest of his kit, all in workhouse brown and gray.

As he looked over his shoulder, he was wary for any explosion, any burst of feeling that would transpose a tame transfer of themselves into the workhouse's world to a battle where both of them would lose. Would but Nolly could see that and it would go easier for them, though Jack had yet to observe Nolly taking the easiest route to anything.

He was a little surprised to discover that Nolly was as submissive in the tub as he'd been in the chair, soaking himself quickly before standing straight up, his shoulders back, as if being in a state of nature with a man destined to do him harm with a stiff brush and harsh soap were completely beneath his notice.

Jack couldn't see Nolly's face, but those clenched fists against Nolly's thighs told their own story. As did the shiver that ran down Nolly's back as Mr. Bassler raked the brush before and behind without much notice that he was leaving dark pink scratches along tender skin. When Mr. Bassler dumped the final bucket of water over Nolly's head, Jack let out a whoosh of air that caused Mr. Bassler to look over at him.

"Your friend here is a better inmate than you already, I can see that," said Mr. Bassler. "Now you, Oliver, get out, get dressed, and I'll take you to the men's dormitory, where you'll be sleeping."

Again, Nolly did as he was told, putting on the collarless, gray-striped shirt, and the dirt-brown jacket and trousers, but slowly, as if he were putting on a skin he'd long ago shed.

Jack found himself moving close, his hands raised, his whole body expecting that Nolly would lash out and Mr. Bassler would be forced to call someone to his aid. Jack didn't think he could bear watching Nolly get such a chokehold on him he would be unable to breathe, though Nolly's whole posture, head up, shoulders straight, signaled to Jack that Nolly could jump either direction.

It was when Mr. Bassler moved to open the door that Jack got a close-up look at Nolly's expression, and it made him draw a sharp breath. Nolly's eyes were glittering and narrowed, which meant it would take one twitch from Mr. Bassler, one more indignity, however slight, to tip Nolly into the ferocity that tightened his mouth that way, his fists clenching and unclenching.

Jack moved in, close to those hands, that temper, which could do so much damage, though never to him. He reached out and touched Nolly on the sleeve, the dark brown wool rough beneath his fingers.

"Nolly," he said in a whisper, wishing with all of his heart that there was something else he could do, in this moment, before they went through that door.

But there wasn't. Nolly shook his head, as though disagreeing with the entirety of what Jack represented to him, in that moment, and Jack felt very disappointed with himself for not doing better by Nolly.

"Come along, then, don't dawdle," said Mr. Bassler, while he was scratching something on a slate that had been hung on the wall next to the door. It had to do with supplies and schedules, Jack could see, and how to keep the workhouse on target with the appropriate number of outfits for the poor paupers trapped within its walls.

They stepped out into the passage. Jack cast his eyes about, trying to take in everything, where the main door was, where the windows were, which way they were headed, all the while trying to look as though he were not doing this very thing. All the while trying to walk shoulder to shoulder with Nolly, who was staring straight ahead and walking stiff-legged, as though marching directly to something more dire than the processing room from which they had come. But what could be more dire than that?

Depending on his mood, Fagin had gone on about work-houses as pits of despair some days, a well of laziness other days. Workhouses were filled with the aged and infirm, and all they had to do was sit about and get fed three times a day. Sometimes the paupers were called upon to do a little light work, but they had a soft life compared to anybody who had to hustle each day for a meal.

Jack had gotten the idea, as anybody would, that workhouses were more like a rest stop between jobs. If you didn't have a job, you went there, and when you got one, you left. And that was it. The only thing was, Nolly's expression, his lack of words to Jack, was giving Jack some pause that this might not be the case.

They walked along the passage that bent to the right, at the end of which was a set of stone steps leading upward. From the top of the landing came the sound of feet being scraped along the floor, and that of metal clanking, tinny, high sounds, and low, echoing ones. And the smell of something boiled, of old steam, and sweat.

WHEREIN IS SHOWN THE
CONSTANCY OF WORKHOUSES

"Up you come, then, boys," said Mr. Bassler, leading the way, grunting with each step upward. "I'd have sent for someone to take you, but they're all busy with supper for the inmates just now, so the task is mine."

Jack didn't know what to say to this, so he followed Mr. Bassler up the stairs, which dipped into a dark gloom, as there were no windows or sconces with candles, only the light from above, sifting down like a draped fog, and from below, through the rain-spattered windows beside the very-much-locked front door.

With Nolly at his side, Jack could manage this, but though Nolly was there, walking just as Jack walked, he seemed focused on something quite distant from what was directly going on. Jack wanted to talk to him, and to get him to answer, to say something, but they'd arrived on the landing.

The room before them was laid out with long tables beneath a high, gray ceiling. Men, dressed in brown with gray-striped shirts, much as Jack and Nolly wore, stood in a line with crockery bowls in their hands and metal spoons, single-mindedly watching while they waited to be served, or were served.

Jack couldn't see what the men were being given exactly, but it was pale and white and thin as it slopped from the curved-shaped serving ladle into each bowl. The measurement was standard; each man received the same portion. No bread was handed out, so there was nothing else but what was in those bowls.

Jack's stomach shifted at the thought of it. He couldn't imagine what Nolly's stomach was doing, though this, though Nolly's silence, his angry attitude, now made more sense. If a single ladle of white-flavored slop were what grown men were served? The male paupers would soon starve, all of them. They looked starved now, their faces slack, their eyes deep within their faces, as if being sucked inward by their own hunger.

Jack looked at Nolly and shook his head, just slightly. He didn't know whether Nolly would understand him, that he wasn't disagreeing with Nolly's attitude at all. He was simply disbelieving the sight that lay before them both. The line of men, no more than forty in all, shuffling, being served what might not supply a delicate lady's tea time meal, and accepting it. As if no more were their due, and they wouldn't ask for more, because—because why? Why didn't they leave? Just leave?

He wanted to ask Nolly this, to ask him all kinds of questions about his time in the workhouse, when he'd been the wee thing that had run away and struck out on his own, marching all the way to London to meet Jack. That wee Nolly had survived this was some consolation, though Jack imagined that the Nolly standing next to him now might have some objections to make, if allowed.

Which he wouldn't be. Mr. Bassler motioned to Jack and Nolly to get at the end of the line and then went to speak to the man in the dun-colored apron, standing by the cauldron, ladling out the glop. They talked a moment, and the man with the ladle nodded. Without another word, Mr. Bassler left and hefted himself down the stairs. Which left Jack with only a moment to get Nolly to talk to him while the line moved, with the men, some old, some infirm, some more able-bodied, shuffling forward, all intent on the bowls they carried, the spoons tucked in their fists.

"Nolly," Jack asked, barely above a whisper, for he noticed that no one in the dining hall was talking, not even a little bit. "Was it like this? For you? When you were small?"

They shuffled forward together while Jack waited for Nolly to speak. He wanted to grab Nolly and shake him to get him to say something, anything but this sharp-eyed silence that still threatened to break into violence.

When Jack was about to mention that they had no bowls, and ask what were they to eat in, Nolly opened his mouth at last, and looked at Jack. His eyes tilted downward at the outside corner, and he looked as though he were quite sorry for Jack.

"It was," he said, slowly. "It was *exactly* like this."

They were halfway up the line now, to where Jack could smell the vapor oozing out of the kettle, kept warm over a small fire encased in red brick and branded iron. The air smelled slightly sweet, with a tang of something else that told Jack the bottom of the cauldron had been heated too hot and had burned.

"Exactly?" asked Jack, still in a whisper.

He looked about him, at the gray walls that looked faded with damp in places, and at the iron bars over the windows, the dull concentration of the men as they sat on the long benches at the long tables that ran lengthways down the room. At the rain on the windows, streaking down like tears. And failed to notice the man coming up to them with two white crockery bowls and two spoons and a hard smack for Nolly.

"No talking in the dining hall, you," said the man. He was dressed much like the man behind the cauldron, who was still dishing out the white slop with concentrated slowness. "You're new, but rules are rules. No talking in the dining hall."

Jack took both of the bowls and spoons and felt their weight clank in his hands. He longed to throw them down with a loud, disruptive clatter, to grab Nolly by the wrist and drag him out of there. But Nolly only blinked at him, making no objection to the blow, merely moved along, and reached out to take one bowl and one spoon from Jack.

He let him, and promised himself that wherever they might sleep, he'd pull Nolly to him and kiss him in the dark, and whisper whatever it took to take that expression from his face, the one that meant Nolly believed that this certain hell was his just punishment. For Jack had never seen him take a blow like that so calmly; even Mr. McCready's scoldings in the courtyard, however gentle, had made Nolly's eyes spark with temper.

Only now, there was nothing. Or almost nothing. As the handprint on Nolly's face blossomed to red, he rubbed his hand along his jaw and tried to shrug, as if it meant nothing. But that lasted only a moment, and then it was gone.

When they were next in line at the cauldron, they held up their bowls to have the white slop ladled into them, which was done slowly and carefully, as if it were the finest broth served in all the land. Once served, Nolly tucked the rim of his bowl against his belly. Jack did likewise and followed Nolly to where they were directed, to two spots on a bench seat, at a table near the end of the room.

As Jack sat down, he was glad that he could see the top of the stairs, the width of the room. The length of it. If he could situate himself and Nolly as to where they were inside the workhouse, it might be easier to determine their exit route. He would learn the layout as best as he might, and keep the map in his mind always, for when the opportunity presented itself. Which it would. It had to.

Nolly might be keeping his temper in check, his anxiety, but it wouldn't last long. Nor would Jack, not on these rations, getting knocked about, and especially not while watching Nolly getting knocked about.

The entire room waited while the man at the cauldron bowed his head to mumble grace. The entire room bowed its head, a collective gesture that Jack copied, and Nolly as well. When grace was done, and as the men began to eat, one of the attendants spoke briskly, and in a complete monotone, about the deaths that had occurred in the workhouse that week, and the inspection by the board that was to happen the following week.

No one seemed to be listening, and Jack took his first spoonful of the slop. And almost spat it out. It was sweet. He could taste the treacle, but there was too much salt, making it foul. There were oats in it, cooked soft until they melted, but this gave them an unsavory texture, like regurgitated pap.

"What the fuck is this?"

"It's gruel, Jack," said Oliver. "Just eat it."

Jack made himself swallow that spoonful, then made himself swallow another. Nolly was doing the same with a twitch to his shoulders as he took the large spoon into his mouth. It was as if his fate, his destiny, had brought him to this very meal, a meal that represented everything Nolly had ever feared.

Suddenly Jack wished that they'd not ever come to Lyme, for then they would not have been arrested for merely borrowing books. He suspected Mrs. Heyland had been responsible for the arrest, as she'd always had a sharp, hateful eye for Jack, even while she'd been all smiles and solicitude for Nolly.

But that was behind them now.

Finishing up his bowl of treacle gruel in a few concentrated mouthfuls, Jack laid his spoon in his bowl, as he saw the other men doing. Nolly finished a few heartbeats behind, his expression so marked and closed that Jack considered that Nolly might be going slightly mad, driven to it, so quickly, by this place.

When the men stood up, Jack stood up, nudging Nolly with his elbow to do likewise. Everyone was taking their bowl to the end of the table closest to the cauldron. There, two young boys in brown aprons gathered up the bowls and spoons to load them into long wicker baskets with handles on them. Jack felt Nolly's whole body start when he saw the boys; they were younger than either Jack or Nolly, and kept their eyes down, concentrating on their work.

No one could linger, though; the attendants were directing the men to go back down the stairs, and Jack tugged on Nolly's sleeve to make him follow. At the bottom of the stairs, they went along the passage again, only to go up another flight of stairs.

Jack paid attention even though he kept most of his focus on Nolly, waiting for when Nolly would give the signal, surely he would, for them to make a dash for it. The front windows had no bars, and even though the porter's room was directly next to them, the porter would, at some point, be otherwise occupied, and they could give this whole place the slip.

Nolly only followed where Jack led, his eyes on the ground, his hands at his sides.

"I'm right here, Nolly," said Jack as they climbed the second set of stairs. "Right here with you."

The landing at the top of these stairs led them into a narrow hall, which was filled with beds. About halfway down the hall was a doorway leading to another room that had more beds. In the closed space, the smell of damp rot rose, that of urine, and some other dank smell Jack couldn't identify and wasn't sure he wanted to. Jack stood even closer to Nolly now, not wanting them to be separated.

The men lined up to wash at the basin set by each doorway, and Jack followed suit, though he never cared much about soap and water. Especially not after Mr. Bassler's kind treatment. He could imagine the water would be cold and the soap harsh. Which it was. Still, he daubed his hands in the murky water, and motioned for Nolly to do the same.

Nolly shook his head, mostly at the water, and a little at Jack, and Jack wasn't surprised. The water was cold, nasty, and had been used by many hands without ever having been changed out for fresh and Nolly couldn't stand that.

An older man came up to them; he was dressed much as the porter, wearing a brown suit a little more refined than what the paupers wore. In his hands, he carried a ledger book, his carved pencil waving in the air.

"You lads, surely you should be with the boys, under Work-master Chalenheim's care."

"They got assigned," said someone from the other room that Jack couldn't see. "They're of age, Mr. Bassler said. It's at Mr. Pickering's direction."

"Oh, very well," said the man. He licked the tip of his pencil and wrote something in his ledger. "You'll share that bed."

He pointed to the last cot in the row. It had a rolled-up mattress and two pillows, and what looked like two gray blankets.

"When the candle is snuffed out, there'll be no talking or larking about. Is that understood? We need order in the dormi-tories at all times."

Jack didn't quite know what to say to that. The men around him were so dull-eyed that they could not possibly be the source of any mischief. Besides, what harm could talking possibly do anybody?

"You mind me, now," said the man. His comment was directed at Nolly who, for all his grace and dignity, was the one sporting a bruise from a blow on his face. "Well?"

With a long, drawn-in breath, Nolly nodded. "Yes, sir," he said, low.

Jack nodded too, though he'd not been asked for any reply. But an attitude of obedience never hurt nobody, and it was easy to do, at this point.

The man pointed at the cot again, indicating that they should go make it up and get in it, as the rest of the men were doing. It couldn't be more than eight o'clock in the evening, going by the darkness that streaked through the glass windows. Yet the men were taking off their shoes, and hanging their jackets and trousers on pegs beside each bed, and were getting into the beds in their shirts and stockings. As if the slow time of evening after supper wasn't a time to relax and talk, perhaps play cards, or listen to a merry tune. In this place, it was bedtime.

Going over to the bed, Jack concentrated on that, and not on his growing worry that he was in over his head. The mattress unrolled evenly, proved to be thin, and was splotched with stains that could either be blood or rust, he couldn't tell which. The pillows had thin cotton slips on them, but there was no sheet over the mattress, nor between them and the scratchy wool blanket.

In normal circumstances, he would expect Nolly would make one, if not several, acid-laced remarks about this, but as Jack looked at him, Nolly just looked at the bed. There was no telling what thoughts were racing in his head, and Jack made himself wait. In the dark, once the room had gone quiet, he could whisper in Nolly's ear, and get him to whisper back. It wasn't as if Nolly were giving Jack the silent treatment, but it felt like it, just the same.

He undressed, as the men had done, down to his shirt and stockings. Nolly did the same, still looking at the floor, and they each climbed into the bed, he on his left side, Nolly on his right, so they could face each other. They laid their heads on the thin pillows and pulled the wool blanket up to their chins.

The attendants made sure everyone was in bed, said some quick prayers, then they snuffed out the candles that hung in sconces at each door, went out into the passage, and locked the door behind them. This stunned Jack into stillness, all thoughts of getting Nolly to talk to him wiped from his mind in an instant.

The workhouse was as much a prison as Newgate had been, as the *Bertha May* had been. They were locked in, and he had to fight down a queasy panic that stirred just below his ribs. In a room full of strange men, anything might happen, though he tried to console himself that the men were too beaten down and starved to go on a rampage to rise up in violence.

He made himself focus, and did not reach to itch his rash, which had sprung to life along his ribs.

"Nolly," he said, very quietly. He moved closer to Nolly in the dark. "Nolly, sweetheart, it's Jack, please, *please*, say somethin' to me, to let me know I'm not all alone."

Reaching out, he found Nolly's chin and cupped it in his palm. Nolly's heartbeat was racing beneath his skin, which was icy cold. Jack longed to strip them both of their rough muslin shirts and push their bodies together, skin to skin, until he could warm Nolly up. Himself too; his teeth were chattering, for the room was as cold as a cellar.

He felt Nolly shake his head, so he moved in close and kissed whatever he could reach, soft, gentle kisses. Nolly's ear, his cheek, his temple. Until Nolly seemed to give up all resistance, and moved into Jack's arms and tucked himself beneath Jack's chin, his arms going around Jack's waist, and finally, *finally*, Jack could draw a deep breath and felt his own shoulders come down.

"Nolly." He put all the tenderness he could into it, to get Nolly to talk to him, to get him to calm from his shiverings. "Tell me what's wrong. Tell Jack what's wrong so he can fix it."

"It's as if a great, dark blanket has come over me, Jack," said Nolly, at last, against Jack's neck. "Nothing's getting in and nothing's getting out, no light, no sound, no feeling. Nothing."

This Jack understood. Directly after his glorious trial in the courtroom, he'd been at ease with himself, preening a bit, and having gratifying conversations in his head about what Fagin was saying to the lads about Jack's arrest. All the variations had involved Fagin singing Jack's praises one way or another.

Later, this had proved itself true. Noah had been there at the trial, and reported to Jack every little moment. Fagin *had* been full of praise about the whole affair, and Jack always considered the arrest part of his glory. Newgate, in light of this, hadn't seemed so bad.

But the first night on ship aboard the *Bertha May*, the glory had left him, and in the vacated spot where his fame was a thing to be marked in the history books had come a bleakness that he'd been at pains to describe. He could not work his way out of it, but could only suffer through it for weeks while the *Bertha May* had plied her way across the ocean to a distant land that blazed with heat and sun. He had been so low, during that time, before he'd settled himself into his new life aboard the ship.

And then the emptiness had come again, when he'd landed in Port Jackson, and had to get used to the extreme heat, the duties he'd been assigned, the native blacks who spoke no English. The farmer that yelled and beat Jack with a stick. The marines who treated Jack like a nameless beast who only existed to polish their boots and bring them hot water to shave with.

"It'll pass, Nolly," he said. "This blackness, it'll pass. 'Tis the change from one life to the next, you see. I felt it when I was arrested; I never told you, but it was so. That same blanket folded itself around me till I could almost neither speak nor move nor eat unless directed. The only thing I could do voluntarily was sleep."

"Truly, Jack?"

Jack had to pause at this. It wasn't a lie, not entirely. He'd slept when he could, but then would be shoved awake and forced to do things for other people. Forced to fetch and carry. To eat strange food and move about in a strange place, as though there'd been nothing painful within his heart.

Sometimes he'd missed London so much, it was as if he was being clawed alive from within. When those times came, he'd find a place in the barn that was dark and quiet and curl himself up into a ball in the hay and stay there until someone found him and made him come out. That was the part he could tell Nolly, that while there was no hiding from it, you *could* get through it.

"After a time it will," Jack said. But that was all he could promise.

He could almost feel Nolly staring blankly ahead, though it was far too dark to allow him to see more than the dark gray shape of Nolly's head, the curve of his shoulders.

"I do not think I can bear it, Jack," said Nolly. "Being in this place."

"You will. You can. We'll find a way out, I promise."

"Oh, Jack," said Nolly, and there was a cruel humor in his voice. "You do not know, do you. The walls are ten feet high and the doors are always locked. The gates have spikes on them. You must understand, there's no way out unless someone lets us out."

"Paupers can always leave, Fagin said so. Said workhouses was a good place for stoppin' when the need arose."

"You have to have a ticket to get in," said Nolly, and Jack could sense him shaking his head. "And when you leave, you have to prove that you won't be coming back. You can't just come and go; they keep track of the people within their walls."

Nolly spoke of the workhouse officers as if they were a single entity, focused on the control of a people so poor that they would welcome white slop with too much salt, too much treacle. Who would go to bed at a signal, at eight o'clock, as if they were young children. Who allowed themselves to—

"We'll figure it out, Nolly, trust me, we will." Jack nodded his head, though he knew that in the dark, Nolly would barely be able to see this. "Stick together, that's what we have to do. Stick together. Never get separated. Don't know what I'd do if I lost you in this place."

With a shudder, Nolly pressed close, and Jack drew his arms around Nolly's back, feeling his pounding heart that Nolly was trying so hard to control. He kissed the top of Nolly's head, his mouth feeling the roughness of Nolly's cropped hair, the whisper of sweat along his brow. But kisses were good, as Nolly's breath eased out, and some of the shivering had left him. He would focus on that, on helping Nolly, and never mind that his stomach was racing, his back all stiff, and that blasted headache thundering in the distance.

"Let me kiss you," said Nolly, and Jack felt him tip his head back. "Let me kiss you now, before it's too late."

"Whatever do you mean, Nolly?" asked Jack, but he obediently brought his hands up to cup Nolly's face, to bend low and find Nolly's mouth with his. To savor the kiss, sweet and soft, that tasted of treacle and watery gruel.

He brushed his thumbs across Nolly's cheeks, to soothe him, and kissed him again, and rested his cheek against Nolly's mouth, to feel Nolly's kisses there, as innocent as if from a newborn child. Then he lay back on the bed, with the narrow, hard mattress biting into his shoulders, and made Nolly settle against him, pulling the blanket up, breathing the still, closed air of the locked dormitory.

Hearing the nighttime sounds of the men around him, each two to a bed, he wanted to laugh at his earlier fears. No one in this room was capable of rising to violence, so there was nothing to fear from that. It was only keeping Nolly's spirits up that he had to do; that was his current job, and Fagin would have approved of Jack's singular focus on this. Keep Nolly's spirits up until he could find a way out.

As to his own spirits, that didn't matter as much. It wasn't as if he was in a strange country, far from home. This was still England, and London was just beyond the horizon. Within walking distance. Close by, when he needed it.

THOUGH JACK SOON FELL ASLEEP, IN THE DARK HIS ARMS becoming slack, his breath going deep, Oliver could not join him. His wide-awake state was not because his surroundings were unfamiliar, but the opposite. He knew the feel of this dark, the dampness, the dank smell of an uncovered piss bucket in the corner, the mold from the mattresses, the sound of water dripping from somewhere—there was always water dripping. And a high-pitched sound from someone that could be snoring or sobbing.

All of this was so familiar that he had to blink against the darkness to assure himself of where he was. That he was in Jack's arms, that between them they shared a bed, and that Jack was not Dick, and that none of this was from so long ago, when he'd been in the Hardingstone workhouse. He had to shake his head now, to rid himself of those thoughts, though others came soon to chase it.

Oliver did not believe in fortune-teller cards, or the runes found in tea leaves, but he did believe in the gentleman with the white waistcoat. Whose prediction was coming to pass, and directly the June assizes would be held, then Oliver would face the hangman's noose. His heart raced at the thought of it, and he stifled the urge to get out of bed and pace the floor, to rub his arms with his hands and keep his blood flowing that way. To distract himself with the feel of the icy floor beneath his feet.

But he could not do that, because to stir was to wake Jack who, fast asleep, seemed to believe the workhouse held only the most ordinary of terrors. That a workhouse was just another building, and that leaving it would be a task far beneath his need to concentrate on it. Though Oliver dearly wanted to disabuse Jack of that notion, the daily grind of the workhouse would do that for him, soon enough.

Or maybe not, as perhaps his current fears merely magnified those of his nine-year-old self, when Mr. Bumble and his swift cane had ruled Oliver's world. When even the simple darkness had scared him badly enough that he'd cowered in the corner.

Well, of course, he still didn't much care for the deep of night, though he'd never told Jack this. Nor would he, not about that, or about how bad the workhouse would get. Because either Oliver would be proven wrong, and Jack might mock him, or he'd be proven right and both of them would suffer for it. What good would it do to speak of something that could not be avoided?

He turned himself in Jack's nighttime arms, somewhat loose around him, but solid and still and quiet. Tucking himself beneath Jack's chin, he buried himself there, with Jack's scent all around him, in spite of the workhouse soap, and Jack's breath, all of it. He anchored himself to Jack, as he could not bear the coming storm alone.

All this movement, in spite of his best intentions, bestirred Jack to a sleepy wakefulness.

"Hey?" asked Jack, and Oliver could hear him lick his lips. "Ain't you asleep? Why not, eh?"

Those arms tightened around him, and while Oliver felt badly for having woken Jack, he took a deep breath, grateful that, for the moment, he was not alone with his fears.

As to why Oliver was not asleep, Jack did not seem to need an answer to this, for along with providing the shelter of his arms, he bent to kiss the top of Oliver's head, and pressed his cheek there. He took a long, slow breath so that Oliver was lifted and lowered against Jack's chest.

This should have been enough, but it wasn't. The ache in his heart told him so. But he could not still the shake in his arms as he wrapped them around Jack's waist, and dipped his head to pillow against Jack's chest. And, curling his legs up beneath the blanket, made himself as small as possible, as if he were using Jack as a shield against what was to come.

"Nolly," said Jack, petting Oliver's head, his neck, the length of his back.

"Don't say it, Jack," said Oliver, his jaw stiff, "because it's not true and it's not going to be true."

"Surely it will," said Jack.

"Trust me, it *won't*."

For a moment, Jack was silent, though his hand was never still, always moving up and down Oliver's back, a constant warmth in the dark that Oliver made himself believe would always be there.

"I'll be with you, though," said Jack. "You know I will."

Oliver almost jumped out of his skin as the man in the next bed coughed and rolled over, and Oliver became quite aware that not everyone was asleep. At Hardingstone, a boy could turn in another boy for breaking the rules, and would be rewarded by extra food, or a thicker shirt to wear beneath his jacket. Perhaps it was the same here, and what other way would it be?

Workhouses were the same, as he, dismayed, had pointed out to Jack. So Oliver unlatched himself from Jack's middle, shifted up till their legs tangled together. They were belly to belly, now, and Oliver could feel Jack's mouth with his mouth.

"I do know it," said Oliver, kissing him, once, very gently. "I've always known it."

As Jack's arms came up around him, the darkness of the room became soft, and the sounds of water dripping distant and unimportant. He told himself no one could see them or, if they did, they would not be able to discern Jack's hand as it came up to touch Oliver's face, Jack's body shifting under his so it was Jack on the mattress, with Oliver upon him, pressing down, shielding Jack's face with his arms, so he could kiss him in the further dark created by his body.

Jack tipped his head back, his breath warm on Oliver's cheek as he turned and whispered his mouth along Oliver's jaw. Oliver shivered and dipped his head into the hollow of Jack's neck, and took a long slow breath, feeling Jack's chest lift and fall beneath him.

In a short time, they would be too hungry and tired, too sore, for any niceties such as this. There was nothing the workhouse wouldn't be able to wrench out of them, and after hours of labor and not enough food, sweet kisses from Jack would be the first thing to go.

But were he to tell Jack of this, Jack would deny it, and however quiet their voices as Oliver attempted to convince him otherwise, someone would hear of it, and that was one too many witnesses for Oliver's liking. In a workhouse, there was not only nowhere to go, but no escape. No refuge. Only cold and want.

What made it worse this time was that he'd been outside the wall, and had breathed free air, and had walked along the street, and had a hot meal waiting for him at the end of the day. In comparison, the dark maw of the workhouse was even darker than he'd ever thought possible.

"You shiverin', Nolly. C'mere, slide down next to me, an' I'll pull the blanket over us both."

Oliver did as Jack bade him, slipping into the curve of Jack's arms to rest his head on Jack's breast, and for a moment, only a moment, let himself be taken care of, closing his eyes as the rough blanket drifted down upon him. Jack reached over to sweep Oliver's hair back from his forehead and, as Jack took his hand away, Oliver felt the contrast of the cold, damp air, and the *plink plink* sound of dripping water. Inhaled the smell of urine in a tin bucket, and the tartness of unwashed skin filling the night air around him.

"Sleep, sweetheart, sleep. Jack's here w'you, I'm here w'you now."

Jack needed to sleep, so Oliver needed to let him and get some rest himself. The morning would come, as it always did, to occupy them with hard work of an untold nature. It might be picking oakum or it might be scrubbing floors; it might be anything. But he could not let his own fears bring Jack down with him. He could not bend beneath the pressure that surrounded him, of the dark night, of the smells, the uncertainty. He would not let it break him, and he would not let it hurt Jack.

Setting his jaw, he made himself stop shivering, made his grip around Jack's middle relax, and felt Jack sigh beneath him.

"Sweet Nolly," said Jack, with a faint exhale of breath, half asleep already, untroubled by the promise the workhouse made to each and every pauper who entered its doors that the morning would come quick, and death not quick enough.

From that fate, Oliver promised himself Jack would be safe, even if Oliver had to work himself to the point of collapse to make sure of it. He'd come this far to be with Jack; he would go further than that to protect him. This was how it felt, then, to love someone so much it hurt. To be willing to be hurt to protect another. In a workhouse, yet. In the dark, cold work-house night.

"Goodnight, Jack," said Oliver, pressing his mouth to the slope of Jack's neck. "Stay with me till morning," he said, "stay with me, say you will."

But Jack was already asleep, and Oliver was once more alone.

❧ 3 ❧

BECOMING ACQUAINTED WITH
STONES AND BONES

T he morning light through the high, narrow windows brought Jack to wakefulness, his arms full of Nolly, who had curled his body around Jack's during the night like a ribbon blown in the wind. Gently, Jack shook him to wake up, to get up and get dressed as the men were doing around them, with the attendant at the door marking their every move.

In a moment, they would be spotted for not moving, and be denounced as sluggards or some such workhouse nonsense, and then be sent off to that refractory room that someone, perhaps Mr. Bassler, had spoken of. If it was a room where they simply locked you away for a time, that wouldn't be so bad. At least Jack wouldn't have to watch old men trying to get dressed, their hands so shaky they could barely put their own trousers on. One man stumbled and had to sit down; the attendant didn't move to help him, but merely stared and scowled.

Nolly got dressed quickly, though not as cheerfully as he usually did, and Jack did likewise. Then together they folded their blanket at the foot of the bed, with the pillow on top, as the men were doing.

Part of staying out of anyone's notice was doing exactly what everyone else was doing until you ceased to be anything remarkable. With Nolly's cropped hair, and him keeping his eyes on the ground all the time, Jack was certain Nolly would escape most notice, but anybody looking at his face, his beautiful face, would be hard pressed not to stop and remark upon it. Perhaps Jack could get hold of some coal soot to rub into Nolly's skin, to disguise his fair features, to help keep him safe from the world.

The men, now dressed with the room tidy behind them, stood in line at the door, and Jack followed suit, tugging at Nolly to come with him. Nolly had that same expression as yesterday, stoic, though far from passive. When Jack did catch Nolly's eyes, they were sparking with something repressed, which Nolly had tamped deep inside of him. Jack hoped that would hold, for in this closed space, being monitored all the time, having that flash-paper temper explode would do neither of them any good at all.

When the attendant was satisfied with the line, he nodded. The men plodded forward, down the stone steps to the main floor, along the passage from the night before, now lit with weak watery light from some tall, narrow windows, around a curve, as if they were going around a tower, and then up the flight of stone steps to the dining hall.

The room smelled the same as the night before, exactly the same, with the same two men in their dun-colored aprons, standing with ladles at the cauldron that billowed the same white, weak, slightly sweet steam as the night before. This morning there was a low table from which each man took a bowl and a spoon. Jack took his and nudged Nolly to do the same, and marched in line till they got up to the cauldron.

At least the gruel didn't smell burned, but it was exactly the same meal as before. As Jack got his share, he tried not to scowl at it, tucking it against his belly to warm it, and sat at the table on a long bench that was too far from the table to be comfortable. Nolly sat beside him, and they waited through the short prayer and began to eat.

The gruel was lukewarm at best. The steam rising from it was due to the fact that the room was very cold this morning, though the rain had stopped. And though Jack knew he could eat pretty much anything and be satisfied, the gruel wasn't sitting very well in his stomach, and the taste was, frankly, foul. But he made himself eat it all, and watched Nolly doing the same.

When they were done, everybody stood up, and, eerily, the same two boys from the night before came with long wicker baskets to collect the bowls and spoons. Nolly didn't even look at them this time, but rather looked away, purposefully, as he had done with Martin in the yard at the haberdashery.

There was nothing Jack could do about this, no chance to try and get Nolly to talk to him, for they were being marched back down the stairs, and directed along the passage through a narrow wooden door that led out into a dirt yard. There was a high wall around the yard on the outside with blue-painted spikes along the top and one-story buildings tucked against it.

Along the inside of the yard, the walls of the main buildings of the workhouse walls rose, the dining hall and the men's dormitories, as near as Jack could figure it. In one corner of the yard, small boys were pumping water from a well and carrying large buckets of water back inside, staggering beneath the sloshing weight, with Workmaster Chalenheim standing over them, directing their every move. Jack had to look away this time, as did Nolly, and he made himself concentrate on what the attendant was doing.

The men were set in pairs over square metal boxes with no lids, and given large poles, blunted to dull at one end and pointed at the other. An attendant poured something from a hemp sack into each square box, and Jack could see that it was bones that he was pouring.

Chunks of white, porous and gray at each end, some still glistening with sinew, some dripping with a pale green fluid. The smell was pretty rank, but the men started working, each pair of men gripping the pole to force the blunt end into the box, and begin the horrible job of breaking bone.

Jack had seen bone before, fresh from the fire, or dripping

red from slaughter. Or baked hard in the sun of the southern hemisphere. But bones were to be tossed, not touched, not handled like this. The smell from the nearest box was dank, a rotten, low smell, and Jack had to bring the back of his hand to his mouth.

"You two, over here. This is your bone tub. Here's your crusher."

Jack made himself go over; he was about to be forced to hard labor, and it was in him to rebel, much as Nolly had wanted to do since the moment they'd arrived. He wanted to take the pole and stab the attendant in the heart with the sharp end, and make a break for it. He looked around for a moment, taking in the high walls, the spikes, the gray and cloudy air whipping overhead. The door from the yard was locked, and the other low buildings all had doors that were locked. There was no way out of this.

Nolly grabbed the pole and hefted it in his fist, as if his mind was reflecting Jack's thoughts of quick murder and escape.

"What does it weigh?" Jack asked, coming up close.

"It's heavy."

Jack took the crusher from Nolly and hefted it as Nolly had. It was almost thirty pounds of iron, and could do some damage if aimed at a man's head, even without the spike at one end. He looked at what the male paupers were doing, taking the crusher and ramming it in the box. He heard the splinter of bone and saw the small spray as fragments spun themselves about.

"Get working," said the attendant.

While the man didn't even mention the refractory room, Jack knew it had to be on the tip of his tongue. But if that was the worst of punishments the workhouse could dream up, then they would make it through this. They would make it through this any way that he could manage it, even if something bad happened, the way Nolly seemed to fear that it would.

Gripping the iron rod near the top, he looked at Nolly, nodding that he should do the same. As Nolly gripped the rod below Jack's clenched hands, he waited for the jest that Nolly might make about Jack finally doing some actual work, but it never came. Instead, completely focused on his hands, on the crusher, the bone box, Nolly began to pound on the bones. As if Jack's hands weren't even there, and Nolly was alone in the dirt yard, using his shoulders, putting his back into it, smashing and pounding, and sending the bones into flakes and damp, white dust.

It flew up to dapple his skin, the length of his temple, his wrists. In Nolly's eyes, Jack could see, was a grim determination to get the job done. As if the job mattered at all. Hell, they weren't even getting paid for their work; it was being done for the workhouse, and who knew who would profit after that.

"What's it for, all this bone?" Jack gripped the rod and made himself do the work, though it made his shoulders feel stiff and his head began to ache almost directly. "Nolly?"

Nolly looked up at him, his expression completely blank. The beautiful blue color in his eyes was faded with exhaustion, as if he'd already crushed ten boxes of bone. He seemed to barely recognize Jack, his gaze soon jumping to the left or the right, and Nolly continued to look at nothing. Nothing, rather than at Jack. Working hard away at it, as if it would make any difference in the slightest.

Lifting up the crusher, Nolly slammed it down in the bone box, as if to state, quite plainly, that he didn't want Jack looking at him. To punctuate this, a spray flew up from the box, catching Nolly in the face, and it smelled just as rotten and nasty as the refuse bin in a knacker's yard.

With a gagging sound, Nolly stepped back, wiping his mouth with his brown sleeve and spitting, working up more spit, and hawking it out on the ground. Like a common sailor, something which Jack had never seen him do. But it was foul marrow he'd gotten a facefull of, and Jack couldn't really blame him. Then the smell hit Jack, and he staggered back, covering his mouth, trying not to swallow.

"What's going on here? Why have you stopped?" It was the

attendant, dressed as they all were, in a finer shade of brown, with a brown apron and a belly that looked as though it had had its share of good suppers. "You need to keep working, we've a schedule to keep."

"'Tis rotten, mister," said Jack, pointing at the bone tub, where even now, a dark liquid oozed over the edge and down the outside. "You can't give us rotten bone to crack, it ain't right."

"Sometimes the bone is that way," said the attendant, though he too stepped back and covered his mouth with his hand. He gestured with his head, and another attendant came and poured yet more bone into the tub. "You'll need to get cracking if you mean to be fed today. Anyone down on their quota will have their dinner meal withheld."

"Oh, we'll have our quota," said Jack, not really believing that they could be fed any less than they already were. "But what's it used for, all this bone mash?"

"Not that I have time for your idle questions," said the attendant. "But it is for fertilizer, for the farms nearby. Now get back to work."

Jack turned back to the box, shrugging his shoulders to loosen them, and reached out for the crusher.

All this while, Nolly had said only two words to Jack. It was as if he was keeping his mouth shut to lock the raging fury inside of him. But Jack was here now; he wasn't going to leave Nolly by himself, and he didn't want to feel that Nolly was so far away from him, even though a mere foot or so separated them.

"Nolly," he said, now, very low, not sure of the rules about talking in the yard. "You all right? Can I get you some water to rinse your mouth?"

Pounding the crusher so hard that Jack was pressed to keep up with him, Nolly scowled at the white flakes that flew from the box, and then at Jack. His eyes were narrow and dark.

"You simply don't understand, do you." Each word was accompanied by a dull thud as the crusher hit bone. "You don't get to ask for water. You don't get to ask for anything. You get it when they give it to you and not before."

"Even water?" asked Jack. His shoulders were starting to throb, and in his mouth was growing a terrible feeling of thirst.

"Not water, not food, not freedom, not *anything*. The sooner you learn that, the better off you'll be."

"Then why did you do it? Why did you come with me?" To ask this, Jack had to lean far forward, jerking back when Nolly lifted the crusher and almost stabbed Jack in the face with it.

Surprised, Jack thought that Nolly was angry with him. But while Nolly was pale, his eyes when they looked at Jack were soft.

"I had to, Jack," said Nolly. His gaze was level, and it turned Jack's heart inside out.

"Wish to God you hadn't," said Jack. "An' how could you, knowin' that it would be like this?"

"I had to," said Nolly again. He looked away, his hands resting on the crusher, fingers curling around the sharpness of the end, as if the words themselves were too much of a burden to bear. "I didn't know they would bring us to a workhouse, but I would have come anyway. I couldn't let you go alone."

Jack felt his soul rip outwards, bare to the wind-tossed gray sky. Nolly was prepared to take the hangman's noose for Jack, if that's what was called for, though coming here was probably worse than that. No one, not even in Fagin's gang, would have been willing to do as much.

The attendant was looking their way, as if he would soon be prompted to come over and release them from their duty of eating their dinners.

Jack knew he wouldn't be able to make it without food all the way till supper, and if he couldn't, then Nolly certainly would not be able to. Which might lead to his temper getting the best of him. So Jack put his back into it, and his elbows, his whole body feeling the echo of each pound of the crusher until they ached.

When they got down to a level where the bottom of the box

was filled with mostly flakes and white and gray bits, the attendant came over to scoop out the crushed bone, where it was taken over in a thin tin bucket to be weighed on a scale that sat on the ground near the well. Then more bones were poured into their tub. Short, blocky white pieces, long thigh bones and jawbones, and a long, horse-shaped skull, empty of brain matter, but still fresh around the eye socket.

Jack looked away and kept pounding, his whole body vibrating with each slam of the crusher. Blisters grew up along the webbing of his hands, both of them, and along his forefingers, breaking open and making the iron slick beneath his hands. So slick that he almost pierced the middle of his palm when his hand slipped up, but Nolly was there, quick as anything, stopping the crusher, and pulling Jack's hand back, grabbing him by the wrist.

As Jack looked at their joined hands, he saw that Nolly's fingers had blisters too, though maybe fewer, on account of he'd spent several days gutting fish at Lyme. But the blisters, the sore skin, was the least of it for Nolly, Jack knew. He'd gladly do rough work, it seemed, even gutting fish, if it was honorable work, if it had a purpose, such as paying Jack's doctor bills. But not for this. The work was shitty, Jack knew, but to Nolly it was degrading as well as foul. And there was nothing for it but to keep going.

~

OLIVER HALF-IMAGINED, WHILE THEY POUNDED BONE WITH their hands on the pike end of the crusher together, or when one of them rested, that Jack thought that this morning's work would be it. That come dinnertime, they'd have a fine meal and then be at their leisure. Or at least it seemed that way.

And it wasn't that Jack wasn't pulling his weight, doing his share, because he was. He was lifting and slamming the pike down with as much muscle as Oliver, but all the while with a puzzled look on his face, his brows quirking in the middle, as if he couldn't quite figure out why he was working so hard. Jack simply didn't understand the purpose of the work, which was to degrade and exhaust the paupers to keep them from rebelling.

Oliver felt the heat of anger low in his belly colliding with the cold, gnawing feeling of hunger. He'd let himself take his temper out on Jack, which he hadn't meant to do. While Jack wasn't new to being in a cage, he was perhaps unused to one so sere and caustic as this.

For it felt like that, felt raw to the bone, and they'd not even been there a day. Who knew how long his resolve to behave would last him? If they didn't meet their quota, then they wouldn't eat and, come the nighttime, Oliver knew he'd be willing to trade his soul for something to eat. He could only pray it didn't come to that.

But he shouldn't be cross with Jack simply because Jack was right there; Jack didn't know how the workhouse controlled every moment, every sip of water, every breath of air, and how could he? Even Fagin had never denied a boy a bite to eat, if he had the coin to purchase it.

So, stopping to swipe at his forehead with the back of his sleeve, Oliver took the pike from Jack again, who hopefully was now more attentive to the way broken blisters could slick up the metal. Jack let him, but shook his head a bit, as if to say he wouldn't be spelled for very long, only as long as it took for his hands to stop throbbing so much.

They had to keep up. To fall behind was to risk being singled out, and the way to survive in a workhouse was to blend in. So Oliver timed the thuds of the crusher with each breath, making it regular, making it steady. He'd get the work done so Jack wouldn't have to work so hard and ruin his beautiful and skillful hands.

The bottom of the metal box rocked each time the crusher slammed into it, with bits of bone spraying up all the while, the smell from the broken bone mixing in the damp air, the rotten smell of it, so much like a funeral parlor that for a brief flicker he felt as though he were there. Or just had been there, such a short time ago that the memory of it was fresh and real. The disaster of taking down the shutters and cracking the window. Being fed the dog's leftovers, or the slice of pork so old that nobody wanted it anymore.

As Jack took the crusher from him, or tried to, Oliver was startled and his grip tightened.

"Give it here, it's my turn, ain't it?"

"We'll do it together," said Oliver, feeling the warmth of Jack's hands on his for a moment as Jack's fingers circled the crusher.

Oliver shook his head and took a breath, raising his eyes to the high walls of the workhouse. The newness of it was still startling to him, the pale stone on top of the darker gray, streaked with rain from the night before. The walls were so sturdy and so thick that there'd be no digging their way out, even should they find a private moment to do so.

Then he looked at the men in the yard around them, two by two, smashing bone with crushers far too heavy for old men to be lifting. The scattering of white flakes of shattered bone that would now never be measured against the quota.

He wanted to shout at them to get moving or none of them would eat, wanted to urge them on or smack them, or both. But it wouldn't do, and he turned his attention back to Jack, almost shaking.

"Nolly?"

Before Oliver could speak, one of the attendants came up; his dun-colored apron and the finer cloth of his jacket and trousers set him apart at once. He was carrying a bucket of water, and a tumbler on a long handle that he used to dip the tumbler in the bucket, bringing it up full. He held the tumbler out to Oliver, who set down the pike with some haste and took up the tumbler in both hands. He brought the cool metal edge to his mouth and emptied the tumbler, gulping down all the water in three huge swallows.

"Say, now," said the attendant. "That was for both you and your friend here." He gestured at Jack with his head. "But that's all you get."

"What?" For a moment Oliver could not believe he'd heard correctly. "What did you say? That's all the water? But there's a well right over there." He pointed at the circular stone well that was along the inner wall below a bank of windows.

"I'm only accountable to making one stop per pair. Maybe next time you'll learn not to be so greedy."

The attendant, with the tumbler securely in his hand, and the bucket nearly full, moved off to the next pair of men. Who, evidently, knew that the one tumbler of water was to be shared between them, and drank their allotted portion, and no more.

With his heart quite thudding within his breast, his throat closed up, Oliver looked at Jack. Who was standing there, holding the crusher upright in one hand, the other hand half reached out for the tumbler, now quite gone. On his face was a look of some surprise, his mouth open, and that puzzled expression, brows drawn together, firmly in place.

"You didn't know," said Jack. "You didn't. Besides, there'll be water at dinner."

"If we get dinner," said Oliver, snapping, and then he winced, turning away from Jack, who did not deserve his ire. His lips felt so numb that he could hardly speak the words, but he said them. "I'm sorry, Jack, I'll go to him, and *make* him——"

"You won't do any such foolish thing," said Jack. He gestured for Oliver to come over to him, and when Oliver was close, Jack touched him on the back of his hand. Three fingers, a single stroke. "You're not even in here a day, an' you're already causin' trouble."

He meant it to tease, but beneath that was a warning. Oliver heard him, and felt the blood start to boil behind his eyes. He could barely see Jack's face now, let alone imagine he would follow orders if it meant that Jack would be thirsty. Did they imagine he'd be willing to let that happen? For even a single *moment?*

"Nolly."

Oliver blinked, feeling Jack's fingers encircling his wrist now, a touch of warmth and pressure, and made himself take a deep breath. He focused on Jack's face as he licked his lips. Lips that were dry. Which was *Oliver's* fault.

"Wouldn't have been more than a swallow anyhow," Jack said.

It barely flinted across the surface of his skin, Jack's forgiveness, but Oliver knew he was heartfelt, so he took the crusher from Jack's hands and began pounding at the bone in the box, shattering the pieces so that they flew up right to the box's edge. He slammed and slammed, and wouldn't let Jack take the crusher from him, not even when the attendant came around again to shake more bones from his hemp sack into the box. He did let Jack help him, but not spell him, and kept it up until his hands were numb and his shoulders ached.

THEY SMASHED AND POUNDED ALL THROUGH THE MORNING, quickly learning to spell each other, with one of them doing the real pounding and the other guiding the crusher and lifting it up so the other could bring it down again. Bone flakes flew over the edge of the tub, making Jack want to sigh with the waste of it; each ounce was to go toward their quota, and he couldn't believe he was even thinking like this. Except for the fact that food was on the line, he wouldn't be.

At one point, Nolly thrust the crusher down so hard it rang against the bottom of the bone tub and bounced back up. A red spray burst up from the crusher, and for a hollow, panicked moment, Jack thought that Nolly had truly speared himself. But it was the bone that had exploded.

Nolly wiped his cheek with the cuff of his jacket and kept

going. So Jack kept going. Together they pounded and pounded and turned their heads aside to breathe air that didn't have bone flakes in it, or not as much. They pounded and thudded until the tub was emptied one last time and no hemp bag was brought over to give them another serving of bone to crush.

The other men in the yard were done as well, but they waited by their tubs, the pointed crushers placed within, as if the crushers were taking a rest from their many labors. Jack took the crusher from Nolly's hands, and Nolly let him while Jack put the crusher in the box, tipping it to the side to rest in the corner. Then he turned to Nolly, jerking his chin up.

"D'you think we made the quota?"

Nolly took such a hard breath that it came out in a shudder. Sweat had dampened his hair to dark gold and the flush on his cheek was a hard red, as if he'd run miles and his lungs were about to burst. He didn't answer out loud, only shrugged at Jack.

Jack echoed the gesture, rubbing his hand across the back of his neck, realizing too late that his palm was befouled with bits of bone, a fine mist of them that seemed to be pressed into his skin. The only way to get the bits off was with a good wash, and wouldn't Nolly be amused to know that Jack was thinking like this?

Looking up, meaning to tell Nolly of this thought, Jack saw the attendants at the scale writing something down in their blasted book. Nobody in the yard moved, so Jack stayed where he was and kept his mouth shut.

Plainly, that was the trick of this place; the less you said out loud, the better it would go for you. Which was why, most likely, nobody was talking. The men just stood there, young and old, their shoulders bowed, covered with a thin, white film of crushed bone.

"You may line up," said the attendant. He snapped his book closed and tucked his pencil behind his ear. "We made the quota, but barely. I expect you'll do better in the morning, or it will be reduced rations for everyone."

The attendant did not shout this, or even raise his voice, but then, he probably didn't have to. All the men hung their heads, as if grievously ashamed of their lack of focus and industry.

"That's some soulless bullshit," said Jack.

The comment was mostly to himself, but Nolly heard him and turned his head, horrified to hear Jack not only saying something so foul, but saying it out loud. One or two other men heard him, but Jack couldn't be bothered with what they thought. Besides, they were going inside for their dinner meal, two by two, and Jack hustled Nolly along. Even so, they were last in the steady, slow line as it went indoors.

❧ 4 ❧

COMPRISING FURTHER
PARTICULARS OF AXMINSTER
WORKHOUSE

Sucking on the web between his thumb and forefinger, wincing at the taste of the thin pus on his tongue, Jack shuffled in line with the rest of the male paupers. He stood behind Nolly, who was staring ahead of him as if his whole body were made of stone, his eyes the only thing alive about him.

He wanted to give Nolly a fond pat, a nod, a glance, anything. To whisper that it would get better by-and-bye, as Nolly seemed to like him to do. But any movement untoward that might draw attention would have Nolly sending a glare his way, or a sub-vocal warning, as though he were a hissing cat.

The workhouse, in less than a day's turn of the sun, had brought out in Nolly somebody Jack was unable to recognize. A frightened, scalded thing, ill at ease, and as wound up as thin, rusted wire that Jack would never be able to untangle, which he needed to do, lest Nolly find himself frozen in place, unable to break free from the hold the workhouse had over him.

Jack suspected that, should enough time pass, he himself would become ensnared, so it was important this not happen to him. He needed to be free, at liberty, to save himself and Nolly.

Their current circumstances, however, of marching two by

two up the stairs to the dining hall, denied him this. The dining hall's stone walls were bathed by the weak yellow light coming through the high windows. The tables were laid out along the floor just the same as the night before.

The men lined up in front of the cauldron over the little fire as they had done that very morning. Though should the contents of that cauldron turn out to be the same, weak, watery treacle-flavored gruel, Jack knew he would raise some severe objections, and hang whatever warning Nolly might angrily send his way.

Nobody had even stopped to wash their hands. While normally Jack wouldn't give a squirt of piss regarding this, he could see that the men's hands as they cupped their bowls, young and old alike, were reddened by the bits of bone that had gone into the flesh, begrimed under the nails with dried fluid, and finally he understood what Nolly was always going on about. Washing your hands was not just a nicety of polite society, it was—

"Here's your bowl."

As Jack took the bowl from Nolly's dirty fingers, he did not quite know what to say in response to the spare way that Nolly said it to him. He took the spoon Nolly was offering him as well, delivered by the merest sense of recognition from Nolly, but Jack was distracted from this by the fact that what was being loaded into his bowl was indeed not the pale gruel of both that morning and the night before. Instead, it was a watery soup with floating bits of cabbage and potato and perhaps bacon, though he could not be sure.

Into his other hand was shoved a hunk of brown bread. While this was, normally, not enough bread to even remark upon, it became a feast to his eyes. But, as he sat down next to Nolly, and even waited through grace before nudging him to share the small miracle, all he got for his pains was a snarl from Nolly and a show of teeth. The message was obvious; the work-house had rules and Jack was a fool if he didn't already know them.

Well, he did not know them, but even if he did, that did not mean that he would follow them. Or, he might do if it assisted him in getting out of this place. Only trouble was, Nolly was following them for no other reason than to follow them. And that would be both his and Jack's undoing.

"Nolly," he said, moving his elbow so that it would brush Nolly's elbow without jarring him. "Is the bread any good? Tell me true, for I would rather not waste my stomach on it if it ain't."

Nolly was halfway with the spoon to his mouth, saving the bread for dessert, it seemed. He kept his left hand tucked about the bread, as if he feared that someone might take it from him. As someone had done, as someone *must* have done throughout the years, at the workhouse, or at that baby farm Nolly had mentioned once in passing.

Withholding food was something Fagin had never done. Though, to be sure, extra work or a clout to the head had occurred when Fagin had deemed the occasion warranted it, but Jack had been spared this extreme deprivation. Nolly had not.

"Nolly," said Jack, as he shifted the bread along the wooden tabletop. Jack was hungry, but he was not fearful about it and so could begrudge the taste of bread. "D'you want my bread? You c'n have it if you want."

All at once, Nolly's face changed, crumpling into that of a young child who had been scolded and punished once too many times for something that was simply beyond his ability to control. And even though he was staring fixedly at his now empty bowl, Nolly's eyes were wet and he was blinking, as though grabbing for even an ounce of control.

It was bad, so very bad, to see him like this. Jack could almost feel what Nolly was feeling, just then.

"No, Jack," said Nolly, very gently, his shoulders hunching forward, as if that could hide his hand as it pushed the bread toward Jack. "You must eat it to keep your strength up."

Their fingers touched as Jack took the bread, a brief caress between them as Jack watched Nolly scrub at his eyes with the back of his other hand.

Jack stopped chewing the bread.

"Nolly," he said, the bread suddenly turning to an unappetizing wad of sawdust in his mouth. "It'll be all right—"

"By-and-bye, Jack?" asked Nolly, wiping his sleeve along his chin. "D'you promise?"

"By-and-bye, Nolly," said Jack. "I promise."

And watched as an unimpeded tear slipped past Nolly's scrubbing hand and hit the tabletop, anyway.

HE TIGHTENED HIS WHOLE BODY, FEELING THE HEAT IN HIS chest as he tried to stop. To stop his tears, to stop feeling the crushing sense of having failed himself, failed Jack, and all because of Jack's kindness. His forgiveness about the water. His willingness to give, when there was precious little to be given.

Jack would have done without his own meager share of bread, had Oliver desired it, and it was because of this that Oliver was undone. Once a coiled spring of righteous anger could have given him strength, he now became unraveled, and all because Jack cared for him.

When he'd been a child in Hardingstone, the sense of being alone, of being lost amidst the bewildering lack of anything good, anything comforting, had been his whole world. As for his friend Dick, with his sweet smile, his tiny, courageous heart, Oliver had left him at Mrs. Mann's baby farm when Mr. Bumble had collected Oliver to take him to the workhouse on his ninth birthday. From that moment, Oliver had been alone and considered the workhouse to be a place that *was* his existence; he could know no other.

Now he had Jack, which made it worse, because he knew, even if Jack did not, just how easily the connection between them could be broken. One of them could be taken away at the whim of the workhouse master, and the other would never know whither he had gone.

The tabletop before him was damp; he wiped it away with the sleeve of his jacket and tried to blink to clear his eyes. He felt Jack beside him, sitting close along the bench so their hips connected, Jack's warmth easing into him.

Would he have had this when he was nine, he would have fared better, cried less. Perhaps not gotten caught up in the drawing of lots where the short straw had propelled Oliver into a life for which he'd not been prepared. Jack would have stopped him from participating in such foolishness as a game of chance, of that Oliver was quite sure.

But then, he would not have met Jack.

It was a mirthless moment, but the realization of it, that he'd had to go through all of that to have this, his Jack, beside him, struck him. It was a twisted laugh that built in his throat, and he swallowed it back down, for he couldn't draw anybody's attention to him. Not at that moment. Not when Jack was so close, his arm half around Oliver's waist, holding up the bread that Oliver had yet to eat.

"It tastes like straw," said Jack, very low, so only Oliver could hear. "An' not meant for anythin' but a cow to eat, but you need to eat it. Go on, now."

"Cows don't eat straw," said Oliver, his voice thick, ragged. "They sleep in it."

"An' you're meant to eat this, for in this place, such a thing 'tis precious an' rare."

Oliver made himself look at Jack now, at the bit of bread in his hand, his fingers sparkling with bone flakes. And at Jack, his green eyes, so earnest and dear. This, Oliver knew, sitting beside him, was what was precious and rare. So he took the bread and ate it, and nodded, wishing for a bit of water to wash it down.

"It does," Olivier said, talking with his mouth full, but only to amuse Jack. "It tastes just like straw." The bread was sticking to the roof of his mouth, and Jack pulled a tumbler of water over and gave it to Oliver to drink.

Oliver's hand froze on the tumbler as he took it, thinking to make a gesture of it, to make Jack drink it, to make up for what had happened in the yard. But he saw the look in Jack's eyes, the tiny shake of his head. The push of Jack's hand on his, that he should just be quiet and drink.

Jack picked up a tumbler of water for himself and, with a little lift of his hand, as though he were making a toast at a formal gathering of kings, Jack drank down the water. And with a sigh, a moist exhale, he all but slammed the tumbler on the table.

The meal was ending, and the men were directed to carry their spoons and crockery to where the small boys waited with their wicker baskets, holding them high, bearing up as the baskets grew heavier with each item placed in them. It took four boys, then, to carry the dirty dishes off.

As Oliver watched them go, he had a vague memory of never having been selected to go anywhere else in the workhouse. For only good boys had special tasks, and he remembered thinking it might have been interesting, even exciting, to have been picked for such a task as the other boys had been. Even if only once.

Now, his gaze raking over the crowd of men, aged, infirm, thin, sickly, all shuffling and shambling into two matched lines as they made their way to the stairs to go down, he was glad that he'd not been picked. For he would have seen what a future in the workhouse would have brought him, and he would have thrown himself on the nearest pike.

When dinner was over, an attendant lined the men up to march back downstairs. But instead of being taken to the men's dormitories, they were led across the yard, along a short passage, and out through two large, brown-painted wooden doors that now stood open. A man stood at the doorway counting them as they walked and jotted down something in a ledger.

Jack and Nolly were told to get into one of two long wagons and, for a moment, Jack could only stare. The wagons were rough, with wooden poles sticking up along the sides of the wagon, much in the way of a hayrick wagon. But since it wasn't harvest time, and even Jack knew that hay was harvested in the autumn of the year, then they were going to be taken where they could do some other sort of work, some sort of spade labor. The muddy, iron-rimmed wheels gave the destination of the carts away.

Nolly was getting on the wagon, sliding along the bench seat, so Jack could do no less than join him. Besides, his heart was racing a bit at an as-yet-unexamined idea. If they were being taken to a field, then there might be a way to get away.

He didn't want to tell Nolly of this just yet, in case his guess was entirely wrong and they were simply being taken to work in a different building, or indeed, a different workhouse. So as the cart jostled into motion, he only grabbed the edges of the bench he was sitting on, and kept his head down, making himself focus on the boots the men were wearing, how they seemed worn thin, had holes where upper met sole, the laces broken and knotted.

There was a brisk wind moving over them as the wagon went along the road, setting the chill into Jack's bones. Had he had enough to eat, he knew he would not be feeling the weather as much, but he was. In the distance was a tall, gray church spire and the shapes of buildings, a grove of trees blocking the complete view.

But the way they were traveling, albeit slowly, was parallel to the town, heading into the wind; the town shifted by on one side, while the quarter-sections of newly plowed dark earth moved into view. Circled around the field was a winding tree line, the branches still winter-gray, but with tiny green edges to indicate that the trees knew that spring was well on its way. Amidst the trees, Jack saw the thick line of sparkling water.

For a moment, he just sat there until forced to get out of the wagon, Nolly tumbling into place beside him. The attendant gave every man a bucket, and they stood in two rows, waiting for their orders, as if duty and obedience would get them anywhere at all.

"You will find rocks in the soil and carry them in the buckets to the edge of the field. Should you find a weed, you should pull it. Anyone shirking their duty will be on reduced rations. Now get working."

Jack walked with Nolly to one of the newly plowed furrows, going past the older, slower men, his feet sinking into the loamy, damp soil. For a brief, precious moment, his eyes met Nolly's, which he thought would give it away, but it seemed that Nolly only wanted to look at him rather than the old men, the infirm paupers, working so slowly, so painfully stiff as they bent to the task assigned them.

The field must have been picked before, as there seemed to be a lot of digging with frail, bare hands and not a whole lot of finding of the stones. But there were spar-thin weeds to pull at least, so the paupers could work on that and earn their meager supper that night.

As for him and Nolly, if all went well, they'd be very far from here by that time. It occurred to him, then, that Nolly might feel differently about trying to make a run for it; it would be crucial to bring him along slowly.

So Jack did. He shrugged his shoulders, and bent to the task, bending over to stir the turned soil for small rocks, large pebbles, breaking it up in his fingers when he found nothing. He pulled weeds, and put them into the bucket, all the while acting as if this were his only object. And this rather than, when he straightened up, the bucket banging against his thigh, what he was actually doing, which was moving further down the row than was needed, leaving large swathes of untouched earth amidst which nestled unsearched-for stones and weeds.

He'd thought Nolly would simply follow along in that mindless, silent way that had possessed him since the moment of their arrest. Jack would have to keep doing what he was doing until they were close to the curve of trees by the river, and hustle Nolly out of his far-focused gaze and make him run by any means he could think of. Including a swift kick to the arse, if that's what was called for. But after the third shuffle like this, with his boots clumped with mud and the bottom of his trouser legs swamped with damp, Nolly came up behind him, bucket banging against his leg, his brows all furrowed and cross.

"What are you doing, Jack? We've missed an entire yard of furrow." Nolly gestured with the bucket, and Jack had to sidestep out of the way or get smacked with it, almost tripping over a clump of dark brown earth.

"That's the idea," said Jack, ducking his head, keeping his voice low, although there was simply no one in earshot. "We keep movin' towards the river, nice an' simple, workin' all the while, an' then, we make our move, scoot through the trees an' cross the river an' away."

"They'll *see* us," said Nolly, the harsh tones of his words coming out in a hiss. "You're mad if you think that will work. It won't, you know. They'll *catch* us, and then—"

"They won't, not if we run fast. There's two wagons, two drivers, two guards, or whatever they are, an' around thirty or so paupers. Now, who d'you imagine is goin' to be able to catch us, let alone notice that we've gone?"

Nolly shook his head, and Jack knew he wasn't convinced. And was terrified, Jack could tell, at the mere thought of such disobedience. Jack wanted to shout at how foolish this was. But not only would this attract the wrong type of attention, it would just shatter in the air against Nolly's wall of resistance, and any chance of getting Nolly to come with him would be gone.

"Let's keep goin' then," said Jack. "Keep workin' an' movin' this way an' we'll see what comes of it."

The wind was kicking up again, bringing down slats of rain that Jack thought surely would signal the end of the workday, for who could work in such weather? But the attendants only turned up their collars, tipped down their hats, standing in the lee of the wagons and simply watched as the paupers continued working. Paupers who surely knew that their supper was at risk if they so much as complained.

This was further proof, as if Jack needed it, of the dreadful lie that Fagin had told him, then, that workhouses were good places to doss down for the night, or to hide for a while, if you needed to. It was quite clear that Fagin had never once, not in his whole life, used this ploy to escape the law. Well, every other thing that he'd advised Jack on was true, so this was less worrisome than it might have been. The important thing was to keep Nolly moving in the direction of the trees, the silver ribbon of river that wound its way along on the other side of the trees. And to move slowly.

5

TEMPTATION BENEATH RAINY SKIES

With the mud clumping on the heel of his boots, Oliver did as Jack bade him, and as he worked, he kept close to Jack while they slowly moved toward the river. The sky overhead boiled with low gray clouds that brought rain in unwanted handfuls.

If Oliver stood up, the rain drizzled on his face. If he bent over to sift through the dirt for rocks or stones, the wind whipped his jacket about and let the rain crawl up his back.

There was no stopping the work, not even for weather, though he could hear Jack muttering about the pure foolishness of it. For again, although the task was straightforward, Jack was put in the position of actually having to do the work to earn his supper, and this he earnestly despised, if the look on his face was anything to go by.

As for Jack's plan, it was more than half-mad. They would never make it to the river, but even if they did, they would be spotted before they got very far. Oliver needed to convince Jack of this, that there had to be a better way, an easier way to escape than running through the mud-thick field and crossing a river.

Oliver paused, straightening up, the bucket banging against his thigh, and looked at Jack, bent over at the waist like a common field gleaner, his dark forelock falling into his eyes. He wasn't working very hard at it, for he was merely turning over the stones in his hands, as if working the tendons of his fingers to keep them flexible. As well, his bucket was mostly empty, and if the workmaster were to measure each bucket individually, Jack would get no supper.

Shaking his head, Oliver looked up the field to where the two hayrick wagons stood, the horses content with their feedbags, the workmasters tucked in the lee of the wagons to keep out of the rain.

As for the male paupers, they were spread across the field, two to a furrow, bent over like brown curls against the darker mud. They moved slowly, as if half asleep, even though moving faster would have kept them warmer. But, as if in a dazed state, chilled to the bone, they stumbled, and bent, and pulled, and put stones and weeds in their respective buckets, all slowly, arms thin, uncovered heads slick with rain.

Oliver did not want to end up like them, of that he was certain; Jack's plan, however mad, would bring the better alternative.

"Jack," said Oliver, blinking against the rain, bending at the waist at Jack's side, as if he too were a gleaner. "Tell me again this plan? What will we do on the other side of the river? And say we do get away, how will we manage?"

"Eh?" asked Jack, looking up from where he was now hunkered down on his heels. "How will we manage? What kind of question is that? Don't you know who I am? Why, I'm the Dodger, that's who, an' I'll soon be able to get enough money to keep you from havin' to sleep beneath a hedge. Unless that's your dearest wish, of course."

Laughing a little to himself, Jack stood up, leaving the bucket wallowing half empty in the furrowed earth at his feet as he brushed his hands against his trousers. He tilted his head and looked at Oliver, the corners of his mouth curling up to smile, as if the whole idea presented itself to him as a rather jolly joke.

"Jack, I'm perfectly serious. How will we manage, how will we—?"

"We'll manage, dear Nolly, we will." Jack gestured to the field behind them, to the wagons and men that from their vantage point seemed muzzy and far away beneath the lowering skies. "No one's attendin' to where we are. They ain't even noticed how far we've gone from them. An' after we get away, why, there's pockets a-plenty in the village, I'll be bound. Never you worry; let tomorrow's problems belong to tomorrow."

Jack reached out and gently patted Oliver's cheeks, but only that, because Oliver jerked his head back, suddenly aware of where they were. That they were out of doors, and there were men not too far off who might take just that moment to look their way. Instantly he felt badly about it, as he knew he should trust that Jack would be circumspect with so many witnesses to hand.

As Jack gave him a lazy blink in lieu of a kiss, Oliver knew he was again forgiven for drawing such a strict line about it. Would that they had privacy and darkness, and would that they could be well on the other side of the river and far away from Axminster. Then he might feel bold enough to tumble Jack to the ground, be it nighttime or daytime, and smother him with kisses and touches and sweet words.

"All right, then?" asked Jack. "We just keep workin' and walkin', you an' me, and we'll soon find ourselves beyond the tree line."

"Yes," said Oliver, nodding. He hefted his bucket in his hand and, looking inside of it, shook it around to settle the rocks beneath the weeds. Not that it would matter, as he'd soon be putting the bucket down and there would be no reckoning to the amount he had gathered within it. "You're right, you *are*, I'm just—"

"You did this before," said Jack, bending over again, pretending to gather stones into his bucket, but really only tossing them around and back into the mud. "When you were just a wee lad, you did this very thing, only this time, you'll be with me. We'll be together."

This, of course, was quite true. Oliver had run away from a workhouse once before, marched all the way to London on his own, and had arrived in one piece with no one the wiser. Well, later, Uncle Brownlow and Mr. Bumble had shared hard words, but Oliver had not been dragged back to the Hardingstone workhouse.

And here he was, set to run away again, though the prospect of Jack picking pockets always filled his chest with a cold fear that Jack might get caught. That was always, and always had been, a risk for Jack with what he did to survive, and a part of him that just was. Still and all, Jack's picking pockets would be what would allow them to survive until they might settle somewhere, and Oliver could find work, maybe in a bookshop and—

"Hey, Nolly," said Jack. "C'mon, keep movin'. You'll attract more attention standin' still."

"You're right, Jack," said Oliver.

He knew that it was true. Jack knew things that Oliver did not. Things that seemed quite obvious to him once Jack had pointed them out, but had been previously unknown to him. And whether it was from Jack's experiences with Fagin's gang, or whether he'd learned it while being a convict in Port Jackson, it always came down to the single, inalienable truth that Jack was clever. Like a fox constantly able to outwit the hounds on his heels.

Oliver thought about it for a moment; Jack's plan was actually a good one, and it was Jack who had come up with it, and not himself. He knew that he normally would hesitate in telling Jack this, as if to protect Jack from his own pride, but he needed to tell him now. It needed to be said, not in repayment for all the kindness Jack had shown him, but because it was true. Jack deserved to know that.

Hunkering down next to where Jack was bent over, Oliver was able to look at him directly. He must have surprised Jack, for

Jack started and then, with a little shrug of his shoulders, hunkered down as well. Now they were knee to knee, the rain pattering on their heads, their trousers soaked, mud up to their ankles. The smell of dark, damp-soaked earth was all around them, with the faraway sound of the bell in the church steeple in the village.

"Eh?" asked Jack. He wiped his upper lip with the back of his sleeve and then ran the heel of his palm across his forehead to keep some of the rain out of his eyes.

"It's such a simple plan," said Oliver. "I'm overthinking it, as usual. You're—you're smart to come up with it, for I know I wouldn't have."

"Oh, you might've," said Jack, but his cheeks were bright, and though he tried to hide his smile, Oliver knew he was pleased just the same.

With a pat to Oliver's knee, Jack stood up and then reached down to help Oliver up.

Oliver let himself be helped, glad that he'd let himself be so lavish in his praise, and wondered why it had been so difficult. Though upon consideration it might have been that whenever Uncle Brownlow had given him a compliment, Mr. Grimwig would turn whatever Uncle Brownlow had said upon its ear while stoutly insisting that the virtue was a fault. And that Oliver was, and would always be, the antithesis of the good thing that Uncle Brownlow had found worthy.

This thought, entirely new, might take a while to settle within him, but he would let it, and vowed that when taken with the impulse to be lavish in his verbal adoration of Jack, he would let it have sway over any other, perhaps more prudent, action.

"Just give the word when it's time," said Oliver. "And I shall be right behind you."

∼

IT TOOK THEM AN HOUR SCRUBBING THROUGH THE DIRT TO move fairly close to the tree line, for there was simply not that much to find. Since it was early spring, it might be that the paupers started with this field, and moved on to the next field each day, grooming them, as if collecting the stones for a spectacular presentation at some local farmer's cotillion. Not that Jack planned to be at the workhouse in the morning, doing the disgusting bone breaking, nor any of this bloody stupid useless picking of stones, no, sir.

"Nolly," said Jack. He moved as close to Nolly as he could without stepping on Nolly's mud-clumped boots. He put the bucket down and nudged Nolly to do the same. "Put it down. We're goin' to run now."

"Now?" asked Nolly, frantic, almost breathless.

He put the bucket down, and Jack watched him wipe his hands on his trousers. They were shaking, but he did it as he looked up at Jack, a mere glance from the corner of his eyes, dark with the fright that was surely overtaking him. But there was one thing that Jack knew about Nolly and that was even when he was afraid, he was very brave.

"Yes," said Jack. "Run. *Now.*"

They could have run faster but for the clumped earth, the clods of mud clinging to their boots, the fact that they'd not eaten any real food since dinner two days ago. But the fear of being caught, Nolly's fear, which Jack had somehow taken unto himself, made him fast. Gave his legs a jolt of something that surged him forward, reaching back, making sure Nolly was with him.

Nolly was with him, running on those long legs of his. The earth churned beneath his feet, a flash in his eyes, his demeanor fierce, which Jack had not seen since their arrest. At the moment Nolly passed him by, Jack sped up, running as fast as he could go to keep up, the spring-bare trees looming overhead as they raced together up the hump of the river's border and over the top to stumble down the steep, rain-slick bank and into the water.

The river was fast and wide, swollen with spring rains and snowmelt from somewhere that Jack didn't know. The banks were slick with mud and bogged with silt. Jack slipped down and almost got stuck, reaching out to grab on to overhanging branches to keep himself steady, to keep from being sucked into the water-logged mud as the river sped by, silver and blue and brown and gorged and racing past, almost at eye level.

"Jack," said Nolly, half-shouting as he turned back.

Nolly was already waist-deep in the swirling water, his brown jacket swirling about his waist, his elbows above the surface of the water, poised, as if ready to dive in and swim his way to the other side. Which, now that Jack was looking at it, was a great deal further off than it had first seemed.

The water was a vast, roaring thing, and Nolly was unaware that Jack could not swim. Not that this was Nolly's fault, of course, for Jack had never told him. There had been no need, and so, thus, Nolly was prepared to swim, not knowing that Jack could not follow.

Well, he would let Nolly go on ahead. It would be worth it if Nolly got away. Jack could move along the bank on this side till he came to a bridge or some narrow piece of the river where he could walk or wade across. Then they could meet up somewhere.

"Whatever is the matter, why are you waiting? Come on!"

Jack heard the words as clearly as if Nolly had been standing close by, and Jack wondered how far that same sound could travel beyond the river. But he only shook his head.

"Can't swim. I'll go down this side of the river an'—"

But before Jack could finish his sentence or push off to back up the bank a small way, Nolly was backtracking. He slogged through the water and the silt, his brown jacket black with water, soaked up to his chest now as he reached out for Jack.

"You hold on to me and I'll swim for both of us."

The words bestilled Jack as he took in the expression in Nolly's eyes, the way his chin jutted out, determined.

"All right," he said, "but if I get too heavy an' you can't make it, you just let go, yes?"

Nolly shook his head and turned his shoulder to Jack so that Jack could take hold of it.

"I'm not going to do that, Jack. Just hang on, and I'll get us to the other side."

The river picked that moment to surge, as if a giant foamy hand had pushed a wall of water up from the bottom of the river. But Nolly walked into it, and when the river got up past his waist, he kicked off from the bottom and started to swim, with Jack hanging on. Only not very well, for they had only reached the middle of the river when the current snatched Jack away, his uncertain grasp on Nolly taken from him so easily he was breathless with shock.

The cold water took him, brown and muddy and swirling, an unending force that slammed him down and wouldn't let him up. For a long moment, the river swirled him around, making him blind, filling his mouth with water, but when the water shoved him upward, he broke the surface, gasping, spitting out brown water, thrashing his hands, his arms.

He tried to see through the spray to where Nolly was. But Jack couldn't even move beyond where he was, though he saw Nolly on the far bank, on his hands and knees, head bent forward, as if retching out a lungful of water.

Something held Jack fast, gripping his boot, and he kicked at it, going under, taking a mouthful of water. He pushed furiously at the water and managed to come up to the surface again. It was only if he held his body upward, letting the water push him back, that he could keep his face out of the water. It would only take one large rise to smack him in the face and drown him fully.

"Jack!"

Jack tried again, wiggling his foot rather than trying to jerk it out of what might have been a submerged branch, or the grip of a watery devil intent on his demise. And just as he thought he might have managed to get free of it, and not having any idea of how to advance through the water toward Nolly, he saw two men on horseback charging down the bank, across the river, and up the other side, before Jack could even draw breath.

They rode directly to where Nolly was, and Jack could see by their clothes, thick blue coats and black top hats, that they were fine gentlemen out for a gallop in the rain, and certainly not workhouse folk.

One of them dismounted from a large gray horse and went over to Nolly and jerked him up from the ground by his collar. He had a crop in his hand, and his mouth was open, as if he were shouting at Nolly. For a moment it looked as though he was going to strike Nolly with the crop, but Nolly grabbed his arm, heedless of the danger to himself, and pointed at the water. At Jack.

Wishing he could hear what they were saying, Jack moved his leg and almost got a mouthful of water, so he pulled upright, and hung onto the branch that was sticking out, and tried to figure out what was going on. Teeth chattering, cold to the bone as he watched.

The man with the gray horse dragged Nolly to the other horse, a rain-streaked brown one, though it looked as much like Nolly was going willingly as being dragged. The man on the brown horse took his foot out of the stirrup and leaned an arm down for Nolly to use. Which Nolly did, putting his foot in the stirrup and mounting the horse even as it danced about.

Once Nolly was behind the saddle, hanging onto it, he looked for Jack.

Jack could tell Nolly blamed himself for the failure of the plan, even though he couldn't make out exact features, for Nolly's shoulders slumped forward, and he was sitting there, as if lost, somehow. Distracted from this, Jack looked up as the man got back on the gray horse and plowed through the thick water toward Jack, and Jack understood.

Nolly had gotten on the horse willingly if the gentlemen would go and rescue Jack. Who had been too damn stupid to learn to swim, a fact he regretted now with all of his heart. For if he had learned to swim, then he could have made a break for it and come back to rescue Nolly. Which Nolly would have appreciated, and it would have been a glorious story they could have told to each other for the rest of their lives.

The gray horse loomed large in front of Jack, cutting a swathe in the river as it moved sideways. The horse blocked some of the force of the river away from Jack, for which he was grateful. The man on the gray leaned sideways in the saddle a bit and pointed the crop at Jack.

"You're due for rescue, young scamp, for which your friend has made us a bargain to not give us any trouble. And, as well, the workmasters who've promised us half a guinea each for your return to the workhouse. Well, come on, get up."

"M'foot is stuck," said Jack. His lips were numb, and his whole body felt sore, and the water just kept rushing past him. "Can't get loose."

"Well, I'm not getting off," said the man. He appraised the river as he held the gray in place, his gloved hands on the reins. He was wet up to his boot tops, but it was probably a grand adventure to him, rather than anything dire. "Hold on to my leg and we'll ease you free. Grab hold."

He had the voice of a man used to being obeyed, much as Nolly did when he was in a mood to be that way, like a young gentleman with a houseful of servants. In that way, the voice sounded familiar so Jack let go of the branch and grabbed hold of the man's booted foot.

The leather was slick beneath his hands, so Jack wrapped his arms all around, feeling the length of the man's leg, the damp, hot pelt of the gray horse, and closed his eyes. The horse heaved beneath him at the man's urging, and Jack felt the wrench of his leg before it slipped free, intact and mostly unhurt, though he didn't doubt it would be sore come morning.

The water parted to make way for the horse, and Jack was banged about as he was dragged until he felt the hardness of the river bottom as it rose up along the bank. Then he let go and the horse lunged up the bank, spraying water and mud, leaving Jack on his hands and knees in the silt, head down, his legs and arms shaking.

The man on the gray made the horse turn, and he leaned down to give more orders.

"Get up, you whelp. You've been rescued, and we're to collect a reward. Never knew a pauper was actually worth anything before this, but I'll know better now."

Half-crawling up the bank, hands in the mud, Jack made himself stand up, looking over to where Nolly was riding pillion on the brown horse. Nolly had a good seat and long legs, and it was a pity that the only one to appreciate this was Jack himself, for Nolly was probably completely unaware. Not that it would matter, for quite soon they'd be back at the workhouse, and nobody would care at all.

"Come on, mount up. We need to get going before it rains any harder and we all melt."

The man on the gray took his foot out of the stirrup, much as the other man had, and leaned down to give Jack an assist in mounting. But Jack had no idea how to begin.

It wasn't that he didn't know how it was done, as he'd seen plenty of folk mounting and dismounting. He'd even made his linked hands into a stirrup for a muddy boot a time or two. But he'd never actually mounted a horse this way, and the large wall of gray flank and four large-hoofed legs was enough to remind him why: horses were just too fucking big.

Jack could only shake his head as he thought of a way to convince the man to let him *walk* back to the workhouse, in spite of the fact that his left ankle felt quite sore, and the workhouse was the last destination on earth he might wish for.

"Blast it," said the man. "Here comes the rain. Drummond, be a good man and let the other one down to help."

In a quick moment, Nolly had dismounted, landing unsteadily on the ground before coming over to Jack. His hair was plastered to his head, with mud streaked along his face, and his eyes were enormous circles, his mouth white. As he shook his head, just the once, Jack knew Nolly didn't want to help him up, that he wanted to help Jack escape somehow. Only there wasn't any way, as the man on the gray horse could easily outpace Jack and, perhaps, force him back into the river where he would surely drown.

Jack shook his head in response and jerked his chin at the gray horse to let Nolly know it was all right. That he should help Jack up, and when they returned to the workhouse, they would figure out another way.

Nolly made a stirrup of his hands, and Jack stepped into it with his boot. His ankle protested, but there was no other way, as he had to get on from the horse's left side. As well, he hated the fact that he was getting mud all over Nolly.

He reached up to where the man in the blue coat was reaching down, and pulled as Nolly lifted him up. He was able to swing his leg over the animal's broad back just as the pressure from Nolly's hands left him, and the man let go.

It was only with a flustered grasping of the man's blue coat that Jack didn't spill himself over the other side, which would have been, no doubt, inglorious and painful. He couldn't even watch Nolly get back on the brown horse, for the man on the gray clucked under his tongue and gave the crop a snap, half-hitting the horse, and then again, right across Jack's wet leg.

Jack yelped, and the gray bounded into action, taking them down into the river, rushing and galloping through the foam and up the other side, wet and moving through the trees so fast that the branches were like fine whips made of wire that snapped against his arms and shoulders. He tucked his face in the middle of the man's back and hung on.

They sped across the field, he and Nolly, on borrowed horse-back; Nolly sitting atop the edge of the saddle like a fine horseman should, and Jack himself, feeling like an untrained monkey who has not quite learned how. But the gallop was short, for both horses pulled up to where the wagons were and the four attendants waited.

As well, with all the male paupers lined up, with half-full buckets in their hands, their dismay pulled at their faces. For now they were standing in the rain, and their work was not quite complete, on account of it had been interrupted by this befouled escape attempt. The judgment on this would determine whether or not they got their supper. Jack could see it all in a glance.

"You there," said the man on the gray horse, addressing one and all. "Whom should I speak to at the workhouse? From whom shall we get our reward?"

"Ask for Master Pickering," said one of the workmasters. "Tell him Workmaster Foxall sent you, an' he'll do right by you."

"Thank you," said the man on the gray horse. "'Tis been a pleasure."

Both riders tapped their top hats with their crops and spurred their mounts into yet another gallop across the field to the road and along the edge of town until they arrived foam-flecked and breathing hard under the double weight that they carried.

No doubt alerted by the commotion, the porter came out with Mr. Bassler, whose apron was undone. The porter was settling his hat on his head, as if they'd disturbed him from some unknown indoor activity, and he eyed the horses, and the gentlemen who guided them. Then he looked at Jack and Nolly, riding behind the men, and shook his head.

"I've no doubt what happened here," he said.

"Workmaster Foxall sent us to speak to Master Pickering. Said there was a half guinea each for the return of these two."

"Indeed, there would be," said the porter. "I'll take you to the master directly, gentlemen. Will you dismount and come this way? Mr. Bassler here will take your horses. As for you two, get down and look lively, I'll warrant that the master will want to have words with you."

6

RELATES THE INTERVIEW IN MASTER PICKERING'S OFFICE

Master Pickering's office was as dull and dry as it had been that first day, well appointed with high, clean windows and the somber, dark desk. Only now Jack was dripping wet and shivering, trying to warm himself up, as he'd not been invited to stand closer to the fire. Nor would he be, though he would have relinquished that small favor if Nolly had been invited. It was all Jack could do to move a little that way so that Nolly might be closer to it, at least, even if neither one of them could afford to relax.

"I don't normally have to receive paupers in my office more than once, if ever that," said Master Pickering, standing up from behind his desk. He pointed at them. "And you're dripping on my carpet. Back up at once and apologize for creating a mess that someone else will have to clean up."

Jack looked down. His boots, muddy and soaked, were leaking about the eyeholes for the laces, and Nolly's were as well. Their boot tips were just on the carpet's edge and would have done exactly no harm if they'd remained where they were. But this was the workhouse, and the master's word was, apparently, law, so Jack scooted back, wincing as Nolly did the same, for Nolly belonged on the carpet, even if Jack did not.

"Now ask my pardon."

Before Nolly could even open his mouth, humble as he looked down at his clenched hands, Jack swept a mud-streaked hand across his forehead, as if doffing his hat, and took a bow, as wide and as generous as any proper gentleman might. Then, with his mock hat off, he straightened up and nodded at Master Pickering.

"Beggin' your pardon, sir, ever so much, for standin' an' drippin' on your carpet after a long day in the field pickin' stones in the rain."

As Nolly drew in a shocked breath, Jack knew that Master Pickering heard the jaunty tone in Jack's voice, the mockery, for all he only acknowledged it by narrowing his eyes. He rang a bell on his desk, sat back down, and picked up the single piece of paper that lay on the dark green blotter.

"You boys are in here because of theft. It is my responsibility to keep you locked up until the June assizes. It was my error to let you roam free, and so now you will be kept with the under-eighteens, under the more watchful eye of Workmaster Chalenheim. Meanwhile," he laid the paper back down, barely looking at it. "I'm going to send to London to see if there is anything the constabulary there can tell me, for you seem far too wild to have limited yourselves to stealing only books."

Jack had a record, as did Nolly, though as to the local law being able to find the right court with the relevant paperwork, Jack had his doubts. Still, Master Pickering's threat made his heart leap in his throat, though he tried not to show it.

Nolly, beside him, jerked into a wary stiffness, and Jack made himself take a breath. He would deal with that later and explain to Nolly how unlikely it would be that Master Pickering would be informed of any of their past actions; magistrates had mountains of paperwork, this he'd seen with his very eyes. Still, this was Nolly's worst nightmare come to haunt him, for what if they did find out about Cromwell? And never mind that Jack would be deported back to Australia straightaway.

The door opened and in walked Workmaster Chalenheim. He was, as before, dressed in workhouse brown, though the cloth was of a finer type than the paupers wore, his dun-colored apron stain free. He carried himself as a man would who was in charge, even if his fiefdom was a group of young boys, too small and starved to prove any resistance. His thick brows were heavy over his dark eyes, and his mouth seemed to slip against his teeth as he nodded at Master Pickering.

"You sent for me, sir," said the workmaster. His eyes took in Jack and Nolly, standing there in perfect silence, even if not in perfect obedience.

"Yes, indeed," said Master Pickering. "These two attempted to go over the wall, as they say, this afternoon, thinking that they could avoid the legal induction which is surely due them."

"I see," said the workmaster. He looked them both over, one at a time, and if his eyes were too bright and attentive, Jack tried not to wonder. "How might I assist you with them?"

"You're to take them under your care, Workmaster Chalenheim, for I need to secure them until the June assizes. They are, under no circumstances, to be allowed outside of the workhouse until that time."

"Then I am the most perfect person to take charge of them," said the workmaster with a small bow that contained none, absolutely none, of Jack's mockery.

"Yes, indeed," said Master Pickering. "You're to take them under your care." Master Pickering waved his hand at Jack and Nolly, as if they were mere pieces of baggage that needed to be placed in storage. "That one is Jack Dawkins, and that one is Oliver Twist. As I cannot tell you which one is the ringleader, I will let you determine that. All jurisdiction I hand over to you, as per usual. Just don't let them get out of hand, do you understand?"

"Yes, I do, sir," said Workmaster Chalenheim, and he seemed very satisfied with his additional responsibilities.

As Master Pickering turned to the pen in the holder on his

desk to dip it in the inkwell and jot something down in one of his many ledgers, Workmaster Chalenheim turned his attention fully to Jack and Nolly.

"I don't believe I will have any trouble with these two. Will I, boys?"

This was not a question for which there was an answer other than the negative, so Jack shook his head. Nolly just glared because that was how he was when confronted. He looked as though he wanted to charge right through the question, as though it were a brick wall and he made of a battering ram.

With no spare moment between them as Chalenheim gestured for them to precede him from the master's office into the main hallway, Jack could not signal to Nolly to tame his temper down, for Chalenheim would see, and perhaps call them to task for talking and breathing at the same time, or some other foolish attempt at control. For that was what the workhouse was made of, rules and control, and the desire to squash anything remotely resembling kindness.

Chalenheim moved ahead of them, his boot heels clicking on the stones in the hall as he led them into the bathing room where they'd been received some days ago. There the porter waited with two stacks of clean brown clothes, blissfully dry.

At his nod, Jack stripped off his damp clothes, not caring that both men were watching him, eyeing him with distaste, as if his eagerness to change out of muddy, wet garments were somehow a reflection of his low state. Well, Jack couldn't care less what they thought, even if Chalenheim's eyes tracked his every move.

Chalenheim tracked every move of Nolly's as well, though Nolly, Jack was glad to see, was demonstrating some forbearance as he followed Jack's lead and changed clothes without a word. The porter even gave them dry stockings, which they were allowed to sit down and untie their boots to put on, and a rough towel to dry their still-dripping heads. When they were fully dressed again, the porter shook his head.

"I should have known these two would have been trouble," he said to Chalenheim, as if Jack and Nolly were not even there. "But they'll be in the proper hands, if they're in your care, sir."

"I should hope so," said Chalenheim. "Come along now, lads, it's almost time for supper."

Making himself obedient, and hopefully an example to Nolly as to how to avoid particular notice, Jack followed Chalenheim out into the main hall, where they turned left to go through a broad door, where there was another dining hall.

This hall was as wide as the men's dining hall, though not so long. It had the same long tables and benches that groups of young boys of various ages and heights were moving into place in preparation for the evening's meal. There was even a smoking cauldron over a low brick-lined fire that emitted the same sour-sweet treacle smell, with a man and woman, dressed in pauper brown with dun-colored aprons, standing and waiting.

"Stop," said Chalenheim.

Though his voice was not very loud, every movement, every sound, even the smallest breath, came to a complete and utter halt. All of the paupers turned, very quickly, as one body, to face Chalenheim as he pointed at one of the tables.

"Move those tables and benches back to the wall, but leave this one in the middle." Chalenheim's voice echoed off the stone walls and seemed to rattle the windows.

There was a scurry of movement as the young paupers jumped to do his bidding, dragging the benches and tables away from the middle of the room, struggling with the heavy, clunky wood, faces pale, while they did the best that they could. Even the benches on either side of the table were removed, leaving the table in the middle of the room, a long, dark, wooden island.

"I cannot imagine," said Chalenheim, suddenly addressing both Jack and Nolly, "which one of you was behind today's foolishness, but I will hazard a guess, and simply deal with the consequences if I am incorrect."

Before Jack could figure out what that meant, Chalenheim pointed at Jack.

"You will stand on that side, and you," he pointed at Nolly, "will stand across from him. *Move.*"

Unable to puzzle it out, Jack did as he was told, which seemed safest at the moment. The table was not quite a yard across, with three rough-hewn planks making up its surface. If they were to stand on top of it to be made some example of, he wouldn't mind that, but it seemed Chalenheim had some other action in mind.

"Mr. Louis, bring the strap if you please."

Chalenheim barely had to raise his voice, for yet again his bidding caused immediate action.

Jack only wanted to reach out to Nolly across that table, to push the still-damp hair back from his forehead, to get Nolly to look at him. To assure Nolly that it would be all right, that everything would be all right, that they would get through this, because Jack could take a beating with the best of them. It was only a strap, after all.

When, with a hurried bow, Mr. Louis handed over the leather strap to Chalenheim, the room became quite still and, even with the number of boys, young boys and tall boys, absolutely silent.

"You, Oliver Twist," said Chalenheim, pointing at Nolly with an assured manner. "Bend over the table, directly in front of you. And you, Jack Dawkins." Chalenheim pointed at Jack, and Jack felt the sweat break out along the back of his head. "You will grab his wrists and pull him tightly to. If you let go, or ease up, I will double the whipping I'm about to deliver. Is that understood?"

Jack could not do it; the beating should be for him. It didn't matter that Nolly obeyed, and bent himself over the table without even a glance at Jack, as if he'd known this moment was coming all along, a foregone conclusion to the downward spiral they'd apparently been on ever since they left London, and perhaps, even, from before that.

As Jack looked down at the curve of Nolly's head, the length of his back garbed in pauper brown, at those hands, still mud-stained as they uncurled themselves to lay flat on the table, Jack felt his breath catch in his throat, hard as if he were trying to swallow shards of ice. In his heart was the pain of a clenched fist, for he could not hurt Nolly. He could not be a party to it.

"You will do as you are told, Jack," said Chalenheim from the end of the table where he stood, though Jack couldn't bring himself to look up. "Or you will suffer the same consequence as your friend here."

"I would rather that," said Jack through gritted teeth. "I would rather *that* than—"

But as he was about to lash out, as he'd hoped to prevent Nolly from doing, he felt a faint brush on his hand and looked down. There, Nolly had reached out with his hand, his whole body still pressed against the table, but his fingers brushed Jack's fingers, a gentle curl. There was a turn of Nolly's head, as if he meant to shake it and tell Jack *no*.

"If you do not do as you are told this very moment, I will triple the whipping."

He was unable to balance the moment in his head. He could only be guided by what he felt Nolly would want, even if it would cause him pain, for it would cause Nolly far less grief to do it this way. At least he hoped so.

Jack would kick himself later for it, good and solid, but he took Nolly's hands in his. He gave them a squeeze before moving his grip to secure it around Nolly's wrists. He felt Nolly's skin twitch beneath his touch, and settled himself against it, tried to remove himself from the moment, as he knew how to do, hating himself all the while as Chalenheim moved around the table to stand to Nolly's left side.

Jack didn't know if he could close his eyes or not, whether that would constitute some disobedience that would be vented against Nolly, so he kept them open. Stared straight ahead, and cursed his vision for being able to see everything that was happening just the same.

What was worse was hearing it, the low hum of the strap through the air, the crack as it found its mark. The feel of Nolly jerking back, and of his own hands, just a bit slippery, almost losing their grip. Startled, his heart beating fast, he hefted his grip, making it more firm while Nolly tried, Jack knew that he did, tried hard to stay in place, so as not to pull away from Jack's hold on him.

He heard, very faintly, Nolly's exhaled breath upon the boards, almost a sigh, low and oddly gentle, and it made Jack want to let go and crawl under the table to hide. But Chalenheim was cocking his arm back as far as it might go, so Jack had to hold on to Nolly with everything he had, and not let go as the strap came down with enough force to jar the table. There was no sound from Nolly this time, as if he'd tucked everything away inside of him, and would not let it out, no matter how hard he was hit.

Chalenheim continued with the whipping, swinging wide and bringing the strap down hard across Nolly's backside each time. Jack was forced to press his thighs against the table to keep it from moving across the floor, as he felt the low thud of the strap, each flinch of Nolly's body, down to his bones.

He was pressed so close to the table that he could feel Nolly's fists hard against his thighs, and the quiver that ran up each arm, and still Jack did not let himself let go. He felt the shudder of Nolly's body echo within his own, and counted each time the strap landed, and lost track when the number rose above thirty, opening his mouth to speak that that was enough, *surely* that was enough.

The count might have been higher than fifty by the time Chalenheim stopped, not even breathing hard, and he leaned close, pressing his front along Nolly's back.

"Will I have any more trouble out of you, Oliver?" he asked, his mouth moving against Nolly's ear.

Nolly shook his head. Jack could hear him try to take a breath to answer out loud, as must surely be required, but Chalenheim straightened up, apparently satisfied, and looked down at where Jack was still holding on with a death grip on Nolly's wrists.

"You may let go now, and Mr. Louis, here is the strap. Boys, put the tables in order for supper. And you." Here Chalenheim yanked Nolly upright, gripping the collar of his brown jacket, giving him a solid shake. "No supper for you, as you'll be spending the night in the refractory room."

Jack's hands were empty, ghosts of Nolly's skin echoing in the space of his still-curved fingers. He lunged, yanking on Chalenheim's sleeve to stop him, taking a breath to raise his voice, for surely it would be inhuman for Nolly to have nothing to eat, and never mind that Jack would suffer the night without him in this horrible place.

"You can't do that," said Jack through his teeth, certain that this would give Chalenheim pause and make him rethink his decision. "You can't starve him, you *can't*."

Jack pulled so hard that he almost felt the cloth tear in his hands, but that was only Chalenheim, breaking free of Jack's grasp to shove Jack hard, right against the table, bending him backwards against it.

"Can't I?" asked Chalenheim. It was obvious he already knew the answer, his hand pressed hard in the middle of Jack's chest making it difficult to breathe. "Indeed I can, for I have complete jurisdiction as the master said, and this is the usual method for dealing with runaways."

Jack had not a moment to consider whether he should continue to struggle against that hand when Mr. Louis came up beside them.

"I'll take him to the refractory, sir," said Mr. Louis, exchanging Chalenheim's grip on Nolly's collar for his own.

Nolly's head hung down, his forehead glistening, his chest heaving jaggedly, gray-striped shirt all rucked about his waist. All

Jack wanted was to go to him, but Chalenheim pulled Jack upward by his shirt front and nodded at Mr. Louis.

"Thank you, Mr. Louis. You are always useful, and I will not hesitate to tell Master Pickering so the next time I encounter him."

As Mr. Louis marched Nolly out of the boy's dining hall, Jack would have chased after him had it not been for Chalenheim's solid grip on him. The workmaster's fist, as Jack looked down, was wider than Jack's breastbone, and was well fed and powerful. Even as Jack tried to pull away, Chalenheim yanked him up and walked him backwards till he was slammed against the brick wall. Chalenheim pressed his fist hard against Jack's chest until he almost couldn't gasp a breath.

"The two of you are more trouble than ten paupers, but we'll soon have that worked out of you." Chalenheim looked at Jack with his dark eyes, his mouth quirking into a lopsided smile. "Soon have it worked out of you."

In another moment, that fist released from Jack's chest, and Jack took a huge breath. But it was too late, for the door out of the dining hall was already closed, and Nolly was somewhere beyond it, beyond Jack's help. And Jack was almost beyond his own help, fatigued beyond measure, unable to think whether he should make a run for it.

He would chance it, if he knew where the refractory was, if there weren't at least five doors between him and the outside, for even he couldn't pick locks that fast. And, as well, as he stayed against the wall, leaning, rubbing his chest, still looking toward the door that Nolly had gone through, he noticed that one of the paupers was looking at him.

The pauper was small, but then they all were, with close-cropped dark hair and a wary look about his eyes. When he saw he had Jack's attention, he shook his head quite slowly, casting a glance at Chalenheim's back, who was turned away directing the organization of the tables, and calling for the attendants to get the gruel ready to dish up.

When Jack looked back at the boy, the boy was already joining with his fellows, taking a bowl and a spoon from the end of the far table, and getting in line down the center of the room. Taking a shuddery breath, Jack ran his fingers over the jagged hem of his jacket, feeling the thick stitches there, the cold draft about his ankles from the boots that had not yet dried.

Had Nolly been the one left behind while Jack was dragged to refractory, he might have taken to kicking the tables and throwing bowls, for all the good that would have done him, though Jack could entirely sympathize. The smarter thing to do was to keep a level head, so rather than try to bash it against a brick wall that simply would not budge, he would, instead, keep his head low and make himself still, to watch for whatever opportunity might present itself, both to find Nolly, and to find a way through the many locked doors to freedom.

MR. LOUIS WAS TALLER THAN OLIVER, AND THE ANGLE OF HIS hand on Oliver's neck forced him to tip his head forward, otherwise those long fingers bit into him like sharp claws. Mr. Louis marched him down the passage from the boy's dining hall, as quick as he might, in spite of the fact that Oliver's whole body throbbed from the waist down.

The back of his thighs, his backside, felt numb, even as the blood pounded through them, his belly scraping against itself, his head whirling with emptiness. But he kept up as best as he could as they went past the bank of windows, dark with rain, and past the series of doors on his right, where groups of women, aproned for work in a kitchen or scullery, stared out of the open doorways as he was marched along.

It was a walk of shame, of this Oliver was sure, meant to engender him with the very solid idea that he was a bad orphan, and it almost made him laugh in bitter remembrance, for he'd taken this walk before. This *very* walk, when Mr. Bumble had sought to teach him the lesson about wanting more than what was offered him, for wanting more than what the board of directors felt he deserved. And, to that, in their minds, he hadn't even deserved as much as he was given.

The smell of the kitchen swamped over him, burnt gruel, cleaning rags, salt, treacle, the acid of cleaning soda. And the layer of effort required to cook three meals a day, the sweat of unwashed bodies and grimy aprons. The sense of exhaustion, even, as Oliver was dragged past the open doorways, while he kept his eyes down and tried to keep up with Mr. Louis, slipping on the damp stones beneath his feet, the blood pounding through him, as if he were being beaten from within.

Perhaps he'd deserved the beating he'd gotten, for not being faster across the field, for having let go of Jack mid-stream in the river, for being unable to hold them both up as the spring current had rushed past them both and broken Oliver's hold on Jack.

That Jack had not been swept away completely in the brown and roiling water was a miracle in and of itself. That two gentlemen had come on the hunt for them and had been able to rescue Jack was another sort of miracle. For which the price to be paid was the confines of the workhouse for them both, and the refractory room for Oliver.

Jack might not agree, and were Oliver to ask Jack of it, Oliver was quite sure that Jack would not. This was a comforting thought, that Jack would not consider Oliver to blame, though this was all the comfort he could take with him, for Oliver stoutly knew that he *was* to blame. And for that, he deserved whipping and deserved the refractory room.

At the end of the passage, Mr. Louis jerked Oliver to the right, and made as if to push him down a narrow flight of stone steps. The stairway was quite steep. It led into a maw of darkness, and for a moment, Oliver teetered at the top of the stair, then pushed back, reaching for the wall, and jerked his neck out of Mr. Louis's grasp.

"You're to go down," said Mr. Louis, as if quite startled by this unwarranted event, and puzzled by Oliver's refusal.

Oliver could smell fresh air coming from somewhere above, beyond the stairway, untainted air that indicated a doorway to the outside. From below came the acid tang of coal and dust, and the dank, low odor of rot beneath heavy stone.

He might think of escape, if it wouldn't mean leaving Jack behind. But he could not leave Jack, he *would* not leave Jack even if he could escape, and yet he was unable to make himself go down those stairs. It was too dark, and the cold reached up at him as if to embrace him in an overly fond and familiar grip, and though he deserved his night of misery, he suddenly could not allow it to happen.

"Get along, you," said Mr. Louis, reaching his arms out to block the way to the passage, forcing Oliver to take a step down into the darkness. "Don't make me call Workmaster Chalenheim, for he will lay into you as soon as he sees you."

Oliver opened his mouth, wanting to make a strong retort that he wasn't afraid of Workmaster Chalenheim, and that the beating had not cowed him. But then he heard the weight of a tread in the passage and saw the outline of a man coming to stand next to Mr. Louis.

"Is there aught amiss, Mr. Louis?"

It was Mr. Bassler, with his half-bald pate and his dun-colored apron streaked from the day's labors. In one hand, he carried a candle-lantern that was burned almost to the stub. He held it up, as if to reveal what was before him, but instead sent streaky, dark shards to layer against the walls of the stairway.

"You can assist me with this one," said Mr. Louis, almost hissing. "For he won't go down."

Oliver almost laughed again at Mr. Louis's surprise at this, though it also made sense, as he would typically only have to deal with much smaller, weaker boys. A shudder went through him at the thought of any of the boys in the workhouse's care having to go down these steps, forced by Mr. Louis's less-than-tender grip.

"You *will* go down, boy," said Mr. Bassler, moving forward to the point where he blocked the light from the passage. "Or I'll know the reason why not."

The two men took a step forward almost at the same time, though Oliver clawed the gritty stone wall of the stairwell and did not move out of the way. But his moment of defiance was for nothing, as both Mr. Bassler and Mr. Louis each grabbed him, hard, their fingers circling around his upper arms, and dragged him backwards to the bottom of the steps.

Once there, Mr. Bassler hung the candle-lantern on a hook in the wall, and with Mr. Louis's help, forced Oliver to sit on the stone bench against the wall. He landed hard, an arc of pain shooting from his legs up to his spine, the cold from the stone coming up through the numbness with jagged edges.

For a moment, as the candle-lantern flickered, all was still. Oliver stared up at the two men, and then at the faint light coming from down the stairway, thinking, very briefly, of how quickly he might gain those stairs, and how much it might cost him if he failed.

But it seemed as if the men, well fed, well-endowed for their labors, had not even the slightest concern that together they could not prevent Oliver from doing any such foolish thing as to attempt to escape. For they only shook their heads, almost in unison, because, for them, his obedience was a foregone conclusion.

"Well, what are you waiting for?" asked Mr. Louis, nominally in charge, for Mr. Bassler seemed the bigger threat. "Take off your boots and stockings, for I have other work to do this evening, and cannot be held up with any lollygagging."

"Off with 'em," said Mr. Bassler, nodding. "And be quick about it."

While this had not been the standard preparation for a night in the refractory room in the Hardingstone workhouse, in this parish, it seemed to be. Though for what purpose, Oliver could not imagine, as the refractory in his memory had a locked door, and no other way out.

"Take them off," said Mr. Louis, "or you'll be in for another beating as quick as I can get the strap."

This was announced in the calmest of tones, for Mr. Louis surely knew he had the upper hand and, with Mr. Bassler to back him up, there was nothing for it but for Oliver to do as he was told. So, sitting on the cold stone bench, the chill from the brick wall behind him leeching every ounce of warmth from his back, Oliver bent forward. His hands quivered, but he stilled them, undoing the laces and slipping his boots off, then his stockings, sticking the stockings inside, as to put them on the floor was to have them soaked through in moments.

Mr. Bassler grabbed the boots and stockings and slammed them on the stone bench next to Oliver.

"Do you have the key?" Mr. Bassler asked.

"No, it's just there, on the hook next to the door," said Mr. Louis, as he stood there blocking the way to the stairwell, and blocking any light that might come down it.

Mr. Bassler opened the second of two doors, which was directly across from where Oliver sat. As it swung wide, the smell of rot that Oliver had sensed before poured out at him, and the blackness hove to, spreading itself about until it almost ate the small light from the candle-lantern.

"In you get," said Mr. Bassler. He gestured at the dark doorway, as if he expected Oliver to hop to his feet with some eagerness, if not exactly obedience, and march himself directly within the bowels of the refractory room.

The alternative to that obedience was resistance, which would bring the threatened strap. Of that, Oliver was not afraid, though he did not imagine that any battle fought on his part would keep him from spending the night in that room.

"Don't make me call Workmaster Chalenheim," said Mr. Louis, hissing again.

If it was his only threat, it was a good one. Oliver's whole body still ached, and his backside was flecked with sharp pain that grew alongside the numbness. Still, as he stood and went to the doorway of the refractory room, his hand reached out as if to stop himself from actually going in. The room was too dark and too dank and too still to be desired of and, at the last moment, Oliver found he could not go in. Could not force himself to go in.

With a slam of a large palm in the middle of his back, one of the men pushed Oliver in, and his bare feet stumbled beneath him, splashing in a layer of water, icy water that soaked immediately into the hems of his trousers. As he spun around, he glared at the men, blinking against the hard light that ringed the still-open doorway.

"There's water on the floor," Oliver said, though he was not sure what he expected them to do about it, for surely they would not give him his shoes and stockings back, nor even a bit of hemp sacking with which to dry off.

"Nasty problem, that," said Mr. Bassler evenly. "The well is on the other side of that wall and has a tendency to leak. Pity we aren't able to afford repairs."

And then he slammed the door shut.

While Oliver stood there with his bare feet in a layer of icy water, enveloped by pure darkness, he heard the key turn in the lock and the faint jingle as the key was replaced on the hook in the wall. There was the sound of feet going down the passage and up the stone stairway, but the sound became more and more muffled until Oliver was left alone in the black air of the refractory room.

The darkness seemed to swallow him without any effort at all, leaving him standing there, quite still, with his arms wrapped around his waist, his feet becoming numb, water soaking into the hem of his trousers. From beyond the wall, or between the stones themselves perhaps, he heard the faint sound of water dripping. It might be falling directly from the ceiling and into the puddle, or from further beyond, deep within the earth where the well leaked.

He knew he could not stand in the water all night; his feet were cold already and by morning he'd be frozen through. He could only pray that as the floor slanted in one direction, that there might be higher ground, where he could get beyond the water and huddle against the cold until morning.

With a bit of a splash, he felt his way, his toes tender upon the grit beneath the surface of the water, and held his hands out to get the size of the room. Which proved itself to be a wise action, for the ceiling sloped down as though it were a half-circle, coming down in a curve from the doorway to the inner wall. There his hands encountered brick, mostly dry, though the grout was starting to crumble away, and then a stone bench beneath that, much like the one outside the refractory room. He swept his palm across the surface and found that it, too, was mostly dry, and merely chilled rather than damp from the cold air.

Clambering, he was up on the bench and out of the water, though he was careful to keep his feet at one end, so the bench would remain dry for most of its length. He balanced on his backside, the welts from the strap feeling charred-hot against the marble-cold of the bench, and attempted to rub his feet dry.

As the hem of his trousers was also damp, he couldn't use that, so he peeled off his jacket and rubbed his feet with it. Any bit of him that touched the stone seemed to burn in contrast to it, so he alternated resting the heel of one foot while rubbing the other. Then he wrapped both of his feet with the jacket and curled over his knees, cupping his hands beneath his arms to warm them.

For a moment, he sat there, rocking a bit forward every now and then to be certain his heart was still pumping, that the breath in his lungs might not stop. His teeth chattered and his stomach growled, and all amidst the common animal impulse to roar at the ceiling were his thoughts of Jack.

When Workmaster Chalenheim had bid them each to stand on opposite sides of the table, Oliver had been certain Jack had still not considered that something quite harsh was about to happen. Up until the moment that Chalenheim had called for the strap, Jack had looked about him as if wondering, merely that, with almost no concern whatsoever, whether or not they were to be served their suppers any time soon.

When Chalenheim had called for the strap, it might have occurred to Jack that he would be the recipient of it, though Oliver could have told him his notion was false and that without any hesitation at all. That Oliver would take the punishment because, as with the way of the world everywhere, his part was to lead, because he came from a more privileged background because he looked as if he should be in charge, and had failed to lead in the proper manner.

But there hadn't been enough time, nor could Oliver dare to explain it out loud. It was the same as it had been in Lyme, when Mrs. Heyland had made her assumptions about who was more elevated, and had never thought to question it. Only this time, when Workmaster Chalenheim had ordered Oliver to bend over, he was glad of that assumption, for it meant that it would be he, and not Jack, who would feel the sting of the strap and the dark abandonment of the refractory room.

Would that he believed any longer in the power of prayer, he might say one in the hopes that Jack would not think Oliver had abandoned him. That his Nolly had not wanted to leave him, but would have fought with every breath in his body to stay at his side, had he been able. That Oliver had no prayers was perhaps less comfort than the thought that wherever Jack was at this moment, either eating his supper or preparing for sleep, that the stone harbor of Newgate would prove to have been less foul than a workhouse, or that Jack's experience of a night alone in a work-house might be less arduous than any time he'd spent aboard ship being transported away from his native land.

Though, at the same time, not for one moment did Oliver

want Jack with him, for even as Jack could have withstood the deprivation, Oliver knew it was better this way. Oliver would take the punishment, and Jack would spend the night in relative comfort. And in the morning, they would see each other again, for he'd never known a stay in the refractory to last longer than a day and a night, and, typically, it was even shorter than that.

He took his hands from beneath his arms, and wrapped them around his knees, tucking his chin low to warm the hollow there with his breath. He kept his eyes closed against the darkness, for this time his imprisonment was accompanied by not even a single candle, and no light cast a bit of itself from beneath the closed and locked door, nor along the side, nor anywhere. The room was total darkness, so instead of searching through it to find even the merest glimmer, it was best to pretend he was asleep, and keep his eyes closed, lest he become panicked at the feeling that his whole body had gone blind.

If Jack were with him, he'd tell Oliver, in that way that he had, so soft and sweet, that the morning would come, by-and-bye, and that Oliver was not to be afraid, for Jack was with him. And he was, in a way, inside of Oliver's head, with his voice saying nice things, and within Oliver's breast, where his heart felt sore and misused, easing it into stillness with an imagined touch. That Jack was with him, in that way, was the only thing that was going to enable him to suffer through it until morning.

"Thank you, Jack," said Oliver, finding himself whispering this aloud. He rocked a bit forward to tuck his head low, till he could feel his chin against his chest. "I'll kiss you when I see you in the morning."

For morning would come, by-and-bye. Jack had told him this and Oliver knew it was true, and that was the only thing that mattered.

7

OLIVER CONTINUES REFRACTORY

"Get in line, Jack Dawkins," said Chalenheim, though he'd not yet turned around, and could not possibly know that Jack still had not moved from the wall.

Jack pushed himself away from it and took up a bowl and a spoon and stood in line. There was nobody at his side, for now the count was off, and it was no longer two by two.

When he got up to the cauldron, he saw that the supper being served to him was a tad more substantial than it had been in the men's dining hall, in that there were small chunks of potatoes and ribbons of pale cabbage in dark broth, and again he was handed a hunk of brown bread.

The two attendants scowled at him as they served him, for of course they had determined that he was a bad thing, but he just scowled at them in return and made his way to a blank spot on a bench as far away from Chalenheim as he could manage. He was still shaking as he sat down, spilling a bit of his supper on the table. He licked it up with his finger. The boy next to him hissed at him and shook his head, pointing at Chalenheim at the front of the room with his spoon. For of course, prayers had not yet been said, so they must wait.

And wait they did, their heads bowed, except for Jack, who

looked at the whole of the dining hall that was kept waiting while Chalenheim bowed his head and seemed to contemplate his clasped hands in front of him.

Jack saw him smirk and knew that the man was drawing out the prayer for the benefit of his own amusement, because he knew the boys were hungry, and it pleased him to make them wait. Jack made himself wait as well, for he was the one with the level head. He told himself this, even as his fist shook as he gripped his spoon, and he felt some of Nolly's fury building up behind his eyes.

"Amen," said Chalenheim, lifting his head to give the nod that signaled permission for the boys to eat.

While one of the attendants rattled off that no one had died that day, and that the board was still coming for its inspection, Jack ate his supper. He barely tasted it, and felt hollow inside as he thought of Nolly in some room somewhere, by himself. Going hungry. Jack would sacrifice his own supper if he could, but there was the door to the dining hall, and doors after that, all locked, probably, and there was just no way—

Jack made himself stop. It wouldn't do anybody any good. He needed to finish eating and then steel himself to spend the night alone in this horrible place, confined to a room with a bunch of strangers. How had he ended up here, alone like this? The workhouse was Nolly's past, not Jack's, yet here he was.

Giving himself a mental shake, he finished his supper, ate the bread, and took one of the tumblers of water from the center of the table, as he saw the other boys doing, to wash the meal down with. When everybody was finished, two of the boys gathered up the bowls and spoons in those same wicker baskets and took them off through the door that Nolly had gone through.

Jack was watching this time. The door, though it opened only briefly, showed a small passage similar to the one they'd gone through when eating with the men, but that was all he managed to see as the door was quickly shut behind the retreating boys.

"Two by two, now, lads, get a move on."

As Chalenheim gave the order, Jack got in line. He could pretend obedience fairly well, when directions were given. Besides, as the line moved, and Jack followed, it went through the very same door that Nolly had gone through.

He was all eyes, then, but there was not enough time but to mark that there was a passage that went straight along directly ahead, and one that curved away to the right. There was no way to determine which passage Nolly had taken, so Jack turned his eyes to the front and followed the paupers up the stairs and into a dormitory.

This was set up just like the men's dormitory, except that the plain frame beds were newer and the room was shorter. Each pair of boys went to a bed and took down from a peg in the wall what looked like a long white sack, which turned out to be night-shirts. After the boys changed into their nightshirts, and hung up their day clothes, they lined up at the end of the room to use the washbasin in a small alcove. Some of the boys, the smaller ones, went through a doorway where Jack imagined there was a similar layout.

It was early, as it was not yet half past seven. Though, at this time of year, the sun was already set, and the night through the windows, which were set evenly in the thick walls, was dark, and the rain was speckling the walls with high, clinking sounds.

"You're there, Jack," said Chalenheim, turning to him amidst the orderly bustle of the other boys.

Jack looked at where Chalenheim was pointing. There was a double bed in the far corner where two nightshirts still hung; the bed was empty and nobody else was getting into it.

He did not want to disrobe in front of these small strangers, did not want to be vulnerable while sleeping, did not want to wash at the basin without Nolly to set an example for him. But Chalenheim was staring at him as if there was only one small item on his list he needed to account for before finding that strap and giving Jack a good, sound beating with it, as he obviously wanted to do. And would do, before too long.

Feeling tall and overgrown compared to his fellow inmates, Jack went to the bed and changed into the nightshirt, and left his stockings folded over his boots as he saw the other boys do. He hung his brown clothes on the peg and waited in line for his turn at the basin.

There was only cold water as far as he could see, and when one little boy began to cry when the soap got into his eyes, Chalenheim pulled that boy out of line, still damp with soap and water, and took down a cane and whipped the boy quickly, three times, on the back of the legs. At which point, the wail got even louder.

Jack thought of what Nolly would do. Nolly would have jumped to the boy's defense at the expense of his own hide, comforted the boy, and demanded that Chalenheim get a clean cloth, one free of soap, for the dear thing to clean his eyes with.

None of this happened, of course, because he was not Nolly. Not in this lifetime, not in this place. Jack let the wailing go on. When it was his turn, he washed his face and hands and dried them on the damp cloth that hung on a peg by the basin and returned to his bed.

"Knees," said Chalenheim.

Every boy in the room, including the wailing one, as well as the unseen boys in the other room, got down on their knees in their nightshirts by their beds, two by two, clasping their hands in prayer and bowing their heads. Their immediate obedience was complete.

Jack watched as Chalenheim's eyes raked the room. When he saw that Jack was doing neither of these things, instead of calling him out, he only pointed at Jack, which was strange. Jack copied the other boys, even though the prayer meant nothing to him, and his knees hurt, and he was chilled through, and he'd be damned if he'd pray to anybody who let Nolly get taken away from him.

"Bed," said Chalenheim.

Every boy got into bed, and Jack did as well, cursing the thin mattress and the woolen blanket, though there was a thin sheet between him and the wool. And then he complained silently, for Nolly's sake, about the lumpy pillow.

Chalenheim walked down the row of beds with his candle, as if reviewing every bed, every boy, and went through the doorway at the end of the dormitory, and did not come out. Jack heard a door close, and imagined that Chalenheim had his own room back there, but what he would do with the length of the evening ahead of him, Jack had no idea. Nor did he care. Chalenheim could rot in his own boredom for all it mattered to Jack.

His stomach was still growling at him, so Jack turned on his left side, pressing his rash against the mattress, hoping that he wouldn't want to scratch it. With his back to the wall, he looked out over the dark shapes in the room before him, sensing the empty place next to him in the bed.

Nolly should have been in that place to keep him company in this horrible place. It was disconcerting to have that ache within his belly at missing Nolly, to become so dependent on him always being near. The scent of him, the darling curl behind his ear, the serious look in his eyes when he would talk to Jack, because to Nolly, the world was a serious place.

Having previously found it slightly irritating, that sense of seriousness, Jack found he missed it now. Would have wanted Nolly to be in that bed with him, to hear the mutter of complaint about the lack of softness in the blanket, and the fact that the slats beneath the mattress could actually be felt *through* the mattress, and who on earth could sleep with that wailing going on?

Jack couldn't help it. He got up in the dark and went over to the wailing, and found a little boy, curled on his side, sobbing into his hands. The light from the night outside had grown a little brighter while Jack had been in the dark, so he could see the boy's bedmate looking up at him.

"He's new," said the boy in a very low whisper. "He only got here two days ago."

Jack could imagine this little boy, so frightened by the horrible newness of the workhouse, might have been like Nolly had been, back in those long ago days. Nolly had been scared and alone all those years ago before he met Jack, and might have needed someone to comfort him in the beginning.

While Nolly had had no one, because Jack had not been there, Jack was here now, and might be able to do something about it. And then tell Nolly of it later, to get that smile, the small one, that would let him know Nolly was quite pleased with him, only wouldn't want him to truly know, in case he got a swelled head about it. But that was Nolly, and Jack wouldn't change him for a moment.

"Won't you come with me, little one?" asked Jack, reaching out.

Jack was surprised when the boy stopped crying and cringed away.

The little boy's bedmate patted him and said to him, "It's not Chalenheim, it's the new boy. The tall one."

Feeling very tall, Jack reached for the little boy's hand and took it. The boy got out of the bed, and Jack led him to the wash basin. He used a bit of the damp cloth to soak in the pitcher of water, and washed the boy's face with it, taking care to gently sweep the cloth over his eyes to get the rest of the soap out. Then he lifted the pitcher and urged the boy to take a drink to soothe his throat, at least. When Jack put the pitcher back, the little boy took Jack's hand again, and clasped it tight with skinny bones and a determined grip.

"May I go with you, please?" asked the little boy, and Jack found the soft spot inside of him that he'd never known he'd had.

"Yes, you may," he said. "But we must be very quiet, right?"

He gave the boy's hand a brief squeeze and padded back to the bed in the corner. He looked at the two pillows and the one blanket, and listened to the way the wind started to rise and squeak through the window leading. Then he climbed in and, expecting that he would take one side of the bed and the boy on the other, was surprised to find the boy climbing into bed and curling up in a little ball against him.

Jack tucked his arm around the boy's shoulders and pulled the blanket up over them both. He lay on his back, quite still, and felt aged and full of knowledge that the world was a bad place, and that this wee thing was on his way to finding that out.

He did not think he would fall asleep, but he did, and woke up, facing the wall. He felt the gust of air as the little boy climbed out from beneath the covers to scamper over to his own bed. Jack heard Chalenheim's door opening as well, and rolled onto his back to see the commotion and activity, with the sun barely coming through the windows, and groaned to himself.

There was no getting through this day except to grit his teeth and bear it. As well, he actively thought about punching something, preferably Chalenheim, who was marching, fully dressed, the cane in his hand, prepared to dole out immediate correction to any boy who was not promptly ready and lined up two by two to go down to their meager breakfast.

"This line is waiting for you, Jack Dawkins," said Chalenheim. "No boy will get his breakfast unless you are also with us, so quickly, quickly, we're waiting."

As to why Chalenheim didn't come at him with the cane, Jack couldn't hazard a guess, though he scrambled into his clothes and laced his boots and got in line. All the paupers looked at him, and not one of them seemed cross with him at the delay. Instead, they looked tired and hungry and pale and so, so small. Jack shook his head and when the line began to move to go out into the passage and down the stairs, Jack went with them.

HIS NIGHT HAD BEEN TIPPED WITH SHALLOW SLEEP AMIDST silver-sharp awakenings, until Oliver could no longer bear it, and opened his eyes. The refractory room was still dark and cold, the water still dripped beyond the stone somewhere, and the air still smelled of the deep, wet earth.

He took a deep breath and felt the cold shiver through him, rippling up and down his spine, as if he could never get warm again, no matter how much he rubbed his arms. When he shifted, sharp spikes lanced through his backside, and his feet were two blocks of ice.

The dark, it seemed, was not as fearsome a thing as the cold, though had he a candle, he could have borne freezing to death a little bit easier. After the hours spent in the darkness, there did seem to be a thin, gray hem of light that slithered across the puddle of water on the floor.

Or it could have been his imagining, for the moment he attempted to focus upon that light, it went away and he was pitched into darkness once more. If he looked out of the corner of his eyes, however, he could see it, so he concentrated on that, and rubbed his arms with his hands, and took deep breaths and felt the light sparkle of his own frosted breath landing on his skin.

But it must be dawn, else he would not be able to see the gray light. His body was telling him it was morning as well, with his stomach scraping and pushing on his spine like a mad creature trying to gnaw its way out of his belly. The ache from that, that emptiness, clawed up into his chest, curling around his heart, it seemed, as if trying to feed upon that. Maybe the gray light was his faintness from hunger and nothing more.

At least Jack wasn't with him. At least Jack was getting fed, even if only something paltry and half-tasteless.

Oliver's whole body was shivering now, a deep, internal shiver that seemed to come from inside of him, racing with itself to warm him up, though it failed, no matter how hard his teeth chattered together. There was a sense of the room moving about him, and he had to reach out to press his palm to the wall in order to stay upright.

But in the midst of the pitching darkness, a seam of light widened, slowly, until the whole of the refractory room was bathed in it. Part of the light was from a candle-lantern held high in the doorway, but the remainder of it seemed to come from some ambient source, a wider gold that promised warmth without actually delivering it, and upon which was carried the sound of voices, a whisk of clean air, and the sense of movement.

"Get up, you," said a voice Oliver recognized as Mr. Bassler.

For a moment, he thought to object, that it should be Mr. Louis letting him out of the refractory room, but he shook his head, since this was foolishness. What did it matter who let him out, as long as he was out and would see Jack soon?

Loath to put his feet in the cold water now that they were dry, though the hem of his trousers were still damp, Oliver stalled by pulling his jacket from around his feet and putting it on. But then, needs must, so he slid off the stone bench and trod in the water for a step or two before surging through the open doorway, pushing Mr. Bassler out of his way as he did so.

He splashed only the merest bit of his heel, but once barefoot on the stone floor of the cellar, the cold shot up through him as badly as if he'd soaked himself from head to toe. Crossing his arms over his chest, and hugging himself tightly, he looked about for his boots, his stockings.

There they were on the stone bench, where they had been put the night before. But as he went to reach for them, Mr. Bassler grabbed him by the arm, squeezing hard, and pulling Oliver's face close to his.

"You gave Mr. Louis quite a troublesome time last evening, didn't you."

"N-no, sir," said Oliver between chattering teeth. But of course he had.

"I ought to give you a thumping here and now, except I'm charged with bringing you to breakfast afore they run out. D'you hear me?" Mr. Bassler tugged hard enough that Oliver would have been sent sprawling to the damp stones but for Mr. Bassler's grip upon him. "Do you?"

"Yes, sir," said Oliver, blinking hard as he tried not to wince, not sure of what it was that he was agreeing to.

"Now, put them on and hurry yourself, as Workmaster Chalenheim don't care for latecomers."

Mr. Bassler shoved Oliver hard at the stone bench; he had to duck his head to keep from hitting it against the wall, but he managed it, slithering into place, grabbing his stockings with shaking hands and pulling them on. The boots followed, with his fingers almost numb to the laces, tying them up into convoluted knots.

When he was ready, Mr. Bassler grabbed him by the back of the neck and proceeded to march him up the stairs as if he had no sense of direction and might not find his way up them.

At the top of the stairs, Oliver tried to tug himself away, but Mr. Bassler's grip grew even harder, the fingers digging in. Pulling him to a stop, Mr. Bassler blew out the candle and hung the lantern on a hook at the top of the stairs. Then, as if he were guiding a reluctant beast, he pushed on Oliver's neck to make him walk down the passageway that abutted the kitchen and scullery.

They were headed straight for the boys' dining hall, it seemed, for Mr. Bassler never paused as he pushed Oliver before him, giving Oliver barely enough time to open the door before he was forced through. Oliver was glad enough, if it meant he was out of refractory and in the light of day, with the windows showing the sky scudding with clouds through which a bit of sun oozed through.

When Mr. Bassler let go of Oliver's neck and grabbed him by his jacket to pull him into the boys' dining hall, Oliver felt as if all eyes were upon him.

And there was Jack, sitting by himself at the end of the last table along the wall. It was a long walk to where Jack was, and Oliver lost all his resolve to be brave and bear up. If Jack was kind to him, with a gentle word, as was his way, then Oliver was not going to be able to get through this.

Mr. Bassler pushed Oliver onto the bench seat next to Jack, and an attendant put a bowl of gruel in front of him.

It was too late to be brave, for Jack was there, handing over his bread ration. Oliver could not suffer him to do it, but he could not refuse him either, for Jack would insist, and the wrong attention might be brought upon them. So Oliver took the bread, shivering hard, not looking at Jack, for if he did, he would break. Right there, in front of everybody.

❦ 8 ❦

IN WHICH THEY PICK OAKUM

As Jack sat with his bowl full of gruel and the hunk of bread, and looked at the collection of tumblers in the middle of the long table, and waited for grace to be said, he did not know what to do. If he ate this meal, and carried on doing as he was told, it would be tantamount to letting Nolly be taken from him. Almost as if he'd given Nolly up with both hands.

Should he not eat, and surprise everyone in the room by demanding Nolly's return to him at once, as he imagined Nolly might do were Jack far from his side, he would be trounced good and proper and taken, no doubt, to the refractory room. Which would have the benefit of being with Nolly, so it was worth a shot.

Chalenheim dragged grace out as long as he possibly could, and upon the moment he said *amen*, and Jack was about to stand up and hurl his bowl of gruel across the room to get everyone's attention, the door to the passage and the stairs opened. Mr. Bassler came in, hauling Nolly by his jacket collar, and walked him straight over to where Jack was, to the only open seat in the room, on the bench, next to Jack.

As Mr. Bassler manhandled Nolly into his seat, one of the

attendants came over and slammed a bowl of gruel in front of him. Nolly ducked backward to get out of the way, flinching, his eyes narrow, as if the room presented him too much light to bear. There was no accompanying bread, so Jack used the side of his hand to push his hunk over to where Nolly's bowl was.

Grace was over, and the other boys were eating, so Jack snuck a glance at Nolly, shocked at his gray pallor, the way he was shivering. The way he wouldn't meet Jack's eyes. It was the day before all over again, and Jack didn't like it.

"Nolly, eat this bread, here." He shoved the bread a little closer to Nolly, where Nolly's hands were on the table, one holding the heavy spoon, the other touching the edge of the bowl, as if he couldn't quite believe it was real. "You must eat. I know it's glop, pure an' simple, but you must eat it. An' the bread, I can't abide it myself."

With a small nod, Nolly hefted the spoon in his hand, curling his fist around the handle the way a common laborer might, and it made Jack sad to see the once elegant manners reduced to this. When Nolly scooped up some of the gruel, his hand was shaking, and the gruel spilled on the table. Jack longed to take up the spoon and feed Nolly, as Nolly had him when he was ill. For it was surely that Nolly was ill, and tired, and when Jack reached out to touch him, the brown jacket felt cold to the touch.

"You keep shiverin'," said Jack, bending low, taking up his spoon to show Nolly how it was done. "It'll warm you up. Bend close to the bowl, then you won't spill. Eat the bread. *Nolly*."

Finally, *finally*, Nolly took up the bread and broke it in half, to give Jack half. Jack knew he had to take it, otherwise there'd be a row because Nolly would raise his voice and insist that Jack take it. So he did, and dunked it in the gruel, and ate it that way, breaking up bits of bread in the bowl to give the gruel more heft.

Nolly did the same and soon they and the rest of the boys were scraping the bottom of the bowls with their spoons and the meal was over. As they stood up to take their bowls to the end of the table, Jack could hear Nolly's stomach growl, and he longed to feed him something; if he got anywhere near where the kitchen was, he'd be able to manage it.

As it was, they were being led, two by two, out of the dining hall and down a narrow passage to the right that had windows that opened up to the yard, where nobody was. The rain was coming down, a hard gray pelt that bounced off the flat stones that paved the yard.

Chalenheim took them to one of the low buildings at the far end of the yard, into a room where the long benches were set in rows, with spiked poles in front of each place. At the end of each bench were wicker baskets of coiled pieces of thick rope, and near each spike were smaller, empty wicker baskets.

Jack had no idea what this was all about, but Nolly groaned almost out loud and turned to Jack with the first bit of pluck Nolly had shown since their arrival. The meal had done him some good then, for all it had been so meager.

"It's oakum," said Nolly, ducking his chin as they sat down on the bench furthest in the back, along the wall, so Chalenheim wouldn't hear him. "We have to pick the rope apart to be reused for caulking ships."

Jack could hardly imagine what Nolly was talking about. The rope pieces were thick and squat and the strands were almost seared together with some kind of tar. It was black and sticky when he hefted the piece in his hand, as he saw Nolly do, and he watched as Nolly took both ends and began to break it on the end of the pike.

The pikes were probably the same as the crushers they'd used to break bones with, as they had the same weight, only these had the flat end bolted into stands, which were quite sturdy beneath the pounding they were getting. Even the smallest boys were going at it, elbows and arseholes, as if it mattered.

Chalenheim marched to the front of the room, stopped in front of the room's only window, and slashed the cane in his hand through the air.

"Each boy must pick three pounds of oakum this morning, or he will have his dinner rations reduced."

Which explained why the paupers were already so hard at it, for while the meal would be paltry, none would want to miss it. And Nolly, of course, had already known about the measurement that would be taken at the end of the morning and was already working, picking off strands of rope, curly, stringy, sticky strands with shaking hands and throwing them in the basket at his feet.

Jack knew he had to pick his portion too, or else Nolly would be tempted to share his bounty with Jack and leave himself short. So it was no wonder that every boy in the room was racing at this task, intent upon it, for it would be their own saving if they were successful.

So he started pulling the fibers apart, as he saw Nolly and the other boys do, peeling back each strand that wiggled around his fingers and stuck to his skin. The pads of his fingers quickly grew quite raw, as though he'd taken a razor to them, and he bemoaned this even as he didn't stop, for it would surely leave scars that would make it more difficult to be deft-handed drawing a fat wallet out of a plush pocket.

He found his back growing stiff, his neck aching as he leaned forward in order to see in the poorly lit room how many strands he was trying to draw off. You couldn't pull too many, or they wouldn't come, and the oakum would slip beneath a fingernail and embed itself there. Or it would whip around, leaving a red mark that smarted and tasted like tar.

They kept going all morning, without even a break for some water or to stretch their hands. Jack saw some of the little ones in the front row start to cry, their tears slipping like fat, silvery balls down their thin cheeks.

His only thought, his selfish thought, was that Nolly would not see it and think he needed to do something about it. For that wouldn't do anybody any good, not with Chalenheim marching up and down, swishing that cane, keeping an eye that everyone was diligent at their task. So Jack licked his lips and kept going, trying to catch Nolly's eye and failing each time.

"Nolly," he whispered finally, giving Nolly's knee the gentlest of nudges with his knee. "Please talk to me, an' tell me you're all right."

He bent forward to hear Nolly's reply, which was spoken in the lowest of tones, with the sad pacing of a bell over a churchyard.

"I'm all right, Jack," said Nolly. "And if I am not, 'tis nobody's fault but my own."

"Do you—d'you regret comin' with me then?" Jack asked this with some dismay, for whatever else could Nolly mean?

Jack heard the sharp inhale of breath, as he found, suddenly, and inexplicably, that Nolly had dropped his hands in his lap, tarred rope pieces and all, and was looking straight at him.

"No, Jack," Nolly said with that firm voice that Jack knew so well. Nolly seemed to have pulled himself out of his own bewildered state, for his eyes were clear and steady as he looked at Jack, in that way that told him Nolly was speaking from his heart. "Never that. *Never*. It's only that I cannot keep myself out of trouble, as it always seems."

"Oliver *Twist*."

There was a swish and a crack. Jack looked up to find Chalenheim standing at the end of the last row, *their* row, tapping the cane in his hand, as if counting out the mere seconds it would take for him to lose his temper.

"There is no talking during work hours. Come up here at once."

"We weren't talkin', mister," said Jack, loudly. Casually, as if this were an ordinary and friendly conversation between acquaintances. "Surely it was somethin' in the yard that you heard. A stray cow an' like that."

"A stray cow?" Chalenheim's eyebrows rose unexpectedly and then came down to beetle together over his eyes. His mouth worked, and he swished the cane against his leg. "There are no cows in the workhouse!"

"There might be," said Jack, ignoring Nolly's looks of astonishment.

"Don't contradict me, and you, Oliver Twist, get up here this instant. You boys, keep at your work."

The entire of the room became diligently attentive to the darkened pieces of rope, while Jack sat there watching the moment play out because he could not believe Chalenheim would whip Nolly simply for talking. But he was going to, and there was nothing Jack could do to stop it. Or was there?

"Workmaster Chalenheim," said Jack, standing up, the rope in his hands, as if he were holding his cap and twisting it. "'Twas me doin' the talkin' there. Me, babblin' on like a brook. Not Nol —not Oliver, not him. Me."

Grabbing Nolly by the collar, Chalenheim glared at Jack.

"Sit down, Jack," he said, and his voice was low and calm, as if he knew he had the upper hand in this. "Know your place. If I hear another word out of you, this one," he gave Nolly a stiff, hard shake, "will spend another night, starting from this moment, in the refractory room with no dinner or supper."

Jack jerked back, as if he himself had been struck, and shook his head, trying to get the words out before Chalenheim's threat became a reality. He shook his head again and tried to say *no* out loud, but Chalenheim marched Nolly up to the front of the room, and shoved him against the narrow deal table that stood beneath the window.

"Bend over the table," said Chalenheim, and when Nolly started to do so, Chalenheim stopped him with a tap of the cane to his shoulder. "Unbutton your trousers first," he said.

Jack felt cold even before Nolly's fingers moved to his waist, and wondered what he should do, what Nolly wanted him to do, when Nolly stopped and looked right at Jack. And shook his head *no*, just once, to warn Jack off, and Jack could do nothing but watch.

Nolly pushed his trousers down just past his hips and bent over the table. Jack fully expected that the whipping would begin, when Chalenheim paused, moved in front of Nolly, as if to block the view of him from the rest of the room, and tapped Nolly again with the cane.

"And these as well."

Jack could see that Nolly was taking down his underdrawers, doing as he was told to do, though Chalenheim stood between Nolly and the room full of boys and all Jack could see of Nolly now was the top of his head, a dull gold in the gray light coming through the curtainless window.

He saw Nolly shrug his shoulders forward and bury his head in his arms, as if he were merely resting on that table to nap, taking whatever respite Chalenheim would give him. But Jack knew what a cane could do on bare skin, knew the marks it left. That sweet round backside would be marred forever, and none of Jack's touches, however tender, could ever remove those marks.

He found himself twisting the rope in his hands and, looking down, dropped it at his feet, for what did he care? Besides, he could go up there, and take Chalenheim unawares, and pull Nolly up from the table—

There was a soft movement at his side, and just as Chalenheim raised the switch in the air, Jack looked down to see the little boy from the night before, the one who had cried and slept in the bed with Jack. He was slipping his hand in Jack's and moving close. Only this time, he was offering comfort rather than merely taking it.

As Jack heard the switch come down, he took the little boy's hand and gave it a squeeze. Shook his head in return, and tried to keep breathing steadily, even as his ears were ringing and the room was cold, so cold.

The table beneath Nolly jerked against the wall, everything seemed to be happening as if it were moving very slowly, and all there was was the switch rising and falling, a flash of white against the rainy-dappled window, and a sharp whistle as it came down, the sound that it made echoing in the absolutely still room.

Chalenheim was putting his back into it with each blow, twisting sideways to put his whole body as the cane came down. And the sound it made. Six times. Whistle-white, like a high shriek, and out of Nolly came only one yelp as the last blow, the sixth, came down.

The workmaster stepped back, letting the cane fall to his side, his fist gripping it as he turned to face the boys. To face Jack.

"And *that* is what happens when you talk, when there is no talking permitted." He half-turned back to Nolly, who had remained motionless on the table, as if he knew better, as he must do, than to move before being given leave. "You may get up and go back to your work, as you must make up the full three pounds before dinner, or you will have none."

Nolly stood up from the table. Every eye was upon him as he pulled his undergarment and trousers up over his thighs, where a thin line of blood trickled down, and he hadn't even the privacy to hide his more intimate parts as he did this. His hands were shaking as he managed to button his trousers closed and begin to limp to the back row where Jack was. Eyes cast down, mouth a thin, gray line.

Jack had never wanted to kill anybody as much as he did in that moment. He'd never been in a raging fury like Nolly could get, where his eyes went blind and the power surged through his limbs that made Jack sure, quite sure, that if he could get his hands around Chalenheim's neck, he could break it in two.

But Jack could not do that, not with Nolly coming near to him, almost hobbling, boots scuffing across the stone floor, not even looking up as he pushed past Jack to see the little boy standing there, holding onto Jack's hand. This seemed to calm Nolly for some reason, for instead of shoving the child off, he cupped their joined hands and gently broke them, easing the boy onto the bench and sat in the space on the other side of him.

Gingerly, and oh, so slowly, he flinched as he bent forward to pick up another hunk of blackened rope, and began to pick it apart. The little boy began to work also, putting broken, untwisted strands into the wicker basket that had been Nolly's.

Jack knew Nolly was going to work as fast as he might to fill the little boy's basket so he could meet the required weight when the call came at the dinner hour. And that Nolly was specifically not looking at Jack, as if he knew that, at the least hint, Jack would break and actually stand up and do something about all the anger surging inside of him.

The little boy was now between them, perhaps so Nolly could pretend Jack wasn't there, so that he wouldn't have to think about him. But Jack could not take offense. He knew how Nolly thought about things, and that if he were to look and see how furious Jack was, he himself might fall apart. Which he could not do, not in front of Chalenheim.

He would not want to shame himself if he started to cry, or object in some way, to say something that would simply earn him another beating. So, in order not to have this happen, he had to shut Jack out. Just for a little while. At least Jack thought so, for had he been the one beaten, he might have reacted the same way himself.

Jack bent to pick up the hunk of rope he'd dropped at his feet and began to work on it, stabbing it on the pike in front of him to loosen the strands, using his nails, already black with tar, to untwist the strands. His jaw felt hard, and he realized he was biting his lower lip, so he moved his jaw to ease it and looked at his hands and the basket at his feet and nowhere else. And not at Nolly, because he didn't want it.

THE MOMENT OLIVER SAT DOWN ON THE WOODEN BENCH
next to the little boy whom Jack had, perhaps, befriended,
Oliver knew there would be bloodstains on his underdrawers and
his trousers. Not that it would matter overly much, as workhouse laundry soap was strong enough to take out deep stains,
and if it didn't, well, nobody would care.

Except it would sting when his clotted skin pulled away from
the cloth. It hurt now, in a way that vibrated up from his bones,
in the same way that the cold of the refractory room had. So
cold he felt frozen where he sat, a sense of gray light descending
all over the room, as if someone was lifting shutters outside the
window and latching them into place. Those shutters were heavy,
he knew; a boy could stagger beneath their weight and accidentally crack the window without meaning to.

Shaking his head, he shifted forward and pulled up a hank of
rope and began untwisting the strands, beating the heel of the
rope against the spike, pushing the spike through, and pulling
the rope apart, piece by tar-covered piece. His hands knew what
they were doing, even as his fingers shook, because he'd done
this before, a hundred times before, on dark days and light, with
hands so small that the rope had often bunched bigger than his
fists.

The rope felt smaller now, beneath trembling fingers, but no
less difficult to unravel and pick apart. His whole body wanted to
curl forward and crawl under the bench to come to hide behind
Jack's feet. For only there could he rest, his eyes closed, safe in
knowing Jack wouldn't let anybody harm him.

But that could not be so, for as much as Jack might want it,
he could keep the dark maw of the workhouse at bay, but he
could not save Oliver from what had always been his destiny.
This place, this room. This spike. The strands of picked oakum
filling up the basket in front of him. The brown-garbed shoulders of the boys in front of him, bent in the gloom, at their
work, not one of them looking up to check the light through the
window. Or even to whisper to one of his fellows, to chance a

glance at the level in someone else's basket, or to send a smile of encouragement.

It was odd how familiar all of this felt and looked, though the difference, this time, was Jack. Who, Oliver noted, was tending to his own work as if it were the most important task in the whole wide world, head bent forward, mouth crooked in concentration, shoulders hunched as though he were attacking each strand rather than merely unwinding it. And studiously, it seemed, he was not looking at Oliver.

For a moment, Oliver looked down at the little boy who had been holding hands with Jack. That such a mite had been so emboldened was one thing, though as to why he'd singled Jack out another. Still more puzzling was why Jack had let him.

There were, in the oakum-picking room, about thirty boys, ten to a row, in three tight rows, any one of whom Jack might have befriended. All facing forward toward the window, in front of which Workmaster Chalenheim paced, the switch held in both hands behind his back. He flicked it like a cock's tail, and he the cock marching back and forth, as if in search of a fight or a boy to discipline.

But as to Jack and the little boy, Oliver had no explanation. Perhaps he shouldn't ask, for Jack had a habit of befriending small, friendless boys such as this one. A fact to which Oliver could attest, and did as his throat closed up and the welts on his backside twitched with every breath he took.

Each mark still vibrated, as if laced with a metal string upon which someone was constantly tugging at each end. The thought of it made him feel sick, a vapid whey taste rising up as his stomach seemed to rebel against his breakfast. He struggled against the saliva in his mouth, for the breakfast, as ugly as it had been, had included bread Jack had given him.

He would not be wasting it, he would not. So he swallowed the bitterness in his mouth, and breathed through his nose, and kept working. Always working, for he knew that Workmaster Chalenheim's threat was anything but idle; any boy caught shirking his duty, and coming short of his quota would be given exactly the treatment that had been promised him.

As for why the little boy had befriended Jack, it didn't matter. Jack was taller than all of the boys in the room, including Oliver, and even though broad-shouldered and rough about the edges, he moved with a casual ease that was more likely to be deemed as friendly than anything else. Had Oliver, when nine and friendless, alone, in the workhouse, found someone like Jack to hide behind? Oliver would have done it in a heartbeat.

Would that he had had someone like Jack then, would that he had. He had Jack with him now, though, and while it didn't change anything about their circumstance, it made all the difference in the world.

Oliver's hands jerked so hard across the pike that he almost stabbed himself dead in the center of his palm, though he did graze his thumb and had to suck on it to ease the sting. Tasting the tar and the dust of dried sea salt from the rope, Oliver let himself, at long last, look directly over at Jack. Enough to gain his attention without having to ask out loud for it.

In the barest flicker of a heartbeat, he had that attention, so dear to him, so utterly needed. And just then, Chalenheim stepped out into the passage with a warning flick at all of them to keep quiet. The whole room seemed to draw a breath, and a sense of ease filled it.

"Jack," said Oliver, in a low, hushed whisper, for though he was certain none of the workhouse boys would say anything to Chalenheim, it wouldn't do to tempt fate.

"Yes, Nolly?" asked Jack, equally low, his gaze resting on Oliver, green eyes meeting his with a casualness that might have belied any concern on Jack's part, except for the fact that Jack looked quite pale, with marks on his lower lip, as if he'd bitten it.

"I'm sorry about before, that I couldn't hold on to you in the river."

He meant it. With all of his heart he wished he could have been stronger, enough to hold on and to swim across with Jack's grip around his neck, whatever it took to have taken them to the other shore. Then perhaps they could have out-maneuvered the gentlemen on horseback.

But all of these thoughts flittered into confusion when Jack shook his head.

"No," said Jack. "It wasn't your fault, Nolly—"

"Yes, it *was*," said Oliver, insistent. "I should have done better, for had I, we wouldn't be here now, with you ruining your hands for anything else." He looked down at Jack's hands, streaked with tar and laced with long, narrow red slices from where the oakum had nipped at him.

"They'll be fine," said Jack, shaking those hands as if shaking off the sting of the cuts. "Once I get a chance to soak them in tea an' honey, they'll be right as rain. You'll see."

"But the river—" Oliver's voice rose with his desperation to get Jack to understand how badly he'd wanted Jack's plan to succeed. Had Chalenheim been in the room, he surely would have pulled Oliver to the front of it for another whipping.

"Nolly," said Jack, stern now, shaking his head. "Not only was the river stronger than you, I could not swim. You'll have to teach me one day, an' you'll make a fine teacher I reckon, so next time, we'll both swim. You see?"

Oliver had to look away, for Jack's forgiveness came to him, as it always did, easy and clean, like a gift, the kind Jack seemed to have plenty of. But one day, Oliver knew, those gifts, and the sense of ease with which Jack distributed them, would end. There would be an end to them, and Oliver would be left, his hands empty, his heart aching, all alone—

"Nolly," said Jack again, "you won't be alone, I won't leave you alone, I promise you that."

To accept such a love as Jack always offered him would be an easy thing, *should* be an easy thing. And it wasn't that Oliver didn't believe Jack, for he did, with everything he had. It was just that he felt he didn't quite deserve it, that he would never deserve it. For coming from Jack, that love was so heartfelt, so easy, so generous, that then, as now, he became overwhelmed with it. And tipped his head down to look at his hands, his mouth working as he tried to keep it from quivering, from showing Jack that his love was wasted on a mere stripling of a boy who could not comport himself as he ought.

"Hey," said Jack, as if from some distance. "*Hey.*"

Jack was touching him, reaching over the head of the little boy between him, his fingers brushing gently along the back of Oliver's neck. "It'll always be you an' me, you know. An' we'll get through this, if you remember that I—"

Just then, Workmaster Chalenheim marched into the room, the cane swishing in front of him as he scanned the room, as if he hoped to find a miscreant upon which to pound into the dirt. But there was no one for him to select; every single boy in the room was bent to his work, studiously, almost frantically. The room was, once more, bathed in a silent, anxious gloom of industry.

As for Jack's words, they'd been cut off, for Jack had to attend to his oakum picking, as did Oliver. But Oliver knew what Jack had meant to say. In his heart, he knew it. And while he hoped that the knowledge would be enough to bolster him, he feared that it would not be.

9

WHEN AFTERNOON GROWS
BLACK AND DEEP

The end of the morning's work shift came with little incident, unless Jack considered the one slender boy who'd sat in the front row, whose weigh-in of his oakum had come a bit short. Chalenheim had offered the lad a whipping instead of missing a meal, and the boy had chosen the cane.

Jack had opened his mouth and then shut it, dismayed to see how all the boys lowered their gazes as Chalenheim took the boy over his bent knee and gave him three swift whacks of the cane. Nolly had resolutely looked the other way, and even when the whipping had been over, and the boys had lined up two by two, his expression seemed to take in nothing, acknowledge nothing.

If Jack couldn't figure out a way to get Nolly out of the workhouse, he was going to be this way more and more until he was sucked dry of all life and feeling, and would simply be drawn into the next cold wind and would cease to exist.

Jack shook his head and blinked, thinking that hunger was making him have these fanciful, dark thoughts. He knew hunger, had experienced it before, but not like this. Again, the thought came to him that Nolly, having been brought up in a place like this, would have the focus such as he did on food, good food, served steaming hot, and piles of it, as though he couldn't even bear the thought of going without for even a moment.

Jack promised himself that, in future, he would always have a spare shilling on him to purchase for Nolly whatever he cared to eat, or carry, folded in a napkin, a corner of a meat pie, or a bit of cheese, even. So that Nolly wouldn't have to go through hunger ever again, even for a short while.

When they got to the boys' dining hall, Jack gathered his bowl and spoon, and nudged Nolly to do the same, hoping that the bit of food that they were going to get would bring some color, some spark, however small, back into his face, his eyes. But it was even before they'd gotten up to the cauldron, where the two attendants stirred the glop, when he found Nolly turning his head to look at him.

Though Nolly's mouth was still a hard white line, there was an expression in his eyes, now a dull blue, and he half blinked at Jack, as if he were glad Jack was there. As if it had been he that had been arrested, and Jack had thrown himself into the fray so that they would not be separated. As if the sacrifice had been Jack's and not his own. Which told him how addled Nolly was, addled with pain and hunger and exhaustion. That was the plain truth of it. And it made Jack angry all over again.

"I'll get you out of here, Nolly," said Jack, whispering, ducking his chin as he held up his bowl. "I promise."

"I know, Jack," said Nolly, doing the same.

Then walked over to the last bench by the wall where Jack could see the top of the stairs and all of the windows. They sat side by side, their thighs touching, and Jack suddenly realized that he was on Nolly's right side where, surely, Chalenheim's switch had hit the hardest, went the deepest. He tried to move away, but Nolly's hand was on Jack's thigh, light as a feather and bold as brass.

Jack kept looking straight ahead, waiting for the signal to bow his head and clasp his hands and listen to Chalenheim say grace over their pitiful, scant meal. Nolly's hand stayed there all through the meal; he ate with his left hand, steady and slow, bending forward a bit, as if to rest on the front part of his thighs. Never letting go of Jack, as if he was the only thing that calmed him.

~

As they lined up to go out of the dining hall, Mr. Bassler came, and Mr. Louis, and two other men Jack did not know who began to count off the boys by fours. Jack was instantly in a panic because he was standing right next to Nolly, and they would be separated. But the counting happened too quickly, and Chalenheim pulled Jack to one side with three other boys, and Nolly went the other way, looking over his shoulder before disappearing down the passageway.

"You boys," said Chalenheim, in a voice that was meant to get their attention, "will be scrubbing the day rooms for the men and women. As you know, we're to have an inspection next week, and the workhouse will be in order by that time, or I will know the reason why not."

He pointed with his finger at the four sets of buckets, scrub brushes, and brooms. Across the handle of each bucket was a cloth.

"You will draw water from the well in the men's yard, and you will wipe down the windowsills, sweep the floor, and then scrub every inch of it. You must move the furniture. If I find any boy has merely swept and scrubbed around the tables and chairs, and believe me, I will look, you will be marked down for punishment before supper."

Each boy bent to pick up his bucket, setting the cloth aside, as though they'd done this before, which Jack supposed that they had. And though he followed suit, dreading the damage the work would do to his very useful hands, Jack did not know where the well was. He had to ask. He had to actually open his mouth and say civil words to this monster. But if he didn't—

"Sir," said Jack, ducking his head in a way that he hoped might appease the man's vanity.

"You have a question, Jack Dawkins?"

Though Jack didn't look up, he could almost see the sneering look on the man's face.

"Which way is the well?"

"Yes," said Chalenheim, as if Jack had just confirmed every single bad thing about himself that could possibly be thought. "Boys, let's show Jack where the well is."

The way to the well, it turned out, wasn't difficult, just along the passage and out a door that was new to him, but that led out to the yard where they'd broken bone. The yard was empty of men, though the bone boxes and pike crushers were lined up under the eaves, ready for the morning's use.

Along the interior wall was a well, an old-fashioned one with a crank that drew up a bucket rather than a sensible capped-off well with a brightly painted pump. But seeing as how they were in a workhouse in the middle of nowhere, he couldn't be too surprised.

He threw himself into the task. He turned the crank, his hands still sore, and brought up a bucket of water for each boy, and helped them pour the bucket from the well into their buckets, seeing as how they were all so thin and pale and still.

At one moment, when Jack was about to turn the crank one last time to fill his own bucket, Nolly came out into the yard from an unseen door. He was dressed in a brown apron, and his jacket was off, his sleeves were rolled up, and he was carrying two empty buckets.

It took Jack's breath away to see Nolly all of a sudden like that. It was rather as though a spell had produced Nolly after a long absence, though it could only have been ten minutes since he'd last seen him. But since he'd not expected to see him until the evening, and there he was, well, it was like a miracle. A miracle of a beautiful painting of a sad boy who did not want to look at Jack, though Jack wanted him to.

So, conscious of all eyes upon him, including Chalenheim's, Jack lowered the bucket into the well and slowly, very slowly, cranked up a full bucket of water, and poured it into Nolly's bucket, which he'd placed on the ground. Then he filled the other one.

"Thank you," said Nolly, as he picked up the now-full buckets. He barely glanced at Jack as he walked back inside, as if he was just anybody. But that was the sensible way to be, not like Jack, who was going all moon-eyed and foolish in this dangerous place.

"Let's not dawdle, Jack. You're holding everyone up. This task needs to be finished or there will be no supper for anyone."

Jack just nodded, gritting his teeth as he filled up his bucket, not willing to risk saying anything for fear of saying the wrong thing that would get him in trouble, get Nolly in trouble, or absent the boys from their supper. Not that they were under his care, but they were, in a way, for the short time he was here. For it would be a short time, as short as he could make it.

In the meantime, Jack followed where Chalenheim led like a good duckling, watching as Chalenheim took the boys into what looked to be the women's day room, for though it was the same as any other room, being fitted with only chairs and some tables, it seemed to have some gentleness about it.

"You three boys, take care of this room. Jack, you're with me."

For a moment, Jack could only stand there looking at Chalenheim.

"Did you not hear me? This way, Jack."

Chalenheim had spoken quite clearly, and as Jack made himself move forward, to follow where he was led, he could not determine what had jarred him so. Only that he had to hustle to keep apace with Chalenheim's long stride as he led Jack around the passage, and to the long set of rooms off it that Jack could easily see were the men's day rooms.

There were long rows of bare windows on either side, and a

very small fireplace set into one wall. The fire wasn't lit, and the room, now quite empty, while it must, at some point, be filled with doddering men and skinny paupers, felt as though it had not been occupied for years.

There was a stillness to it, which had nothing to do with the emptiness; it was as if the room were made to absorb all the ghosts of existence that had ever passed through it, and Jack wondered if all workhouses felt this way. He had no desire to ever find out, of course, for the one was enough for him.

"Start with the windows," said Chalenheim, gesturing about him as he reached the center of the room. "Then sweep the floor. I'll check back to determine when the floor is ready for scrubbing."

Chalenheim went past Jack on his way out, wearing the expression of a man who was quite, quite certain that his every command would be carried out to the letter. In a moment, the vague breeze created by his quick stride out of the room was followed by that uncertain stillness of the room, as if the floor had never been trod upon and the layer of dust created by years of absence.

Jack shook his head and carried his cleaning supplies through a little doorway that led into another slightly smaller room. There were more tables and chairs in the room, lined up in an almost orderly fashion in the spaces between the windows to the far end of the room. At the furthest wall, where there were no windows, and Jack assumed was built into the outside wall of the workhouse, was another small, unlit fireplace.

For a room supposedly set aside for the comfort of the inmates, wherein they might rest from their labors, it had all the appeal of a pile of broken bricks. As for whether the board's examination of the workhouse would take them even this far, Jack highly doubted it.

They would probably want to see the most obvious parts of the workhouse, to be seen to be seeing, and would have no real concern about the condition of its inmates. Thus, the current push to make things ready for that inspection was complete and utter bullshit, a scheme to get the paupers to work harder for no reason.

Jack wanted nothing more than to toss down his bucket, the brush, and to fling the rag as far as he could manage it. Maybe he'd get it wet first by a dunk in the bucket before balling it up and hurling it against the wall, where it would make a good, resounding slap sound. He was not Nolly, who might consider that the best way to get his assigned chores done was to actually *do* them.

But Jack knew better. Nobody cared, at least not any of the board. As for the inmates, with their dull expressions and with their expectations all but beaten and starved out of them, they would not care that there was dust in their day room. Quite possibly they would even be surprised by its removal, and be disjointed and confused in the change in their day room, since at all other times, the room would be left quite as it was, and to hell with the comfort of the men who used it.

Such dark thoughts were certainly not getting the room cleaned, but since it didn't matter, then he couldn't care. Instead, he leaned by one of the windows, his arms folded over his chest, as if he were at his own leisure, looking out into the men's yard across to where the well was, and where a small boy was struggling with the crank on the well.

Jack had an impulse to go and help him, for indeed the boy was quite small. But another small boy came out to help him, and together the two of them managed to pull up the water for their buckets, and trundled back inside to carry on with whatever scrubbing task had been assigned them.

After they left, Jack lingered at the window, and realized that across the yard, just beyond the well, and through the bank of windows, he could see Nolly. His head was bent down, intent on some task that required his concentration. The window was streaked across the panes, and the light wasn't very good, but Jack could tell it was Nolly.

With that particular way he now lifted his head, and seemed to ask a question, and then returned to his duties, because for Nolly, that was the way things were. The way you did them. As if chores and tasks and suchlike were a type of salvation, or a ticket to forgiveness. Not realizing, as Jack did, that nobody gave a damn about why you were doing what you were doing. Some people just liked to tell others what to do.

His only compensation was he knew, for Nolly, that if the task wasn't too beneath him, he would find it soothing. So Jack hoped Nolly was doing something worth approving of, at least in this place, such as peeling potatoes or cutting up a chicken for the master's supper, rather than doing something such as the lowly task that had been assigned Jack, that of scrubbing floors.

Thinking of food, his mouth was watering, and Nolly had moved back from the window so there was nothing to see. There was only the yard, vast and gray and empty in its stillness except for the slight speckle of rain that was now dappling the stones in the yard.

In a moment it would begin raining hard enough to drip from the eaves and make flat, oily puddles across the stone. Jack promised himself he would watch for a while and if a little boy came out to the well, or perhaps even Nolly himself, Jack would go out and help turn the crank.

He thought, even, that he might slip out of the day room and make his way down the passage to end up wherever Nolly was, and pretend he'd been assigned there. But from behind him, Jack heard a noise, a crisp footfall that announced to his body the presence of another person before his ears could make sense of it.

Jack turned, and Chalenheim was right there, directly in front of him, tall, with his broad shoulders almost filling the space around him. Jack almost took a step back, except that he was already against the wall with nowhere to move to get away from the press of Chalenheim's presence in the still, dry air of the day room.

"There you are, Jack," said Chalenheim, smiling down on Jack as if he'd been a lost pup and Chalenheim, his timely rescuer. "Making progress, I should say?"

"I should say," said Jack in echo, though it was easy to see that he'd not done a lick of work.

Chalenheim seemed less concerned with that than his distance from Jack. He moved closer till Jack had to tip his head back or be staring at Chalenheim's jacket buttons, and Jack was less inclined to converse with anybody's buttons than he was to do any actual work.

"There's a proposition on offer for you, if you're sensible enough to take it."

"A what?" Jack knew what the word *proposition* meant, of course; you couldn't be around Nolly and not pick up the definition of fancy words. But the word had different meanings, he knew, so it was best to make certain which one Chalenheim intended.

"An exchange," said Chalenheim, with a small smile.

It made no sense to Jack what Chalenheim was talking about. He was going to say as much when Chalenheim's face gentled as he reached out and, with a small movement, cupped Jack's face and traced his thumb along Jack's cheekbone. Startled beyond all composure, Jack jerked his head back, wincing as it struck the wall.

"Bloody hell," he said, reaching back to rub his head, fearful of the headache that might soon start; his poor head was such a tender thing these days, after the clout that Cromwell had given him.

Fully expecting to be slapped for using profanity, and there was no way Chalenheim could pretend that he'd not heard, Jack was flustered to feel Chalenheim's hand on his face, the curve of his palm, the roughness of his fingers. Stroking Jack's face, as if there were other parts of Jack that he also wanted to stroke.

"So you do understand what I intend," said Chalenheim.

"You give me what I want, and I'll make your stay in the work-house a very comfortable one indeed."

Jack knew he'd given himself away already. Any other boy less experienced in the ways of the world would have asked for clarification with a sweet and innocent, *whatever do you mean, work-master*, and been completely confused by the reply. Even Nolly would have been confused, and Jack hoped that fact would be forever true.

But as for Jack, oh, yes, he knew what Chalenheim wanted, and what the exchange would entail, how he, Jack, would live high on the hog in the workhouse if only he would bend over and take it up the arse whenever Chalenheim looked at him and gave him the signal.

He could imagine the confused look on Nolly's face when Jack started to receive butter on his bread, and a pint of beer to wash down his meat pie with at mealtimes. There would be questions from Nolly, also, as to where the extra blanket and pillows had come from, and—

Worst of all, it would be unpleasant. It would be—it would be painful, for Chalenheim was the sort of man, as Jack had already seen, who enjoyed tormenting young orphans by delaying their meager meals through an overly long pause before prayers.

If Chalenheim had Jack to himself, in a room somewhere, or a less than frequented corner of the workhouse, he would not be kind, let alone tender, and it would be, again, like it had been in Port Jackson. Before Jack had learned to let what was happening to him simply happen. To give in and not fight it. And even then—

He could not imagine going anywhere with Chalenheim, who still hovered above him, that half-smile on his face as if he expected Jack to jump at this chance. Well, Jack would not. Not for all the creature comforts in the world.

"The hell I will," said Jack, standing his ground.

"What was that you just said, Jack? Is that a *no*?"

"Yes, that's a *no*," said Jack, getting to the point, not wanting to go around and around in some polite dance about it. "You're not gettin' your hands on me, so find some other boy to fuck."

As soon as he said it, it hit him that Chalenheim had very likely been using the workhouse as a sort of hunting ground, and his duties as workmaster had given him so many chances, so many opportunities. Had Jack been a better sort of person, he would have volunteered in their place, so as to spare those hungry, wee boys the dreaded moment when they experienced too much of the world too soon.

Nolly certainly would have done it, though it made the sweat break out along the back of Jack's neck to think of Nolly going through *anything* like this. But Jack wasn't a better sort of person, and he had only himself to chide if he grew a soft heart and did anything like this in order to save what were to him complete strangers.

"It's a definite *no*," he said now, shaking his head, giving himself a bit of breathing space by talking to Chalenheim's jacket buttons. Then he made himself look up.

He thought for a moment that Chalenheim would haul back and punch him, knock him unconscious and have his way with Jack right there in the men's day room. It was on his face, a fast, dark-eyed fury, his lips pulled tightly over his teeth as he glared at Jack.

Jack knew, in his heart, that were Nolly here, he would go on the attack to teach Chalenheim the error of his ways, and probably feel those fists that Chalenheim was clenching at his sides, and find himself on the losing end of a battle he could never win. Jack also knew better than to butt his head against a brick wall like this one; it was better and safer to go around it. So with a slight nudge, he made to push past Chalenheim, as if it were the ordinary, the expected thing to do, since Jack needed to attend to his duties.

Chalenheim, who might have been taken off guard, or who might have other plans to achieve his aim, let Jack by.

Jack picked up the cloth from the bucket handle and, with

his heart hammering in his chest, hard enough to break bone, turned his back on Chalenheim and began to wipe at the windowsill.

Through the window, he caught a glimpse of Nolly again, working away, in whatever room he was in, not seeing Jack, and that was fine. Jack didn't want to be seen by Nolly at this moment, not with Chalenheim standing behind him like a silent monster who has not yet determined whether or not to devour his human prey. Nolly didn't need to know about any of this, no, he most certainly did not.

"Was there aught else you wanted, mister?" asked Jack, doing his best to achieve a casual lilt to his voice. As if the workmaster had merely stopped by to check on Jack's work.

There was only a chuffed sound of annoyance from Chalenheim, and then the slow, heavy tread of his steps as he departed.

Jack might have taken the workmaster off guard, and Chalenheim had been put off, but most likely there would be another attempt made that Jack would have to fend off. Which he needed to do without Nolly knowing. Which wasn't the same as lying, as near as he could see it. This was simply something Nolly did not need to be exposed to. Well, and anyway, he could hardly get two words together out of Nolly, so the chances of them having a conversation of any length was quite small, and for this, Jack could be grateful.

He was grateful now for the ghostlike stillness that again crept over the room as the rain turned the yard to gray streaks, and Nolly's blond head became a mere slash of faint gold through the layers of window glass. Jack's heart felt the pain of it, that they were here, together.

If Jack couldn't protect himself, then how could he protect Nolly? Maybe he couldn't do either; maybe he was fated for it, this place, in the way Nolly always said that he was born to be hung. Jack didn't know, and his hands slowed, the cloth dangling from his fingers as he stopped working, and leaned against the sill to stare out of the window into the rain.

BECOMING ACQUAINTED WITH A WORKHOUSE KITCHEN

They were separated, but then Oliver knew they would be. It would only be for the span of work that occupied the afternoon, but it would be too long, for he couldn't bear to be apart from Jack just now. But away Jack was led away by Workmaster Chalenheim, and Oliver was taken by Mr. Bassler, along with three other boys, down the passage to the kitchen.

It felt familiar, that passage, bright on one side, with the turning clouds in the sky letting in a bit of blue, and the doorways to the kitchen and scullery, and two other rooms besides. He could have taken himself there by this time, having already gone up and down the passage twice.

Then he shook his head; focusing on unimportant details would distract him, and he needed to stay focused, on the work, on where he was, on what he needed to do. Otherwise, there would be no reason for Mr. Bassler not to beat him again.

Oliver didn't think he could take seeing that expression on Jack's face if that were to happen. For now, after only a few days, Jack was, perhaps, coming to understand how a workhouse worked, and what happened to the paupers within its walls. Moreover, every time Oliver was the recipient of that less-than-tender care, Jack's face became more drawn, his eyes more fierce, even though there was nothing he could do about it.

"Robert," said Mr. Bassler with a snap, bringing Oliver to the awareness that two of the younger boys had already been sent off, and there were only three of them standing there. "You're to go to clean the grates in the porter's room and assist him in any way that he needs you. And what's your name, boy? You there."

Mr. Bassler was pointing at the younger boy to Oliver's left, a small slip of a thing, with shorn hair and bright, gray eyes.

"Finley, sir," said the boy. His mouth barely moved as he spoke, but it was enough to let Oliver hear he was Irish, though what an Irish boy was doing in an English workhouse, he did not know. However, Finley was the same little boy who had sat on the bench between Oliver and Jack that very morning.

"Finley, you and Oliver will work in the kitchen, and do whatever Cook tells you. Cook, can you come here a moment?"

Cook stepped out into the passageway with a great deal of bustle, her hands on her hips, impatient, as if Mr. Bassler had taken her away from undoubtedly more important pursuits. She was round and dark haired, with her large bosom covered in a white apron that went all the way to her toes.

On her head, she wore a white ruffled cap, the old-fashioned kind that Oliver's nurse used to wear. But she was not in the least bedraggled by her work in a kitchen, for there was not a smudge on her.

Oliver could almost hear Jack's comment in his head, the unruly response that would have brought dire consequences upon his head were he to speak it, but Oliver heard it just the same: *From the looks of her, she certainly ain't cookin' anythin' in that kitchen of hers, that's for certain.* Oliver did not let himself smirk in response to this imagined comment, not even a little bit.

"These two are yours for the afternoon to do the washing up and whatnot. I'll come get them at supper."

Then Mr. Bassler was off, taking Robert with him, and leaving Oliver and Finley to stand in the drafty passage as Cook looked them over. Which she did with some asperity, her discontent radiating from her narrow eyes that were too close together, and her scowling mouth.

As to what she had to be unhappy about, Oliver could not determine, for she certainly, yes, certainly never actually cooked anything worth eating in that kitchen of hers. And, from what Oliver had sampled of her cooking, he could tell her, were she to ask, that her title was a misnomer in all forms.

"I've got no assistant all this week, so you'll have to do. Come along in," she said, in sharp tones, though they'd not yet done anything wrong.

Oliver followed her, giving an encouraging nod to Finley, who looked young enough as to be frightened by a sharp word as well as a kind one in this place, which must seem so strange to him. Finley stuck close to Oliver's side, as though he felt Oliver could protect him from Cook were she to go off in a temper. Which was likely, seeing as how she was already halfway there.

The kitchen was as long as the boy's dining hall, and was broken into two main areas. At one end, toward the center of the workhouse, was the scullery, the half-walls allowing light to come in through the windows. And also, Oliver suspected, to allow Cook to keep her eye on the entire of her territory.

The sideboards on either side of the sinks were stacked with dirty bowls and spoons, though, come to that, both the bowls and the spoons had been scraped or licked clean and wouldn't need much washing. Still, there were a lot of them.

At the other end was the kitchen, with a long iron stove set into the wall. It was as long as two stoves, and might be for baking bread, though Oliver couldn't smell anything baking at all. Against the far wall were two cauldrons, dark with age and use, each which stood on their own brick-walled fire pits. There was a bank of windows that faced what Oliver recognized as the men's yard, where he and Jack had crushed bone only the day before. It was empty, as probably all the men were again in the field.

Cook grabbed two brown aprons and shoved them at Oliver.

"Put those aprons on and roll up your sleeves; you're not at your leisure here."

Oliver did as he was told, taking off his jacket to put it on a hook next to the sink, and tied on his apron. Then he assisted Finley, as the poor boy's hands were shaking too hard to tie the apron around his back. The ends of the sash needed to come around to his front, where Oliver tied a tidy knot around the boy's middle.

"Finley, you're to mix the washing soda with the carbolic soap, and Oliver, we need more water. Buckets are there." She pointed beneath the table that was along where the windows were. "Go and fetch water, well's in the yard. Finley!"

Finley seemed unable to move, so she grabbed him by the collar and pulled him over to the table.

"Mix the washing soda here in these bowls. When you're done with that, you'll polish knives. Use that emery powder and them cloths. What are *you* standing there for? Go get water!"

Somewhat astonished at her quickness of speech, Oliver grabbed the buckets, the handles cutting into his sore hands, and hurried down the passage, wondering how to get to the men's yard from where he was. At the end of the passage, he passed the stairs going down to the coal store and refractory, and hurried on. As he turned the corner and went through an open door, he saw a room full of coffins, which stopped him cold.

He'd heard the announcements at suppertime with only half of his attention, but yes, paupers died quickly and often. At Sowerberry's Funeral Parlor, he'd been witness to several pauper funerals, and each and every one of them had been simple, hasty affairs, with no mourners save the parson mumbling the rites over the shallow grave into which the body was tipped, falling from the oft-used coffin.

Next to that was a doorway, now locked, that Oliver recognized as being the one that went out into the yard at the back of the workhouse, where he and Jack had been loaded into the hayrick wagons and taken to the field to pick stones. This was certainly more of a workhouse than he'd seen at Hardingstone, where he'd been limited to the dining hall, the boys' dormitory, and the yard. If there had been any other place, he didn't remember it.

The door at the end of the very short passage was hanging part way open, as if the last person to use it had forgotten to latch it. Oliver pushed through this and found himself out in the men's yard, as if he'd meant to go there on purpose. And, to his surprise, there was Jack.

He was drawing water from the well, cranking it up by the handle as the rope came up dripping. He was pouring water into buckets for the smaller boys grouped around him. Workmaster Chalenheim was overseeing everything, but didn't offer any help.

Jack looked up and stopped mid-crank, his eyes brightening upon seeing Oliver there, and Oliver felt his breast warm with gladness at seeing Jack there. For even though it had only been moments, seeing him again was like being given a reprieve from the gray-walled workhouse with all its layers of misery. And there amidst everything, was Jack, Oliver's bright bird, a startling contrast even as he merely stood there. Neither speaking nor moving, he was still the most vivid thing in the yard.

But Workmaster Chalenheim was watching them, so Oliver swallowed his joy and brought the buckets to the well, as if he meant to wait his turn and draw water when Jack was done filling the young boys' buckets. Though, when Jack was done, he continued drawing water and poured water into each of Oliver's buckets.

Oliver was not surprised, but felt a rush of affection that Jack would work so hard when the work was so obviously beneath him and, moreover, when he did not believe, had never believed, that it would ever be of benefit to him. Yet he was doing it. To help the younger boys. To help Oliver.

"Thank you," said Oliver as he picked up his now-full buckets.

He looked at Jack with carefully guarded eyes, for he could not bear to have anybody in this place see how much he cared for Jack, how much he loved him. He could only turn on his heel, the buckets sloshing against his thighs, and make his way back to the kitchen.

When he got there, Cook was already yelling at Finley, her hands up as if she meant to box his ears.

"You're to polish them with the powder, not stir it around!"

"Can I help, missus?" asked Oliver, using the form of address as Jack would have, for so common a person did not deserve a more formal title than that.

"He's mucking it up. He's to polish knives, and he don't know how! I should thrash him!"

"I know how to polish knives, missus," said Oliver, for he had often been in the warmth of the kitchen when the servants were bustling around, working, and he'd seen it done, at least.

"What about them dishes, them pots? They need to be washed!"

"We'll do them after," said Oliver. He kept his tone level, as all the shouting was causing Finley to cower behind him. "Finley and I'll do each task together. It'll go quickly, you'll see. If you'll let us."

"This is all too much, for *next* you'll be telling me how to do my job!"

This particular shriek hit the ceiling and bounced off of it, startling Oliver to jerk backward.

"We'll do it, missus," he said, attempting to soothe her now. "Never you worry." For it might be that she'd be upset enough to call for the strap and a strong man to punish both of them. Oliver didn't think he could take another beating just now, nor stand by and watch while Finley was beaten.

Cook threw up her hands and went to the stove, where she began fussing with the oven door, and the coals inside, and put a kettle on as if she meant to have tea. Meanwhile, Oliver drew Finley to him, and picked up the bowl of chloride of lime.

"This stings, so don't get your fingers in it, especially if they're wet, you see?"

Finley watched closely, his eyes as enormous as saucers.

"First, you take the soap, this bar of yellow soap, and you shave off slivers, like this." Oliver picked up the rather dull knife that was on the table, soothed by the familiarity of the motions of holding the soap in one hand while he shaved it. "Always do it away from you, so if the knife slips, you don't cut yourself. Would you like to try?"

Finley looked brave for about all of a moment, then shook his head. He almost flinched, as if he expected Oliver would smack him for saying *no*, but Oliver only nodded, thinking of the times the cook in the kitchen of the townhouse in London had been patient with him, letting him get away with not doing those tasks that seemed too complicated. Not that he had ever been required to do anything remotely resembling manual labor, but from time to time, it had been interesting to involve himself in the servants' occupations.

Oliver pushed the bowl toward Finley.

"You can hold that for me," he said, "so it doesn't move about if I accidentally jostle it."

This Finley was able to do, and Oliver shaved off probably more of the soap than was necessary, but it was soothing to do this while he looked out the window into the yard as it started to rain. Where, if he narrowed his eyes, it looked as though it could be anywhere, that he could be anywhere except where he was.

When he finished shaving the soap, he took the knife and stirred the soda in with the slivers until it was well mixed. Cook came over with the kettle to pour hot water on the mixture, and then went to have her cup of tea and sit in the chair near the stove and stare at them as they labored on.

"Now we'll polish knives," Oliver said. He wasn't as familiar with this task, but he'd seen it done, and it didn't seem to be too hard.

He moistened a cloth with water from the bucket, then

dipped it into the bowl of emery powder. Holding the knife in one hand, he rubbed the paste on the blade, over and over, then flipped the blade and rubbed the other side. After rinsing the knife in the bucket, it shone, and he handed it to Finley to admire.

"Take that cloth, and you can dry it, then lay it on the table in neat rows. Like soldiers." Which is what the cook had said to him, gently guiding his hand when his rows had turned out crooked. "This keeps the knives from rusting, do you see?"

Finley nodded, eager to help, but in his haste as he reached out for the knife, he knocked the bowl of emery powder all over the table. The bowl then bounced on the floor and cracked into two huge pieces.

Cook flew over to them, leaving her cup of tea behind, and smacked Finley hard.

"Look at this mess, look at this bowl!" She pointed, as if they couldn't all very well see the disaster before them. "You're a careless wretch and you'll be taught a lesson!"

Oliver bent to pick up the bowl and, holding it in two pieces, considered what he must do, though his heart began to race at the thought of it.

"I knocked it over, missus," he said. "For I am clumsy that way." He looked over at Finley, whose mouth was wobbling, the tracks of his tears already cutting through the grime on his face. "Finley was reaching for it, trying to catch it."

Cook scowled at them, her hands on her hips, as if unable to determine whether or not he was lying.

Oliver wished that Jack were with him, for Jack would know the exact right statement to make to diffuse her anger and redirect her attention. Jack could have probably even gotten her out of her bad temper with a saucy remark, though, to be more honest, Jack's attitude could just have likely brought down more of her rage.

"I'm terribly sorry," said Oliver now. "Do you have a little broom we could sweep this up with?"

"A *little* broom?" she asked. "A little *broom* you want, is it now? Where on earth do you think you are, the house of the Lord Mayor of London? You'll use your hands and get every bit, or I'll want to know why not!"

She stomped around the kitchen to find them a different bowl and, in the meanwhile, Oliver motioned for Finley to kneel down with him so they could scoop up the emery powder with their hands. How to use the heel of the palm to brush the powder together in a pile in the center of the plank. Though, as Oliver saw now, the width between the planks would serve as a dustbin of sorts and, seeing as she was so agitated, Cook would never see that a portion of the powder had simply gone away.

She came back directly with a metal bowl this time, and they both breathed a sigh of relief when she went to her chair by the stove and glumly drank her tea. Oliver showed Finley how to scoop up the emery dust, carefully in the cup of his palms, to deposit it in the bowl.

"I'll be reporting the loss to Master Pickering, I will. Never will I take the blame for a clumsy pauper."

"Yes, missus," said Oliver.

He concentrated on his task with a little nod to Finley to give him courage. A broken bowl was not the end of the world, and the emery powder certainly wasn't costly. Still, it was a workhouse, where any step out of line, any mistake, no matter how small, always brought down someone's wrath.

Oliver and Finley returned to the task of polishing knives, doing one after the other with good care, lining up the knives, until every one was done. The length of Oliver's legs hummed, an underlying ache that came up to the surface only to bite back down to the bone, till he could hardly stand without swaying.

But in the face of this discomfort, the bruise on Finley's face blossomed, and Oliver knew he could hardly compare his aches, so known to him, almost familiar, to the wideness of Finley's eyes, the rabbit-scared quiver of his mouth. Oliver knew what was in store for himself, while Finley did not. And surely, the unknown was to be faced with more timidity than the known.

Oliver gave Finley a quick nod of approval that Oliver knew for himself, back in the days when he had been as small, would have taken him very far indeed. A simple nod, a quick pat on the shoulder. Something. Anything. Instead, he had gotten nothing, so for that he would encourage where he could, when he could. Finley smiled back and, for that moment, the kitchen seemed a good place, though absurdly damp, and not smelling very nice.

When they were done polishing knives, Cook pointed to the stone sinks, about which teetered a good many bowls and pots in which something had been cooked that had not been fed to the paupers. There was even a wicker basket full of spoons, which had to be washed as well.

Pushing his sleeves up just to his elbows, Oliver settled into the task, pouring the soap mixture into the sink, then adding water from the buckets standing by. He told himself he did not mind the sting of the washing soda, or the reflective thought that the bowls looked practically unused, on account of the paupers scraping and licking them to get every last bit of food.

But with Finley at his side, Oliver washed and rinsed, and let Finley dry, as that was the easiest part. And as long as their backs were to Cook, they could pretend they were alone in the kitchen, doing the rough work to help the scullery maid who was, perhaps, down with the toothache. It was a good enough story in his mind, and the motions of washing and rinsing so methodical and simple that his body relaxed for the first time that day.

Next to him, Finley looked up with a smile, so little as to seem cautious, as if Finley were uncertain what Oliver's response might be. Finley was a good lad, eager to please, and there were so many who would have found him useful, who would have wanted to take him on, perhaps as a boy to watch the fires in the kitchen, or to take down the shutters in the morning—

When the door opened, and heavy footsteps heard on the

stone floor, Oliver was not ready to be disrupted from his state, in which he was at home again, and everything seemed straight-forward and uncomplicated.

"Oliver Twist," said a voice behind him, that of Workmaster Chalenheim.

Oliver's whole body tightened up, stiff through his spine, all the way to the soles of his feet, and he could barely turn around to answer the summons. When he did turn, Finley pushed himself close to Oliver's side, a little behind him. Oliver knew he needed to be brave for Finley's sake, as Chalenheim filled the doorway with his shoulders and whose dark eyes missed nothing.

"Yes, sir?" asked Oliver.

Cook cut off anything Chalenheim might have to say, as she shoved her teacup and saucer to one side and marched to the doorway where Chalenheim stood.

"Yes, Cook, whatever is the matter now?"

"That brat," she said, pointing to Finley with a sharp finger, "broke a bowl with his carelessness and wasted emery powder!" This came out as a shout, as it always seemed to do, bouncing off the walls of the kitchen. "And this one, haughty and high-handed, dared asked me for a little broom to clean it up with. A little *broom*. I ask you, is this workhouse equipped with a little *broom*? He's full of wasteful proclivities and pride too much for words. You're to take them both, Workmaster Chalenheim, and give them a good thrashing!"

For a moment, the room was still as Chalenheim looked at Cook, and at the kitchen, where half the work was undone; her shouting served to emphasize this. Then he looked at Oliver, pausing for a moment, as if remembering the morning in the oakum room, and contemplating whether Oliver, by his very presence, deserved another beating.

Oliver held very still, and did not speak, for he had not been spoken to, listening to the whisper of Jack's voice inside of him that told him this was best. He refused to lower his eyes, however, could not make himself do it, for if Chalenheim was to approach him, he wanted to be ready when that happened. But it did not. Chalenheim merely looked at Finley, who was now clutching at Oliver's shirt, his small fingers tugging hard, the heat of his body close along Oliver's side.

"And who is this?" Chalenheim asked, as if Cook's demands didn't still ring in the air.

"Finley," said Cook, though the question hadn't been addressed to her, and even as she answered, Chalenheim's attention did not waver from Finley. "He's a wasteful wretch, and barely useful, in spite of the fact that the rest of my help has gone missing. Whatever am I to do with only two paupers to help me, I ask you?"

"Finley?" asked Chalenheim. "That sounds Irish. Is it?"

Nobody stirred, nor said anything, least of all Finley, who had glued himself to Oliver's side. Oliver was about to answer when Chalenheim took a step forward.

"You must answer me when I speak to you, Finley," said Chalenheim. But it was not said in strident tones, but only barely scolding ones as Chalenheim tipped his head down to look at Finley. Waiting for him to answer.

Oliver wanted to answer for Finley, but that would only make it worse, so instead he put his arm around Finley's shoulders to give him courage.

"Yes," said Finley, in a voice so faint it was almost a ghost of itself.

"Then why aren't you in Ireland with the rest of your people?"

"Mam sent me on a boat," said Finley with a small gulp. "There weren't nowt to eat at 'ome."

"Ah," said Chalenheim, as he lifted his head and looked about the kitchen. "Well, you assist Cook, and do as you're told, and all will be well."

Oliver could hardly believe the soft tones in which this was said. Workhouses promised work, and that was all. There was never anything good or well that came out of them. What's more, Chalenheim nodded and stepped back, as if to exit the kitchen.

"Ain't you going to thrash them, Workmaster?" Cook said this with a little shriek, her mouth dropping open.

"Why, no, I'm not. Boys, do your work, and someone will collect you come suppertime. Good day, Cook."

Cook sputtered as he left, but there was nothing she could do to bring him back, for his steps were already mere echoes along the passageway. But she glared at the two of them just the same.

"Get back to work, you," she said, her hands on her hips, shaking her head as if they were to blame for Chalenheim's visit. "Or I will find somebody to thrash you, so help me."

Nodding, Oliver gave Finley's shoulder a pat and looked down at him.

"We'll finish this easily, you and me," he said. "All right?"

Finley nodded, gulping a bit, and, looking at Oliver directly, in a way that Oliver could see took more than a little courage, nodded again. "Yes," he said.

"Never mind Cook," said Oliver, bending close, as if he were straightening Finley's apron strings about his neck. "Just stay close."

And with that, Oliver turned back to the mound of dishes, the water now cold and still, with a film of soap along the surface of it. He felt so tired, so worn, and he hadn't been in the workhouse but a handful of days.

How would he survive as much time as it would take till the June assizes were held, let alone get through the work assigned to him each day? With a deep breath, he pushed up his sleeves to just past his elbows and reached into the water for the next bowl, and began scrubbing.

❧ II ❧

SENSELESS WRATH, SENSELESS CRUELTY

B y the time Chalenheim came to get him to lead him and the other boys to the dining hall, Jack had made a very half-hearted attempt to sweep the floor, and that was only to get out from beneath the heavy weight of boredom that had moved into his bones. Besides, after a time of watching through the window and peering through the rain, he'd not been able to see Nolly any longer, and thus the room was the only thing available to occupy his attention. But there were no books, no sharp little knife to whittle away at one of the chair legs, no pack of cards, no pipe, nothing.

As to what the elderly paupers did whilst in the day room besides look at one another as they sat around the nonexistent fire, he had no idea. Nolly's fear and hatred of the workhouse was now quite clear to him, and Fagin had been just plain wrong.

Jack picked up his cleaning supplies and carried them out to the passage to line them against the wall, as the other boys were doing. He felt a little bad about it that the boys looked tired and grimy from their labors while he remained relatively fresh, although he was starving. But they were too young or inexperienced or driven to distraction by hunger to see it as he saw it, so he wouldn't lord it over them that they were fools, and he the much cleverer one to have escaped the labor of the day, or, as was likely, merely sideswiped it for the time being.

It was not certain that on the morrow Chalenheim wouldn't charge him with the cleansing of a more visible location that the board would certain to visit during their inspection. But that was not his to control, so he got in line, two by two, to go into the dining room, scanning the line as it went around the corner, looking all the while for Nolly.

And there he saw him, coming through the far door with a small boy at his side, the same small boy who'd held Jack's hand when Nolly had been whipped in the oakum picking room. Both of them were rolling down their sleeves, and looking sweat-streaked and overly warm. Which might feel nice, being that warm in a place like this, but neither of them seemed to appreciate it. They might have been working in a laundry or a kitchen, some place with a bright fire that needed constant tending, but it seemed that this had been more arduous than pleasant.

At any rate, the little boy went to someone he knew, and Nolly was coming right down the center of the room, bold as anything, coming straight for Jack as he got in line in front of the cauldron for their evening's meal of barely warm, thin, white glop. At least there was bread to go with it, stacked in a basket on a table near the front of the room. At least there was that, for Jack's belly was pressing against his spine as if it had been fused there, and if he didn't eat soon, he was going to start consuming whatever was near to hand.

As Nolly reached the halfway mark between Jack and the door, Chalenheim was there, and he reached out with his large hand to grip Nolly by the upper arm to yank him aside.

"What did you just say to me?" Chalenheim said, in a none-too-quiet voice that almost directly had the dull hum of the room fade away to almost nothing.

"I didn't say anything," said Nolly.

He shrugged to get his arm free, looking up at Chalenheim as if he'd gone quite mad. He even used his free hand to attempt to pry Chalenheim's fingers from his arm, for all the good that was going to do him.

Jack could see it from where he stood that Chalenheim didn't care whether or not the accusation was true; he had the spark in his eyes of a man intent on finding someone upon whom to vent his temper. As Nolly had the most remarkable, most beautiful face, well, Jack could have told him that it was almost a foregone conclusion. Which didn't ease the sudden thud in his stomach as he watched Chalenheim snap his fingers at several of the boys, and gestured for them to pull the bench away from the nearest table.

An attendant brought him the strap and, as Chalenheim manhandled Nolly to bend over the table, Jack felt cold all over, sweat like small icy dots along the back of his neck, a chill running down his spine. And asked himself why he couldn't just jump to Nolly's defense, race over, grab Chalenheim from behind and simply pull him off? To stop the beating before it even began?

But it had begun. From across the room, Jack could see Chalenheim swing the belt in the air, as though to test its heft, and then he looked right at Jack.

Jack looked away, looked until he found a window and his eyes could focus on the gray rain as the night grew onwards, so that the sound of Nolly being beaten could then become, simply, something else. A loose roof slate torn by the wind, banging over and over. Or a door slamming, hard, as a storm raged beyond it. Anything but what it was, that made his heart pound till it might break through his breastbone, and his stomach roll over and over.

He'd been through many things in his time, seen violent men do hard, cruel things with their hands. But nothing like this, where his own, his own Nolly, was being treated like this, like a—

The beating stopped, and Jack, still staring out the window, could hear the tables being scraped back into to place, and the pattering steps of paupers resuming their normal evening's activities, lining up for food that was tasteless at best, and which would eventually cause them to starve to death.

He heard, almost distantly, Chalenheim saying something, and Nolly's careful, low, and respectful reply. Jack felt, just then, as if he'd been smeared all over in tar and rolled in ash to be witness to this and be unable to do anything about it. Or, because he was a coward at heart, he'd been *unwilling* to do anything about it.

When Nolly was beside him in line, Jack looked at him, feeling almost blind with the rush of feeling, of wanting to do something, but being unable to. He blinked when Nolly's hand brushed against his, as if to say it was all right that Jack hadn't done anything to stop it, because Nolly knew it was impossible.

Jack tried to clear his vision, to look at Nolly and acknowledge this, but he was at the head of the line before he knew it and, taking a bowl, held it out for his supper. He took his hunk of bread, as Nolly did, and stumbled behind him to their seat at the far table along the wall, and sat down, somehow without spilling his gruel.

He was unable to feel the bench beneath him until he looked down and realized that Nolly was touching his thigh, as he had before, but petting it this time, soft touches with his curved fingers, as if he were tapping out a signal, meant only for Jack. Jack let out a shuddering breath, bowing his head for the grace that Chalenheim was mumbling as he stood near the cauldron.

Jack didn't even look at the workmaster. He could only look at Nolly, who'd ducked his head, tipping it sideways so that he could look at Jack. Nolly was white faced, pale, smudged circles under his eyes, and while he might be uncomfortable sitting down after a whipping like the one he'd just received, for some reason, his sympathies seemed all for Jack.

"There was nothing you could do," said Nolly, sweet and kind. "Nothing that wouldn't have earned you a whipping as well."

"That's you, then," said Jack, smart mouthed, for he could

bear it no longer that Nolly was so brave, was so forgiving, wasn't angry. Jack had to crush the futility of it all, and hard words were the only thing standing between him sitting at his supper and him curled up on the floor like a wee lad who couldn't bear it anymore. "Bein' the hero, like you always do."

"I'm only a hero in your eyes, Jack," said Nolly, his voice so soft that it rippled all the way through Jack's body.

He had to bow his head for real this time to stare at his knees and the edge of the table. And down to where Nolly's fingers stroked his thigh, as if there was nobody watching. As if they were far away and on their own, in a private place where the message of Nolly's touch might have been a prelude to something far more pleasant.

Chalenheim stopped saying grace. The death announcements were made and, on the heels of that, followed the usual drone about the board's upcoming visit, until finally the boys were at leave to eat their suppers. Not one of them complained, nor did Jack, though his hand shook as he tried to eat, and he could only manage when he felt the pressure of Nolly's hand as he again ate left-handed.

Jack slipped his left hand beneath the table and laid it on Nolly's thigh, their wrists crossing against each other below the level of the table where no one could see. Which was for the best, because if anybody caught them, they'd both be strung up to hang at the workhouse gate, with Chalenheim, no doubt, pulling on the release to let the floor drop beneath their feet. For maybe Jack had been born to hang as well, but as long as he did it with Nolly—but no.

Nolly should die peaceful in his bed, at a long distance from this moment, with a book open on his breast, mid-sentence as he read to Jack. Which meant Jack would be sitting at his side with a knife in his hand to slit his own throat the moment Nolly exited this life. Of that, Jack was quite sure.

❧

OLIVER MADE HIMSELF EAT, THOUGH THE GRUEL WAS tasteless, and felt as though it were riddled with slivers of wood, though he'd watched Cook prepare the meal from nothing but water and ground oats, with a little salt and a little treacle. When an assistant had come in, she'd bossed the assistant around and kept at him to keep stirring. The gruel had scorched a bit in spite of the stirring, and beneath the splintery texture was the tang of burnt bits.

What made it even harder to eat was the pounding along the backs of his thighs as he sat on the bench next to Jack. He did not know what had earned him Chalenheim's ire, where even his attempt at politeness, that, if he *had* bumped into the man, he'd not meant to, had done him no good.

Chalenheim was so strong, a strength obviously not gained from eating the workhouse dietary, his whippings hurt. They made Bumble's attempts at discipline feel like a tap from a lady's slipper. Now Oliver's bruises and welts had him wanting to curl over and simply lie down on the bench, though there was no room for that, and doing it would bring on Chalenheim's rage once again, though Oliver had no idea why he was being singled out.

He was doing his best, keeping his temper in check, though that temper, so readily at hand upon his entrance into the workhouse, seemed to have dried up and had somehow been absorbed into the building. Into the very stones beneath his feet. If he reached for his temper to aid him, he feared he would not be able to hold on to it, let alone find it.

With his hand on Jack's thigh, barely felt beneath his cold fingers, Oliver finished up his allotment of gruel. Jack was not staring at him, but Oliver felt his attention, the slight shifting of Jack's shoulders as he leaned a bit closer, the gentle warmth of his hand on Oliver's thigh. That alone seemed to bring Oliver out of a state that felt akin to dreaming.

Working in the kitchen with Finley had been easy that coming to awareness with the rough grasp of Chalenheim's hand on his collar made him feel as though he'd been jerked into another world. Jack's touch confirmed that he was in a workhouse, but not as he'd been before, as a little boy, but older now, wary and sure that bad things would happen. Had happened. Would keep happening, as if he'd fallen into a bad dream, his past come to eat him alive.

But Jack. Ever there, sitting so still, so attentive. His hand petting Oliver's thigh, wanting his Nolly to look at him.

Oliver would do as Jack wanted, once he'd absorbed the warmth of Jack's hand, the steady stillness of his nearness. The shift of his legs on the bench. The way he leaned close. Letting Oliver know he was there, all without saying a word, bright and alive. As Oliver looked over at him finally, those green eyes looking at Oliver, he was telling Oliver that he was not alone.

He'd already told Jack there was nothing he could have done to stop Chalenheim. To have tried would have been the worst foolishness, for it would only get Jack in trouble as well. And Jack didn't deserve to be beaten, not for anything.

Though as Oliver pushed his bowl and spoon away, sticking an errant crumb to his finger and putting it in his mouth, briefly pretending he did not know it was the worst of manners, he looked at Jack. Truly looked at him. Waiting for the meal to be over, though it would bring nothing but a quick wash in harsh soap, and a night spent in a hard bed, in a room, Oliver was sure, with too many paupers with too few covers.

He remembered this from his days in Hardingstone and, for a moment, he felt ill with the remembrance of it. Of being parted from Dick and thrust into that gray-brown world of dampness and dreary tasks, with no spot of anything joyful anywhere.

At least here was Jack who, for all they had a moment under the bustle of being dismissed from the dining hall, table by table, had said nothing to Oliver. He looked pale in the workhouse light, as if the building had stripped all the color from him. His lower lip was bitten and chapped, his mouth curved downward.

Something tugged at Oliver. Down deep, in his belly, where the too-small serving of gruel was churning, as if threatening to come back up again.

"Jack." Oliver whispered this, ducking his chin. Jack looked at him, steadily, waiting for the rest of what Oliver had to say. "Don't worry about me," he said. "I've been through worse."

Which was true, in a way. His days at the haberdashery had ended so badly that nothing could ever supersede that. Or what had happened at the Three Cripples. Or—well, perhaps it was best to stop listing the events that had made his life horrible, for something had flickered across Jack's eyes, a coded message that Oliver felt too slow to decipher. He'd let himself be too distracted by his own worries, deep inside his own woe, to see it, to understand it.

But then Jack smiled, that slow, lazy smile he showed Oliver when he was truly relaxed, though there was no cozy fire for him to relax in front of, no circle of pipe smoke about his head, no pint of beer in his hand. They were not in a tavern, they were in a workhouse, so the smile seemed a little out of place. But it was so welcome to see that Oliver smiled back.

"Get in line, get in line," one of the assistants was saying, and whether it was Mr. Bassler or Mr. Louis didn't matter much; the shouting would continue until all the paupers were lined up, ready to be taken to the boy's dormitory to get ready for bed.

Oliver got up, and carried his bowl and spoon to where a little boy he did not know was staggering beneath the weight of the wicker basket that was full of bowls and spoons, all licked clean, as he had seen in the scullery. The crockery and spoons would not really need washing, but to keep someone busy, they would be washed three times a day.

He felt a little undone by the futility of it, but Jack was at his side, a little brighter now, as if having Oliver near him was all that he ever needed, and this made Oliver blink hard several times. He wanted to keep some burst of emotion inside of him, for if he let it out, then all of the workhouse would know how much Jack meant to him.

Jack must have seen this on his face, for he nodded, giving Oliver that half-blink, so full of love it could have melted the hardest of hearts. But the message in his eyes was meant for Oliver alone, so he tucked it inside his breast, and followed in line as the boys were led up the stairs and into the dormitory.

As they entered the door of the dormitory, two by two, Oliver was not surprised at the layout of the room, or the paucity of furnishings, the familiar, musty smell of a room where the windows were never opened, or that each boy went directly to change into his nightshirt, hanging up his day clothes on the pegs. He did not stare at the slender legs, the hollow bellies, the yellowed underdrawers that had not seen good soap and hot water since the day of their making. He only followed Jack to where their pegs were, and echoed his motions to Jack's as he undressed down to his underdrawers, and hung his clothes on the peg before pulling on his nightshirt.

He let Jack stare, if he would, for as his arms lifted into the sleeves, he could feel the soreness of his arms, from the work, the stiffness of his hips from the beatings, the bruises where they pressed to bone. He could not hide this from Jack, nor did he want to. But he would rather Jack not look so worried.

"It's not so bad, Jack," he said, standing close to Jack, as though helping him by tugging on the collar of his nightshirt. "It looks worse than it is."

"The fuck it ain't," said Jack. "I know blood stains when I see 'em, those marks'll leave scars, an' I won't stand by an'—"

As to what Jack wouldn't stand by for was lost as the low sounds of the room, of boys changing into their nightshirts and getting in line for the washbasin, sounds that were cut off by the arrival of Workmaster Chalenheim in the open doorway. His presence felt like a blow, and his shoulders filled the frame of the door, cutting off the light from behind him.

Oliver's heart sped up directly Chalenheim caught his eye,

and he held his breath, going over a list in his mind of what might he have done to anger Chalenheim this time, and what dire consequences might follow. He hoped there was nothing Chalenheim could accuse him of, for he could not withstand another whipping. He simply could not.

But as Chalenheim actually entered the room to speak to the attendant presiding over the ritual of getting ready for bed, Oliver felt Jack's whole body twitch, as if from a blow, though there had been none. And Jack, rather than looking about him in the steady, easy way that was his nature, was looking, instead, at the floor. Not as if in shame, but rather, as if he felt that this would hide him from anything untoward.

Oliver wanted to reach for Jack to find out what was the matter, but just as Chalenheim stepped toward the first boy in line at the basin, Jack looked up at Oliver, his eyes bright, and he waved Oliver off.

"There's nowt wrong w'me, Nolly, just hungry, is all. Just hungry."

This seemed to be true, for as the line shuffled forward, and as each boy splashed his face and hands with the water from the basin, and marched past Chalenheim for inspection, Jack nodded and gave Oliver a grin he was quite sure was meant to be saucy, but which could only be seen as sweet, for it was such a small grin, tenderly curling the corners of Jack's mouth.

By the time his turn at the basin came, Oliver knew he had to accept what Jack said. Especially in the face of Chalenheim staring at him, watching so closely as Oliver took his time at the basin, using the sliver of soap that had sat, dry and untouched, in its wooden dish.

In a sort of defiance, Oliver turned the soap in his hands to gather some foam to wash his face with it, and bent to rinse his face and hands with the water in the basin. Which meant that the water had to be refreshed from the large tin pitcher that the attendant held in his hands.

All the while, Chalenheim stood by, his face hard, those eyes glaring as he watched, though his gaze shifted to take in all the boys, in case anybody else got the idea that the soap was actually meant to be used.

As Oliver dried his face and hands on the damp, grime-streaked towel the attendant held, he let that little bit of defiance carry into his whole body as he looked at Chalenheim, as if daring him to do anything about it. Having Jack right behind him gave him the courage to be so bold, but Chalenheim merely looked at Oliver and nodded that he should go back to his bed.

Which Oliver was about to do, except Jack tugged on the sleeve of his nightshirt, bidding Oliver to stay by his side. This Oliver did, though he felt out of place, seeing as how as his turn was already done. Besides, he towered above the smaller boys who were standing by their beds or still standing in line, and he smelled like soap, as nobody else did. But Jack, oddly enough, used the soap as well, doing a less thorough job than Oliver, but doing it just the same, his own defiance, that Oliver knew could come to nothing good.

"Quit lollygagging," said Chalenheim, directly to Oliver, though he did not address him by name even though he knew it. And he did not force Oliver to go, even though Oliver waited with Jack until he was done, drying his hands on the dirty towel, until Jack turned to Oliver with a nod to indicate that he was done.

"Get to your bed, both of you," said Chalenheim with a snap, moving closer, his shoulders looming like a threat. "There are others who need to wash, and we've prayers to say, so quickly now, don't hold up the line."

There had been only a few boys behind Oliver and Jack, so the delay was minimal at best, but Oliver hurried to the bed that Jack led him to, and knelt down as Jack was doing, wincing as he bent his limbs and pressed his knees against the floorboards. He did his best not to show his shock that Jack immediately bowed his head and clasped his hands for prayer. But Oliver could not stare as though he'd never seen such a thing, though he had not:

Jack bowing his head like that, his eyes closed, lashes dark on his pale cheeks, as calm and as still as if he actually believed in the prayer that would be said over his bowed head.

"Jack," said Oliver, nudging Jack with his elbow, but gently. "What are you doing?"

But the whole roomful of boys was doing this very same thing, and while Jack did not lift his head nor open his, he smiled into his clasped hands.

"Doin' what you should be doin'," said Jack, "to keep Chalenheim from comin' over here, as he's bound to do when he catches you not doin' it."

This was said in such teasing tones that Oliver almost laughed at Jack, at his saucy ways, pretending to pray when it meant nothing to him. But it was also better to do what he was doing, for showing defiance with soap and water was one thing. Refusing to bow your head when told to do so was another.

So Oliver clasped his hands and bowed his head, closing his eyes to the brown floor, and the yellowed-white of his nightshirt. But he would not close out the warmth of Jack's nearness as Chalenheim's words rattled over his head. Would not shut out the scent of Jack's skin, laced with soap, and a touch of dust that Jack must have picked up through his labors in the afternoon. And longed for them to be elsewhere, far away from the workhouse, or anybody who might want them there.

They did not deserve this, Oliver knew, for while stealing books was a crime, surely borrowing them was not. Those books had never left the manor, nor had they come to any harm. Only Mrs. Heyland's cruelty had brought them here, and though he might have asked her forgiveness, had he been able, he was sure she would not have given it.

"Nolly," said Jack, touching his shoulder as he stood up to let Oliver know that prayers were over and that he should stand up also.

Oliver sighed and stood up, keeping close to Jack as Chalenheim gave the nod that the boys were to get into bed. He'd spent the previous night alone, shivering in the damp, dark confines of the refractory room. Now he would again sleep with Jack, and he could be glad about that, for when the candles were put out, and the room locked from without, they could be together for a little while. Besides the fact that the room had a gentler feel about it than the men's dormitory, as the younger boys did not seem the type to give them away.

Oliver saw Finley at the end of the room near the door, and just before Oliver climbed into bed, he nodded, and Finley nodded back. Then Oliver crawled into the bed, and settled himself down, feeling the coldness of the room, as if for the first time, in contrast to the warmth of Jack's body.

Jack pulled Oliver to him, almost in a hurry, settling Oliver against him so Oliver could use Jack as a pillow. As long as he had Jack beside him, Oliver knew that he could manage whatever the morning would bring.

12

DIVERSIONS IN THE DARK, OR DISTRACTING OLIVER FROM THE TRUTH

The lights were out, after the brief prayers had been said under Chalenheim's supervision, and Jack could feel the cold seeping up through the slatted mattress, as if pushed there by the wind and rain that beat at the window-panes. At the far end of the room, a small, scared pauper was crying, probably thinking the storm would cover the sounds, but Jack could hear the thin, scared sound as clearly as if the boy had been right next to him. He was grateful the boy was not, because the sound, any closer, would break him.

As for Nolly, he was safe in Jack's arms, half rolled on top of Jack so Jack could be his pillow and enfold Nolly close to him. It made him warm, where Nolly was, the length of his body close and still, and it helped to ease him. To quiet the bestirred worry that simply went round and round in his head and wouldn't stop.

He'd defied Chalenheim today, and in a place like this there would be a price to pay for it, as there always was. Even though nobody had seen it, and that he and Chalenheim would, no doubt, keep the exchange between them, the defiance, although quietly voiced, had been real. Jack did not think Chalenheim was the type of man to let something such as Jack's refusal pass without a challenge.

"So where were you today, Nolly?" asked Jack, stroking Nolly's arm, careful not to jar him too much. "I saw you through the windows."

"I was in the kitchen," said Nolly, in a short way that told Jack that Nolly might need a bit more distracting than a quiet talk in the dark might bring him.

"Eh? Peelin' potatoes?"

"No," said Nolly, and he seemed to press his forehead into the curve of Jack's breast, and his whole body shivered as he shifted forward, as if wanting more of Jack than he currently had. "Mostly I washed dishes and polished silver, and was put in charge of a little boy, Finley, who had been sent to help. It was the same little boy whose hand you were holding this morning. He broke a bowl, and the cook smacked him before I could do anything about it—never thought I'd be working in a workhouse kitchen—he could barely reach the knives on the tabletop and yet he had to."

Jack waited while the storm whistled and howled outside the window until the slight lull pulsed through the dark.

"Oh, Nolly," he said. "He's so very little."

"He is," said Nolly, and Jack could feel the sadness of so many memories pouring off the body in his arms. "He couldn't move fast enough for her, such a small, thin thing, with the biggest gray eyes—lost his whole family back in Ireland, it seems." Nolly shook his head and almost flinched from the thoughts in his head.

"Bloody Christ." Jack bent to kiss the top of Nolly's head in the dark, resting his chin against Nolly's temple.

"I did most of the work, such as I could, but she kept at him the whole while, and there was nothing I could do about it."

"You did your best," said Jack. He was not surprised at how upset Nolly was about this, but he was surprised that all the hardship Nolly had experienced had not turned him cruel.

"But I felt cruel, just the same," said Nolly, very low now, his words almost hidden by the sound of the rain. "For I was as kind as I could be, but will that be the last taste of kindness that the rest of his life will ever show him?"

"Can't say as I know the answer to that one, my sweet Nolly. But you was kind today an' that matters for somethin'."

"Perhaps," said Nolly, and then nothing more, as if working the memory over and over in his head, turning it this way and that, examining it for some flaw in his actions.

Jack sighed. Perhaps they should sleep, for the morning would bring more picking oakum and bowls of bland food, and not enough of it at that. Plus, it felt as damp and as chill as if it had been raining for days on end, and all Jack wanted to do was burrow his head beneath the pillow and never wake up again.

"Say, Nolly."

"Yes, Jack."

"At supper, when Chalenheim grabbed you—he's been at you, yet you never fought back, not even once. Why not?"

It might have been that Nolly understood the comparison Jack was making between how Nolly was outside of the workhouse and how he was inside of it. He drew a breath and let it out, and pressed his cheek against Jack's arm, rubbing it there.

"Because I know men like him, have known them, all of my life. And if I submit, then he'll go easier on us."

Jack wanted to laugh then, but he knew it would come out a harsh bark of a laugh, and that might alert Nolly to what Jack now knew about Chalenheim. So he kept silent, and thought about the world beyond the walls of the workhouse, and how it felt as if it were raining all over the world. Or maybe it was just raining on the workhouse.

At the far end of the room, there was the snick of a door being shut, and then a round, flickering light, like that of a candle being carried.

Jack's whole body stiffened in alert, for there was only one person who would have access to a candle and a match. His heart started racing, uncertain what he would do if Chalenheim would come to their bedside and demand that Jack get out of it. There would be no way that he could keep hidden from Nolly the rest of the story, and what had happened in the day room. What had happened in Port Jackson.

But even as his heart was pounding, the candle flickered as it was carried down the aisle between the rows of beds, continuing to about halfway to the door. The level of the candle fell in the darkness, the sound of crying stopped.

Jack could hear Chalenheim's low voice speaking, and a small voice responding. Then there were two sets of footsteps as the candle went past their bed to Chalenheim's room at the far end of the dormitory. And the sound again of a door being opened and shut.

For a moment, Jack couldn't breathe. Nor could he mistake what Chalenheim had just done, or was about to do, for the sound of the crying child had vanished. In its wake came the rolling, dark sound of the storm on the roof, with rain slatting the windows, and wind rattling the panes, covering any sound of anything else happening. Leaving Jack with his mouth dry, and Nolly stirring in his arms as he propped himself up on his elbow.

He might have been staring at Jack through the darkness, though the position he was in could not have felt very pleasant, not with the welts and bruises that Nolly was currently sporting.

"Jack?" Nolly bent down to give Jack a small kiss. "What is it? What's wrong? Your skin went quite cold."

These words were spoken against Jack's mouth, a soft, little whisper of kindness and care, and Jack reached up and cupped Nolly's face in his hands. He returned the kiss with a little more force, trying to hold back the shout he wanted to make. The rampage he wanted to go on. But in this place, that was the worst sort of way to handle it.

"Let me make you feel better," said Jack.

Giving Nolly even the smallest bit of pleasure would help to distract him from the dark thoughts pounding in his head. Plus, he needed to make sure Nolly received not even the slightest hint as to the kind of man Chalenheim was, nor what he was doing to the wee mite he'd collected in the dark. But he felt Nolly draw back in the darkness.

"You don't have to, Jack," said Nolly. "Not in this place."

"Best reason," said Jack, his lips feeling stiff in spite of Nolly's kiss. "Best reason in the world. Fight off the cruelty with kindness. Best reason."

Nolly could not know all of what he meant, but perhaps some of it had gotten through, for Nolly bent close, leaning once again on Jack's chest, kissing him on the cheek, the corner of his mouth, but slowly, softly.

"No," said Jack. He tipped sideways to roll Nolly off him, pulling up the blanket to cover their shoulders, cradling Nolly's neck in one arm. Reaching down to pull up the hem of his nightshirt with the other.

"I don't think—" said Nolly, quickly.

Jack felt Nolly's hand come up to block his arm.

"Fuck the rules," said Jack.

"No, it's not that, but I don't think I can—manage. Is that the right word?"

"Get hard, you mean?" asked Jack, not caring, for the moment, that his words were coarse, for his hand was gentle as it slid up between Nolly's thighs. "Don't matter if you spend or not, long as I get to touch you, make you feel good."

There was a long pause. Nolly held himself quite still, and Jack could almost hear his heart pounding. Feel the rise of his chest as he drew in a breath. They were lying length to length; every move, every stillness of Nolly's body was known to Jack. If Nolly said *no*, or shook his head, then Jack would kiss him goodnight, draw back, and pull Nolly into his arms to be a pillow for his sleep.

But then Nolly nodded his head, little jerks of his chin that told Jack that Nolly had said *yes*. Yes to Jack, and this moment in the night, in this horrible place.

He trailed his fingers between Nolly's legs where the flesh became warm, Nolly's private hair tickling his wrist as Jack rolled

Nolly's bollocks around in his hand, bending to catch the sweet scent of him. Moving his hand up to the base of Nolly's cock, which was indeed distracted and not very hard.

It was better to concentrate on this, to kiss Nolly gently, and push him back on the bed, being silent as a cat, and stroke Nolly very softly. Not expecting anything, not wanting anything more than to feel Nolly relax beneath him, pliant. Covering Nolly with his own body, as if he could protect him from the cold and the dark. Distract him from his own fears. Sweep him away for a single moment, even.

He brought his hand up from the tangle of the blanket and Nolly's nightshirt, and slicked his palm with his tongue. He brought it directly down on Nolly's cock, cupping the whole length of it with his hand, feeling it, soft in his palm, warm against his skin. And then heard Nolly sigh, unconscious and unaware, tipping his head back, even if only a little, while his cock hardened in Jack's hand.

"Easy, easy," said Jack, kissing Nolly again, swallowing Nolly's breath. "Come quickly for me now, just a little bit. I'll hold you till you're done."

He stroked Nolly's cock, using his wrist to make it easy rather than rough, flipping his thumb around the head of it, feeling the heat spring forth, the bit of slick, and drew his hand back to taste it on his thumb. He closed his eyes over the taste as he absorbed it, very still for a moment, before bringing his hand back down to resume his caress.

Nolly, bestirred by the pause, moved into Jack's hand, clasping Jack on the arm, his fingers pinpoints of sharpness as he dug in. Jack stroked a little harder, covering Nolly's mouth with silent kisses to mask any sound. And pushed down just a bit with his chest, and moved his hand faster, feeling the slip of Nolly's desire along his cock, the strong feel of Nolly's heart pulsing beneath Jack's hand as he came.

Nolly sighed into Jack's mouth then, and Jack kissed him good and proper, like he had wanted to for days, licking into

Nolly's mouth to capture the taste of that sigh. He gentled Nolly's head to the pillow with his hand. Wiped his other hand on Nolly's thigh, then set everything to rights. Nolly's nightshirt, his own nightshirt. The blanket. Cool air wafted down on their skins, the scent of Nolly's pleasure filling his lungs and, for a moment, everything else was blocked out.

"Thank you, Jack," said Nolly, and his voice hovered on the edge of sleepiness, bound with exhaustion and hunger.

Nolly would be asleep in under a minute, Jack knew. That was for the best, because he would be asleep when Chalenheim brought back to bed whatever little boy he'd taken out of it.

"'Twas a gift," said Jack. "Sleep now, my sweetheart. I'll be here when you wake."

He rolled back, feeling along the length of his arm the muscles in Nolly's neck relax warm and easy. In a little moment, there was that low, even sound of Nolly's breathing as he fell asleep.

Jack scrubbed at his eyes with his hand, the scent of Nolly all around him in the night, and he blew out a breath, trying to ease his chest. He was not worried for nothing, but there was nothing he could do. He would waste all of his energy if he let his mind rabbit on like this. He needed to sleep so he could think clearly in the morning so he could keep both him and Nolly safe.

He curled on his side and burrowed his face against Nolly's shoulder. Pulled the blanket up over them both and closed his eyes. He had Nolly with him now, and tomorrow would come soon enough. There was no stopping it.

❧ 13 ❧

SAYING YES BUT NOT
SAYING WHY

W hen the light sifted through the streaked windows, it was low and gold-gray, as if a tired sun was trying to push through the rain-clouds. It only made Oliver more tired to watch it as he lay on the hard mattress with Jack sprawled over him, both of them beneath the rough blanket that did not provide enough warmth.

Blinking through the dryness of his eyes, Oliver tried to make himself stir, for surely one of the attendants was soon to come through that door and demand that they all be up and out of bed.

This he remembered from the workhouse in Hardingstone, and he couldn't imagine that the rituals had changed all that much. They certainly had been familiar the night before, with paupers lining up for a wash at the basin, with soap standing by that they weren't expected to use.

Oliver wished there was a hot bath somewhere that he could take to wash away the grit and tiredness. There probably was one in the master's rooms, though Oliver had yet to see a doorway that seemed as though it led there. The only doors were to the yard, or the kitchen, or the dining hall, and though he'd only been going through them for a few days, it felt as if he'd been going through them forever.

His back, and the backs of his legs, felt stiff, as if they'd been pounded on for hours, but the memory of Jack's hands upon him the night before felt good. He knew it was the hard mattress and the wood-slatted bed that had done the real damage. A softer mattress would have eased him into sleep better, as would have a warmer room, a fuller belly. Something sweet to take his mind off the pain, or, perhaps, a stiff concoction of gin and sugar would have done the trick. None of these were to be had, nor would they be, in this stone-clad place.

But at least he had Jack with him, though that was a comfort torn between being gladdened by the thought and being horrified by it. For a workhouse was full of rules designed to break a pauper down to his very bones, and Jack, who had withstood much, did not deserve to have his liveliness taken away. Even the dull brown of the jacket and trousers, and the laundry-yellowed striped shirt with no collar, seemed to suck away all of Jack's brightness.

Oliver suddenly dearly missed the gaudy plumage in which Jack had been garbed when Oliver had met him in the park on that winter day so long ago. Jack had worn a blue checked waistcoat, a dandy top hat. The glitter in Jack's eyes against the color in his face and neck and hands had just started to fade from a tropics-given tan to the pale of London winter. That it was turning into spring, and they were stuck here, meant that Oliver would not see those rare and much-beloved feathers turning even brighter with the season.

But these fancy thoughts would soon be undone once the day was underway, and the monotony of the food, and the sting of the oakum beneath his fingernails, the threat of Chalenheim's attention—all of this would take any gentle thoughts and musings and rip them clean away.

With a soft sigh, Oliver petted Jack along his back, his upper arm, which was now slung across Oliver's middle. Jack, who had started as Oliver's pillow, had seemed to need his own, and so they had switched sometime in the night.

It hurt to lie on his back like this, but not for anything would he stir Jack from his position, where he was comfortably asleep, as he had not spent hours being awake already, his throat desperate for water, eyelids feeling as though chalk dust had been dusted beneath them, as Oliver had.

The bell from the yard sounded, startling Oliver from the doze he'd fallen into. All along the low-lighted room, heads lifted from thin pillows, the gray blankets fell back.

Chalenheim came from his room at the end of the dormitory, fully dressed and awake, walking into a little side room where Oliver could hear him enjoining the orphans to get up, get up. As if there were anything to get up for but bad food, hard work, and unpredictable discipline. But that meant he and Jack had to get up as well, or their day would start off badly and probably get worse from there. So he pulled Jack to him and gently patted his arm.

"Jack," said Oliver. "Time to get up."

Jack, who usually woke as slowly as he was able to, stirred almost directly the words left Oliver's mouth. He rolled away to push the blanket back, and stared with wide eyes at the room that was full of narrow, hard beds, and thin, under-fed boys pulling their nightshirts off to don their pauper garb.

Something caught Jack's eye, for he stilled, and Oliver followed his gaze. Only to find that one little boy was struggling to pull on his trousers, and that his bedmate was helping him. It was Finley, his large gray eyes full of tears, his mouth screwed up to try and stop them. He barely letting the boy standing next to him help him. He was shaking, demonstrating all clumsiness, unlike the shy, careful movements from the day before in the kitchen.

"That's Finley," said Oliver.

"Who?" asked Jack, as he sat up and scratched at his head, for a moment as casual as if he was, indeed, at his leisure.

"Finley," said Oliver, more carefully now. "Finley, who held your hand in the oakum-picking room yesterday, and who I worked with in the kitchen."

"Oh, yes. Finley."

But Jack's attention was on his own hands, as if he couldn't care less about a little boy whom he barely knew. Jack was ever solicitous of the needs of those he considered to be within the lines of family that he had drawn, Oliver among him. Finley, it seemed, was outside of those lines.

"What's the matter with your hands, Jack?"

For Jack was staring at them as if they were the only thing of interest, and this rather than getting dressed as he ought to do to avoid Chalenheim's temper. Luckily, Chalenheim was busy helping Finley out of his nightshirt and into his clothes.

"Sore," said Jack, keeping his eyes down, still sitting on the bed, the edges of his nightshirt fluttering over his knees.

"Will you get up?" asked Oliver. "I'll help you, if you can't manage."

When Jack looked up at Oliver, his eyes were dark, as if there was something he wanted to say, but would not. Whether this was because the thought was too difficult for him to share, or that he thought Oliver would be upset by it, Oliver couldn't tell, for the look was gone as soon as it appeared.

Jack slid off the bed to stand on his two feet in front of Oliver. Brightly, as if, for a moment, their stay at the workhouse was a jolly lark and something to joke about.

"I can manage well enough, my fussy lad, just give me some room."

Obliging him, Oliver stepped back. He tried to see over Jack's shoulder as to whether Finley had been able to get dressed without any more difficulty, but Jack actually stumbled against him. Oliver helped him to rights, and together they dressed.

By the time they had gotten dressed and made their beds and were in line together, Finley was with his bedmate at the head of the line, and Chalenheim gave the nod that allowed them to proceed. This they did like a brown-clad snake turning along the dark, unlit passage. Oliver's head felt dizzy, as if he were merely repeating the actions from the day before, only in reverse, every day the same, so much the same, that they could be flipped over and started again from the very same moment.

When they at last were at the bottom of the stairs and had entered the boy's dining hall, this feeling was diminished by the light coming through the windows, streaking through cloud-tossed blue-gray skies, as if the clouds were rolling over and over themselves in an attempt to cover the sun, but were failing. This lifted his spirits somewhat as he took up his bowl and his spoon from the table by the door and stood in line with Jack. Jack, who was holding his bowl and spoon as easily as he might a feather, as if there were no pain in his hands at all.

As they shuffled forward in line, Oliver meant to ask Jack about his hands, but Jack spoke first.

"Did you sleep well, Nolly?"

The question was meant to tease him a little bit, and Oliver felt the heat on his cheeks, feeling shy. It was like Jack to give so easily to him, as if the giving were its own pleasure, but Oliver knew it wasn't fair if it was always like this. He'd thought it in the manor house at Lyme, and he thought it now.

He couldn't tell Jack that while yes, he'd slept for a few hours, he'd awoken early before dawn and stared at the ceiling with dry eyes. Jack would consider himself at pains to make it better, but since Oliver himself did not feel at ease within the walls of the workhouse to return the favor, he couldn't allow it.

"Yes," Oliver said, hiding the lie behind a smile. "You are good to me, Jack."

"Nothin' but the best for you, Nolly, dear," said Jack in return.

It was as if, for a moment, they were alone together, their concerns and anxieties tossed to the wind like it didn't matter.

"Quiet, you two. No talking in the dining hall."

The order came from somewhere and bounced off the hard

walls. Oliver obediently ducked his head, and concentrated on the bowl in his hands, and noticed that Jack, at his side, had a grip on his bowl, as if he meant to break it.

"Easy, now," said Oliver, as if Jack were a skittish creature that needed calming.

Jack looked at him, and the second before he looked away, Oliver got a glimpse of the expression he'd seen before. There was darkness in Jack's eyes, as if Jack were standing on the edge of something and needed to tell Oliver about it before he fell. But then the expression was gone, as if it had been nothing, and in a moment, they were up at the front of the line, leaving Oliver without any opportunity to ask Jack what was the matter.

With predictable stinginess, Mr. Bassler, standing to one side of the cauldron, ladled into Oliver's bowl the barest measure of gruel. On the other side, Mr. Louis handed Oliver a chunk of dry bread, and motioned with his head that Oliver should get a move on before the bread was taken away. When Jack got his serving of gruel and bread, they walked as quickly as they could to the table at the far end, nearest the stairs, where the younger boys had left them their places on the bench.

Oliver sat and bowed his head for prayers, checking out of the corner of his eyes that Jack was doing the same. It was still a bit of a shock to see it, Jack so pious and so still, though it couldn't possibly be in earnest, even if he was beautiful with his chin tucked down, his eyes serenely closed. At peace, in a way, and deliciously sweet.

As Workmaster Chalenheim moved to the center of the room to lead the prayer, Oliver knew he had to know.

"Are you actually *praying*?" he asked.

Jack smiled against his clasped hands, the first real smile that Oliver had seen in what felt like a long time.

"Don't be daft," Jack said. "'Tis easier to fit in if you're doin' what everybody else is doin', is all."

This was the sensible thing to do. Of course it was, and was the same truth as Jack had spoken the night before. Though now it left Oliver with a dull taste in the back of his throat because whereas before the idea of church and of praying had seemed a calm, gentle thing, a comfort within his breast, now, in this place, it was a sham. Jack knew how to work the sham, how to hide within it, and, by example, was encouraging Oliver to do the same.

So Oliver did it, praying without praying, though he realized it had been some time since he'd done it in earnest, prayed, attended church. It seemed a long time, as well, since he'd seen a beggar in the street and turned his eyes away so he wouldn't have to look at it. Though it was the worst irony that he was now the pauper and was invisible behind the high stone walls of the workhouse. Nothing he'd not deceived himself about before, long ere this.

While Chalenheim rattled on at the front of the dining hall, Oliver let the words circle in the air over his head without giving them a chance to settle within it. Chalenheim's cruelty to Oliver, to all the boys, and this place as well, made the prayer false, so there was no place for it within his heart. Nor in Jack's, though Jack had figured this out right away, wiser in this than Oliver could ever be, though a part of Oliver hurt at the thought of it, that there was no hope, no gentleness, no soft blankets, no sugar, nothing sweet—

"Nolly, eat now."

This came from Jack, low under his breath as he motioned with his own bowl and spoon, and scooped some of the gruel into his mouth to show Oliver how it was done. Would that he, Oliver, could be more like Jack, seeing the truth of things and knowing what to do directly he encountered a new situation that called for fast thinking.

Oliver did as Jack had bid him, eating the gruel, crumbling the bread into it when he was halfway finished with it to soften the bread and give the gruel more heft. From the middle of the table, he grabbed a tumbler of water and drank it all, though it would not be enough. He'd be thirsty again way before dinner.

Pulling another tumbler, he passed it to Jack, nodding his head to encourage Jack, that Jack should take the water and drink it.

Jack drank the water and set the tumbler down with a little slam, as if he were pretending he was in a tavern, and had just finished a pint pot of beer.

"Thanks, Nolly," said Jack, licking his lips. Slowly.

Oliver opened his mouth to chide Jack for flirting so openly when there were so many people about, but he stopped himself. Yes, it was dangerous to be so bold, but in a way, what did it matter? Their relationship was the last thing that anybody would be looking for. The younger boys would have no idea, and the attendants would be so puffed up with their own importance and looking only for disobedience, that the flirting would be outside of anything they might punish for. So instead, Oliver did what Jack sometimes did, that way he did when communicating affection without speaking a word: he half-closed his eyes, and gave Jack a smile.

This startled Jack a bit, for the spoon stopped halfway to his mouth and his eyebrows flew up.

"Saucy thing," said Jack, looking away, pretending to concentrate on his gruel, but Oliver could tell he was pleased.

When breakfast was over, and all the bowls had been thoroughly scraped clean, the ritual for putting bowls and spoons in the wicker baskets started all over again. This was followed by lining up, and the repetition was starting to weigh heavily on Oliver's shoulders.

They did not deserve to be here, and the comparison between stolen books and borrowed ones pushed upward in his mind again. The injustice of it felt hot within his breast, and he turned to Jack, his mouth open to say something about it, when Workmaster Chalenheim appeared at his side.

"In line, Oliver Twist, in line."

Oliver didn't look up; it would be a sign of respect, so he didn't do it. But as they waited their turn to go along the passage to the oakum-picking room, he noticed Jack go quite stiff, moving closer to Oliver, almost brushing their shoulders together. Then Chalenheim moved to the head of the line, to lead the way and keep watch to make sure no one lagged behind.

Oliver looked over at Jack in time to see his shoulders sag, the bite along his lower lip, and watched him quickly look away. When he turned back, his features were transformed into their normal lines, calm, assured, with a little smile for Oliver.

"All these lines we're standin' in," said Jack, complaining, but with good humor. "Too bad there ain't nothin' good at the end of 'em, eh?"

Before Oliver could puzzle out the rapid changes in Jack, they were entering the oakum-picking room, and Oliver's whole body stiffened. In this enclosed space, sitting on the backless benches with only a single task assigned to them, there was no room for error. For a moment, as he sat down, wincing as the back of his legs touched the bench, he felt as though he could not catch his breath.

Chalenheim's gaze, as he stood in the front of the room with the switch at the ready behind his back, was already upon Oliver, a predatory slice through the air aimed directly at him. Then he looked at Jack, though Jack was concentrating on his hands, on bending over to pick up a bit of tarred rope to start with, and did not see.

Oliver began to work in earnest, to keep both him and Jack from Workmaster Chalenheim's attention. To fill his basket with picked oakum, even denying the soreness of his fingers, the strain on his wrists. That his palms felt shredded. That his heart sped up every time Chalenheim looked at him, or when he marched down along the benches to stand at the end of their bench, to glower as if he judged their every movement. No doubt he did, and no doubt they were falling below some line of equity that would demonstrate that they'd not earned their breakfast, and would soon not earn their dinners.

Oliver's hands fumbled when Chalenheim was watching, but he caught the bundle of rope and somehow continued on with it.

Chalenheim would find no excuse to beat him today. That was his earnest hope. Whether or not it would be proven true was another matter. All he could do was to keep working, to focus on his hands and keep them steady. To drop the oakum in the basket and pick up another hunk of twisted, gnarled rope to slice it on the pike in front of him.

There was sweat on the back of his neck within a moment, and he could only draw breath when Chalenheim moved off to stand at the end of another row with that judgmental glower, his switch at the ready for the next unruly boy, the next boy who was too slow, who was not producing enough, who was not working hard enough.

It was a terror he could taste in his mouth, like bitter dirt, for even if it wasn't he that was beaten, and surely there would be some boy who was soon to be pulled out of the ranks, neither could he stand to watch it done. Though he was not foolish enough to believe any protestation of his would stop it. He just had to hope each boy would do his best, and surely they could all avoid any trouble.

Next to him, Jack was working as well, though not as fast as Oliver, as if he couldn't be bothered but to do the barest minimum, though Oliver didn't have the heart to say anything about it. Or perhaps he should, to help keep Jack safe, even if Jack resented him the moment he said it?

"Jack," Oliver said in a whisper. "You need to move faster; he'll single you out else."

But Jack only laughed, low under his breath; his hands, his fingers, while slow, never stopped moving. "Too late to be worried about that, I should think," he said now, though he didn't look at Oliver, and didn't stop to explain what he meant.

Which meant that the only thing Oliver could do was to keep working and pray that Jack's slowness, or Chalenheim's fickle temper with regards to Oliver, wouldn't earn either of them a whipping.

~

IT WAS EASIER TO PUSH THE WORLD AWAY WHEN YOUR HANDS were busy. Jack figured that out, long about the time they were halfway from breakfast and halfway to dinner, when the meager substance of the gruel had soaked into his bones, leaving only a ghost of itself behind. His stomach was making the type of noises folks in polite society would be embarrassed to hear. Jack didn't care about that, only he could hear the same noises, graphic and unsettled, coming from Nolly. Who, given his desire to eat hearty, warm meals on a regular basis, probably felt as though he were being torn apart from the inside.

What Jack didn't understand was if Nolly had worked in the kitchen, why hadn't he stolen himself some food? There was no need to bring Jack any, but for himself, Nolly should have taken something. Jack hoped it wasn't from a false sense of goodness that Nolly had refrained from stealing, for in this place it might be the only way to get a full belly.

Looking at the paupers on the benches in front of them, Jack could see the backs of their heads, all bowed over their oakum-picking duties, each head shorn close of hair, thin, pale necks hard at work.

The little boy that had held Jack's hand, and that had worked in the kitchen with Nolly, had been the same wee lad Chalenheim had taken to his room to be buggered. Which now explained why Finley had been crying that morning, crying Jack had studiously ignored, though this only unsettled his stomach to the point where even if someone had offered him something to eat, he could not have borne eating it. Nor could he even consider sharing the information with Nolly, as there was nothing either of them could do about it, anyway.

Jack sucked on his fingers, tasting the tar, trying to ease the red lines along the pads at the end of his fingers, the black lines beneath each fingernail. The line on his right forefinger had torn and was bleeding sluggishly. He'd have to soak his hands in tea and honey for a week to get them back to their gentle, sensitive status, to where he could ease his hands into a man's pocket, or flick his wrist and deal a decent hand of cards. Hands were important in his line of business if he wanted to get ahead. Or to even survive.

Beside him on the bench, Nolly was working away as though it mattered, which Jack knew it did not. Jack's basket was half full, as was Nolly's. Going any faster would not earn them more gruel at dinner, but Nolly was working away as if the merest extra ounce of oakum at weigh-in time might earn him that extra bread. A double helping of white glob.

Nolly's cheek was flushed, as if he felt Jack looking at him, and was remembering how Jack had touched him the night before. There was no telling, since Nolly, closed-mouthed about what he would call *intimate relations* at the best of times, was now a veritable mute about anything. But the color on his cheek, like a new spring rose, gave him away, and he shifted, as though he felt Jack looking at him.

"Oliver Twist."

Nolly looked up to the front of the room where Chalenheim stood, watching over the paupers in his care.

"Oliver *Twist*, you will stand up at once."

Startled, Nolly fumbled with his hands to still them, almost grazing his palm over the point of the iron pike.

"Yes, sir?" asked Nolly, standing up, and Jack was close enough to see that Nolly's hands were shaking, that he was unsteady on his feet.

"What have I said about falling behind? If you insist on lolly-gagging, then you will not make your quota for the day, and I will be forced to keep your dinner from you. Is that what you want?"

For a moment, Jack could only blink, because Nolly's basket was as full as anybody's, perhaps even more-so, for Nolly had done this before. He knew what he was about, he knew how to work fast, and would make his quota, of that Jack was certain, and besides, for once they'd not been talking.

In spite of this, Chalenheim charged to the back row, where the taller boys sat on their bench, reaching for Nolly's collar. He yanked Nolly from his seat to the aisle way and gave him a hard shake. Lifting him off the floor for a moment so that Nolly became unbalanced and landed hard, falling against Chalenheim.

The workmaster had the switch in his other hand, and he was going to march Nolly to the front of the room and give him another thrashing, because that's what he did. He had it in for Nolly, on account of his beautiful face, or the spirit in his eyes, or for whatever reason, it didn't matter.

But as Chalenheim gave Nolly's collar a hard jerk, he looked at Jack, and squinted, then smiled. Jack felt it like a slap. This had nothing to do with how hard Nolly'd been working or how full his basket was, or the fact that Chalenheim simply liked to hand out thrashings, whether or not the boy had been unruly. It had nothing to do with any of that.

Chalenheim smiled again at Jack, walking fast, turning his head away, and Jack felt the understanding ripple through him, like a beast set free.

He found himself standing as he tossed the hunk of tarred rope in his basket, his mouth open, taking one deep breath quickly before he had any time to think.

"I'll do it."

Almost all the way to the front of the room, Chalenheim paused, the chancy light from the window limning his broad shoulders. And while normally an outburst such as that would have Jack hauled to the front of the room, Chalenheim merely turned to face Jack.

"What was that, Jack Dawkins?"

Chalenheim's hand was light on Nolly's collar; he was almost not holding on at all. Nolly could have sprinted back to his seat if he'd wanted to, but being Nolly, he stayed where he was, as if obedience would grant him any saving from what Chalenheim was prepared to dish out. It would not. There was only one thing that could.

"I said I'll do it." Jack swallowed hard, doing his best to avoid catching Nolly's gaze, because there would be no way to explain what he'd just said. What he'd just agreed to. As to what Nolly might have said if he *did* find out what this was all about, well, Jack took some comfort in the notion that Nolly would be furious with him. But that would never happen, because Nolly would never find out. Not if Jack had his way. "I'll do it."

The room was so quiet Jack could hear his own heart thudding, and he imagined that some of the paupers, at least, understood what had just happened. And why Jack was agreeing to this unnamed thing.

"Very well," said Chalenheim. He flicked the switch near Nolly's face as he let him go. "You need to get back to work before I'm forced to use this, you understand?"

"Yes, sir," said Nolly, though the color had gone from his face, and he obviously did not understand.

As he came back to the bench, Jack sat down and, grabbing the hunk of rope, began to work again. He used his hands and focused on his task so he wouldn't have to look at Nolly and think of a million reasons why he couldn't explain.

Well, one reason was that there was no talking allowed, so even Nolly's concerned gaze as he sat down was not enough to distract Jack from what he was doing. Even if he felt sweaty and cold, and wanted nothing more than to be saved from this, he could not tell Nolly anything.

"Jack," said Nolly, even though it was obvious that Chalenheim was watching them from the front of the room, and the merest hint of rebellion would get either or both of them in trouble. "What did you just agree to?"

Continuing to work, Jack kept his focus on his hands, and brought his thumb up to his mouth to nip off the ragged edge of his thumbnail between his teeth. Then he spit the thumbnail on the floor and shook his head.

"'Twarnt nothing," he said, working his jaw, as if he were

highly annoyed at Nolly's useless questions. "Just obedience. I'll behave myself if he won't thrash you, is all."

He allowed himself to look at Nolly then, at the furrowed brow, and the thrust of his jaw, the slight pout that might signal Nolly's confusion, his desire to get to the bottom of whatever Jack was up to. But in this place, even Nolly had to back down; after all, Jack had just saved him from a thrashing, so that had to be worth some reticence on his part to kick up any more fuss.

"Don't matter, Nolly," said Jack. He had to look away just then, or he'd start talking, so he looked at his hands, at the pile of oakum, at the iron spike. And took a deep breath that tasted like black tar, and the salt of sea-worn rope. "Just keep workin', that's all we can do."

OLIVER COULD BARELY CONCENTRATE ON WHAT HIS HANDS were supposed to be doing, let alone on what had just happened. He'd been so ready for the whipping from Chalenheim, which would have added layers to the welts already there on his skin, that he'd not been paying attention. A little light-headed, he picked the strands of rope from the hank in his hand, the sharp ends slicing into the pads of his fingers, and tried to make himself understand what Jack had said. Why Jack would have to be obedient to save Oliver from Chalenheim's wrath.

He looked up to where Chalenheim paced at the front of the room, back and forth, the switch in his hand like a saber as he slashed it through the air. Ready at a moment's notice to select a boy from his spot on the bench and march him up to the front of the room. Where beyond those rain-drizzled windows existed only the boys' yard, bound by walls so high that no one could scale them.

Oliver remembered thinking how the misery and sadness had poured over the tops of the walls of the Poland Street work-house. Now, in reverse, nothing from the outside was getting in, as if the miasma of poverty made a cap for itself and kept the hopelessness at the paupers' level.

Giving his head a small shake, for to do more was to make himself dizzy, Oliver stopped the unproductive chain of thought. He also tried to ignore the raw growling of his stomach and tried to think it through.

Oliver had been the one Chalenheim had singled out time and again, not Jack. Jack had not been disobedient, so there was no reason for him to trade obedience for Oliver's safe passage. That Jack would have done anything he could have to save Oliver from the switch was a given, but what he'd said did not make sense. Not at all.

Swallowing against the pain in his belly, the noise in his head that vibrated like untuned piano wire, Oliver lowered his chin, looking at his hands, as if concentrating on picking out a very difficult strand of oakum.

"Jack."

"Yes, Nolly."

Somewhat taken aback at the stoic levelness of Jack's voice, Oliver pushed forward, even though it seemed Jack was loath to have any kind of conversation about anything, just then.

"You've *been* obedient this whole time," said Oliver, low, and as carefully as he could. "Why would you need to agree to any more?"

Jack only shrugged and continued working, his eyes on his hands, at the basket between his feet, at the pike as he shoved a bit of rope down upon it to get between thick strands of tar. He was doing everything but answering Oliver, and this was quite unlike him, unlike the easy, casual manner Jack had about him at all times, whether he was in a tavern or in the basement of a great manor house. But here, in the workhouse, Jack was as stern and as careful as Oliver had ever seen him. As Oliver had *never* seen him.

"Jack," said Oliver again, leaning in close. "Why would you

have to agree to anything? And why would you imagine someone like Chalenheim would keep his promises?"

"Because he will. Now, just leave it, will you?"

If Jack meant his words to stop Oliver from worrying, they only made it worse, for Jack's throat was moving, as if over difficult breath, and the words themselves came out almost as faint as a whisper, with no conviction in them whatsoever.

"Please tell me, Jack, whatever is the matter? What can I do, how can I help, please tell me."

Oliver allowed himself a quick glance at Jack, where he could see that Jack was still concentrating on his work, the work he thought worthless, as if it were important to him, which was the oddest thing of all.

Oliver could see through Jack's words, but he could not make his way through what Jack's hands were doing. Jack's beautiful, graceful hands that he was now using as though they belonged to the most common laborer rather than the best of the best of pickpockets in the whole of London. His sensitive skin was being ruined as the oakum strands poked and shredded, and Oliver wondered where he could get tea and honey for Jack to soak his hands in. And what he would give for there to be a moment when he could tend to Jack's hands.

He heard Jack inhale, long and slow, those hands pausing for just a fraction of a moment, and then heard Jack sigh. When he looked over, Jack still wasn't looking at him. The flick of his eyes took in the room rather than Oliver, but he was going to answer.

"Off m'head with hunger, is all, Nolly," said Jack. "Can't hardly think straight to know what I said. Just wanted to help you, if I could."

"Jack."

"Guess it worked, eh?"

Now Jack looked at him, pale beneath his freckles, his eyebrows raised, as if to punctuate the earnestness of his declaration. Jack's expression was a pale echo of its own self, but Jack's eyes were pleading, so Oliver would have to believe what Jack was saying and force his own puzzlement to tuck itself away for the moment. If he pushed any further, used any more force to find out what he wanted to know, Jack seemed fragile enough to break, and Oliver would rather march up to the front and hand himself over to Chalenheim than be the cause of that.

"Thank you, Jack," said Oliver, meaning it with his whole heart.

If he was less hungry himself, less *starving*, if the truth be told, then he might have been better able to figure out what Jack really meant. But to insist upon the fact that Jack was not telling him the whole truth was to force Jack to lie even further, and would bring Chalenheim's wrath upon their heads. So he tended to the work in his hands, concentrating on that instead of anything else, and listened to the growls that shook his belly.

He worked steadily until the bells rang announcing the noon hour. Chalenheim put his switch away, though when Oliver relaxed his shoulders, his stomach curled around itself until he had to clutch at his middle with his hand, wanting to ease the hunger that now seemed a permanent part of him.

He stood up when his turn came, walking behind Jack to get in their two-by-two line, and did not answer when Jack lifted an eyebrow to question him, because what could he say? That his whole body felt as though it were eating itself from within, that the anticipation of a single serving of gruel was not enough to keep his hunger at bay? That his ears were ringing, a low, dull sound that almost outdid the sound of the bell, of footsteps on stone floors? All of this was known to Jack, surely.

"Hey," said Jack, sounding more normal as they walked along the passage to the boys' dining hall. "I'll share my bread w' you, if we get any."

Oliver could barely feel Jack patting his arm as they walked, and could barely shake his head.

"No," he said, and he meant it. "You eat your share an' I'll eat mine, an' together it'll make a whole serving."

Which was nonsense, he was spouting utter nonsense, and

from somewhere he could smell meat grilling, a whiff of butter and cream, probably in gravy or slathered on thick slices of newly baked bread. There was food in this workhouse, only it wasn't meant for him, or for anyone like him. His mouth watered just the same, and he swallowed and then swallowed again.

"When we get out of here—" Jack started to say, but Oliver cut him off.

"How on earth are we going to do that, Jack?"

But Jack was unable to answer him as they entered the dining hall, and the pattern from that morning repeated itself all over again. It was a kind of madness to imagine it could be otherwise, that they'd serve something other than gruel and bread and water, but of course they did not.

In line with his bowl and spoon, Oliver stood next to Jack, and studied his feet. If he concentrated on them instead of the food they weren't going to be served, on his scuffed boots instead of looking out the window, as if that would provide him his salvation, then he would make it through this.

Wanting something he could not have, that the world had decided he did not deserve, would send him into madness. The workhouse's only recourse would be to send him to a lunatic asylum, where surely Jack would not be willing nor able to follow.

Oliver held up his bowl for the ladleful of gruel, almost grateful beyond words that there was a serving of bread being handed to him. The bread would make the gruel seem as though it were more than it was, which would dull the roar in his head and soothe his stomach with a sense of satiety, however temporary.

"Nolly."

Blinking, Oliver tried to focus.

Jack stood in front of him, bowl and bread in hand, jerking his head that Oliver should follow him. Which Oliver did, feeling like a stray hound who does not quite know which fox to go after. He kept his eyes on the back of Jack's head, and sat when Jack sat, the bowl landing on the table in front of him at a strange angle, where the gruel almost slopped out.

Jack's hand was there in front of him, reaching out to settle the bowl, to straighten the spoon. To move the bread closer to Oliver's hands. Oliver swallowed, his throat feeling dry now, as if all the hunger in his body had taken leave of him, for he could not bear to eat anything now that he had sat down.

"Here's your spoon, now, take it." Jack said this in a steady tone, all business as he curled Oliver's fingers around the handle of the spoon. "An' eat."

For Jack, and only for Jack, would he do this. He tipped the spoon in the bowl of gruel and brought it to his mouth. Shoveled the gruel in and swallowed it as quick as he could, as it tasted like dirt, for some reason. Dirt with salt in it. His stomach roiled with the flavor and his mouth wanted to spit it out, but he swallowed.

"Bread," said Jack. "Water."

Oliver found both of these things in front of him, and as he took a swallow of water from the metal tumbler, he felt a bit better. Then he drank the whole thing and licked his lips, wanting to make himself clear.

"I'm ain't hungry n'more, Jack," he said, his lips numb over the words. He lifted his eyes to where Jack was staring at him. "I just felt dizzy an' now I ain't hungry, so you c'n have mine."

"Fuckin' chance, that," said Jack, his eyes narrowing. "You'll eat it, bread an' gruel, all of it right now. *Mind* me."

For a moment, Oliver stared at Jack, thinking he would fight him on this, then, as Jack stared at him, not wavering, he thought better of it. It was pure foolishness not to eat, even if it didn't taste very good.

He knew this down to his bones, and remembered that sometimes in Hardingstone, after not having been fed very much, a small boy's belly would rebel at finally being fed. This was what had happened to him now, and he'd never thought to feel that way ever again, to ever be that hungry again, yet here he was. Balking at his food, at the one thing that would keep him alive.

Plus, now that he was feeling a bit better, from sitting still, from the water, he didn't know, he could see the concern on Jack's face. The way his brows were furrowed together, the hard line of his mouth, as if in preparation for being even more fierce to get Oliver to eat.

"You will eat," said Jack, his face quite pale and still.

"Yes, Jack," said Oliver, as quickly as he could. "The water helped. I'm sorry I worried you. I didn't mean to."

"You!"

This shout came from Mr. Bassler, who strode over, his dun-colored apron flapping away from his legs.

"There is no talking in the dining hall. You've been told time and again. Do you want me to call Workmaster Chalenheim over?"

"No, sir," said Oliver, doing his best to answer without his jaw trembling.

"Do you?" asked Mr. Bassler, looking at Jack.

"No, sir," said Jack, with a fairly steady voice.

"Then see that you obey the rules, and I won't have to come over here again."

Jack and Oliver both nodded and, as Mr. Bassler marched away, to Oliver's surprise, Jack was almost snickering into his bowl of gruel. Bent over as he was, with his elbows around his bowl on the table, it would be hard for anybody else to tell, yet there he was.

"Jack?" asked Oliver, breaking the rule one more time.

"The two of us, like ladies over their tea, we are," said Jack, swallowing a large mouthful of gruel. "Just can't stop chattin' can we."

Trust Jack to find it amusing. Trust Jack to brighten Oliver's spirits with his saucy grin, and a complete disregard for the serious.

"No, indeed," said Oliver, ducking close to his bowl as well.

"Will you pass me the sugar, then? My tea is simply not sweet enough."

Almost spitting out his mouthful of gruel, Jack hovered forward over his bowl, and laughed, silently, open-mouthed. And suddenly it was a better meal than Oliver had had in days.

❧ 14 ❧

AN AFTERNOON TO REGRET

It was Mr. Bassler who escorted Jack and his cleaning supplies across the rain-soaked men's yard, where the bone boxes still waited under the eaves, and the iron pikes were leaned against the wall in wait for the next fine morning when the rain wouldn't soak the bones and make it impossible to crush them. Mr. Bassler opened the door to a low building on the far side of the yard and motioned him in.

"You're to clean this as you did the men's day room, Work-master Chalenheim says," said Mr. Bassler. "He'll be by to check on you, so no foolishness."

Before Jack could even nod in agreement, Mr. Bassler was gone, closing the door behind Jack. Which left him in a room lit only by the meager light coming through the rain-splattered window. Jack didn't turn around to watch Mr. Bassler go, only noted over his shoulder that the door was closed and he was alone.

The room was long and low-ceilinged, like the oakum-picking room was, and Jack suspected it was the men's version of that room and, indeed, underfoot, he could see the tail ends of yellowed rope, dotted with black tar. He couldn't imagine those old hands attempting to manage such tiny strands; he used his toe to scrape a bit of rope across the stone floor, leaving a faint black streak behind.

Had this been any other day, Jack would have made himself comfortable with a good lean against the window, for across the yard, through the windows of what he now knew to be the kitchen, would surely be Nolly, hard at work. Earning his daily bread. Trying to be good, as Jack never could be.

But it wasn't an ordinary day by any means, and Jack could feel that in his bones. There was no point in pretending to work, for that was not what he was there for. Instead, he carried his bucket to the far wall where the benches were lined, half of them stacked upside down on their fellows. The far corner stank as if someone had pissed in it, so Jack scooted a set of benches in that spot, and hunkered down between the benches in a place where he could watch the door.

It wasn't long before the door opened.

Workmaster Chalenheim strode across the room to where Jack crouched on his haunches, his back pressed to the wall. His eyes were pleased and sparkling.

Jack's bucket and brush were only a hand's length away, but there was no point in using them to fling at Chalenheim to give Jack a moment to slip past him and out the door, no point at all. He drew in a slow breath as Chalenheim came to stand in front of him, and let himself look up Chalenheim's length, stopping just at the angle of his chin, for he did not think he could meet those eyes full on and go through with it.

"Do you have anything to say to me, Jack?" asked Chalenheim, somewhere above Jack's head.

Jack licked his lips in preparation for speaking, when Chalenheim reached down and yanked him up by his arm. As he stood, Jack's head clonked against the wall, but it was because he was bracing himself too hard; he needed to relax so Chalenheim couldn't see how scared he was.

"Anything at all?" asked Chalenheim.

"I do this," said Jack, speaking to the middle of Chalenheim's chest. "An' you stop hurtin' Nol—Oliver. You just leave him be, you *stop*—"

"You have no say in the matter. I hand out discipline where I see fit."

This was true, of course, so Jack took a sharp breath and made himself look Chalenheim in the face. At his dark eyes and heavy brow, the way his mouth moved over his teeth. The way he'd scraped himself shaving or, perhaps, had been in a struggle and been scratched by a small hand.

"I'll come easy, if you do," Jack said, watching Chalenheim's eyes. "Anythin' you want, if you leave him be."

It was easy for Jack to see by Chalenheim's raised brows and the pause his whole body made that this was a new idea for him. That Chalenheim held all the control must be so very obvious; he could have Jack anyway, if he so desired it, but perhaps a willing victim might be more pleasant than an unwilling one.

"I won't fight you," said Jack, then he had to look away, to the window where the rain was coming down so thick it doubled the panes of glass until the light was gray and liquid in the room.

"Then that's a bargain," said Chalenheim, and he held out his hand for Jack to shake.

Jack took it. He felt the breadth and strength in that hand, and thought about what he would say to Nolly when, in the night, Chalenheim came carrying a candle and led Jack away.

"When?" asked Jack. His throat was dry, and his neck was hot, a quiver racing up his back because he'd just said *yes* to it, shook his hand on it. And there was no turning back.

"I'll send for you," said Chalenheim, and Jack sensed he was tipping his head back, that crooked smile exposed as Chalenheim sighed with pleasure. "And for now—"

Chalenheim cupped the back of Jack's neck, where surely he could feel Jack's trembling, but this only made him smile.

"Unbutton your trousers."

For a moment, Jack was confused; surely the men's work-room was too public. But then Chalenheim could have given the other attendants instructions, told them that he needed to have a quiet word with Jack Dawkins, to afford him some personal discipline.

No one was coming.

Jack bent his head and, with numb fingers, slotted the buttons out of their holes, thinking of the time Nolly had dressed him, and teased him about the number of buttons on his fine, only slightly used, new trousers. His throat closed up, so he breathed through his nose, and undid the buttons and left his shirt tucked in and his pants in place, for even if it might surprise Nolly, Jack knew how to follow orders and he'd not been told to do anything else but undo a certain set of buttons.

And, as was obvious, as Chalenheim stepped closer, blocking the view to the window, his shoulders creating a dark line above Jack, Chalenheim wanted to disrobe Jack himself. He stepped in and circled his arms around Jack's shoulders.

"Put your arm around my neck."

Jack did as he was told, lifting up on his toes, his arm along the top of Chalenheim's arm, his hand tucking around Chalenheim's neck, holding onto the brown collar. It couldn't be that Chalenheim would go too far with this, for there was no comfort to be found in this room, cold and chilled from the rain, no fire having been lit for days. But Jack recognized the look in Chalenheim's eyes, the expression on his face, the serious focus that reflected Chalenheim's need to mark his claim.

Then Chalenheim's arm dropped and his broad palm circled around Jack's hip, pushing at his trousers, causing them to slip, just a little bit. This made Chalenheim smile, the edge of a crooked tooth biting into his lip.

Jack let his eyes unfocus to stare at the brown expanse of Chalenheim's workhouse-issue jacket, though of a finer sort than the paupers wore. Felt that hand, calloused at the edges, and strong, push down the back of Jack's trousers. The hand brushed across his hip, pushing the trousers down a ways. Then Jack felt Chalenheim's fingers trailing along the tender crease below his buttock before moving between his legs.

Jack's whole body started, and he jerked backward, pushing at Chalenheim's chest, when Chalenheim gave a deep grunt and yanked Jack's trousers down, leaving Jack's legs cold to the air below the hem of his shirt. Chalenheim advanced even closer, shoving Jack against the wall, his hand rough between Jack's legs, pressing the soft flesh with his palm, almost grinding, as if he wanted Jack's cock to spring to life for his pleasure.

But it didn't.

Jack knew he was shaking as he tried to blink away the panic, his lips numb, Chalenheim all pressed against him, as if he meant to take Jack against the wall, bugger him standing, just as they were.

"You resist me again, and your pretty friend will spend his entire stay at the workhouse in the refractory. On short rations. Do you want that?"

The words came out, solid and assured. Chalenheim knew the moment was his, and all there was left for Jack to do was give in. Which he would do, because there was nothing else he *could* do. Even if he was shaking, now, head to foot, his mouth was full of acid, and he wanted only to fall to his knees and beg Chalenheim to be gentle, for he could not bear it if he was not.

But he had some dignity; at least he had that.

"No," he said, wincing as Chalenheim tugged on tender flesh, swirling Jack's bollocks in his fingers. Then he added, "No, sir," as Nolly might have done, just to slide the words along a little easier. Those such as Chalenheim enjoyed it when honors were paid to them.

"Very well," said Chalenheim, finally letting him go. He nodded at Jack and stepped back, and Jack bent to pull up his trousers, feeling as though he'd been beaten all over, rather than merely submitting to a bit of manhandling. "You may go back to your tasks, Jack Dawkins. Just be ready. When I send, you'll come. Is that understood?"

"Yes," said Jack. He was struggling with his buttons; he couldn't make his fingers work. But Chalenheim stepped closer again, tugged at his trouser waist, and did Jack's buttons up for him. Smirking, with a little snort under his breath, he tugged on Jack's jacket collar to straighten it.

"How do you paupers get into such a state of disarray?"

It amused him to say it, and Jack didn't spit in his face, as he wanted to. Only stayed very still as Chalenheim pulled on his jacket, and marched out of the room, whistling a little as he went, some tuneless tune that Jack couldn't recognize and hoped never to hear again.

But at least that was that. He knew what Chalenheim's hands upon him would feel like, and he had survived it. He could survive the other, when that time came.

Except now, as Chalenheim closed the door behind him, Jack was again alone in the men's workroom, with the smell of piss clogging his lungs, the damp dust in the corners of a room that existed only for the grim duties of the paupers.

Though there was nobody to see him, Jack knew his mouth was quivering. He didn't want it to, so he turned to the wall and braced his arm against it and buried his face in the crook of his elbow.

There, in the shadow of his own body, the smell of lime-washed plaster overrode everything else, and he let himself sink into a time of not so long ago. Into the memory of another lime-washed room, tinged a pale blue, with the scent of sea air coming through the barely cracked window. The sounds of a simple boiled supper being prepared not far off, just down the passage to the kitchen. And Nolly, standing there in a fine linen shirt as he tucked it into his trousers and looked up to see Jack watching him, his blue eyes blazing and a smile meant only for Jack.

He would think of that. Of those days, seemingly so long ago, Nolly's gentle fingers as he leaned over the bed to touch Jack's forehead to make sure that he was all right, and not too feverish. That was what Jack would take with him, when he went, when Chalenheim called.

CONSIDERATIONS MADE OVER
WORKHOUSE GRUEL

The rain sheeted down the windows of the kitchen, shutting Oliver in with the dampness and the low, rotting smell that came from the pipes beneath the sinks. The standing water in the bucket beneath a slow drip from the ceiling in the corner. The sweat of unwashed skin. The leavings of potato peelings in a basin that had not been emptied. All of this created a fug that was one tender note below a full-blown stink.

Just the same, as Oliver polished knives with emery paste and water on the long table in front of the rain-obscured windows, he thought about those shreds of potato, the peeled skin turning to gray and dark brown and normally unappetizing except to be fed to pigs.

He looked down at Finley, who seemed very quiet today, though obedient, rinsing the knives and drying them off with a cloth to set them in lines across another cloth that lay on the table. Like soldiers, those knives, just as straight as might be.

Finley seemed less pleased than Oliver thought he ought to have been; the boy kept his head down, focused on his work, never once lifting his eyes for Oliver's approval. Perhaps the odor of the kitchen was making him feel ill, or perhaps the workhouse had finally broken him down to where all the joy had been taken from him.

Meanwhile, the potato peelings.

Cook was standing at the doorway shouting at somebody, and while Oliver would have never heretofore considered vegetable scraps as food, he now was. If he was asked to carry the peelings to the piggery, for surely there was one somewhere in the workhouse, then he could eat some along the way. If not, well, nobody would be counting the shreds.

As well, if Cook kept her back turned long enough, Oliver could get scraps into his mouth before anybody would notice. He'd take some for Finley as well and get him to eat them, as unappetizing as they were.

Perhaps he could find a way to grab some for Jack, who was certainly no less hungry than Oliver, or even more so, since he'd been going at his tasks with such intensity that surely he was not used to. But where could Oliver carry them? In his stockings, perhaps? For he had no pockets, not even in his trousers.

Jack wouldn't mind being fed potato peels that had been carried in Oliver's stockings, and Oliver's own mouth watered at the thought of being able to do this for Jack. To watch him eat something with substance, and smile at Oliver that he was full now, and might take his ease, and where would Oliver get him a pipe to smoke?

The thoughts all blurred together, and Oliver knew his fancies had taken him too far, for someone came in and took the bowl of peelings and left with it. It was too late to eat them, or take some for Jack, or get Finley to eat some. Or anything.

Swallowing the moisture that had built in his mouth, Oliver returned to his labors, noting with some dismay that only half of the knives were done, and Finley seemed to have fallen asleep over the basin of water.

Amidst Cook's shouting, and a bustle outside the doorway, someone else came in, a woman with a brown apron like the one

Oliver and Finley wore. She carried two buckets of water and tipped them into the cook pot.

Oliver let the normality of this act override his dull shock that there was a woman other than Cook in the kitchen. That she was a pauper was obvious from her skinny arms and the dull glaze in her eyes. But she went about preparing gruel for the boys' supper as easily as Oliver might make toast in his own room. She put in several measures of oats, which surely didn't seem enough for the amount of water she put in the pot, a handful of salt, a glop of treacle, and that was it.

After poking up the fire beneath the pot, she took a long spoon and began to stir the gruel. This was almost mesmerizing, and Oliver could smell the salt and the oat-flavored water. His stomach wanted some if it directly, undercooked as it was. He could have consumed the entire pot of gruel, if they'd let him. But she never left her post and, defeated and somewhat undone by his current willingness to eat raw food, Oliver returned to the knives. He jostled Finley a bit, but gently, to get him to waken, and together they returned to their tasks.

Cook came in and stomped around the kitchen, yelled at the woman, who never paused in her stirring, and then came over to Oliver and Finley.

"You are lazy, *lazy* boys," she said. "I will report you to the workmaster if you don't pick up your pace and get that finished. I've plenty more work that you could be doing."

Oliver held his tongue over what he wanted to say, that if there was so much work to do, perhaps she might lend a hand. Having not said that, he almost smirked at the thought of it, but bit the inside of his cheek and focused on looking at the rain through the window. How the water slid down the panes of glass like thick strands of silver. How the men's yard was obscured by the rain and only came through as chunks of brown or gray.

Just as he was wondering where Jack was and what he was doing, someone came to the door and spoke to Cook in a low voice.

"She can't go!" shouted Cook. "Who will stir the gruel? Somebody must stir it or it'll burn, else."

But go the female pauper did, leaving the spoon in the pot, hurrying out of the kitchen with some haste. Cook gestured at Oliver.

"Come here, you wretch, and put this apron on. No, this one."

Oliver put down the knife in his hand, laid the cloth on the table, and went over to her. She handed him the dun-colored apron of a workhouse assistant.

"Put it on, and stir this till the bell. Then you'll serve, for I haven't anybody else to do it. And you!" she shouted at Finley now. "Get back to work and make sure all those dishes are washed after you've finished with those knives."

Oliver doffed the brown apron of a pauper and put on the dun-colored one. It felt light in his hands, and was much cleaner than anything else he had on, so he handled it a bit gently, not wanting to spread the grime from his hands upon it. It tied easily, as the string was flat and new, and the collar of the apron fit smoothly upon his neck. Then, turning to the stove, where the warmth was close enough to be felt upon the skin, he went over to the pot, picked up the long spoon, and began stirring.

It took him a moment to realize what he was doing, what he had in his hands. He was holding a long-handled workhouse spoon, and he was stirring gruel. Gruel that was thin and gray and had to be stirred or else it would scorch.

He stirred, waiting for the gruel to get thick, as the porridge in the townhouse would have done when Uncle Brownlow's cook would prepare it. At some point, the oats would thicken and be taken partly off the heat to finish cooking. On the table would be waiting cream and sugar, and a tub of butter, all ready to be put on the porridge before eating it.

Oliver's mouth watered all over again, but he kept stirring, and watched as Cook stomped around some more before leaving the kitchen altogether. He had no idea where she might go, but she'd just left them on their own.

"Is everything all right, Finley?" he asked over his shoulder.

"Yes, sir," said Finley in a small voice.

"Not sir," said Oliver. "Just Oliver, yes?"

"Yes, Oliver," said Finley.

As much as Oliver stirred the gruel, no matter how it bubbled in the pot, it still resembled oats mixed with water. There was plenty of water and not enough oats, but it should have started to become blended together somehow, with the heat beneath it and all of Oliver's stirring. It remained, in spite of his best efforts, an unpalatable mess that would provide no sustenance, and would ease the hunger in a pauper's belly not at all.

Then, beneath the table along the inside wall, Oliver saw that the cupboard was open. Normally he would not have been in that part of the kitchen, but he was there now and he could see that the cupboard was ajar.

Laying the spoon along the rim of the pot, he sidled over to the cupboard and eased it open with his foot, keeping his eyes on the door the whole time. A single glance downward told him what he had thought was true. The cupboard contained two cones of sugar, one still wrapped in blue paper, the other partially unwrapped, with the top of the cone lopped off at an angle.

After a moment or two of fussing in his mind about it, Oliver went over as quick as he could, quietly so Finley wouldn't see what he was doing, and would be innocent of any wrongdoing if Oliver was caught, and took up a bowl and a spoon that had not yet been washed. Not that it mattered. Both had been licked clean, and besides, no one would care that Oliver had used dirty kitchenware, not when they tasted how sweet the gruel was.

He took the bowl and spoon, knelt down in front of the open cupboard, and hacked off a bowl's worth of sugar, carried it over to the pot, and tipped it in. Putting down the bowl and spoon, he gave the gruel a quick stir to melt the sugar. It went in quickly, as if the gruel was thirsty for it.

Considering, Oliver went back to the cupboard, hacked off more sugar, and tossed that in the pot as well. He gave the gruel several hearty stirs with the wooden spoon, and then with the tip of the metal spoon, reached in and took out a taste.

The gruel was hot, so he blew on it, and took it on his tongue. Yes, it was sweet enough, but it needed something more, for it was still thin and watery. So he went back to the cupboard, and bent down, keeping his eye on the doorway and on Finley at the same time, his heart pounding with fear, yes, but mostly with righteous gladness. If they put him in charge of stirring the gruel, then they were going to get what he made of it.

The cupboard, whose lock appeared to be not fully engaged, besides the cones of sugar, contained salt and other spices that didn't belong in gruel. The second cupboard contained small bags of oats; Oliver took one of these and poured the entire of it into the pot, and stirred it several times to mix it well. The gruel began to thicken up almost directly and, with the sugar, smelled a great deal better.

He went back to the cupboards one more time, kneeling down, silently opening each one to search its contents. After each search, he closed each cupboard till it locked so Cook wouldn't know that he'd been rustling among her supplies.

The last cupboard at the end of the row toward the wall contained Cook's tea things. There was a tin box of tea, of course; a sieve, to capture the tea leaves while pouring; two spare cup and saucer sets; and, amazingly, a whole jug of milk, thick along the top with cream. Along with this was a full bowl of butter for her toast, just sitting there.

With the amount that Cook took for her tea, the entire of the workhouse could have enjoyed a treat, but she kept it for herself, all the while shouting and stomping that everyone else was lazy and slow.

With absolutely no remorse, Oliver took the jug of milk over to the pot and, using the wooden spoon, stirred the contents in, slowly adding a bit at a time so it went in evenly. He saw Finley had finally noticed what he was doing and was watching with wide eyes. Oliver shook his head in warning.

"You are working," he said, sternly. "You didn't see anything I was doing. Look out the window, now, or at your hands, and don't look at me."

For a moment, Finley hesitated, and Oliver could see that he wanted to help, as if doing what Oliver was doing was a grand adventure.

"Now, Finley," said Oliver.

Finley did as he was told, and Oliver went back to stirring the gruel. He added the bowl of butter all at once, and let it sit on top of the gruel, watching it melt into gold strands among the gray before finally mixing it in. And realized as he stirred that he was no longer cooking gruel, for he had turned the contents of the pot into porridge, which was a proper dish for little boys whose bellies needed feeding.

He put the empty bowl and jug back where he found them and shut the cupboard door till it locked; Cook would think she'd taken the milk in her tea and finished the butter, for with a locked cupboard, she could not accuse them of having gone into it. Besides, the damage was already done, and Oliver smiled at the thought of it, and returned to stirring. His heart no longer pounded, but there was sweat on the back of his neck, on his upper lip. He told himself this was from the heat of the stove.

Cook came back in the kitchen, still stomping, muttering to herself, and went directly into the cupboards to freshen her tea. When she noticed the empty pitcher, she cast not one glance in Oliver's direction, but took it and stomped out of the kitchen to get some more.

Meanwhile, Oliver continued to stir the contents of the pot, the golden-brown mess of porridge, sweet with sugar and thick with milk, bubbling away like a contented thing. Since he was to serve as well, he'd make sure that the ladle was full before he poured its contents into each boy's bowl. There was no telling how far he could go before he was caught. But there was one thing he needed to do before the supper bell rang.

"Finley, come here."

Finley came over with some eagerness. Oliver took the bowl he'd used for the sugar, and served up some of the porridge in it. He handed the bowl, along with the spoon, to Finley.

"Blow on it, to cool it," he said. "Then eat it as fast as you can."

Flicking a glance up at him, Finley held the bowl against his belly, bent close to the bowl, and blew on it. He tried to stir it at the same time, which might tip the contents, so Oliver guided Finley and took him over to the table under the window where Finley could balance the bowl.

"Now try," said Oliver, nodding.

With only a few attempts to cool the porridge, Finley began stuffing it into his mouth in great, huge spoonfuls, which he barely swallowed before taking in more.

Watching Finley eat, Oliver felt his eyes grow hot, and his mouth pulled back against his teeth lest he shout his anger and the fury that it should come to this, that a little boy was so hungry he ate barely tasting what he was eating. When Finley was done, he patted his own belly, smiled up at Oliver and, at a single gesture, went contentedly back to his task of polishing knives.

Staggering back a bit with the force of his rage, Oliver returned to the pot and continued to stir. And kept stirring till his shoulders ached and his face felt burned by the heat of the fire. Soon someone would come to help him carry the pot to the boys' dining hall. There, someone would hand him a ladle. At which point, by God, he would serve those boys something to eat.

≈

WHEN SOMEONE CAME TO THE MEN'S WORKROOM AND CALLED
to him, Jack felt the words echo in his ears, and struggled to
push himself against the wall so that he could stand upright. He
was cold from sitting so still for so long, and damp through
where his jacket had pressed against the wall.

"Come along, Jack, and bring your supplies; it's time for
supper."

Not that the supper would be anything much, but Nolly
would be there, and it would be easier to pretend in front of
Nolly that everything was all right. It was always easier with an
audience.

Jack picked up his bucket and brush, couldn't remember
where his broom was or whether he'd brought one at all, and
went out the door to follow the attendant across the yard and in
through the door that led to the passage to the dining hall.

His trousers chafed at his hips, as if someone had rubbed
them too hard. The memory of Chalenheim looming over him
felt quite distant and, as he placed his bucket and brush in line
with the others, he looked about him, but Chalenheim wasn't
there. Nor was he in the dining hall as Jack got in line at the end,
two by two, not feeling anything in his belly that was remotely
like hunger. But he should eat. When the food came, he would
eat it because he needed to keep his strength up. He had to be
strong, no matter what.

When he got halfway up the line, he looked over his shoulder
to where the door that led to the passage to the kitchen. He saw
a small group of boys coming out of it, looking hot and sweaty,
rolling down their sleeves, but he could not see Nolly. Acid shot
through him, clenching up inside, making his shoulders stiff, for
what if Chalenheim had gone straight to Nolly and taken him to
some distant room somewhere in the workhouse, a far-off room
where nobody went, and gave instructions that Nolly would be
forced to obey?

Almost desperate now, he hung back in line, mouth open,
breath coming in hard shocks, when he heard a noise from

beside the cauldron, where each boy was holding up his bowl to the server. And there, standing next to the cauldron, was Nolly. His sleeves were rolled up, and he wore the dun-colored apron of an attendant, and he was ladling out gruel.

Someone else was handing out bread, but Nolly had the ladle in his hands, his wrists corded as he upturned the ladle into each bowl. His chin was jutted out in determination and as Jack got closer, he could see why.

Nolly was scooping up a whole ladle for each bowl, rather than the half-ladle measurement that was the usual dole for each pauper. No, it was an *entire* ladle that almost filled the bowl to the brim. The boys staggered under the weight, holding the bowls against their bellies as they walked to the tables, quickly, not spilling a drop as they sat down.

Now Jack was almost at the head of the line. He could see that the gruel looked thick and sweet, and smelled very nice indeed, as if something extra had been done to it in the kitchen. As if someone had determined to make the meal as delicious as he could.

Jack looked at Nolly, then, all other thoughts scraped from his mind as he took in this sight, this beautiful, almost comical sight of Nolly, attending to the orphans, feeding them as fast and as much as he could with warm, sweet porridge.

His smile, when he caught Jack's eye, was angry at the same time it was a little sad, and Jack figured he knew why. Give an orphan a full bowl today, and tomorrow his stomach would miss it. It was like giving a stable boy a ride on the back of a rich lady's pony, a taste of something he could never have again. But whether it was better to know pleasure and never again have it, or never to know it, Jack did not know. He merely stood in line, twirling his bowl between his fingers, trying not to smirk too hard in case he gave Nolly's game away.

But it was too late for that, for just as the last boy other than Jack had been served, the attendant on the other side of the cauldron, who had been handing out small hunks of bread in a very bored manner, suddenly became alerted to what Nolly was up to.

"Whatever are you doing, you? That's too much—" The attendant nearly shrieked this as he reached out to the nearest boy and grabbed the full bowl with his fingers.

The bowl full of white liquid sprayed over the cauldron, causing the fire to sizzle and hiss. The attendant reached around and grabbed the ladle from Nolly's hands, which caused more porridge to get on the fire, where it actually began to smoke.

Nolly, as Jack could see as he stepped wisely back, was having none of it. He moved quickly enough, with long strides, marched right up and, with a quick left hook, had the attendant sprawled on the floor, his mouth bleeding. The attendant's piteous cries brought two attendants running from the kitchen, and the cook, too, in her long, spotless white apron, which told Jack directly that she had plenty to help her in the kitchen, doing almost no work herself.

The main thing, the important thing, was to get out of Nolly's way, as people might get hurt. Jack considered jumping in and helping him, but the attendants were rough as they charged Nolly, and Jackwas shaking all over. There was no consideration in his body, nothing left to hold himself in check at the thought of anybody touching him with violence. He shepherded the paupers, with their full bowls, away from the corner where the attendants had Nolly pinned.

"Move it, you," said Jack to one or two orphans who were gawping, letting their bowls tip, the contents splatting on the floor. "Go an' sit down an' eat, don't get in this, don't—"

It was Mr. Bassler who waded into the fray, his belly heaving at the excitement in the dining hall such as he'd probably not seen in recent memory. He walked right up to Nolly, who was being held by his arms, and ripped the dun-colored apron off of him, as if divesting him of some badge of honor. Then he slapped Nolly hard, a solid clout with the back of his hand that was obviously meant to cow Nolly into something far more meek than was standing before him now.

"Workmaster Chalenheim will hear of this when he gets back from the village," said Mr. Bassler in loud tones meant for one and all to hear and be awed by. "You're not here on charity, you know, and you had no right, no right at all to be changing the dietary like that. What will Master Pickering say when he finds out?"

"I don't care."

The words were loud enough for Jack to hear, for everyone to hear, angry and level, as if Nolly were holding back.

"There's more than enough food in that kitchen to feed these boys," said Nolly now. "You know it's true."

"That food is for the board of directors when they come on their inspection next week. It's not for mere paupers to eat."

"But they're the ones who are starving. You're *starving* them to feed those fat fools who think they know—"

Upon those last words, so foolishly, so bravely spoken, Mr. Bassler struck Nolly again. The attendants crowded close, as if to hide what they were doing, and within moments, Nolly was on the floor, sprawled between the legs of the men who stood above him. They hauled him up, and he was almost limp in their grasp as they dragged him off, out of the door from the dining hall, though toward what destination, Jack could not be sure. Unless it was the refractory room—

All semblance of calm left Jack. Shaking, his bowl empty in his hands, he sat down on the nearest bench as the attendants who were left scurried to make order of the orphans standing there with their allotment of porridge and the orphans who were already seated, all of them swallowing large mouthfuls of their meal, whether they stood or sat, before anybody could take it away from them.

"Stop eating, stop eating!" one of the attendants shouted, braying the words to be heard above the uncommon din.

But all of the orphans were more beneficially occupied than

to listen to the attendant, making the sweet gruel disappear inside of a heartbeat or two. All that was left was the fire that smoked, the smell of burned porridge on the outside of the cauldron heating to black, round, charred spots.

Jack could only sit there, even when someone came around and poured a ladle of porridge into his bowl and handed him a hunk of bread, a rather large hunk, as if in an attempt at bribery. But though he bowed his head for the hurried prayers, and scooted along to let other boys sit next to him, he could not eat.

No part of him wanted anything to do with the porridge in the bowl in front of him, for it was clear that the deal was broken. Nolly had been beaten and taken to the refractory room, so the deal was broken.

Jack was grateful, for it meant Chalenheim would have no hold over him, could not come to him in the night with his single candle and take him to his room, where he would tell Jack to lift up his nightshirt and bend over the bed. No, he didn't have to do that now, on account of Nolly's temper having, at last, and at the most unexpected moment, gotten the better of him.

Jack should not be glad, but he was.

His hands shook as he passed his bread to an orphan on his left, and divided his rather large bowl of sweet porridge between two other orphans, scraping the bowl clean. He gave the spoon to yet another orphan to lick, for he could not stomach eating.

Someone pushed a tumbler of cool water into his hands, which he looked down to see were clenched on the tabletop. He made himself drink some of the water, though it tasted bitter and metallic, as if it had been drawn days ago and left in a pitcher that had not been scoured in a long time.

Waiting until the meal was over was less a matter of sitting still than it was of keeping the tumbril of thoughts in his mind at bay. And how they whirled, making his face feel numb as he scrubbed at his eyes with the heel of his hand, of Nolly, who had the heart of a lion. What would he say when he found out that

Jack was glad of the respite that had been paid for by Nolly's skin?

Mr. Bassler was bringing out buckets and cloths. He grabbed some of the orphans and set them to cleaning up the mess from a battle that had been fought for them. Nolly would have been proud, for though the orphans did as they were told, as they always did, Jack thought he could see some of them with a brighter look in their eyes, from having been fed. A proud tilt to their heads that someone had stood up for them. Or tried; though, for an orphan, that was more than they usually had.

Mr. Bassler led one of the orphans to the corner of the room, but the orphan pushed the bucket away and shook his head, and he seemed scared. Then Mr. Bassler looked right at Jack and beckoned him over.

For a moment, Jack thought of refusing, but the meal was done, and if he didn't obey then Mr. Bassler would, most likely, get angry and take it out on one of the small boys. Jack got up from the table, his stomach empty, and went over, his heart feeling as though he'd broken it with his own hands.

"Clean this," said Mr. Bassler, shoving the bucket and cloth at him. "There's blood on the floor, now. What will the board of directors say if they saw this? Clean it up now."

The stone floor was stained with blood. There wasn't a lot of it, just a long circle of scarlet that had been scuffed by someone's boot and ground into the crack between two stones, which was what had scared the little boy who had refused to clean it up.

When you were young, when you were *that* young, a splash of blood like that was a warning sign, and Jack could remember being scared himself, the first time Bill Sikes had slapped one of Fagin's boys so hard that his nose had bled all over his shirt. And though Fagin had pulled him away and taken care of him, the memory stood out like a way sign.

At no urging, Jack got down on his hands and knees and wet the scrub cloth in the bucket and began to clean the floor. It didn't matter that he got blood on his hands, that it was Nolly's blood he was rinsing out in the bucket, taking the cloth down again to circle it around, where the edges of the small puddle were already drying to a dark brown. It didn't matter, and he told himself this as he scooted back to clean the blood beneath his boots, the swipe of the cloth leaving a thin, watery stripe along the stone.

He felt hollow inside, so hollow, as if his guts had been dug out with a spoon, the contents to be dumped somewhere where nobody would find it.

Giving the stones one more good go with the scrub cloth, Jack wrung out the cloth over the bucket. He watched the water turn pink, and stood up, unsteady as he hauled up the bucket in one hand, the cloth in the other.

"Dump that in the yard," said Mr. Bassler, too busy putting order to the orphans, directing the attendants to dampen the fire to pay much heed to Jack.

Jack did as he was told, as though he were some dumb animal who didn't know any better, and had no thoughts beyond that of the moment. It was easier that way.

He went through the doors and out into the men's yard, where he tipped the bucket on the stones. He watched the water swirl around as the rain spattered down, taking the pink trails and mixing them with the leftover dust from pounded bone, and oozed into the cracks, where the rain watered it down.

For a moment, Jack stood there, his head bowed, water dripping from his forehead and down his nose, feeling as though he'd been cut adrift on a vast sea of misery from which there would be no return.

❧ 16 ❧

THE BATTLE IN THE
DINING HALL

Two attendants whom Oliver did not know dragged him from the boys' dining hall, and along the passage, past the kitchen and scullery, his boots scraping against stone as he was taken yet again to the refractory room. For him, there was no doubt as to where he was bound, only the question for how long he would be kept there, and whether or not they would feed him.

They would not, he knew, for the grip on his arms was too tight, fingers pressing hard to set bruises almost to the bone. As his nose bled down his chin, the attendants tugged him around the corner to hustle him down the stairs. As if they thought he would fight back. As if he had the strength to fight back.

But as they threw him to the stone bench to rip off his boots and his stockings, he could not regret what he had done. Cook deserved to have her milk used for a better purpose, and the paupers deserved at least one good, hot meal.

One of the attendants rose with Oliver's boots in his hands and smacked him in the face, sending Oliver against the stone wall, which he held onto, gripping the cracks between the stones with his fingers, trying to push himself upright. Not that it would do any good. Not that he had anywhere he could go.

"That'll teach you to change the dietary," said the attendant, almost spitting the words.

"I'm getting the strap," said the other attendant.

Oliver closed his eyes and did not watch as the other attendant approached, the strap in his hand. But he felt the blows that slammed into him, that knocked him against hard stone, fast and painfully deep, slipping through the air with a heated, leather-scented whine.

He curled away, curled into the stone wall, his head down, bare feet scraping against the edge of the bench as they hit him, all the air taken from him, blow by blow, until he was left gasping. When the strap stopped, he was left unable to take in a breath. Or move. Or sigh.

But it wasn't over. The attendants grabbed him roughly once more, and he saw through squinted eyes that they were unlocking the refractory room. The motion of the key in the lock was slow and clear, and the door opened with the select focus he could not seem to draw his gaze from.

Then, instead of bidding him to walk in, they grabbed him and threw him in with a quick, brutal toss that landed him fully in the depth of the puddle of cold water oozing up from the stone, and filled from where the well leaked. Even as the door slammed shut and the key turned again in the lock, he could barely manage to push himself up on his elbows, his back aching, his legs numb, his mouth sticky with the blood from his nose.

For a moment, in the darkness, he wondered whether his eyes were closed or open, whether he should move to the ice-cold bench, or whether it might be easier to die where he was. His arms trembled beneath him, his thighs started to shake, as if he'd run as far and as fast as he could, only to stumble and fall and to end up where he was, on his hands and knees in icy water. In darkness. Alone.

Jack wouldn't wonder where he was, for Jack had seen everything: the creamy porridge for the pauper boys, the full ladle served into each bowl. Jack had smiled at him, that low, smirk-laced smile telling Oliver that had Jack been in the kitchen with him, he would have approved of what Oliver was doing, every step of the way. That he was proud of Oliver's rebellion, that he would have fought for him if he could.

But Mr. Bassler's punch had taken Oliver to the floor and, with a part of his awareness, Oliver knew Jack was taking the boys out of the range of violence, because there was nothing he could do for Oliver, nothing at all. As Oliver licked the blood from his lips, his head bowed, still on his hands and knees, his only hope was that Jack had gotten a serving of the porridge before it had been taken away, for Jack deserved that at least, for his smile on Oliver's behalf.

Still quivering, Oliver made himself get up on his feet, and dragged himself through the water to the bench beneath the curved wall. He knew enough now to dip his head so he wouldn't clonk it against the brick.

He had no jacket, nor even the dun-colored apron of a workhouse assistant. He rubbed his belly with chilled fingers, his lungs taking shallow, quick breaths to try and keep him warm. The sound in his head hummed, till at last he could do nothing but sink down to lay on the bench and curl his body close, his elbows tucked against his chest, his head bowed, still tasting the blood on his lips.

His bare feet were like ice, and he had nothing to wrap them in lest he take off his shirt, so he gave up and let the cold of the stone bench soak into him, bit by bit, taking his energy, his warmth. The low thud of his heart felt strangled, his breath raspy and shallow. But he couldn't move, for there was nowhere to go. The dampness of his clothes stuck to him, against his skin like wide, thin flakes of ice.

His eyes felt sticky and his head ached, and he longed for Jack. For Jack's arms around him, that easy smile to brighten the dark, the hue of Jack's eyes, like an emerald, to herald in something better, something sweeter. Something gentle and good.

But there was only darkness that swallowed everything, the

still, cold air layering itself along his shoulders. There was only the sound of dripping water, the echo of that drip, and the pounding of blood along his temple. He rubbed at it, wanting it to go away, unable to open his eyes to the darkness. And so he would stay until morning, if not beyond. They would come for him, eventually. Or they might not.

As he sank into his own darkness, it began not to matter so much, the emptiness of his belly, or the numb blocks of his feet, the hard edge of his ankles where they pressed against the stone bench. Or that his heart began to slow down, the low thud-thud of it sinking below his ability to hear, or even feel it. The hum in his head, a sharp, high-pitched sound that seemed to be coring its way into his forehead.

There was so much, there was so much, that he finally buried his head in his hands. He wanted to cry, but could only make a whisper sound that came from between clenched teeth. His eyes, which could not draw on the salt within his body, stung. After a time, he felt drained, and could not even feel enough aches and pains to cry, but could only lick his lips and wish desperately for some water, for he was thirsty and his throat was dry.

But there was water on the floor, was there not? It didn't matter how long it had lain there, or where it had come from, or what earth it had seeped through, or what had been dredged through it. For surely any vileness in the water would settle out, if the water was left alone long enough.

He thought about this for a moment, pulling his mouth against his teeth, tonguing the inside of his teeth where everything tasted like dusty chalk, and the water only a hand's reach away. He could get off the bench and scoop the water into his mouth, he most certainly could.

That would sustain him for a time, and after more water had leaked in from the well, he could drink from it again. He could survive if he had water.

He could survive, but he didn't move, only shivered on the bench and thought about drinking the water on the floor.

Thought about it and then remembered the clean, warm water in the basin Mrs. Pierson had provided before every meal.

There had always been so much water available to wash in, or cool water from the pump to drink. That should be the water available to him, not the swill mixed with mud such as he was contemplating. Mrs. Pierson would be so disappointed in him if he drank it; though, on the other hand, Jack would shrug and tell him that if he needed that water to get through the night, he should have it.

Frowning, Oliver scrubbed his face with the palms of his hands, and shifted within his cold, damp clothes, his shirt sticking to him, his trousers all twisted around his waist. There was no reason he couldn't figure this out on his own and decide whether to drink the water or not. If he drank it now, there'd be more later, but if he didn't drink it now, he never would. So which was it to be?

His mind couldn't seem to settle on one or the other course of action, but only circled around itself like an animal whose tail was caught in a trap, and was unable to figure out how to escape. His whole body shivered constantly now, up and down his spine, rattling his ribs, shaking his teeth so that they clicked against one another—all of this distracted him so that he simply could not think.

Besides which, there was a sharp sound from outside the door, a clonk and then a scraping noise—all from his imagination that suddenly believed, with some conviction, that Jack had figured a way to free Oliver from the refractory room and had just unlocked the door to do this very thing.

Oliver almost sat up, his whole body brightening with joy, but the shape in the doorway as it opened was not Jack's. It was too tall, too broad at the shoulders, and filled up the frame, almost blocking the low light of the candle-lantern behind it. No, it was not Jack at all. It was Workmaster Chalenheim.

"Come out of there now, Oliver Twist," said Chalenheim.

Oliver pushed himself back against the curved brick wall and shook his head.

If Chalenheim was here, it meant he had been informed as to just how much milk Oliver had added to the gruel, and how much of that gruel had been served into each boy's bowl. If Chalenheim's ire could be roused by Oliver having a simple, quick word with Jack, then changing the dietary would make the workmaster angry beyond words. Furious to the point where a whipping with a switch would be the next event.

Oliver shivered and pushed back against the wall even harder, for Chalenheim's whippings hurt, even when the crime that Oliver had committed wasn't so dire. There was no power on earth that would make Oliver volunteer for it by coming out of the refractory room willingly.

Chalenheim would have to come and get him.

This Chalenheim did, stepping into the puddle of cold water with his sturdy boots. He reached for Oliver and pulled him upright, a gesture Oliver could not resist because he simply couldn't. His muscles twitched beneath Chalenheim's touch, but he was easily led through the puddle and made to sit down on the stone bench once more.

There were no other attendants nearby, just Chalenheim and the candle-lantern that burned bright and clear as it sat on the bench next to Oliver. He blinked against the light and looked toward the faded gray light of the stone stairway.

There was no option to try to make a run for it, for he couldn't feel his feet, and his legs felt like damp cloth, and would not be able to bear his weight. Nor would he be able to trick Chalenheim to allow Oliver to make such an attempt, for Chalenheim stood before him now.

He looked down at Oliver, and Oliver looked up, wary. He kept his mouth shut tight, in case something Chalenheim might say would break through Oliver's stupor and allow him to shout out loud and say something foolish that would get him into more trouble than he already was. Though that was unlikely; he was at the bottom of a workhouse, alone with a man whose sole focus had been to mercilessly punish Oliver each and every time he laid eyes upon him. It could not get any worse, he was sure.

When Chalenheim knelt at Oliver's feet, Oliver almost kicked him, his whole body reacting with shock, his only desire to move away, far away, as fast as he could. But Chalenheim, with one hand on each of Oliver's knees, steadied him into stillness, and pulled a towel from the stone bench.

It wasn't even a bit of hemp sacking, such as Oliver would have sold his soul for, but an actual towel, clean and dry, and Chalenheim used it to rub Oliver's feet. First the left one and then the right, rubbing them dry, cleaning off the grit. Oliver winced as the blood started to pound, surging warmth through his feet, his legs.

"Your jacket and trousers will dry on the peg while you sleep," said Chalenheim, as if addressing his own hands. "But here are some clean stockings for you."

Without waiting for Oliver's reply, which was good, for Oliver could not think of a single thing to say, Chalenheim pulled the stockings on Oliver's feet, and then put his boots on for him and tied the laces, good and snug, as was proper. Then he gave the towel to Oliver.

"For as much of you as you can manage," said Chalenheim, standing up and nodding. His eyes glittered in the near dark as he looked at Oliver.

Mouth open, feeling like a gaping idiot, Oliver dried his hands, then his hair, and then the back of his neck. He jerked back only when Chalenheim leaned in close to straighten the line of the collarless shirt around Oliver's neck. Chalenheim took the towel back and sat on the stone bench beside Oliver.

"Here," said Chalenheim, pulling something else from the bench. "Eat this. Drink this milk."

Into Oliver's nerveless hands, Chalenheim placed a slice of buttered bread and a white tin mug full of milk.

For a moment, Oliver went still, his whole body frozen as he looked at the food in his hands. The bread was soft; he could smell the salt in it, smell the fat in the butter, and for a moment he inhaled, taking it all in. The mug of milk was heavy and cool against his palm, as if the milk, sweet and fresh, had just been taken from a sealed crock that had been submerged in a fast-running, freshwater spring. Both would taste delicious, would cool the fever in his head, soak the dried, parched feeling in his throat. Fill his belly.

But Chalenheim was not his friend. Chalenheim was the enemy, the stout-shouldered, strong arm of the workhouse, from whose booming voice and icy glare paupers cowered and Cooks did as they were told. Who had beaten Oliver till he could not stand, and who had left his hard marks on Oliver's skin.

Was Oliver, then, to take food offered by that hand? Though, in the private semi-darkness of the cellar, with only Chalenheim to witness, who was to know if Oliver ate and drank?

He, Oliver, would know, and thus he shouldn't accept it. Though, were Jack here, he would tell Oliver, in no uncertain terms, that he should eat as much as his belly would hold and then, after he was done, he should spit in Chalenheim's face to tell him what he thought of this sham-gesture of kindness.

Oliver didn't think he could manage enough moisture to spit, let alone to speak or to offer his thanks, but his trembling hand brought the bread to his mouth before he could stop it, and his teeth bit through the thickly layered butter to the bread, and sank into it.

The saliva built up in his mouth as he managed to stuff half of the bread-and-butter slice into it, chewing as quickly as he could. He swallowed that mouthful before taking a gulp of milk, not letting even a drop of it escape his mouth to drip down his chin. His whole body shuddered as the food hit his empty stomach, rolling around itself as the muscles cramped up, threatening to make him vomit the just-eaten food all over his knees, the dirty floor.

"Slowly," said Workmaster Chalenheim. He pulled the mug

away from Oliver's face, and the slice of buttered bread; his hands were hard and warm. "You must take small bites, and drink slow sips, understand?"

Oliver nodded, for he did understand how the vast empty spaces in his stomach could rebel when food was given to it too quickly. So, still shaking, jarring the surface of the milk in the mug, Oliver took a small bite of the bread and chewed it slowly. As if he had all the time in the world, and there were plenty more slices of bread awaiting his pleasure.

When he swallowed, Chalenheim released the hand that held the milk, and Oliver took a long, slow drink from the mug, his throat moving over each swallow, till half of the milk was gone.

"There," said Chalenheim, as gently as any nurse had ever done. "Finish that, and then we'll go upstairs, where your bed awaits you."

His bed awaited him, and Jack, who must know, surely, where Oliver had been taken, and was counting each breath and each beat of his heart until Oliver was returned to him.

Oliver smiled over his next bite of bread and butter. Jack wasn't as romantic as all to count breaths and heartbeats, but he would be waiting, worried as to where Oliver was, of that Oliver was quite sure. So he finished the bread and made quick work of swallowing down the rest of the milk. He licked a smear of butter that had made its way to his palm as he handed the mug back to Chalenheim.

Some sense of feeling, of balance, returned to him, and Oliver looked at the workmaster with wary eyes. He was at Chalenheim's mercy now, for Chalenheim could throw him back in the refractory room and shut Oliver into the cold, wet darkness, or he could take up the strap that hung from the wall and deliver a beating that would knock Oliver down so hard he would be unable to get up again.

"Stand up now, Oliver, and come along; it's almost time for prayers."

Chalenheim took the towel and wiped Oliver's mouth and

chin with the corner of it. After which, he closed the refractory door, and hung the key on its hook, then turned back to Oliver to clasp the back of his neck. But gently, almost faintly, feather-light, and Oliver had to clench his jaw to keep from crying out. For he had been certain the workmaster's touch would be painful and hard, and the distance between that thought and reality almost undid him.

Chalenheim picked up the candle-lantern to blow it out. This he left, though he picked up the tin mug and the towel, and led Oliver up the stairs, into the passageway, which was almost breezy and warm in comparison to the cellar.

He led Oliver along to the kitchen, where, to Cook's amazed eyes, and the open mouths of the kitchen attendants, of which there were now many, washing up, following Cook's orders, he put the mug and the towel on the long table under the window. Then he took Oliver's jacket from the peg by the table under the window and let go of Oliver long enough to help him into it.

"He's the wretch what took my milk!" shouted Cook, coming forward, her face red. "He fed it to paupers! Why are you letting him out so soon? He should be in there for a week at least!"

Chalenheim pulled Oliver behind him, a steady pull that put the workmaster between Cook and Oliver so she could do him no harm. This act left a strange feeling inside of Oliver, a raw, sharp knowledge that he'd taken a gift from the hands of the devil himself, and that the devil himself was now protecting him. Well, for the moment, Oliver would let him, for Cook was baring her teeth and, if given the chance, would have torn Oliver apart with them.

"The decision as to what punishment is handed out and for how long is mine, and mine alone."

Without even nodding at her to bid her good evening, Chalenheim placed his hand, fingers still lightly gripping, on Oliver's neck and led him out of the kitchen, along the passage, and up the stairs to the boys' dormitory. Oliver's heart was pounding so hard when they reached the top step, where the door to the dormitory was solidly closed, that he could barely breathe.

Chalenheim turned Oliver to face him.

"I want you to listen to me carefully, now," said Chalenheim, placing a hand on either of Oliver's shoulders.

Oliver swallowed, his mouth tasting foul, though he nodded.

"You have been given a time of grace, and whether that lasts only a moment or more than that is up to you."

Those broad hands squeezed Oliver's shoulders now, with some force, making Oliver wince.

"Do you understand what I'm saying? Speak up."

"Yes, sir," said Oliver, hating himself more than he ever had in his entire life, for he'd sold himself for a slice of bread and a drink of milk, and had betrayed everything he thought he stood for. He was more the monster than Chalenheim was, for the workmaster remained ever true to himself, and Oliver had not. He hung his head, and looked at his boots, and moved his toes within his clean, dry stockings. "Yes, sir."

"Very good," said Chalenheim.

He opened the door with one swift pull and guided Oliver into the room where the boys were already in their nightshirts and on their knees, while Mr. Bassler said the evening prayers, as if Oliver's blood was not still embedded into his knuckles.

But what did that matter when there was Jack, arrayed like a pauper in a laundry-yellowed nightshirt, on his knees, hands clasped for prayer as he lifted his head. His expression upon seeing Oliver was as if the brightest angel had stepped into the room, and it was all Oliver could do not to quail and cower and turn back, to beg Chalenheim take him back to the refractory room, rather than have to face Jack and admit what he had done.

Chalenheim was having none of this, for he guided Oliver directly to Jack, and halted Oliver with a tug on his neck before releasing him, for Oliver was Jack's as ever he had been and even Chalenheim, of all people, knew it.

Jack stood up and welcomed Oliver with open hands and

arms, but there was puzzlement on his face as Chalenheim spoke words that Oliver did not understand, nor had the wits to figure out.

"Put him to bed and remember, I keep my promises."

❧

"GET INSIDE THIS INSTANT. GIVE ME THAT BUCKET AND GET IN line."

It was easier to follow orders than to do anything else and, besides that, it was done now. There was nothing Jack could do, even if he wanted to. So he got in line, at the end, two by two, though he was alone, because Nolly was in the refractory room, and Jack had no one to pair with.

˙They marched up the stairs, and Mr. Bassler shouted out orders for them to get ready for prayers and bed. Jack went to his bed, took down his nightshirt and changed into it, grateful for the moment to hang his damp clothes on the peg and to get out of his wet boots and stockings to arrange them beneath the bed. And to get in line to wash his face and hands. It was all so simple, really, if you just did as you were told.

Mr. Bassler told the boys to get on their knees for evening prayers, and they did, waiting in that pose while he rattled through the words, keeping their heads bowed until he was finished. Just as prayers were over, Mr. Bassler stepped back, and Workmaster Chalenheim stepped through the door, with Nolly in tow.

Jack froze where he kneeled, as if Nolly had caught him in the ridiculous act of being an obedient, pious pauper, hands clasped for prayer, amidst a small sea of paupers in their night-shirts, doing as they were told. Jack's face grew hot, with that, and the memory of being glad Nolly had gotten punished, but as Chalenheim and Nolly came closer, he tucked that away.

Nolly's nose had bled down his chin, though his mouth was clean. The blood dried to dark brown on his shirt, his collar rucked, the side of his face dark with a large bruise. And yet he walked as if mindless, and Jack stood up, throwing every other thought aside as Chalenheim handed Nolly over to him, actually taking Jack's hand and placing it on Nolly's arm.

"Put him to bed," said Chalenheim, his eyes level and serious as he looked at Jack. "And remember, I keep my promises."

Chalenheim stepped out into the passage, taking Mr. Bassler with him as he nodded at the boys that they should get into bed. Which they did, silent as ghosts, while Jack sat Nolly down on the bed, knelt at his feet, and began unlacing his boots. His hands were shaking so badly he almost couldn't manage it, but then he felt Nolly's hands touch his hair and he stopped, the laces curling between his fingers, to look up.

"It's all right, Jack," said Nolly as he took one hand to scrub at his mouth, where little, almost invisible flecks of dried blood dropped on his shirt. It was obvious he'd been hit hard enough to bleed, but someone had taken a cloth and cleaned him up a bit before bringing him back to Jack. "Will you say it for me now? Will you?"

He knew what Nolly wanted him to say, and this steadied Jack as nothing else had that day. He nodded and finished unlacing Nolly's boots, and pulled them off. The stockings and the boots were bone dry, for all that Nolly's skin above his ankles was chilly beneath Jack's fingers. As Jack stood up, he pulled Nolly to his feet, vaguely aware of the candle burning in the sconce by the door, and of the paupers in the room, all still in their beds, trying not to stare and failing.

"Up you get, now. Let me have this off you," Jack said.

He tugged Nolly's jacket and shirt off him, and dressed Nolly in the dry nightshirt. Nolly's shoulders twitched where Jack touched him, the bruises on his arms dark. In the low light, Jack tugged the nightshirt into place before lifting it to undo Nolly's trousers, for he'd be damned if he gave anybody a view, however brief, of that fine backside.

Nor, even if he could admit it only to himself, could he bear to catch more than a glimpse of the welts and black and blue stripes that Chalenheim had left behind with his strap and his cane. There were more bruises, long ones that wrapped around Oliver's ribs, turning his whole back black and blue. These were not marks from the workmaster, but from someone else, one of the attendants who had taken Oliver to the refractory room and beaten him.

When Jack had Nolly to rights, Nolly standing so still beneath his ministrations, Jack cupped Nolly's face in his hands. "It'll get better by-and-bye, you know it will. Now let's wash you up."

It was easier to tend to Nolly than to examine what blackness lurked inside of himself. He took Nolly to the washstand and used the last of the water to wipe the sweat from Nolly's forehead and give him a drink of water straight from the pitcher.

At the end of this task, Chalenheim came back into the room, carrying a candlestick in his hand. He paused to look at Jack and what he was doing before he snuffed out the candles in the sconces. Leaving only the room's shroud to shelter Jack from prying eyes as he led Nolly to the bed, and urged him to get into it with both hands, before crawling in next to him. Nobody needed to be witness to him drawing Nolly into his arms, though he knew Chalenheim could see it plain as day.

He watched with careful eyes as Chalenheim walked past the rows of beds, checking on his charges. He spared Nolly and Jack no more nor no less a single glance than the others, but Jack could feel his consideration, even as the light of the candle danced past them, and Chalenheim went into the other room to check on the younger orphans before finally going into his own room to shut the door behind him.

With the metallic snick of the door latch echoing into the dark, Jack let himself take a full breath. He rolled to face Nolly, wanting to sweeten him with small kisses, wanting to distract him, for surely Nolly would have questions about what Jack had said to Chalenheim that morning.

"I don't understand it, Jack," said Nolly, as he leaned into the fold of Jack's arms. "I don't understand what just happened."

"Well," said Jack, putting a smile into his voice. "You were pretty bold, I must say, feedin' all them orphans that way you did."

"No, no, that's not it." Nolly ducked his head, curving himself beneath Jack's chin, as though he wanted to crawl inside of Jack. "It was what happened after."

Nolly's arms were around him now and he was hanging on so hard that for a moment it occurred to Jack that Chalenheim had gotten to Nolly after all. Jack tugged at Nolly's wrists to pull him back, keeping their bodies under the gray blanket, but tucking himself down so he could feel Nolly's breath on his cheek.

"What happened after?" Jack's heart began to speed up, fear filling him.

From one of the windows there was enough light, and Jack's eyes had adjusted to the dark, so he was able to see the gleam of Nolly's eyes, the hard curve of his cheekbone. But only that. The rest was in shadow.

"In the refractory room, they take off your shoes and stockings to make you docile. It's so cold there, Jack, but I couldn't move from the stone bench, couldn't bear to put my feet on that damp floor. You have to sit up to keep your feet warm, do you see?"

Jack nodded, though the punishment was more barbaric than he would have thought possible.

"I was only there for a little while, when Chalenheim came and opened the door and bade me to come out."

Now Jack's heart felt as though it had stopped in his chest, a large, icy rock that might explode through his ribs at any moment.

"What happened, Nolly? What happened?"

He realized he was almost clutching at Nolly now, for one of Nolly's hands came up to gentle him, and Jack let go.

"He made me sit down and rubbed my feet dry with a towel,

a soft one. Then, while he pulled my stockings on my feet and did up my boots, and he gave me—"

Nolly pulled away, turning away, as though to roll on his back so he wouldn't have to look at Jack while he told what happened. But Jack couldn't let him go, so he looped his arm around Nolly's waist, and petted him amidst the linen of his nightshirt. He pulled the blanket up close beneath Nolly's chin, for Nolly was shivering now, fine tremors that rippled down from his shudders.

"What did he give you, Nolly?"

"He gave me new milk to drink and a slice of fresh bread. From the oven. It was still warm. It had butter on it"

"Nolly." Jack didn't know what to say, couldn't understand what any of it meant.

"I drank the milk, Jack. I ate the bread. While everyone around me is starving, my belly is full because I couldn't turn it down. Couldn't turn him down."

Jack had a reprieve, then, which he'd not thought possible. Nolly had forgotten what Jack said in the oakum room that morning, on account of the unexpected gift from the workmaster. If he remembered it later, then Jack could say he had forgotten and whatever was Nolly going on abou, right?

He cupped his hand over Nolly's brow, feeling in the dark to push his hair back, moving down to pet Nolly's temple, then to slide down his neck, holding him in his other arm, holding him so close that he could feel Nolly flinch where Jack held him too tightly. He loosened his hold enough to hear Nolly sigh and felt Nolly rest his head on Jack's chest.

"I'm sorry, Jack, I couldn't refuse him, couldn't spit in his face, as I ought to have done. I was just too hungry."

"It's all right, Nolly," said Jack. He felt hollow again as he pet Nolly along the length of his back. He kept his touch to Nolly's off side, as the bruises and marks were on his near side, and Jack didn't want to spring those to life, as it was probably a nasty jar every time Nolly took a breath. "I would have done the same," he said now, kissing the top of Nolly's head. "Anybody would have."

"Would they, Jack?" The question came out a small whisper, as Nolly was so ashamed of himself he could barely stand to ask it. "Would you?"

"They would," said Jack as firmly as he knew how. "I would. Anybody would. Don't you worry. You just think about those wee boys that you fed tonight. There was such a confusion after you left. Why, I do believe that most of them got second helpin's. You should be very proud of that, you should."

Nolly huffed under his breath, and Jack took it to mean that the thought was a good one, and another fine distraction from Chalenheim's real goal in all of this.

"Got a charge out of watchin' you like that," said Jack now, resting his cheek on the top of Nolly's head. "Is that wrong, then? Bein' proud of how you fought back? Seein' that left hook of yours strike out like a bolt of bloody lightnin'?"

"No," said Nolly, and Jack thought he could hear the small smile in Nolly's voice. "But I don't understand why everything I do falls apart, almost from the moment I conceive of it. Like feeding the young ones, which all came to naught."

"No, it didn't," Jack said, insisting this, his voice rising in the dark. He licked his lips and lowered his voice. "All of them have full bellies now, thanks to you. They got somethin' to eat, you let off some steam, I got to watch."

He waited for this to sink in, thinking that now would come the question about Jack's declaration to Chalenheim, or some recrimination as to why Jack hadn't joined in the fray in the dining hall.

"Jack?"

"Yes, Nolly?"

"What's a left hook? You've said before that I have one, but what is it?"

Jack smiled for real, his shoulders relaxing as he rolled back on the pillow, taking Nolly with him a bit so Nolly could curl against him.

"Oh, my sweet boy, a left hook is what you got when you're lashin' out like you do. You're a natural. That punch comes straight from your shoulder, an' down the other fellow goes before he even knows what hit him. If I had any money, I'd bet on that left hook every time."

"Like you would a boxer, Jack? Me?"

"Indeed yes," said Jack, and now his body had relaxed enough to where he could yawn and feel the hunger in his belly. It was better, also, with Nolly so distracted, and the troubles of tomorrow feeling so far away. "Bet a fiver on you, if I had it. With a street bet, it'd be double or nothin' an' I'd have ten pounds inside of a moment."

He felt Nolly twitch against him, as if a thought had occurred to him, only he was holding back for some reason. Jack went over in his head what he'd just said, and felt the small chuckle rumble up from inside of him.

"O' course I can multiply in my head. Fagin taught me. You had to know what your cut was of that day's take an' keep track. He was always on about keepin' track of money."

"Oh," said Nolly.

Jack allowed himself to feel a little bit of pride now that Nolly had found out what Jack could do. Like when Nolly discovered that Jack could read. The expression in his voice wasn't amazed, more, it was as if the world had turned at a different angle, and he was doing his best to adjust to that. Never once had he declared, as anybody else might have, that reading was too good for the likes of a street thief such as Jack Dawkins. Instead, he seemed pleased at this new discovery.

And whether it was from the arrogance of discovering that Jack was more like him than Nolly had previously thought, or from determining how useful this newly discovered skill might be, Jack didn't really care. It was better to keep Nolly on his toes a little bit, from time to time. This kept him sharp, kept his senses from being dull, which would keep him safe if Jack wasn't around. Which he would be, for always, for how could he give this up?

This feeling of possessiveness came upon him as Nolly settled against him, using Jack's chest for a pillow, his arms around Jack as Nolly's body relaxed into sleep. This kind of trust could not be bought nor traded for, it could only be given. Would that Jack still had that trust, when and if the day ever came that Nolly found out about the type of lad Jack was. Jack hoped he never would.

But it was time to sleep now, and Nolly was almost already there, warm and still in Jack's arms, trusting Jack to take him into the dark. Trusting Jack to look out for him, in case Chalenheim changed his mind and came out of his room in the dark, carrying his candle, and took Nolly—but he wouldn't.

If Chalenheim wanted to, he could have taken Nolly to his room instead of warming Nolly's feet with his own hands, feeding him out of the stores of the kitchen larder. That would have been his moment, and he would not have hesitated to take it if he'd wanted to. Of that Jack could attest.

He shifted on the mattress to reach down to scrape at the rash on his thigh, wondering that Chalenheim had not commented on it, though he probably knew it was there. But men like that, they liked a bit of the rough trade, of boys not quite schooled in the finer arts of manners suitable for a front parlor. Wanted boys like Jack, with grit beneath their nails, their knuckles begrimed with dirt from the street. Which was fine with Jack, for that would keep Chalenheim from ever even considering Nolly for what he wanted from Jack. Jack would stop washing at the basin each night, if that was what was called for, and hang what Nolly might have to say about it.

Jack closed his eyes and gave Nolly's shoulders one last squeeze, pulling the blanket up as far as need be so Nolly could still breathe, and the warmth of their bodies could combine beneath the blanket. As he fell asleep, he thought he might have heard someone crying in the dark, but then it stopped, and he made himself forget about it.

There would always be orphans crying somewhere, but as long as he could keep Nolly safe, he couldn't let himself care about it. For as he had told Nolly, he could not save the world, only his little corner of it.

❧ 17 ❧

AFTER BEING RESCUED FROM
REFRACTORY

When he opened his eyes, Oliver knew he would not be able to move any muscle in his body without aid. That Jack was half on top of him again did not matter as the warmth of Jack's body was a comfort against his skin, but it could not reach the ache that went up and down his entire body, starting with his jaw and ending at his ankles. It might be amusing in another lifetime, if he didn't have more of the same coming at him that day. Every day. As long as he remained in the workhouse.

Jack had been right on the first day, of course he had. They couldn't stay in the workhouse because the magistrate in June was sure to find them both guilty and either hang them or deport them. Either way, they would be separated forever.

All of these thoughts raced around in his head as he struggled to lift his hands to pet Jack's arms, to wake him without startling him, because the bells of the churches in town were beginning to ring, and the workhouse bell, also. Jack liked to take his time waking up, so it was important he started now so he could finish before Chalenheim got up and came out of his room and determined that Jack was nothing but a laggard, and any deals Jack had made with him would be canceled completely.

"Jack," said Oliver, but it was too late. The bell rang out over the walls of the workhouse, and Chalenheim, as if he'd been primed for this very signal, marched out of his room and began shouting for the orphans to get up and to be quick about it, or he'd be doing more than shouting.

Obliging in an unexpected way, Jack lifted his head and scrubbed at his eyes in that way he had, his forelock a short, dark swirl on his forehead, which Oliver indulged himself by sweeping away with the edge of his hand.

Of course they must pull apart now, before anybody caught them, though the two boys who shared the bed next to theirs had surely seen, but would not know what it was they were seeing. Still, they were being unwise to cuddle as they were.

Sadly, Oliver pushed Jack away from him as if Jack were an annoyance, and swung his feet to the floor. He curled his toes on the ice-cold floorboards and wished with all of his heart for some of Mrs. Heyland's willow bark tea, for his pounding head, the stiffness of his neck, the entire soreness of his body that thumped and thrummed with the pulse of blood below his skin. Even if she was bound to refuse him merely upon the principle of who he was. Who Jack was.

Sitting next to him, his naked knees poking up through his nightshirt, Jack regarded him.

"You look like hell, Nolly," said Jack.

"I know," said Oliver. "Just get dressed."

"An' stand in line," said Jack.

"Yes, and stand in line."

Being obedient had taken Oliver as far as it could. Chalenheim had singled Oliver out every day, though for what reason Oliver could not hope to fathom. Yet the workmaster had rescued him from the damp darkness of the refractory room for a supposed deal with Jack. Which might be why Chalenheim, striding up and down the room to make sure no pauper took the time to do so much as yawn before getting dressed, never even looked at Oliver and Jack.

Of course they must join the line, but it didn't look like Chalenheim was going to punish either of them for being at the end of it.

They got dressed and made the bed together. Jack helped Oliver with the laces on his boots because he was simply too stiff to bend over that far, for his shoulders throbbed and his waist wouldn't let him do that and breathe at the same time. Finley and one of the other little boys, when Chalenheim's back was turned, came over to Oliver, looking up at him as though he hung the moon.

"Thank you for the supper," said Finley. The other boy, who was missing one of his teeth, which showed as he smiled, nodded and clasped Finley's hand, as if he were afraid of Oliver, and was using Finley as his lifeline.

"You're welcome," said Oliver.

He felt a warmth rush through him that eased the soreness a little, and made him feel good for the first time since they entered the workhouse. Pride was a sin, of course, but just for a moment, he felt it, and saw Jack smiling at him, for Jack saw nothing wrong in pride, nothing at all.

Then Chalenheim turned around, and the paupers jumped, and Jack and Oliver got in line. When they were in line, Chalenheim ignored them still, though Oliver felt the level of his attention was as quick and sharp as it had ever been, as if he were merely pretending not to lie in wait for either of them to do or say anything impertinent, let alone downright disobedient.

But Oliver was bewildered by his near miss with the refractory room, and how, with Chalenheim's dismissal of Cook's complaints, the exorbitant crime of feeding paupers had just vanished. The stealing of milk and butter and sugar, surely worth at least a week in the refractory room, was written off somehow. For some reason.

That it had to do with Jack's trading obedience for Oliver's safe passage was the reason, of course, but nothing in Oliver's mind could convince him that Jack's behaving himself carried the same weight as what Oliver had done in the kitchen, in the dining hall. The small meal of bread and butter and milk. None of it made any sense.

The brown snake of boys made its way down the stone stairs and into the boys' dining hall, where Mr. Bassler and Mr. Louis stood on either side of the cauldron, their dun-colored aprons clean and starched and firmly in place. Though Oliver was at the end of the line next to Jack, the attendants seemed to espy him coming through the doorway, and their faces were dark with unexpressed anger.

Had they been able to get him in a dark corner, he was sure he would get another thrashing, yet, as he knew, Chalenheim had called off Cook, so he'd probably told Mr. Bassler and Mr. Louis that Oliver was not theirs to discipline. Which only left Chalenheim, which was a shoe that would be very loud when it dropped.

Oliver kept his body some distance from them as he stepped up to receive his serving of gruel and was, begrudgingly, it seemed, given a chunk of brown bread, just as everyone else had been. As Mr. Louis grunted when he gave the bread to Oliver, it was obvious it would have been his preference to cut Oliver's rations off entirely, had he been able. Oliver lifted his chin, an insulting salute he was not afraid to give them. They couldn't hurt him after all; at least not for now.

Still, when he sat down, his whole body hurt from the movement of walking, from stopping the movement and sitting down. Even taking a breath hurt his ribs.

Bending his head for the prayer before the meal strained his neck in a way that got his head pounding, but he clenched his teeth against this, so as not to worry Jack. That is, overly much, for as soon as Jack dropped his clasped hands, his expression as he looked at Oliver, the raised eyebrows, the frown of concern, meant Jack was watching him, knowing he must be in pain and wanting to do something about it, even though there was nothing.

The gruel, meanwhile, was as thin and gray as it ever had been. Oliver stirred it about with his spoon, thinking he'd never gotten a taste of yesterday's porridge.

"Was it any good?" asked Oliver. "Yesterday at supper?"

"Oh," said Jack, obliging Oliver with a smile. "Hell, those boys, they swallowed it so fast that it couldn't be taken from them. I saw them, pattin' their bellies afterward, an' lickin' their lips. I had some as well, an' it was very sweet an' thick. Like the porridge you said Mrs. Pierson used to make."

This offhanded compliment pleased Oliver; his skin shivered with it, thinking about the haberdashery, and the pleasant warmth of the kitchen. And all that food.

Well, he'd enjoyed it when he had it, so at least that was something. But the memory of then, that kitchen, made the current bowl of thin, watery, undercooked oats an unpalatable substitute. Oliver made himself eat it anyway, and the dry bread, and the water from the tumbler that tasted as though it had been poured from a pitcher whose bottom was coated with old moss.

With breakfast over, the boys were led into the oakum-picking room where, at the doorway, Oliver halted, falling back on his heels, bumping into Jack.

"Steady on," said Jack, his hands on Oliver's waist.

"Keep moving," said Workmaster Chalenheim, and for the first time that day, Oliver was not invisible. The workmaster was looking directly at him as he took down the switch from the pegs on the wall and swished it in the air, where it made a snapping sound.

There was no avoiding the oakum-picking room, for it was where he was bound, with Jack right behind him. Oliver swallowed against the dryness in his throat, the surface of his skin prickling with the thought of Chalenheim calling him to the front of the room again. Which he would, he surely would, for this was his room, and he was the master of his domain.

As Chalenheim closed the door, the snap of the wooden door

against the doorjamb felt like a blow, and Oliver jumped. He saw Chalenheim smirking at him, and Oliver turned away to find his place on the last bench against the wall, fumbling with shaking hands for the basket to settle it next to the pike between his feet as he sat down.

"Everythin' all right, Nolly?" Jack asked, his hands full of a chunk of tarred rope, but idle.

"Yes," said Oliver. He shook his head to clear it, and wanted to push everyone aside and lay down on the bench. "It's just been a very odd day, is all, and it's not even noon."

This made Jack laugh under his breath for some reason, and even though Chalenheim was looking right at them when it happened, he did not do anything about it. That was what made it odd.

It was as if Oliver was beneath some strange canopy of protection and, having been provided by Chalenheim, it was not guaranteed to hold back even the slightest of foul weather. So Oliver did not reply to Jack's feeling of good humor, but instead went to work, grabbing up a hank of sticky, black-streaked rope, and began to press it upon the metal pike.

He toiled for some time, growing stiff along his shoulders where he held himself so still, watching askance as Jack messed about without actually picking any oakum at all, but seemed completely at his ease, and unconcerned that he could be caught out for it.

But just as Oliver was about to say something, he heard Chalenheim shout, and watched as a brown-garbed pauper was hauled up to the front of the room and forced to take his trousers and underdrawers down so that Chalenheim could thrash him.

With the first snap of the cane against bare skin, Oliver allowed himself to look away. He found Jack doing likewise, his eyes focusing on the window over Chalenheim's shoulder where there was nothing to be seen but the slash of gray sky, the silver slurry of rain on the window, and the looming rise of the work-house walls.

The whipping was over before Oliver could draw two breaths, for which Oliver was grateful. Jack seemed grateful as well, for he looked at Oliver as if the small boy had been his dearest own, and he unable to do anything to protect him.

"I'm sorry, Jack," said Oliver, whispering, though he did not really understand what he was apologizing for.

"Me too," said Jack, but he looked as though he were talking about something else altogether, his jawline firmed, as if he were prepared to resist the worst altercation.

The work in the oakum-picking room continued, dulling down to a repetitious pattern of taking the rope, and splitting out the oakum, trying not to spit out the taste when he sucked his fingers into his mouth after the rope or the pike jabbed him. Beside him on the bench, his shoulders slumped, Jack continued not to work very hard, idly playing with the rope instead of making any use of it, yawning at one point, as if completely unconcerned about the repercussions, should Chalenheim determine that making a check of the level of their baskets was his next course of action.

Of course, Chalenheim did this, but only got as far as the end of the first row before pulling out another boy to whip him with the cane, and then again, whipping a boy from the second row. But that was as far as he'd gotten when the noon bell rang, and Oliver got up, grateful as he could ever be that he'd not come under Chalenheim's scrutiny the whole morning.

But he might have been noticed and called to the front of the room, as he had been before, so by the time he was sitting down with his bowl of gruel and hunk of bread, next to Jack, he was as tired from the weight of anxiety over what had *not* happened as if he'd stayed up the entire night and done the work of five.

There was no telling when the dam would break, and Chalen-heim would determine that now was the time to bring Oliver to heel. When he did, and he would, everything would come crashing in and Oliver would find himself in a worse state than a night spent in the refractory room would bring.

He could only eat his dinner and wait for the ax to fall.

~

AFTER THE NOON HOUR, WHEN THE BOYS WERE COUNTED OFF, Oliver found himself, along with four other boys he did not know, and Jack, facing off Mr. Bassler with a queasy feeling in his stomach, as though his dinner were turning into something rotten he'd just eaten. For he was in a narrow passage with few witnesses, and Mr. Bassler could do anything he liked to Oliver, and lie if Oliver said anything about it. Plus, he'd been assigned to the kitchen for the past two days, and was desperately hoping he wouldn't be sent there again to be put in the care of Cook's less than tender clutches.

But Mr. Bassler surprised him, for after he sent the other four boys off on various errands and tasks, he turned to Oliver and Jack, but he was glaring only at Oliver.

"You're not to be assigned to kitchen duty ever, ever again," said Mr. Bassler, his belly puffing up, his face streaked red with his barely held-back rage. And this said as if the loss of this task were something to be mourned over, so Oliver kept his expression suitably solemn. "You are tasked with cleaning all of the grates in preparation for the board's arrival next week."

"Which grates?" Oliver asked, and though the question was an honest one, Mr. Bassler looked as though he wanted to strike him for being impertinent, only he didn't dare, for Oliver was under a cloak of protection, albeit a dark one.

"The men's day room, the men's oakum-picking room off the men's yard, the other workroom off the men's yard, and the oakum-picking room off the boy's yard."

That didn't sound like very many grates to clean, but given that Oliver had never seen smoke from any fire, nor seen the flicker of a fire's warmth in any room he'd been in inside of the workhouse, those grates were probably rusted black and coated thick and would be very difficult to clean.

"Then you're to get coal from the coal store in the cellar and see that a fire is laid in each grate, ready for lighting."

The workhouse was going to put on quite a show for the members of the parish board, to be sure, but while Oliver didn't really want to play a part in that kind of hoax, there was nothing he could do. Besides, if Mr. Bassler was giving instruction to both of them, it meant that they were working together and that would make the taste in his mouth less bitter.

"Me as well, mister?" asked Jack, ever bold and unafraid.

"Yes," said Mr. Bassler, his teeth clenched together as if he'd rather spit at them than agree.

Again, as before, the word seemed to have come down that Oliver was to be spared any discipline, and while this lightened the weight on Oliver's shoulders, he knew he could not count on it. For when Chalenheim's mood changed, and it would, his focus on Oliver would be knife-sharp.

"Here," said Mr. Bassler.

He handed them a box like a carpenter's box, long and with a wooden handle. Inside were a bottle of blacking, a grate brush, a blacking brush, and several cloths. The whole of it smelled like old glue, and Oliver's hands were smudged the moment he took the handle from Mr. Bassler.

"Someone will be by to check on you," said Mr. Bassler, "so you'd best be at it, and don't slack. Those grates need to shine."

"Yes, sir," said Oliver.

As he hefted the supplies, he was beginning to feel a bit of Jack's lackadaisical attitude toward the work, for none but the parish board would appreciate the gleam in the fireplace grates, and certainly none of the paupers would benefit from the warmth of the coal he and Jack would lay, for none of the fires would ever actually be lit.

Of this he was certain, for the only place he'd ever seen an actual glowing fire in a workhouse was in Master Pickering's office. So all the old men, and the old women, and the stick-thin boys, and even the girls, though he'd not seen even a single glimpse of one, would remain cold, hunched over their bowls of gruel in this remorselessly daunting place.

For a moment, Oliver ground his teeth together, thinking of it, unable to stem the tide of fury making its way up his chest, furling hot fingers around his jaw that urged him to do something about it. To hurl the box of supplies at Mr. Bassler's retreating back and hang the consequences.

But Mr. Bassler went through the doorway that would lead him toward the front of the workhouse, perhaps with the intent of going to the boy's workroom to see what stories of Oliver's wrongdoing he might carry to the other assistants and, eventually to Chalenheim, so he was too far away and beyond Oliver's reach. What's more, he felt Jack's fingers on his wrist, a slight touch that sent shivers up his arm, making the hair on the back of his neck prickle.

"Nolly, dear," said Jack, speaking as if he knew why Oliver had set his shoulders, and why he was still looking at the door at the end of the passage. "We won't work hard, just make a show of it, right? You an' me? It ain't so bad, long as we're together."

Jack wanted Oliver to stay calm, and while it might have been that from anybody else this sentiment would have only served to ramp him up further, coming from Jack, it had the opposite effect, as it did, because it came from Jack.

"I am always stronger when I am with you," said Oliver, looking directly at Jack. At his pale face grown thin beneath the tangle of his dark hair, at those brilliant green eyes that the workhouse had not yet been able to dim.

Jack grunted, looking pleased, his mouth curling up in the corners, as if he were unable to hide his pleasure as he might have done. Hiding it behind something else, in that way that he'd had at the Three Cripples, or even in Lyme. But here, when so much of them had been stripped away, Jack's ability to hide behind it became rather less hiding than deferring, as if that type of statement had no place being made in the dank, narrow passageway of a workhouse but he could not help himself.

But Oliver knew better.

"You are my strength," he said, curling his fingers around the back of Jack's neck to hold him still for a quick, soft kiss.

As he drew his hands away, his fingers had left smudges, like four commas drawn across Jack's skin.

"I'm sorry," he said, though it was foolish to be concerned about it because not only was there no place to really wash, Jack never seemed to mind the dirt.

"Let me carry that," said Jack, his voice gruff, taking the tool box, clenching his fist about the handle. "Fuck, there's only one of each tool in here, an' we can't both be at them grates at the same time."

"You carry," said Oliver, moving to go through the doorway to the men's day room, letting Jack hide the flush of color on his cheeks with bluster and movement. "And I'll clean the grates, I don't mind."

The men's day room was as wide as the boys' dining hall, but longer, separated about two-thirds of the way down by a doorway that had no actual door, but perhaps served to separate the room into two areas for different activities. What activities those might be, Oliver had no idea, for there were only a few tables against the wall, an array of mismatched chairs, and absolutely no books to read or ornaments to look at. Only the pale drudge-brown walls and the scuffed wooden floor.

The light from the rain-spattered windows on both sides only served to accent the gloom and the stillness of the room where the older paupers might sit when at their leisure. Except they never seemed to get any.

Along one of the walls was a fireplace with a gray, choked grate, as if there had been fires in it once, but so long ago the ash had turned to stone. The other fireplace at the end of the room was in the same condition, with signs of rust along the tips of the grate's ribs.

Oliver swallowed the feeling of futility that the work they did here would make no difference, and resigned himself to doing it anyway. Him instead of Jack, for the work meant nothing to Jack, and would give Oliver's hands something to do besides clench in rage.

As Oliver put the tool box down in front of the fireplace along the inside wall, Jack obliged him by getting a chair and plunking it down, and then himself in it, backwards, with his arms along the chair's back so he could watch Oliver toil away. And this Oliver did, thinking back on how the maids in the townhouse had done this task when he'd been in his room and too lazy to leave while they tended to it. Or how the girl at the haberdashery had done it, though she had been sullen, and Oliver had too many thoughts in his head to follow her slovenly example.

First, he needed to cart out the ash, then he needed to scrub the grate with the wire brush. Then he would polish the grate with the blacking and wipe it down with the cloth. At the end of this, he would be black with coal dust clean up to his elbows.

"Hand me that—never mind," said Oliver. He grabbed the bucket and, using his bare hands, moved the cool chunks of frosted-hard ash into the bucket, bit by bit, the gray ash turning to powder and flying about his head, until the last of it could be sieved away between the bricks beneath the grate.

"I could help," said Jack with a sigh.

But as he was about to get up, Oliver sat back on his heels and waved him away.

"I told you I don't mind. This'll keep my mind off it."

"Off what exactly?" Jack asked this, as if he didn't know, though his voice sounded a bit strained.

"Off this place, of you and me being here, of needing to get out."

There was no point going over why that was so important, so

Oliver shook his head and returned to kneeling in front of the fireplace, taking up the wire brush to scrub the grate.

"An' when we do get out," said Jack, shifting to a more comfortable position in the chair, his chin resting on the backs of his hands. "Tell me, then, about your bookshop. I know you want to own one, but you never tell me what it's like. You c'n tell me now, right?"

"Oh, I could indeed," said Oliver with a little half of a laugh. "But I'd bore you insensible after about a moment of it."

"No, you wouldn't," said Jack, sitting up, his hand to his heart as if he were truly wounded to be so thought of. "You wouldn't, I swear it."

"Besides," said Oliver now, shaking his head, "you truly don't deserve to be witness to the argument in my head as to whether the door should be green or blue."

"Oh, blue, for certain, blue."

Oliver shifted so he could look over his shoulder at Jack, uncertain as to why Jack was so adamant, when those sorts of details had often seemed beyond his reach of interest.

"Why blue?"

"Oh, it'd be the color of your eyes, that door," said Jack, and while his tone sounded teasing, the look on his face was fond as he tilted his head to one side, as if seeing the door before him. "We'd get all sorts of patrons wantin' to come through it."

"We?" asked Oliver. He took up the wire brush again, scrubbing down the length of the spines of the grate and then across them, hearing the high scraping sound of wire against metal, gritting his teeth against it. "Would we own this bookshop together, then?"

Jack paused, and when Oliver turned to look at him, his eyes flicked away from Oliver's gaze, seeking the wall as if it offered refuge to his thoughts.

"I'd help out now an' then," said Jack, as slow and as careful as if he were delivering unpleasant news. "But it'd kill me to be cooped up like that, to wear an apron an' dance when I'm told to dance. Stuck indoors all the time like that?"

Concentrating on getting all of the burnt-on fingers of ash off the grate, Oliver thought about this a moment. To him, being indoors and safe from the weather, in some snug little shop, where perhaps they could—

But he stopped and, clearing his throat, spoke his thoughts out loud instead. For Jack.

"Of course, you could come and go as you liked, or you could sit in front of the fire and smoke your pipe and read."

"A fireplace? In a bookshop? Ain't never seen nothin' like that."

Oliver smiled at the tone in Jack's voice that was obviously meant to get Oliver all embroiled in the details of his story, even though Jack had probably never been in more than one bookshop in his life, and then only to steal something for Oliver to read.

"Indeed, there is, at least in my bookshop there will be one in the front, crossways from the front door. There'll be another one in the back room, as well, where our patrons can linger over their books. Perhaps we'll serve them coffee while they sit at a fine, round wooden table, because there's a kitchen where we can make the coffee, upstairs in our little bedsit over the shop."

"Our little bedsit," said Jack.

Jack was silent for a good long while after that, perhaps entertaining the notion of how nice it might be to reside in a cozy place where only he and his Nolly lived. Or perhaps he was contemplating what it would mean to have a place like that, where the shop below the bedsit earned them their living, and in which nothing was stolen or paid for with money fenced from stolen goods.

That was not Jack's way, but the silence told Oliver that at least Jack might think about it, and want to share in Oliver's domestic dream. Or perhaps it was too staid a way of living, being in one place all the time, cooped up in four walls. It might make him uncomfortable enough to leave, so Oliver changed the subject.

"As for the books," he said, reaching for the blacking brush and the bottle of blacking, "I've heard there are book auctions in London, you know, near Tottenham Court, I think. I could go alone, but I'd rather have your company."

"Go with you for that," said Jack. "Sure I would."

"We'd have to get a line of credit to be able to bid, but, with my inheritance, that shouldn't be too hard."

"What books would we get, then?" asked Jack.

This was the bliss of it, this list, which had been tucked in the back of Oliver's mind lo these many years. He already knew the kinds of books he wanted.

"Adventure books," said Oliver, "like *Gil Blas* or *Robinson Crusoe*. And the one you stole for me at the Three Cripples, *The Arabian Nights*, that was a good one that we never got to finish. And *The Castle of Otranto*, which I've heard is rather scary. And poetry, of course, some sonnets, the ones you love so well."

"An' a copy of that book you was readin' out to me in Lyme," said Jack. "The one about the old man and the sailor."

Oliver could almost feel Jack nodding his emphasis, in complete alignment with this particular choice of Oliver's. "Well, yes, of course, that book. We'll have several copies of that one. It will display prominently in the window each day."

"Will it sell, d'you think?" asked Jack. "Bein' as it's about a foreign sailor doin' all them illegal things."

Of course, Jack was teasing; the book had clearly been about more than that, it had been about revenge and love. Spread out as those ideas were amongst the danger, and the remorse, the guilt, and the loss, the more sophisticated theme tended to get lost amidst the swagger of the story. Though, to be honest, he knew Jack could well understand it, were he to have it explained to him.

Oliver paused in his scrubbing and scraping to sit back once more on his heels, his hand that held the spiky wire brush resting against his knee, to look back at Jack. Expecting a smile, or some added appeal from Jack for more books like that one, ones about smuggling, and highwaymen, and Jack Sheppard, the most famous and daring highwayman of all who had escaped Newgate only to be caught and hanged in the end. Those were the types of books Jack would want, and Oliver would agree that those would be exciting books, ones that people would want to buy—

Only when he turned to look at Jack, Jack was looking out the window, as if he were alone in the room with his thoughts. Sitting quite still, his chin resting on his hands along the back of the chair, gazing through the bull's-eyed panes at the sheets of rain in the yard, as if he'd never seen the sight of it before. As if that particular view was so engaging it had absorbed all his thoughts, every movement, as if the liveliness of his spirit was so solidly encased in pauper brown that he could not move.

"Jack?" asked Oliver. "What are you looking at? What do you see?"

That wasn't the actual question he wanted to ask, but something had turned his tongue a different way. Perhaps what had stayed the question was the unease he felt at seeing Jack so still, and not really listening to him, though he chided himself that Jack did not have to focus only upon Oliver every moment of every day.

This, however, felt different than Jack being merely distracted, so Oliver shifted to his knees, and rose up as if he might shuffle forward on them, toward Jack to touch his face and bring him back from where he was. Though to bring him back to the men's day room was quite an unkind thing to do, so Oliver was loath to do it.

But Jack drew himself up and saw Oliver there, on his knees, with the wire brush in his hands that he held as though it were a scepter.

"Is everything all right, Jack? You look quite—"

"Quite what?" asked Jack, as if this were a conversation about someone else entirely.

"Quite worried, I think," said Oliver. "We'll get out of here before the court sessions in June, you'll see. I've not been thinking about how, as I've been distracted, but I'll think about how we'll manage that, I will. So you're not to worry."

"Ain't worried," said Jack, "'cause I know that together we'll manage it, an' we'll manage this, you'n I." He made a gesture with his hand that drew a line in the air between them. He said it more as if he hoped it was true, rather than he actually believed it.

"Of course we will, Jack," said Oliver. "If only you will tell me what's troubling you. Besides us being in here, I mean." He meant it as a little joke, but it seemed to make Jack cross, for he frowned and looked out the window again, scraping his cheek across the rough, brown sleeve of his jacket.

"There's nowt wrong," said Jack, almost mumbling. "Nowt wrong w'me or with anythin'."

That wasn't strictly true, but Jack's attention was truly gone now, and the pleasure of their conversation about the bookshop had been sucked away by the far more present and immediate situation. If Jack couldn't think of a way out and Oliver couldn't, then there would be no getting out. They'd be brought up before the magistrate, and that would be the last day he'd ever see Jack, for the courts would send Jack one way and Oliver another.

Turning back to the fireplace, Oliver examined the grate and determined it could do with more scrubbing. After that he'd polish it, for he didn't mind the actual work, even if it was for a false purpose, with no real pleasure or warmth at the end of it for anybody.

Still, he worked until the grate was cleaned and polished, getting blacking all over his hands and beneath his fingernails, as he had expected, and Jack began to stir in his chair like an unruly charge who has been left unattended too long. So Oliver determined they should move on, and get coal for the grates later; he could not bring himself to admit to Jack that actually going to the coal cellar to get the coal was making him feel cold deep in his belly.

They took the tools and went along the passage, past the kitchen and scullery and dead room to cross the yard, in the rain, to the men's work room, whose windows were directly across the men's yard from the kitchen. The work room was a single room, such as the oakum-picking room was, with the same low roof and sets of chairs instead of benches, but essentially it was the same. It had only one fireplace, which, again, was choked with ash that was coated with dust, and Jack again dragged a chair to the windows, and sat upon it backwards to watch Oliver work.

"You should be ashamed of me, makin' you do all the work." Jack chewed his lower lip as he mused over this.

"No," said Oliver. "I'm not ashamed. I enjoy your company. Besides, you'd ruin your hands even further with all this gritty dust, and then how would you pick pockets, eh?"

"You don't mean that," said Jack with a wide-mouth grin, making a scoffing sound from the back of his throat. "You'd rather I quit the business, you know it." His eyes glinted green at Oliver as the grin changed into a real smile.

"Oh, I don't know about that," said Oliver, shaking the bottle of blacking to loosen up the hard bits inside. "You wouldn't be you doing anything else."

"That's just 'cause we're in here, ain't it."

"Probably," said Oliver, laughing a bit beneath his words. "But if you were to be taken from me, for any reason, then I'd be alone, and how could I possibly go on?" He looked at Jack through half-lowered eyes, somehow fortified to make such a flirtatious game of it, for, of course, it was a far more serious matter than that. If Jack were to be taken from him, he really did not know what he would do.

"Oh, a fancy man would take you in, for sure, in a heartbeat, ever he gazed upon that face."

"Jack," said Oliver, almost hissing the word. "A *man*? I would never go with another man, let alone a fancy one. A man? Me? Don't be ridiculous."

"Well, I'm a man," said Jack. "And I'm pretty fancy, when I got my own clothes to wear, that I picked out myself."

Of course, that was true, but it was just the idea of it, of being with another man, doing those things that Jack and he had done with someone other than Jack. Jack, in Oliver's mind and in his heart, was just Jack. The idea of *another* man—

"Nolly, don't get all fashed about it. 'Twere only a joke, you see, an' not meant to make your eyebrows do that thing they do when you're put out about somethin'." Jack pointed his finger at his own eyebrow and drew a harsh, back-and-forth line in the air.

"I don't want to be with another man," said Oliver now, feeling his mouth pull down, as if prepared to argue the point to a standstill.

"Only do go on with your housework, would you, an' quit goin' on; it was only a joke."

With a low sigh, Oliver did as Jack asked him and returned to his scrubbing, following it with polishing, using the blacking brush and plenty of blacking to get the grate so glossy, it almost looked new.

"Are you ready?" asked Oliver. "We can move on now."

With a nod, Jack got up, and followed him out the door, taking the box in a gentlemanly fashion to carry it across the yard to the men's oakum-picking room. "We forgot to lay coal."

"You're right," said Oliver, tamping down the rush of fear in his belly. "Let's just do it quickly and get it over with."

❦ 18 ❦

CONTAINING REVELATIONS OF
THE DARKEST SORT

They had been assigned the task of bringing coal to every room the board might choose to visit, and to build an arrangement in each fireplace that looked as though it could be lit and that the warmth from it would spread to the room where the paupers huddled around it.

As Jack followed Nolly down the passage to where the coal was stored, Jack debated saying what a lie it all was. The fireplaces might be lit in the dead of winter, at least Jack hoped so, but now that spring was coming, the cost savings in not having fires all through the workhouse was enormous. Thus their task today was pure folly. At least, as Jack trudged behind Nolly with a large bucket banging against his thigh, the two of them were allowed to work together. At least there was that.

And, so far, nobody had laid a hand on Nolly, not even when Nolly had stumbled in the line for breakfast that morning, knocking right into Mr. Bassler and stepping on his foot. Mr. Bassler had merely waved Nolly to continue on, and that had been that.

Workmaster Chalenheim had been standing next to the cauldron, which Jack felt might have had something to do with Mr. Bassler's restraint. That Chalenheim was looking out for Nolly now, for which Jack was glad. Of course he was. Nobody deserved a little peace and quiet more than Nolly. Not that he could explain to Nolly why he'd been given a reprieve, for the questions that would come from that would be unanswerable.

"What's that, Nolly?" asked Jack, now. He hefted his grip on the bucket and walked a little more quickly to be at Nolly's side.

"So many rooms," said Nolly. "They want coal and built fires in so many rooms."

"Which ones again?"

"Men's oakum-picking room, men's day room, the boys' oakum-picking room, and the other workroom off the yard, whichever one that is."

Jack wasn't surprised Nolly could rattle all of this off, though he was loath to admit he'd not been listening when Mr. Louis had handed them their instructions. At the time, he'd been too amazed and pleased to be with Nolly all the afternoon, which meant he could keep his eye on him to make sure Chalenheim kept his word. Which, perhaps, in light of thinking about it, was why they were paired, so Chalenheim would know that Jack knew Nolly had made it through the day without anybody determining that Nolly needed to be hauled up to the front of the room for another whipping.

"Where are we goin'?" Jack asked.

Nolly was moving so fast as he led the way up the passage that Jack could barely look through the open doors. Though he imagined by the smell that they were passing the scullery and then the kitchen. He could even hear the clang of pots and pans and the low hiss of something cooking. Bacon, maybe. Possibly. Hopefully.

"Cellar," said Nolly, his tone clipped. "That's where the coal store is."

Nolly slowed for a moment, shaking his head, as if remembering where he was and that Jack was there. It might be he was trying to keep his head down, being completely unaware of the fact that, for the moment, there was a protection around him. A flutter of angel's wings all around Nolly that Jack intended should keep fluttering for as long as he could manage it.

Nolly, as confident as if he'd been this way before, and perhaps he had, led Jack to the end of the passage and down a flight of stone steps that seemed to descend into darkness. At the very top of the stairs, Nolly stopped to light a small lantern that was hanging there, a candle lantern such as one might use in a stable.

It occurred to Jack that this knowledge of where the lantern hung, where the matches were to light it, came from something more than a memory from Nolly's childhood about how work-houses worked. But he kept his questions to himself, for as Nolly led the way down the stairs to the stone landing, the cold air swept up at Jack like a slap in the face. It tasted of winter, and coal dust, and a deep stillness that abided no disturbance. He didn't want to go down, but Nolly paused, holding the lantern up to look at Jack.

"Come on," said Nolly, "I'm not afraid of the dark if you are with me."

Jack didn't like it, no, not one little bit, but he couldn't let Nolly go on his own, now, could he. So he pressed his hand against the wall, his palm against the weeping, damp stone, and followed as best he could, the darkness seeming to swallow him up like a mouth. When he reached the bottom of the stairs, he was almost squinting against the brightness of the lantern as it shone against the curved walls, the plaster gleaming in some places, showing a dull patchy greenness in other areas.

"Is that water?" asked Jack.

"It's leaking from the well," said Nolly without hesitation.

"Which well?"

"The well in the men's yard. It's above us, or a little ways more along. But no need to go that far, for this is the coal store."

Standing back so Nolly could unlatch the door to the coal store, Jack's eyes had adjusted to the sparking light of the lantern. Now he could see that the passage against the curved wall went further into the darkness, and that there was another door. It was painted a dull green, like the door to the coal store, but after that the passage ended, and it was difficult to understand what the room was for.

"How do you know the well leaks? Does it leak in that other room there?" Jack lifted the lantern in Nolly's hand to point.

"Yes," said Nolly. "It leaks into that room there." He tugged the lantern out of Jack's hand, picked up his bucket from the floor, and began to enter the coal store.

"Is that the refractory, Nolly?"

Nolly didn't answer him, which meant that the answer was *yes*.

From where Jack was standing, there were no windows to the room, not even a set of bars. Just stone piled on stone till it met the curved ceiling, and that one door. From far away, Jack could hear a slow dripping sound that was the leak from the well in the men's yard. And this was the place they'd sent Nolly, his sweet Nolly.

Jack made his way into the coal store, where the dust hung in a black-gold cloud in the light of the lantern, and Nolly was busy piling chunks of coal in his bucket, using his hands, getting them blackened and dusty.

"Nolly."

"I don't want to talk about it, Jack. I've been in a refractory before and no doubt I'll be in one again. It just doesn't matter. Help me with this coal."

Nolly, crouched down to get at the coal, had his back stubbornly turned to Jack, and though Nolly needed something tender and kind to happen to him, there was nothing more Jack could do than what he already was doing.

Jack didn't imagine Chalenheim would hold back from walloping Nolly again if he or Jack openly flouted the workhouse attendants by not doing their assigned tasks. Jack's time in the men's day room and the men's workroom, where he'd done no work, had been a time unto itself, so Jack needed to work now.

He hunkered down at Nolly's side, echoing Nolly's movements, brushing their shoulders together. After a few more lumps of coal had been stacked in the buckets, he felt Nolly sigh, as if his whole body was relaxing.

Nolly made a shrugging motion that Jack quickly realized was a way for Nolly to pet him a little without getting coal dust all over their clothes that no doubt someone would take objection to and blame them for. Jack shrugged back and, for a moment, they crouched together, their thighs resting on their heels, the light of the candle-lantern sparking gold through the black coal dust, sluggish in the damp air, falling like dark snow, flecking against their skin.

"I'm glad you're here with me, Jack," said Nolly. He turned his head to look at Jack, and perhaps the flash of his temper the night before, and the fact that he'd not been beaten that day, gave him some courage, for his eyes were blue and steady. "I could not bear it if you were not."

"You got it all backwards," said Jack, giving Nolly a hard push with his shoulder. "You're the one that came with me. Remember?"

Ducking his head, Nolly seemed to laugh, a low vibration that went straight to Jack's heart. "Well, yes, that's true, but it seems as though it's actually the other way around. That you're the one who followed me into this hellish place."

"I would, you know," said Jack, feeling the words rush out of him before he could temper them with something more light-hearted. "Follow you into hell."

Jack thought, at that moment, from the quirk of Nolly's brows, that Nolly would ask Jack for more clarification, to get Jack to say more such profound things. He would do that, if Nolly needed him to, but Nolly just nodded, a single jerk of his chin.

"You would, wouldn't you," said Nolly. "I know you would. As would I you."

"You've already done that," said Jack, coughing to clear the thickness in his throat that, were anybody to ask him, came from the coal dust in the air. "Now let's get moving on this afore someone comes down to scold us for lollygaggin'."

Their buckets were filled and Nolly was already standing up, prepared, as if it were his bounden duty to dupe the board into thinking that the paupers were properly warmed all the year round.

Nolly made his way out the door, pausing to latch the door behind Jack, going up the stairs, stopping at the hallway point so they both could catch their breath.

Jack could keep up; his ankle was mostly fine, but his hands, marred by the common work, required that he change the bucket from one hand to the other, and still it was that the handle bit into his palm, pressing the coal dust where he could feel it, black speckles under his skin.

When they came up into the light at the landing, Nolly had black smears on his cheek and Jack knew he must have some as well, though he'd taken such pains to avoid it. And just as he'd thought Nolly would scold him for it, as Nolly was ever so particular about those sorts of things, Nolly blew out the box lantern, hung it on its hook, and turned to Jack, looking as though he was trying not to smile.

"There's nowt to laugh at, is there, Nolly?"

He'd not seen a smile from his Nolly smile for days, years it seemed now, and with them standing in the center of a fortress that would never let them go, it seemed completely out of place, that smile.

"You no doubt will find me foolish," said Nolly and, in spite of the dark smell coming from the cellar, the flat fish odors leaking from beneath the door to the kitchen, in spite of the fact that any amusing thoughts were forbidden, it felt good to hear Nolly talking this way.

"No doubt I will," said Jack with mock solemnity. "But tell me anyhow."

"You look like a smuggler," said Nolly and quite unexpectedly reached up to touch the ends of Jack's hair. "With your forelock falling just like that and your skin, as if you'd dusted it with soot to better hide in the shadows while you wait to haul in kegs of brandy."

"Haven't lost all your fanciful thoughts then, eh?" Jack said this quickly to hide the way it moved him, that his sweet boy hadn't been trampled so much as to destroy all the stories within him. As well, a smuggler was, in Jack's book, and anybody's, he was certain, a very dashing fellow. Full of swagger and daring, and quite a draw for the ladies of less than sterling repute. And, perhaps, the idea appealed to his Nolly as well.

"Was this a book?" Jack moved close in case someone should catch them at their leisure in the passage so at least they would not be overheard. "One you read?"

"Yes, it was," said Nolly, his face brightening, as if he was very pleased to be asked. "It was called *The Rascal of Dover,* and the cover had a painting of a smuggler—he looked like you do just now. It would be a good book to sell in the bookshop, you know—"

Just then, Nolly's belly gave a low growl, reminding them both where they were. Jack knew, though he did not say it aloud, that at this rate, if Nolly was able to open a bookshop, it would be in Port Jackson. If they even made it to the June assizes without starving to death, that was.

But he didn't say it, though he could see the thought reflected in Nolly's eyes as he scrubbed at his forehead with the heel of his hand and pushed the soot even further into his skin and left a black streak there.

"I'm sorry, Jack," said Nolly, looking as abjectly apologetic as he might have been for a far more serious offense. "That was foolish of me to say, in this place."

"What a feisty thing you are," said Jack, daring to lean in close as if for a kiss. "Havin' them dreams of yours in spite of these bastards what keeps us here. Fagin would be proud."

For a moment, Nolly scowled at him, and then he looked as

though he understood. For of course, Fagin approved of having dreams, as long as they were the right sort, where you wanted to be a housebreaker one day, or develop the perfect shell game.

"I'm only messin', Nolly."

"I know," said Nolly. "But he wouldn't be pleased. He'd be yelling that we'd not already broken our way out of here."

"Maybe we should," said Jack, feeling more serious now. "Maybe we should have another go at gettin' out."

It was obvious Nolly had his doubts that any attempt would be successful, but at the same time, he didn't want to believe it would be futile. Jack didn't want to believe it either.

"We'll keep our eyes peeled, just that. See what comes up, eh?"

"Yes," said Nolly. "Now heft that bucket before someone catches us not working."

In the next moment, Mr. Bassler was coming up the passage that led from the center of the workhouse. His brown apron was clean and firmly round over his belly, and he was puffing a bit as he hurried up to them.

"Get on with it, boys. You have at least five grates to do this afternoon, so you better get at it."

Mr. Bassler turned and went back the way he had come, and because Nolly knew his way around, he led Jack out into the yard, where the sun was struggling behind the clouds that seemed to be whipped by an airy hand. At least the air in the yard was fresh, and except for the fact that it blew fragments of bone around in circles, it might have been a fine afternoon. But it was fine anyway, because Nolly was there, and Chalenheim wasn't going to knock him about anymore.

"This is the men's workroom," said Jack, as Nolly walked all the way to the end of the yard, to the last door on the left.

"Yes, it's on the list, right?"

Nolly was inside the door before Jack could think to hesitate, but of course, it was better because Nolly was focused on the task at hand. Of cleaning and blacking the grate and laying coal upon it. He was already halfway across the room before Jack thought to follow him, taking a deep breath and letting it out slowly so Nolly wouldn't hear.

"This grate hasn't seen a fire in a while, I'd say."

Nolly stared at the fireplace, as if it had personally disappointed him. When he looked at Jack, Jack hurried to school his features into something resembling interest. Then Nolly put the box of supplies down and picked up the bottle of blacking to open it. As he shook it, he peered inside of it, squinting with one eye.

"This bottle is empty," he said. "Here, you take this brush." He paused to pick up a square-handled brush that had wire bristles at the end of it. "Take it and give it a good scraping. I'll go fetch some more blacking."

He was off before Jack could suggest that maybe he should go instead of Nolly, because he didn't fancy himself on his hands and knees scraping a grate with a wire brush without Nolly to tease him about it.

For a moment, Jack stood there, flipping the brush in his hand, catching it by the handle. It was easy enough to do that it wasn't amusing after three successful catches, so he hefted it by the handle and knelt down, his knees on the dirty floor, propped up on one hand, and began scraping the grate, just for something to do. The wire bristles made a high scratching sound, but it was satisfying for a moment to feel the old rust and burnt bits of coal coming away, something he was sure Nolly could appreciate.

The door opened behind Jack as he was scraping away, but he didn't turn around, for surely it was Nolly, back so quickly with the bottle of blacking that Jack hadn't even had time to miss him.

"Quite the domestic, aren't you," said Chalenheim.

Jack heard the quick strides and shot to his feet, losing the brush in the fireplace as he moved quickly around the table in the center of the room, trying to get to the door before Chalenheim could get to him. But Chalenheim had caught him off guard, and Jack wasn't quick enough on his feet, though his heart was already racing because he needed to get away from Chalenheim before Nolly came back.

"Where are you going so quickly, Jack?"

Chalenheim was on him in a moment, grabbing hold of Jack's face and pushing him backward until he was flat against the wall by the door.

It was to Jack's shame that his knees were already knocking together, and that even as he squirmed, he couldn't get away from that single handhold. Then Chalenheim let him go, but barred his way by leaning in close, placing his forearms squarely on either side of Jack's head.

"Didn't you make a promise not to resist me? What happened to that promise, then, eh?"

"Mister, you can't be about this now. Oliver's just gone to get some blacking, and you *can't*—"

"He'll be ten minutes or more," said Chalenheim, and Jack could feel the breath from his mouth, so close and smelling like sweet tea.

"No," said Jack, "no, he's quick, he'll be back—"

Chalenheim drew back and hit him, using the flat of his big hand, shocking the breath out of Jack, and a high, startled sound that he was trying to believe didn't come from him. Then he felt his nose start to bleed and tried to wipe it away, but Chalenheim had him pressed against the wall, using the weight of his arm to keep Jack pinned there while he leaned in.

"Thought I might have a bit of you now. What do you say to that, Jack Dawkins?"

"No, *don't*—"

But Chalenheim's hand was already at Jack's crotch, the rough palm of his hand so startling that his cock went hard, the blood rushing from his head, making him breathless, making him unsteady on his feet. Twisting his wrist, Chalenheim rolled Jack's cock through his trousers, and though Jack tried to shift his weight and move away, he was held fast, mouth open, on the verge of begging.

"Come on, now, Jack, you know what this is about. You've done this before, eh? I'll reckon you know plenty of ways you could pleasure a man while standing."

When Jack didn't answer for want of breath, Chalenheim merely smiled.

"Unlike your friend here."

For the door had opened, and Nolly stood there with a full bottle of blacking in one hand, his other hand on the panel of the door where he'd pushed it open.

There was no place to hide, no way to pretend that the tableaux wasn't exactly what it was. Jack wanted to weep. Chalenheim gave Jack's cock another hard pet, then stepped back, tugging on Jack's jacket as though to straighten it, even brushing away a stray bit of coal dust.

"Do us a favor, Jack," said Chalenheim, and he patted Jack's cheek just short of hard enough to leave a bruise. "Don't scrub too well come Saturday night, there's a good boy."

It was obvious, now, why Chalenheim had picked Jack over Nolly, surely the more beautiful one. Chalenheim liked a bit of rough trade, and preferred boys who weren't so clean about their persons. But Jack was sorry the moment he thought it, that he wished Chalenheim had picked Nolly over him.

With a tuneless whistle, Chalenheim shouldered his way past Nolly and out into the yard. Leaving Jack alone in a room so silent and still, he thought he could hear white feathers from angels' wings falling to the floor like snow.

"Jack." Nolly closed the door and put the blacking down on the floor. "What did he mean? What was he doing?"

Jack turned away, grinding his shoulder into the wall, curling over himself, trying to soothe his groin into restfulness, but when he put his hand upon himself, he flinched. He dropped his head, wincing.

"Go away, Nolly, please, just go away."

But Nolly didn't go away as Jack wanted him to. He came up close and put his hand on Jack's shoulder. Jack couldn't bear to look at him.

"Is he telling the truth? That you have an agreement between you?"

"What the bloody fuck am I supposed to say to that?" demanded Jack, half laughing, half growling.

Jack tried to pitch Nolly off him, but the wall was so close that Jack banged his shoulder against it and fell, slamming his knees on the floorboards, sending a cloud of dust up from between the cracks. He folded himself over his knees, neck bared as if for the chopping block, elbows tucked in, all the fury and despair locked up so tightly inside of him that he feared it would rattle him apart.

"He's hurt you, Jack," said Nolly, kneeling down at his side, those strong hands stroking down his arm as if they wanted to draw his hands away from his body, as if Nolly was afraid that he'd do himself harm.

"For fuck's sake," said Jack, snarling. "Leave me with my dignity, at least."

He reached out and, blind to all discretion, slammed Nolly hard in the chest with the flat of his hand, sending Nolly sprawling to the floor.

Jack pressed his hands to his eyes; he could hear Nolly's gasp of breath and knew he must have landed on all those welts and bruises Chalenheim had been so freely handing out. That was Jack's fault as well, that he'd not stopped it before he had, that he'd not come up with a better way to protect Nolly from the hard lessons the workhouse so wanted to teach him.

But then he heard something behind him, and looked to where Nolly was crawling on his hands and knees across the floor, favoring his right side, his eyes as blue as the sky. He reached Jack in a moment, and hunkered down beside him, brushing Jack's shoulder with his own, but not touching him anywhere else.

"Help me to understand. What did he mean you've done this before, were you a—a *whore?*"

The laugh barked out of Jack before he could stop it. He couldn't believe it had come to this: his darkest secret had been buried so deep that not even God Himself could find it, and here Nolly had managed to stumble upon it and was digging it up as easily as if it only needed bare hands to uncover it.

"It's called a rent boy, Nolly, if you must know."

"Were you a rent boy, then? Is that how you know all the things that you know?"

"No!" said Jack, but the words came out so harsh that Nolly drew back from him, so Jack softened his tone. It was too late anyhow to do anything other than tell the truth. "Yes—no. I don't know what I was."

"But you were—*something.*"

It was not a question. Nolly already knew the answer, so Jack nodded, his face feeling stiff from where Chalenheim's hand had held him. His lips were numb, and there was a low hum in his ears, as if from the approach of a far-off storm.

Nolly reached out to touch him, on the shoulder, his hand, his face, but Jack didn't know because Nolly pulled back at the last moment, as if aware, somehow, that Jack couldn't bear his touch, no matter how gentle.

Somewhere inside of him became tender with the faint awareness that Nolly wasn't entirely horrified by this new knowledge about Jack. Though he might become so when he knew the details, Jack had no idea how to make it any less bleak than it was.

"Is this about the promise you made him that day in the oakum-picking room?"

"Don't ask me that, Nolly, please, *please* don't ask me."

"No," said Nolly, nodding a bit. "Not just now. But later, you'll tell me later. Now let me help you up. Let me help you."

Nolly stood up and reached out his hand for Jack to grab onto. This was done as calmly as if they'd been in any street in

London and Jack had merely stumbled and fallen, and Nolly was his friend, holding out his hand. So steady, which was, Jack knew, not what he might have expected from Nolly, who enjoyed lashing out first and considering the matter later.

But the flash-paper temper was nowhere to be seen, and this unsettled Jack so much that when Nolly pulled him to his feet, he was shaking again, his teeth chattering. He half expected Nolly to slap him, to tell him not to be so foolish. To get angry that Jack had lied to him, had kept this from him.

Nolly did none of these things. Instead, as he let Jack's hand go, he stood quite close, but left some space between them that Jack knew was for him to cross if he wanted it. And Jack did, feeling as though ice water had been dumped all over him and had settled in his veins, sizzling and hissing as it melted against the heat of his heart.

"Don't leave me alone," Jack said, ducking his head, almost unable to hear himself over the din in his head. "Stay with me, stay with me, Nolly, please, *promise* me—"

He was shaking all over, his bones rattling with it, when Nolly put his arms around Jack's shoulders and, as sweetly as a dove, pulled Jack to him, embracing him, tucking Jack to him. His hand swept up to push the hair from Jack's hot face, and he felt Nolly kiss him on the cheek.

"I will never leave you, Jack," said Nolly. "Not ever."

But that could not be. It could not last forever that Nolly would stay with him. For at some point, the workhouse would separate them, and Chalenheim would find his moment between now and Saturday night. And then, come that time, after baths had been had, Chalenheim would send for Jack, and he would have to go, lest Chalenheim unfold his strap and beat Nolly with it until Nolly could no longer stand.

Jack would sell his soul for that not to happen.

WHEN THE BOUGH BREAKS

Oliver had jumped back when Jack snapped at him and shoved him on his arse before he could even register what the words between the workmaster and Jack meant. His own hiss of pain came to him as though from far off as his mind whirled. Had he heard it right? Did he understand it correctly?

He got to his feet, pushing himself up with his hands, and stepped forward, his mouth open as Jack curled up on the floor, his arms tucked close to his chest, one hand between his legs, pressing on his groin. Shaken, his face white except for two spots of hectic color and Jack's refusal to meet Oliver's gaze.

As he looked at the evidence before him, Oliver began to understand it all. That Jack's obedience to Chalenheim actually involved Jack having intimate relations with him. Chalenheim was certain Jack knew how to pleasure another man, and Jack had not denied it, which, at least in part, explained how Jack knew all those things, those pleasurable, nighttime things he had shown Oliver and shared with him.

But Chalenheim wanted to use that knowledge to hurt Jack.

All of this churned together in Oliver's head, until he could not quite sort it out, and he grit his teeth, and narrowed his eyes as he struggled his way through it.

The worst of it wasn't that Jack had had other close acquaintances, perhaps even sweethearts, before he'd professed his devotion to Oliver. It was that Chalenheim had been prepared to use Jack for his own purposes and, knowing how fierce the workmaster could be, those purposes would not be pleasant. His hard words directed at Jack, his rough treatment of Jack's person, was proof of that. As if Oliver even needed proof.

What Chalenheim was going to do, come Saturday night, was evil. *Boys get buggered every day,* Jack had once said. Now, finally, inexplicably, Oliver knew what he had meant.

"I'm going after him," said Oliver, his lips feeling numb as he hunkered down next to Jack. "He's not going to touch you. I won't let him lay a hand on you."

The anger, which had no longer been ready to hand in the workhouse, now rose, an animal thing that wanted to roar and race through the workhouse and find Chalenheim, and *tell* him— and *hurt* him—

"Nolly."

Almost his whole body shivered, head to toe, a hum in his ears, the pounding of blood along his jaw, boiling hot behind his eyes. When Oliver looked at Jack, he could barely see him. Jack, who was standing up, getting up, one shoulder curved into the wall as if it were a steadying lifeline, his only one, a wall built to house paupers and keep them obedient and starving, and available for that despicable beast of a man—

"Don't," said Jack, his voice coming from a far-off distance, though Oliver could sense the slight shake of his head. "There ain't no use in it. Them walls are too high, with all the doors locked, with you an' me trapped inside these fuckin' walls. Bloody, *fuckin'* walls."

Struggling to steady himself, Oliver blinked hard, wanting to focus on what Jack was saying, on Jack himself, in this room, where this terrible knowledge, which he'd been hiding as a secret for all the while they'd been in the workhouse, had come to light.

"I'm glad I'm with you," said Oliver, hurrying through the words. "I'm glad I came, so I can protect you from that man, that *monster*—"

"Well, I ain't." Jack said this low in his throat, the words rising to a pitch, to a growl, his whitened lips pulling back from his teeth.

"What?" asked Oliver, astonished. "What, Jack? What are you saying?"

"I wish you'd not come because then he'd have nothin' to hold over me, an' I would have had a chance, a *chance* at least, of sayin' *no* to him. And holdin' to it. 'Stead of givin' in so easy, like I did, on account o' you."

Oliver's jaw dropped, and he felt as shocked as if Jack had slapped him, hard and without warning. He'd been doing everything he could to take care of Jack, he'd turned himself over to the law, hadn't he? Got himself locked up in a workhouse, in the space of a moment, for God's sake, so he could be with Jack. Entered the nightmare to end all nightmares. In a moment of loyalty to Jack. Who now was rejecting all of that, as if turning away this veriest act of fidelity, as if turning away Oliver's *love* because the winning of it had gained him nothing but pain.

He took a breath, his eyes clear now and focused on Jack, still half-curled against the wall. Ready at Jack's slightest twitch to lash out, to defend himself, to make it known exactly what he thought of this turncoat behavior, what he thought of *Jack*.

Jack looked at Oliver, a single glance, quick and hard, that showed the whites of his eyes, the brilliant green now dulled. Then Jack closed his eyes and looked away. Still standing against the wall, as if waiting for Oliver's ire, his fury, his bite, as if he would stand there and take it, stand there as if this were his due, as if he *deserved* it.

It was this submissiveness that stilled Oliver in a way he'd never experienced before, and it felt strange. It felt as if the world beneath his feet had stopped turning, a stone-quiet still-ness overtaking him.

Then he saw, as if stepping back from himself, the whole of it. He and Jack, on this journey that they had begun, oh, so long ago, should not come to a place where one would fault the other for something beyond either of their control. Jack had done everything he could, everything within his power, had been prepared to sacrifice the sanctity of his own skin to protect Oliver. For that gift, Oliver should be worthy, but he was not.

And why not? Because he had been absorbed in his own concerns, cloaked within his own woe, of being in a workhouse, of going hungry, of taking beatings he'd done nothing to deserve —all of these things, so familiar to him, he had examined and fretted over and complained about. But he was used to it, could take the whippings and the bad food, because it was nothing to what Jack had been going through, *nothing*.

His insistence upon his own struggles had been at Jack's expense, as he had never truly noticed anything about Jack at all that should have given him pause. He'd been acting like a spoiled, self-absorbed child with the attitude that his needs must be served first, before anybody else—well, no longer. He swal-lowed his rage, wincing at the bitter taste of it, and looked at Jack, truly looked at him. At their situation.

The distance between now and only a moment ago seemed immense and irrefutable, as if he'd been behaving like the young, nine-year-old boy he once had been, rather than a young man who had his wits about him and his beloved Jack to protect and care for.

Jack did not deserve Oliver's anger, only his patience. Jack did not deserve to be bitten with words, or smacked, or beaten, or hurt in any way. He never had, never would. Oliver could not let it happen, this heinous thing. Would *not* let it happen.

"I'll stay with you," said Oliver, feeling out of breath, as though he'd run a long way and come to a sudden halt. "I won't leave your side, not for a moment, and if he tries to take me or you away, then I will—I *will* hurt him. Do you understand me, Jack? I love you more than anything, please say that you'll let me protect you." He stopped, for he was asking again, asking for something Jack might not be able to give, and that was a selfish thing to do. Licking his lips, he tried again.

"I'll stay with you," he said again. "And give you anything you need, if you'll let me. If you'll *tell* me—"

Jack's whole body twitched and suddenly he was scrubbing his eyes with the back of his hand, the green of his eyes so green against the unshed tears that Oliver went to his side, standing close, his hands coming up and then stilling, just as he was about to touch Jack. He was waiting for permission, such as had come so easily before, but Jack needed to know that now Oliver would do what *Jack* wanted. Would give where before he had only taken.

"Yes, stay w'me, Nolly, just stay w'me." Jack's voice was wobbly, his lips thin and white against his teeth, as though he were holding everything back for fear of upsetting Oliver.

"I will, Jack," said Oliver. "I promise, I promise, I promise."

He moved forward till he stood so close that he could feel Jack's shattered breath upon his cheek, and smell the sharpness of Jack's sweat, see the glitter of sweat along the back of his neck, and knew just how scared Jack had been. How scared he was, still.

He lifted his arms to circle them around Jack, and pulled him close in a slow, steady way so Jack could pull away if he wanted to. But Jack came to him, shaking as he tucked his head beneath Oliver's jaw, trembling like a wild thing that had determined that the touch of a human hand was the only thing that might save him from the jaws of the hunter's trap.

Oliver thought to speak aloud the apology in his heart for being so stupid, so blind to everything but his own needs. But that would entail either Jack's acceptance or, perhaps, his refusal of that apology, and right now Jack did not need to do anything but feel that Oliver was with him. That Oliver would do anything for him. That Oliver would stay with him always.

"I love you, Jack," said Oliver, pressing his cheek to Jack's temple, his face dampened by the sweat in Jack's hair, now cooling as Jack's breath slowed. "I love you. I won't leave you. I'll stay with you. I will. And I'll think of a way to get us out of here before Saturday night."

Beneath his touch, Jack shuddered, and Oliver bit off the thought of the timeline looming in front of them both.

"I'll think of a way, but for now, would you like to sit with me beneath the window? We can press our backs to it and look at the lovely grate I've just cleaned."

"W'about the work?" asked Jack, his lips moving against Oliver's neck.

"The work?" Oliver almost laughed as he asked this, but turned it into a kiss on the top of Jack's head, his inhaled breath tasting of the sweet oil in Jack's hair. "Bloody work, none of it matters. You know it doesn't. I don't care about the work, only about you. Would you like to sit with me?"

Now he did get a response from Jack, a little puff of air along his skin. The sound might have been astonishment at Oliver's language, or might have been an echo of the sentiment of Oliver's repudiating work and all that it stood for, even if only for this particular circumstance, and it could have been either made Oliver feel a little bit better about it.

As well, he finally understood why Jack had been so ambivalent about getting anything done in the workhouse, for it wouldn't matter. The parish board would come and take their notes and march out again, well satisfied that everything was in order, whether or not the paupers were dressed in clothes too thin for the weather or were starving on the assigned dietary. The only thing that mattered was that he and Jack escape from the workhouse.

In the meantime, Jack needed to sit down, for he was still shaking beneath Oliver's touch, and when Jack nodded, Oliver guided him to sit on the floor. He sat next to Jack and tucked Jack into his side, and petted his arm, and held him close. Breathed with him until the shaking stopped and Jack sighed, as though taking his first full breath that day.

"Rest against me now," said Oliver. "We'll go back when the bell rings for supper, but for now, you rest and I'll keep watch."

Jack nodded against him, his shoulders relaxing a little bit from their tight lines, Jack's hands slipping about Oliver's waist, as though he was a ship mooring himself to solid ground after a long storm at sea.

"Nolly," said Jack, in a voice that sounded on the verge of breaking.

"What Jack? What is it?"

But Jack only shook his head, and pressed hard against Oliver, almost sinking down upon him.

Oliver held as still as he could and didn't wince or pull away when his bruises jumped to life so hard he wanted to cry out loud. Which is what he would have done before today, vent a pain that had been given so carelessly, but that would fade with time. Or remain as scars, but which would never terrify him into an aching, terribly still thing such as Jack had been when Chalenheim's hands had been upon him, and even after. Of that brutality Oliver had never suffered, so his only concern was for Jack, who had.

"I'm here, Jack," he said now, low, wishing he knew what to say other than what he'd said.

Perhaps words were not needed now, since Jack had been unable to speak beyond saying the pet name he had for Oliver. The one that made Oliver's heart beat quicker within his breast, the one that made him feel wanted, and loved, and safe.

"We're together, Jack," said Oliver, saying Jack's name again, for it might do the same for Jack, and make him feel wanted, and loved, and safe. "And I'll stay with you. All night. All day. Always."

Then he kissed Jack in the mess of his hair, and let his head rest on the top of Jack's head, and held him close as they sat on the floor of the men's oakum-picking room, with the smell of tar-coated rope, and the leftover flakes of rust from the pikes that were lined up like soldiers against one wall. And waited for the sound of the supper bell to call them to the boys' dining hall.

~

THE BELL OVER THE WORKHOUSE WAS TOLLING THE SUPPER hour and though the rain had let up, the men's oakum-picking room was filled with a chill that had the low, cloying smell of something burnt and soaked in water until it turned putrid.

Oliver lifted his head, feeling the soreness where he'd rested it against the wall, the tingle where his shoulder had fallen asleep beneath Jack's head. His buttocks as well, his thighs, felt akin to wooden boards, warped in foul weather, and he honestly did not think he could move to get up.

But that didn't matter, seeing as how Jack had not awoken, for Oliver would not bestir him to do so until he absolutely had to. Besides, there was no rush, for they were next bound for the boys' dining hall, where Chalenheim would no doubt be presiding over all.

Oliver had a very great many things he should like to say to Chalenheim, that he would like to announce to the dining hall, to one and all, as to the proclivities of the man they had placed over them to maintain order. Regardless of Mr. Louis and Mr. Bassler's collective opinion of Oliver, and it could not be a gracious one, he doubted whether they would want to keep such a man in their midst.

Which was, perhaps, the answer. Oliver might report Work-master Chalenheim; he might ask to speak to Master Pickering so he could tell him whom he had in his employ. Then Chalen-heim would be summarily marched off the grounds. Then, while Oliver and Jack might still be trapped within the gray walls of the workhouse, and would still have to undergo the indifferent treatment of the attendants, they would not be subjected to the vagaries of a man for whom buggering a small boy, or a young man, against his will was considered his due, his *right*—

"Nolly," said Jack in a very soft voice.

"Yes, Jack?" asked Oliver, bending close, brushing his jaw gently along the top of Jack's head.

"Only do stop."

"What? Whatever do you mean?"

"You're thinkin'. I can feel you thinkin', an' it can't be about anythin' good, for I know the way your head works. So you must stop afore it goes too far."

Blinking in confusion, Oliver considered this. Of course Jack knew him fairly well, but surely he was not able to suss out the contents of Oliver's mind.

"How can you tell?"

"Oh, your breathin'. It picked up, like you was prepared to start runnin'. Like you do when you're all worked up, as you are. I c'n always tell."

Oliver's mouth worked silently as he petted Jack's arm and tried to still the slight tremble in his fingers.

"I only thought—what if we reported Chalenheim to Master Pickering, or to one of the attendants, even. Surely they would not want such a man working among them. He coerced you, Jack, to have relations with him, and it's wrong, it's so *wrong*."

Jack laughed a bit as he sat up, pulling himself from Oliver's arms so he could look at him. But it was a sour laugh and sounded strange and Oliver could not return the smile that Jack tried to give him.

"You know you'd never get in to see him in time, an' even if you did, he'd not believe you. Over Chalenheim? His best an' brightest what keeps this place runnin' for so cheap? Never in your lifetime."

Oliver hung his head for being so foolish in the face of Jack's hour of need, so stupid as to believe that running to the authorities would do them any good at all. For it had been the authorities who had hired Chalenheim, and men like him, to hand out beatings and withhold food. Who had built workhouses all over the country and determined they should be hellish places, as grim and miserable so as to deter anybody entering them, even those in dire need. Who allowed small boys, to allow his Jack, to suffer at the hands of such a man.

"Nolly," said Jack. "C'mon, up now, there's the bell. Someone will be in soon."

Jack stood up and held out his hand for Oliver, and Oliver chided himself for once again falling into that sink-trap of behaving like a needy child instead of a young man who might stand beside Jack so they could look out for each other. Protect each other instead of making Jack look after him all the time. So he firmed his jaw and took Jack's hand and raised himself up, and kissed Jack rather quickly, for there was someone coming to get them, striding across the yard with a candle-lantern in their hands.

"It was a foolish idea," said Oliver quickly.

"'Tweren't so bad actually," said Jack. "In any other place, goin' to the top might have worked, but today's not that day."

In the echo of this bit of praise that made Oliver feel a great deal better, even though, yet again, it was as if he'd shown himself to be needy of reassurance. Then the door swung open and there stood Mr. Bassler, holding the candle-lantern high and peering beyond the yellow-gray light spreading upon the floor to see whether they were within.

"Come out, you boys, you'll be late for supper, now, march!"

It was on the tip of Oliver's tongue to announce that they did not give a tinker's curse whether they had supper or not, seeing as how the meal to be served would be so poor. He didn't even need to see the slight shake of Jack's head to know what a bad idea saying such a thing about Chalenheim would turn out to be. For even with the new-found knowledge that Oliver was beneath the cloak of Chalenheim's protection, Mr. Bassler wouldn't take kindly to being spoken to in such an aggressive manner and, without Chalenheim around to stop him, would surely take Oliver to task.

They grabbed the buckets and the box of cleaning supplies, and followed Mr. Bassler across the yard in the growing dark, the wind whipping over the workhouse walls, chill and damp, as if the rain, having held off this long, was once again on the way. He led them around the corner, past the dead room and the gate to the outside, along the passage next to the kitchen and scullery and, finally, to the dark door that led to the boys' dining hall. There, he halted them to blow out the candle-lantern, which he hung on a peg by the door.

"Give me them things and go on in; he's holding prayers up for you, and it's put him in a temper, I can tell you."

This was not unexpected news, of course, but it made Oliver's heart flutter in his chest and his mouth go parched. He licked his lips and opened the door, leading the way, Jack close on his heels. The door handle slipped out of his hands and the door swung open, lumbering heavily on its loud hinges, like a tumbrel turning, and smacked into the wall.

The entire of the room, the boys already seated and waiting for prayers to begin, the attendants at the cauldron in the front of the room and, as well, Workmaster Chalenheim, who stood apart from the gathering to watch over the room, were perfectly silent. Everyone's attention upon Oliver Twist was blended together as a single hard and expectant eye. All on him, who had dared not only to come late to supper, but who had also made a spectacle of himself by banging open the door loudly upon his entrance.

"Oliver Twist," said Chalenheim, not unexpectedly, perhaps, but loudly, like thunder against stone, his hands held behind his back, but if he held a switch or a strap, Oliver did not see it. "You are late."

"I am," said Oliver, his voice coming out clear and level with a calmness he suddenly felt spreading through him. He lifted his chin.

"You will apologize to me at once for delaying prayers, for delaying the boys' eating their supper."

"I will not."

Again, he sounded in his own ears like someone who knew the ground he stood upon, and he felt something within himself, a steady, strong rush filling him, like a sea tide coming in. He also felt Jack poking his back, and the hiss of Jack's breath urging him to stop.

Which of course he should, but as Chalenheim began marching over to them both where they stood by the door, Oliver moved in front of Jack, and drew a hard breath and looked straight up into Chalenheim's face. At those eyes, so angry, sparking dark, his gaze quick, flicking over them both to land on Oliver, because of course he'd determined who the usurper was, and with whom his battle would be.

"Excuse me, did you say that you would *not* apologize?" Chalenheim's brow drew together over this, as if it were an unbelievable notion.

Had this been any other day, any other evening, when the situation between Jack and Chalenheim had not been known to Oliver, then of course Oliver would have backed down or faced Chalenheim's wrath. That Chalenheim had not yet boxed Oliver's ears was an indication he would not, in spite of the witnesses all around that could attest to the fact that Oliver had just denied the workmaster's request and, frankly, had it coming.

"Yes, I did," announced Oliver loudly and clearly.

Jack's touches turned into full-blown tugging, for it was clear Jack did not think he could get Oliver out of harm's way, either fast enough or far enough. With a gentle pull, Oliver twitched out of Jack's grasp, and clenched his fists and stood his ground.

"You will apologize at once," said Chalenheim, on the verge of a shout.

Oliver took a breath and settled himself, feeling it deep within, in that place where the right course of action had made itself known, and had been there all along, from the very beginning.

"I will apologize to all present for delaying their supper; it was rude and I should not have done it." Oliver made his words loud enough to be heard by everyone in the dining hall, from the attendants at the cauldron to the boys in the back row. Then he lowered his voice, and spoke only to Chalenheim, fierce, the words coming through grit teeth that he bared in his fury. "But I will not apologize to you, not now, not ever, for you are not just cruel, you are *evil* and deserve no courtesy from me or from anybody. And I will never forgive you for what you have threatened Jack with. *Never.*"

"Nolly!"

At that moment, when Jack was tugging on him, as if imploring him to stop, Chalenheim slapped Oliver with the full of his palm, a blow that numbed the side of Oliver's face entire and made his ears ring. Jack was there, holding on to Oliver's shoulders, pulling him back, out of range, though it was too late to save him.

"Please, mister," said Jack, even as Chalenheim was grabbing Oliver by his jacket collar to pull him up close. "Please don't, he ain't—"

But what Jack might have used to explain away Oliver's actions was cut off as Chalenheim gave Jack a hard shove to move him away, which left Oliver struggling against the hand upon his collar until he lifted his head to look at Jack and realized what he'd done.

Though the words had been true, and Chalenheim deserved to be told them, saying them out loud as Oliver had just done only served to put Jack in a worse position than before. For who knew what extra favor Jack might determine he should curry to keep Oliver out of the refractory room, to save him another whipping?

Oliver knew he was not wrong, he was *not*—but this was not the time to be so righteous in his anger, however much it was justified. What he'd just done with his intemperate, unpropitious outburst could only bring Chalenheim's anger more firmly upon his head, and cause him to be cruel to Jack. *More* cruel, in fact, and for that Oliver was horrified with himself.

He would apologize and say whatever needed to be said, and he was resolved to draw Chalenheim's anger upon him rather than Jack. That Oliver was so easily swayed because of his affection for Jack would not be lost on the workmaster, but that could not be helped.

"I apologize," said Oliver, his lips numb, his left ear ringing like a low, continuous, brassy note. "I should not have spoken that way to you, or said those things, and I'm sorry for it."

Chalenheim shook him and turned him to face the room. The boys sitting on the benches, waiting to eat while their bowls of gruel grew cold and their hunks of bread dried rock-hard, were motionless, eyes wide, mouths open.

"Say it again, boy," said Chalenheim. "Fully inform the present company of your ill manners."

Oliver was not shamed by the eyes looking at him, as he might heretofore have been before finding out what Chalenheim had been doing. But in the shade of the workmaster's despicable behavior, Oliver knew his pride and his explosive, uncontainable temper was the far lesser sin and, besides, he did not imagine any boy in the place actually felt Chalenheim was in the right, regardless of the fact that none had actually heard what Oliver had said to him.

Oliver swallowed against the dryness in his throat. The words would taste bitter, but they needed to be said.

"I apologize for my behavior, in arriving late and in my rudeness to Workmaster Chalenheim, for which I hope I will be forgiven."

The entire room sighed. Oliver wanted to imagine that it was in sympathy, or perhaps it was in disappointment that Oliver had not stood his ground in putting Chalenheim in his place. But as Jack had said, today was not that day. Would that it ever arrived,

Oliver could celebrate and feel himself worthy for having defeated an evil man. But not just now.

Letting Oliver go, Chalenheim gave him a last smack to the back of his head.

"Go and sit down and count yourself fortunate that I have not determined to deny you your supper ration."

Oliver did not let himself look back, but walked steadily to his place at the last table, in the last row at the end of the room, with Jack at his side, ducking his head the whole way to try and catch Oliver's eyes. When they sat down, Oliver gripped the table, feeling his balance waver as if the floor were moving beneath him. Jack grabbed his wrist and gave it a small squeeze.

"Steady on, Nolly," Jack said, low, for one of the attendants was bringing them over bowls of gruel and hunks of bread, and they had to remain absolutely still or it might be taken from them.

"Bow your heads, boys," said Chalenheim from the front of the room, and all the boys, as one, instantly obeyed.

With his hands clasped, Jack scooted close until his thigh was warm along Oliver's thigh. This steadied Oliver in unexpected ways, the closeness of Jack's body and the intent behind the gesture. All of it felt a balm to his still-pounding heart, his breath jagged in his throat, for how could he, in the face of promises to himself and to Jack, have been so foolhardy?

"Oh, Nolly," said Jack, when the prayer was over and the evening's announcements had begun and they were at liberty to eat.

"I'm sorry, Jack," said Oliver, as he'd meant to since he'd first wanted to storm after Chalenheim. "I'm the worst of companions, the most foolish—"

"No," said Jack. "You were as brave as a lion, as you always have been."

"But I put you in worse danger, for now he will want—"

"You put him in his place," said Jack, nodding, looking as if he wanted to take up his spoon and start eating. Only the gruel was quite cold now, and there was a scum upon its surface. "I saw it in his eyes that he's never goin' to disremember what you said to him, what you said he was."

"I shouldn't have said anything to him."

"Ah, but you did, an' with style, that, proud as a king."

Jack sounded quite smug about this, though he should have been upset that Oliver had very probably made things worse for him. Oliver looked over to where Jack was merely stirring the gruel around and not eating it, and determined to follow up on his desire to take care of Jack.

"You should eat, Jack," said Oliver. "You won't keep up your strength if you don't." As to what that strength would be used for, Oliver did not quite want to examine. Still, Jack could not starve, for Oliver would not stand by and see him do that to himself. "Please eat, even if only a little."

And this Jack did with slow, small bites, as if he'd become the fussy miss about it that he'd often accused Oliver of being. But that didn't matter, as long as he ate something, and as long as Oliver could remember to keep his thoughts to himself and concentrate instead on how they were going to get out of there before Saturday night baths were over.

❦ 20 ❦

IN WHICH BARGAINS MADE
BECOME REVEALED

The supper hour provided Jack with a bowl of gruel and a hunk of bread that he could not bear to eat. Only Nolly made him with a shake of his head and a stern glance as he pointed his spoon at Jack's bowl. He need not do anything more than that, and while Jack was not fearful of making Nolly cross, he knew Nolly was right.

So he ate the gruel in great tasteless mouthfuls, choking it down, wanting to choke himself with the spoon itself as he swallowed the gruel and ate the tasteless, dry bread. All the while, Chalenheim stood at the cauldron in the middle of the room, finely garbed in his dun-colored apron, eyes narrowed as he monitored the room to ensure that there was no dissension in the ranks, no outbursts as had happened the day before.

Jack, in the part of his mind that could still muse on these things, wondered if that would be Nolly's legacy, as Jack's day in court had been his. That Nolly would be talked about, that the story about the meal with full helpings of delicious porridge for each boy would be told and retold, a legend among the paupers, the tale of their hero told and retold of their hero, the golden-haired boy who dared defy the dietary.

Leaping from mouth to mouth, the story would grow in size,

until it grew so big that at the end, it would be said that the angels themselves had drawn the mysterious orphan up to heaven with them, where the bread was warm and fresh and the butter melted off it.

"Butter, Jack?"

Jack shook his head, realizing that he'd been talking to himself, and put it off to nerves, plain and simple.

"Just tellin' myself your story," said Jack, though he knew that wouldn't make any sense.

He considered for a moment, creating another story, one of his own, to distract Nolly with, for when they were in bed. For when the light was gone from the room, there would only be the sound of rain echoing in the boy's dormitory when Chalenheim came to collect another little boy for his own pleasure.

Should he share that fact with Nolly and let him know the whole truth of it? What difference would it make whether he did or no? Anything more about Chalenheim that might tarnish his reputation wouldn't matter, for Nolly would take Jack's side in this. But Jack's belly told him something else, roiling against the gruel that Jack had pushed into it, aching enough so that Jack had to curl forward to make it stop.

He shook his head to dissuade Nolly from asking him whatever was the matter, because the answer was obvious, and he was ashamed that his troubles had brought him so low. To the point where he was no better than a frightened child cowering in the corner, waiting for his fate, and doing nothing about it.

Nolly touched his thigh, as though to make him look up. Jack did, wincing a bit, but doing it, for who was he to resist anything Nolly wanted of him?

The expression on Nolly's face was almost unreadable, those dark brows furrowed, that beautiful mouth tight, as if Nolly were irritated with him.

"I'll find a way, Jack," said Nolly, a low whisper that skittered up Jack's spine. "I promise."

"How can you," said Jack in return.

Then he saw Chalenheim was looking at them, looking at *him*, so he straightened up and shrugged his shoulders, and made as if he was scraping the last of his gruel from his bowl. And indeed there was some, a small white glob that was tasteless and cold as he scooped it into his mouth with the metal spoon. He jerked his chin at Nolly to let him know they were being watched and made a show of swallowing what was in his mouth.

Nolly bowed his head, looking at his hands, his thumb brushing up and down the handle of the spoon as he held it against the edge of the table. He looked as though he was about to pray, and maybe for a good Christian boy such as Nolly a prayer might be what was called for right about now. Then he turned his head, keeping his chin down, as if to keep anybody who might be watching from divining his feelings.

"I can—" Nolly's jaw worked, his shoulders tight, as if he longed for a meat cleaver then and there for him to use to hack their way to freedom. "I can try. I can do my best. For we can't stay here, I know that now. I was letting fate have its way, but I cannot any longer. Cannot let fate have its way with you, at least."

Nolly caught Jack's eye at this last statement, a little surprised at what he'd just said, the horrible comparison that he'd just made, and Jack snorted, for trust Nolly to get all balled up inside of a problem not of his own making.

"You are dear to me, Nolly," said Jack. "Now please shut up before he comes over here."

That wasn't the last of it, Jack knew, but it would do for now.

THE RAIN DID START, RIGHT AFTER SUPPER, CREATING A ROAR that slipped between the leading in the windows, drops of damp falling from the window ledges, oozing into the air, bringing with it a chill that was worse for the effect it had on an empty belly.

Across the room, only a few beds away, one of the boys was

crying. He must have been new, for new boys always cried, though he could barely be heard above the roar of the wind.

Jack grit his teeth and turned in the bed to face Nolly. He couldn't make out Nolly's features, the sky through the windows was too dark, but he could feel Nolly's closeness as Nolly's hands reached out for him, settled on his chest, Nolly's strong hands, pressing so gently.

Jack knew he was in for it now that Nolly knew what he knew, knew that there was something more to know. The moment Jack had dreaded, that he should have known was inevitable all along, had come at long last.

"So," said Jack, opening himself up to it, hoping it wouldn't hurt.

"Only tell me, Jack," said Nolly with soft, broad pets of his hand across Jack's breast. "Why would you go with him if you weren't willing? For it didn't seem as if you were."

Jack felt the question slip into silence, the darkness absorbing it while the storm pounded the windows and the child's wailing died down.

"Jack."

Bringing his hand up, Jack felt for Nolly's face with his fingers and traced the warm curve of Nolly's mouth before pressing lightly to keep it closed.

"Hush now, an' listen," Jack said, his voice shaking only a little. "I'll tell you, for I love you so, but you mustn't do anythin', d'you hear?"

For it occurred to Jack what Nolly might do when he found out the whole of it, what with Chalenheim's chamber door only a short way in the dark.

He felt Nolly nod, which had to be as good as a promise.

"He wanted me," said Jack. "He wanted me an' he came to me an' he asked an' I said *no*." Jack drew a quick breath, not knowing if Nolly understood what he was telling him. "Then he came again an' I said *yes*, because—"

He could only imagine Nolly's expression now, and felt the

shift of the form beside him as Nolly struggled to hold himself in check and not interrupt and turn the conversation to a direction of his own liking.

"I made him a bargain, if he would leave off hurtin' you, my own sweet Nolly."

"Leave off?"

"No more strap for you, no more cane. He wasn't to lay a finger on you, an' I would—"

"Go to him *willingly*."

Jack nodded, though he knew Nolly couldn't see it. Then he closed his eyes and dipped his head, waiting for the force of the storm to pulse through Nolly and reach him at long last.

He thought he heard Nolly make a strangled sound, and prepared himself to take Nolly's fury and perhaps clamp a hand, albeit carefully, over Nolly's mouth to keep him from drawing any undue attention while he roared with anger.

Then he felt it, the weight of Nolly's body as he pressed close, moving half upon Jack as if to hold him still, but not hold him down in a way that would make him feel trapped. He felt Nolly's hands finding and clasping his face, Nolly's mouth almost upon his, the sweet treacle smell of his breath, the rose-soft touch of his lips.

"Nolly," said Jack, whispering it, his voice coming out all quivery, as though he were a fool with no backbone.

"You must never, never *ever* do that again." Nolly's voice reached Jack's ears in the dark, for he was speaking quite clearly, not whispering at all. "If it comes to that, you must let me die rather than subject yourself to—Jack, you looked as though you'd just been visited by the devil."

"Please," said a young voice in the dark from some beds away. "Keep it down or he'll hear you and come out."

Nolly's whole body jerked against Jack's, but he only paused long enough to move his mouth to Jack's ear. He was whispering low now, but with enough force in his words to make Jack quiver, alarmed.

"I'll take a strap to you myself if you ever do such a foolish, *horrible* thing. I'll offer myself up in your stead, now, and how will you like that then? I'll tell him to take me instead of you. Why, I'll do it first thing in the morning, directly after breakfast. He'll touch me instead of you. He won't hurt you, Jack, for I won't *let* him."

Jack had to blink a moment to take this all in. His hands moved to circle around Nolly's waist to bring that warmth closer, cloaking his whole body with the angry, beautiful boy who loved him so, who would be willing to make that exchange, to bend over the edge of Chalenheim's bed in Jack's place, even though he was still unaware of what it all meant. Though, knowing Nolly, he was so angry on Jack's behalf that *had* he known what it meant, the full of what it entailed, he still would have been willing.

"Nolly," said Jack, wanting to bring Nolly to stillness with his voice and the slow strokes of his hands along Nolly's back. "He only wants to bugger street boys, rough boys, boys who know things. Dirty boys. D'you see? Not beautiful golden boys such as you."

"I'll put soot in my hair," said Nolly, and though he wasn't trying to get out of Jack's hold, he was thumping Jack on the chest. "I'll roll in the mud. I don't care how dirty I have to be."

"Oh, Nolly, sweet Nolly," said Jack now, and for a moment Nolly's fierceness made his heart unclench and some of the fear left him, for nothing bad could happen to him when Nolly was near. "It goes more than skin deep, for one like him."

He petted Nolly's back for a moment, though the tense, taut line of him did not seem to ease beneath his hands as it normally might have done.

"You can't be the hero this time, Nolly," said Jack, low. "I'll just let him bugger me an' it'll go easier for the both of us whilst we're in here. Maybe we'll even get more food out of him afore he tires of me an' moves on to bugger the next boy."

"Jack, buggering, that's—"

"Stickin' your cock up another lad's arse. It could be nice, or it could be not, an' w'men like him—"

"It isn't."

This was not a question; Nolly picked things up quickly, it seemed to Jack, even something like this, something not talked of in polite society.

"No," said Nolly now, almost in a tone that was him speaking to himself, asserting something until he was sure of it. "No, he won't have you that way. He won't hurt you, he won't even *touch* you."

"Hush, Nolly, sweetheart."

While Nolly was the sort who would take objection, even offense, to being forbidden to express something so heartfelt, Nolly only twisted in Jack's arms and burrowed his head in the hollow of Jack's shoulder.

"He shan't have you, for you belong to me, for you are mine as ever you were."

Jack kissed the top of Nolly's head, and stayed there a long moment, until Nolly settled against him. Jack's belly churned with worry, for what would happen come the morrow?

Chalenheim would not select Nolly for this ugly task, no matter that Nolly rolled himself in pig shit, so he needn't worry about that. But Jack needed Nolly by his side for as long as could be managed, for he knew that come the moment, his own knees would buckle from beneath him and he'd be helpless to stop what was coming.

✌ 21 ✣

CROSSING THE RIVER STYX

I t was after breakfast that the sun determinedly made its
way through the clouds, and filtered through the windows
of the oakum-picking room, warming the glass so as to
obscure any blue sky with steamy streaks across the surface.

Oliver could not actually see the blue sky from where he sat
in the back row, but even if he could have, he was unable to
appreciate it. Jack had told him so much, and shown him such a
deep vulnerability, that he was even more determined to figure a
way out of the workhouse.

It was Saturday, which meant baths after supper, and however
much he might have enjoyed getting clean, at least for a moment
or two, there was no way he would contemplate leaving Jack to
suffer for it. Chalenheim, after all, had said he always kept his
promises, and Oliver had no reason to doubt him.

"Jack," said Oliver in a low, whispering way that until their
time in the workhouse had seemed so strange to do, but that
now seemed to come very naturally. "Are you quite sure that
going to Master Pickering, or even to the board when they come
next week isn't a good idea?"

He felt Jack stir on the bench next to him, watched him as
he cast his eyes to the front of the room where Chalenheim was

marching up and down, scowling, observing the paupers at work, just waiting for his chance to snatch a boy from his seat so he could scold him and beat him. If Oliver never saw another man discipline a child much younger and weaker than he, he did not think it could come too soon.

"Nolly," said Jack, pretending to be busy with the tarred rope in his hands. "We talked of this already, you'n me. There ain't no chance of it workin', an' besides, there ain't no time. It'll be too late."

"But, Jack, we could at least try, for it can't make it worse than it already is?"

"Oh, believe me, it can," said Jack, shaking his head, gripping the rope in his hands so tightly that his fingers were white.

"But if we—"

Finally, Jack slammed the twist of rope in his hands squarely down upon the pike, which broke it in two narrow slices as neatly as if Jack had been picking oakum for years. Then he turned to Oliver, his eyes fierce, his mouth a drawn line.

"Bloody fuck, Nolly, will you please stop?"

His voice was loud enough so that several boys in the row in front of them turned their heads, not to listen, exactly, but to warn them. So Jack dipped his head and leaned toward Oliver, and lowered his voice, though the fierceness was still there.

"The only way—are you listenin' to me—the only way we're gettin' out of here is if we're dead. But that ain't goin' to happen, 'cause I'm goin' to do this thing, do it willingly, an' save us both a lot of trouble."

"Jack, no—"

In the front of the room, Chalenheim whirled around and slashed the cane through the air, making it whistle and snap. Several of the boys in the front row jumped in their seats and cowered back.

"Who is talking?"

Nobody spoke; the entire room was still and quiet, brown-shouldered paupers hunched over in their places, staring at their hands, as though praying that they would not get drawn to the front of the room.

"I will hear no more talking, or every boy in this room will miss their dinner. Is that understood?"

The room, as a body, nodded, and the noise of industry and diligence began to fill the air. Oliver breathed out a slow breath and did not look at Jack.

It was obvious Jack meant what he said, that to save them both, he was going to go through with it, sacrificing his own skin to save Oliver's. And while, had it been the other way around, Oliver would have been glad to stand in for Jack and subject himself to the workmaster's vicious and unpalatable tendencies, he could not endure Jack doing that for him.

Jack would not be the first boy Chalenheim had buggered nor, as Jack had informed him with much regret, would Jack be the last. The workhouse was a place where Chalenheim could pick and choose as he pleased with no one to report him, for no boy dared, and no one in a position of authority seemed to care.

There was nothing Oliver could do, it seemed, either to change Jack's mind, or overhaul the system by the time the supper hour was over and they were marched down to the bathing room and told to strip to their skins. Only one boy, Jack, would be excused from the ritual, and nobody would think a thing of it.

So Jack was right. The only way they were getting out of the workhouse was if they were dead, just like the paupers who had been reported in the nightly announcements at suppertime. Taken to the dead room and wrapped in a winding sheet to be measured for black-painted coffins, and then hauled off to the churchyard where they would be dumped into a hole, mumbled over by a half-drunk parson, and remembered by exactly nobody.

Oliver had not been apprenticed to Mr. Sowerberry for very long, but an undertaker's life was quite simple. Build the coffins, wrap the bodies, haul them to the churchyard, and start all over again the next day. The only time anything ever happened was when they ran out of black paint, or someone forgot to bolt the door, or to leave a crack of a window open so the smell of the rotting flesh wouldn't fill the room and make everyone within the house ill.

That had been the worst of it, the smell of death and the turpentine odor of the black paint, which got on absolutely everything. Oliver remembered scrubbing the bricks in the passageway because Noah had trod on a spot of black paint on the floor and tracked it everywhere.

Death wasn't complicated, but it did leave a mess behind. A scrap of a ribbon that had fallen from the fist of a man who had died, only nobody had been able to explain where the ribbon had come from or why the man had clung so desperately to it while his last breath left him. That is, nobody had been able to explain it because nobody had inquired after it.

Oliver had tried asking Mr. Sowerberry, especially with the notion of giving the ribbon back to whomever it belonged to. Alas, these ideas coming from a small boy of young years, had been swept aside, and Oliver had been sent to dust the coffins on display in the front parlor.

Oliver looked toward the front of the room where Chalenheim was marching up and down as though he were keeping time with his feet, when the workhouse bell announcing the dinner hour began to clang, and Chalenheim gestured that they should bring their baskets up to be measured.

Everybody came in at the near limit, except for Jack, whose basket was almost empty. Nobody seemed to begrudge Jack this as they got in line, and perhaps it was that they all knew, somehow, what Jack was in for come nighttime.

Finley, as well, had picked his fair portion, but shook so hard as he came near Chalenheim that he almost tipped his basket out and was not soothed when Chalenheim reached to take the basket from him to pour the oakum onto the scale himself.

"Well done, Finley," said Chalenheim, but it made no difference to Finley's agitated state, only Oliver was too far away to comfort him.

Two by two, Chalenheim led the boys out of the oakum-picking room and along the passage to the dining hall. By now, Oliver was quite familiar with, at least, the male side of the workhouse, and knew that the passage led past the kitchen and scullery to the stairs to the coal store and refractory room.

Beyond that, the passage led to the dead room, where the door was open from time to time, to allow the dead bodies to be carried in. While still wearing their pauper-brown outfits, the bodies were wrapped in a winding sheet to absorb the odors and the fluids that leaked out and to make the body easier to handle. Or perhaps they stripped them of their garments so as to take the clothing to be cleaned and disinfected for the next pauper who would wear them.

It was odd that he should consider what clothes paupers were buried in because at the undertaker's, the dead were buried in their finest, with their hair tidily combed, their hands neatly folded in front of them. Sometimes their jaws were wrapped shut with a strip of cloth and sometimes, for the very religious, they had shiny sixpences placed upon their eyes to pay the ferryman when they got to the crossing of the River Styx.

Of course, that was nonsense. Souls went to heaven or they did not, depending on the character of the person. Oliver knew with every bone in his body that Chalenheim would go directly to hell, to the lowest level, or perhaps the second level, since that was the level connected with lust.

As the boys rounded the corner to go into the door into the dining hall, Oliver reached out, meaning to ask Jack if he knew on which level lust was supposed to be found, which was ridiculous because while Jack might understand the idea of levels of hell, he would not know which one was which, because Oliver had not read Dante's *Inferno* to him yet. He'd like to, some day, though Jack might be more amused than impressed by the idea of sinners being stuck upside-down in the ice than anything else.

And this, in spite of Oliver explaining the idea of an allegory to him, that in Dante's time, that type of story was a way of communicating the different kinds of sin, because when people died—

Oliver stopped, distracted by the fact that they were standing in line for food, and even though it wasn't very much, he wanted to attend to it. Catching no one's eye, Oliver patiently got his serving of gruel and a hunk of bread and, along with Jack, sat at their usual places, and bowed their heads, waiting for prayer.

"Nolly?"

Oliver nodded that he'd heard Jack, but stared at his clasped hands. He was doing it again, going off into his own world, thinking thoughts that had nothing to do with the situation at hand. Rolling around in memories of books he'd read, and all while Jack would be growing more concerned, more anxious as the day went on.

But in spite of his concern about Jack, Oliver's mind seemed stuck on the idea of people dying and, as he listened to Chalenheim droning his way through prayers, he thought again of the distance to the dead room, along the passage past the kitchen and just at the end. The door was sometimes open and, being within the workhouse, would be unlocked.

There would be coffins within the dead room, either empty and waiting for bodies, or already nailed shut and waiting to be carted out of the gate and into town, where they would be dumped into an open grave, where nobody would stop to remark upon the contents.

He smacked his palm against his forehead, startling the boy on his other side, which served to focus Jack's attention solely upon him.

"I have been so blind," Oliver said, girding his teeth. "So bloody *blind*."

Since their arrival, he'd been so wrapped up in himself that he'd been scarcely able to attend to his surroundings. Then, with

Jack's sad revelation, he'd been wholly concerned with what Jack had told him, and Jack's fate, come Saturday evening. When all this time, the answer had been directly in front of him. Well, almost in front of him, but certainly within reach.

His distracted state had been because while he'd been thinking of death, it had not been because of Dante and his levels of hell, but because of the Abbot Faria and Edmond *Dantes*, the former who had begun a plan to escape the Chateau d'If and the latter who had completed that plan. They had dug their way out, and Dantes had been freed from their prison wearing the guise of a dead man. In a dead man's shroud, a burlap sack sewn at each end and thrown into the sea.

Well, they needn't go *that* far, he and Jack. All they had to do was make their way to the dead room and empty two coffins of their cargo. The rest would be up to the system, the one that so indifferently took care of their paupers, both alive and dead.

It was so simple an idea that either it would fail utterly or it would succeed utterly.

❧ 22 ❧

OLIVER'S ORDERS MUST BE
FOLLOWED

True to his word, Nolly had stuck by Jack's side in line, at breakfast, in the oakum-picking room, where either his shoulder had brushed against Jack's, or he'd tucked himself against Jack's body, the back of his shoulder against the front of Jack's, as though he were a type of shield made of human flesh and bone and all that bravery.

Jack had caught him more than once glaring at Chalenheim, sticking his chin out, as though daring the workmaster to make even a single move toward Jack. At which point Nolly would have done something dreadful and irreversible, but Nolly had promised, and Jack hoped that his warning had not just been heard but also heeded. You couldn't go up against a man like Chalenheim, for even with an audience, the workhouse system would back him up. So Nolly had agreed to not let his temper get the better of him. Still, he glared.

At dinnertime, Jack made himself eat his gruel, and his dry bread, and longed for a large slice of roast beef, and boiled potatoes so badly he could almost taste them. He was concentrating on this, on trying to remember what they tasted like, when with a sudden start of his whole body, Nolly went absolutely still beside him.

Jack allowed himself to look out of the corner of his eyes, for he sensed Chalenheim looking their way, and watched, somewhat puzzled, as Nolly leaned forward and thumped at his forehead with the heels of both hands, using his fingers to pull at his hair.

"I have been so blind," Nolly said, to himself, but fiercely. "So bloody *blind*."

Shocked for a moment that Nolly was even using profanity the way Jack would have, so casually, Jack's hand stopped, his spoon halfway to his mouth as he finished off the entirely too small portion of gruel from his bowl.

"Nolly," said Jack, talking behind the shield of his spoon. "He's lookin' at you, better sit up."

Chalenheim was looking as he scanned the room, always on the alert for a boy to step out of line, to cause a ruckus, anything that might need his instant and fiercely painful attention.

Jack nudged Nolly with his elbow, hoping to stave that off. To have Chalenheim come even a step closer, even if Nolly would not feel the back of his hand, would be too much for Jack to bear.

"Nolly."

Nodding, Nolly sat up and took his hands away from his face, attending to where he'd thunked his spoon on the table, eating his gruel with steady, careful bites. But he didn't look at Jack, nor say another word for the rest of dinnertime. Only waited attentively until every boy was done and Chalenheim gave them leave to stand in line, two by two, until they could be divided up for the afternoon's duties.

Jack didn't know how Nolly managed it, but he found himself paired off with Nolly, then Mr. Bassler took them to the end of the passage past the kitchen and handed them brooms and buckets and cloths.

"You're to go to the cellar, where the coal store and refractory is. Give it a good sweep. With any luck the board won't be troubled to go down there, but it pays to be careful."

"Yes, sir," said Nolly, as politely as Jack had ever heard him. "Would you like us to scrub it as well?"

Before Jack could think of a proper reply to Nolly's actually volunteering them for extra work, Mr. Bassler was nodding.

"Yes, come up when you've swept, and there'll be soap waiting. You'll have to fetch the water yourself, mind." Mr. Bassler made shooing motions with his hands. "Now go on, quit dawdling, there's more work waiting when that's done."

Nolly led the way up the passage to where the stairs were, but instead of going down them, Nolly placed the broom and cloth at the landing, and looked at Jack, carefully, as if appraising him.

"We should fill the buckets with water first," said Nolly, and it was then Jack considered that Nolly had gone completely mad.

"Whatever for? 'Tis bollocks anyway, us scrubbin' down there. We'll make the sweepin' last as long as anything, anyways."

But Nolly had that look on his face, the one that meant he expected to have his way, and he tugged on Jack's arm till they were going through the doorway that led into the men's yard. On the left was the door to the back fenced-in area, from whence the wagons had taken them to haul them to the field where they were to have picked rocks and weeds.

There was another door, yawning open, that also led to the fenced-in area. As they walked slowly past it, Jack saw Nolly take a long look, but all Jack could see were some black-painted coffin lids.

"Have you got a fever, Nolly?" asked Jack as they walked over to the well and set their buckets down beside it.

The yard was windy, but for once it wasn't raining, and Nolly set to work. He dropped the bucket into the well and used the crank to draw it up, the back of his jacket flapping in the wind. Nolly could crank on his own, of course, but Jack couldn't manage to stand there and watch him do it, so he reached out to curl his hands around the handle next to Nolly's, when Nolly shook his head.

"Let me do it on my own, and listen to me? Do you hear? Just listen."

Jack jerked his hands back and felt his shoulders tighten, not understanding the tone in Nolly's voice.

"You must do as I say," said Nolly, turning the crank ever so slowly, so slowly that Jack wanted to snatch it out of Nolly's hands and take over, and hang what Nolly wanted. "You must do *exactly* as I say, when I say it, do you understand?"

The hair on the back of Jack's neck began to prickle as the wind whisked around the yard, chasing bits of dirt, flecks of bone. The men were probably in the field again, thanking their lucky stars that they didn't have to slog through the mud and rain that day, though they were probably still hungry and cowed.

"Jack?"

"Yes, Nolly, fine, I'll do as you say, but whatever are you on about?"

"And ask me no questions," said Nolly, quite firmly.

He filled the bucket that sat on the ground, and then he dropped the bucket into the well and began to let it down to bring up water. He was quicker with the second bucket, motioned for Jack to carry his bucket, picked up his own, and led them back through the doorway that led to the passage where the stairs to the cellar were.

As they passed the gate, now closed, Jack could see that the door to the room with the coffins was also closed. As Nolly motioned to him to do, Jack put his bucket down at the top of the stairs and expected that they would pick up their brooms and cloths and go down into the cellar and at least pretend to work.

But Nolly shook his head, took a few steps backward and, briefly turning to check the passage and the doorway, opened the door to the dead room. There was no one in it, only three freshly painted black coffins that rested on the floor with their lids on. Jack couldn't even imagine that Nolly meant to go into such a place, but he grabbed Jack's arm and pulled hard, and Jack went where he was bid, his heart racing as Nolly closed the door behind them, sealing them in with three coffins.

"We ain't supposed to be in here," said Jack, keeping his voice down, doing his best to figure out what Nolly was up to.

"No, we *ain't,*" said Nolly, mocking him. "And that's the point."

Nolly went over to the largest of the coffins, bulky at one end, tapered at the other, and gave the thick lid a yank. Jack opened his mouth with shock as the lid came right up. There was a form inside of it, wrapped in a white winding sheet in the shape of a man. It must have been one of the men who had been listed during one of the evening announcements as having passed away.

"Help me with this," said Nolly as he bent, hunkering down a bit, putting his hands inside the coffin as if he meant to lift the corpse out of it.

Jack reached out to grab Nolly's arm and yank him back from doing such a horrible thing, when Nolly looked at him and shook his head.

"I told you; help me with this, and ask no questions."

For a moment, Jack could only stand there, smelling the black paint, and that of wood shavings, and the undercurrent of rot and sweet stink, like that from a slaughterhouse. As he looked at the corpse, he noted the splotches around the head, and not only were Nolly's hands just *there* as he tucked them under the corpse, there were maggots, already crawling on his wrists.

"But there's maggots, Nolly, *maggots.*"

"It doesn't matter, just keep your mouth shut and clap your hands over your ears if you have to."

Then Jack understood everything, in the flash of a moment.

"D'you mean me to crawl in there?" His voice rose on the last word, and he pointed, completely forgetting Nolly's instructions.

"Yes, now, c'mon, help me lift him. We'll put him behind those planks along the wall."

Breathless, Jack went to the other side and helped to lift the white-shrouded figure out of the coffin, and stumbled beneath the bulky, icy weight to carry it and lay it against the wall. Nolly arranged the planks and kicked some curls of wood shavings against them to make it look as if the planks had been there a while.

"D'you want me to get in now?" Jack knew his voice squeaked as he asked this but he couldn't help it.

"No," said Nolly. "Help me with this one."

With a bit more gentleness, Nolly pried off the lid of the mid-sized coffin, whereupon was revealed another shrouded corpse. This one had a winding sheet that was a bit more streaked, as if fluid had soaked through, and across which even more maggots were swarming like wiggling, blond blobs.

Without even pausing, Nolly took off the lid of the other coffin and looked at that corpse, a smaller one, that of a child's, as if deciding. And all as calmly as though he was packing a series of wicker hampers and merely needed to balance the load between them.

"You're bigger," said Nolly, "so you'll go in that one." He pointed to the first coffin where the maggots were starting to scurry away into the panels of the wood, and thence to the floor, as if in search of something to eat. "And we'll put this body with that body, and I'll go in the second biggest one."

"How did you know that the lids would come off the way they did?" asked Jack, for Nolly had been able to pry them off with no difficulty whatsoever.

"I worked in a funeral parlor, that's how. For pauper's funerals, when they get to the churchyard, they'd dig a hole, open the lid, and dump the body in, without the coffin. They reuse the coffins over and over until the holes for the nails become quite soft."

Nolly spared Jack a glance, as if daring him to question this, but then Jack realized how brilliant it all was. If they could keep from getting their necks snapped when they were tumbled out of the coffins, they'd be halfway to being free of the workhouse.

"Help me now," said Nolly, his voice a little softer.

Willingly, Jack bent to the work, though his skin prickled as the maggots fell from the shroud and onto his sleeve, his wrists, beneath his boots. He couldn't even manage to squash them as they crawled on the floor, as it was making his stomach churn just to watch them. Together they placed the bigger body in with the little one. Then Nolly pressed the coffin lid down, hammering on it with his fist once or twice, with as much ease as if he'd done this before.

"I'll help you," said Nolly.

Now that it came to the moment when Jack would actually have to be as obedient as Nolly had asked him to be, Jack hesitated. This was a mad course that Nolly had set them on, and there was no way it was going to work, and he opened his mouth to say so. But Nolly got up close and, without touching Jack at all, looked him straight in the eye.

"It's just like the sailor and the old man, do you remember?"

"But that was a story—"

Jack stopped, and closed his mouth, thinking of the maggots that might want to crawl in it. While that had been a story, the sailor's scheme had worked because nobody would think to open a sack that they thought contained a dead body, especially not since it had been sewn shut.

"Get in," said Nolly now, "and I'll pound the lid shut over you."

"What about *your* lid," said Jack, looking about, having wild thoughts of them being in the same coffin together, except that would be too heavy for anybody to think it only contained a bag of bones.

"They'll give it another go with the hammer, I expect," said Nolly. "Though the nails will still be loose when the time comes, so never worry."

Jack would just have to do as he was told, this time, so he

lifted his foot and, with gingerly care, stepped inside of the coffin, feeling the dull thunk of his boots on the wood, watching the last of the maggots squirm into the cracks between the boards. He turned around to sit down as he might in a bathtub that was the length of a man and completely empty of water.

Scooting and worrying about splinters, he lay back in the coffin, feeling the tightness of the wood around his shoulders, the smell of death, the low odor of it, sweet and thick in his throat, and eyed the lone maggot scurrying away along the lip of the coffin.

"Don't be afraid, Jack," said Nolly as he lifted the lid and prepared to settle it in place, the nails sticking out all around, a ragged row of thin metal teeth. "And don't make a single noise, all right? No matter what. Stay put till I give you leave to move."

"How will I know?"

"I'll say your name when it's time. Just lay still, just lay still."

Jack closed his eyes as the coffin lid came down over him, shutting him in darkness, the smell of new paint and something old that he couldn't define filling his lungs with every breath. He felt the planks of the coffin jar around him as Nolly pounded on the lid. Heard the scuffling sounds of Nolly pulling the lid on his own coffin, the high plinks of loose nails dropping on the floor, and wondered how Nolly was managing this, how he'd kept his wits about him to come up with the idea in the first place. And determined that Nolly had ice water in his veins for being so brave as to get into a coffin without aid and *then* to pull the lid of his own coffin over his own head.

They waited in silence. Jack could feel the cold from the ground beneath the wooden planks of the floor soaking up into him. It might help a corpse from rotting too quickly, that cold air, but it was setting him to shivering, his teeth almost chattering. He clamped his mouth shut, and tried to breathe deeply and quietly, his mouth closed in case there were any maggots about that thought he was a dead body.

When finally the door opened, and Jack heard footsteps and

voices and the low squeak of a rusty hinge, he almost shouted with relief, for either they would be on their way or they would be discovered, but it would be over, for he did not think he could bear the confines of the coffin one moment longer.

"Not too many this week," said a voice, one Jack didn't recognize.

"Still enough to make a good profit, I expect, eh, Mr. Berg?" That was the voice of Mr. Louis.

"Yes," said Mr. Berg. "For it's a good, sickly spring this year, bless the saints. Well, help me heft these onto the cart, and I'll take them to the churchyard."

The week had starved him and Nolly both, but they couldn't be a great deal lighter, and must be heavier than an actually dead pauper. Jack had frantic thoughts of jumping out of the coffin to surprise both men, for if there was a cart, it meant the gate was open, and he could grab Nolly and they could be away—then he had to stifle a squawk as the coffin he was in was lifted and tilted so his feet were higher than his head, and he slid backward, his head banging against the wood.

"This one's heavy," said Mr. Louis.

"They get heavier when they go, with no soul to prop up the weight."

The coffin tilted again, shifting Jack's whole body on its side, making his stomach feel as though it were being flipped about. If he'd had anything substantial to eat, he might have vomited the contents. But there was nothing but thin gruel in his belly, so he swallowed and, with his eyes still closed, reached out to brace his hands along the sides of the coffin, which was hard, since the coffin was tapered at the shoulder. But he managed it, the rocking motion making his head spin till at last the coffin was slammed on a high, flat surface that he determined must be the cart.

"Let's get these other two. C'mon, it might rain later, and I fancy having a pint along the way today."

There was more grunting, and Jack felt the cart rock beneath his back as the other coffins were placed upon it. He wondered which coffin Nolly was in, and whether it was next to him now. Whether the horse would go too fast and the coffins would tumble off it. Whether the lids would come off in time to save them from being buried alive. Whether—

"Will you need assistance at the other end, Mr. Berg?"

"No," said Mr. Berg, huffing a bit as if he were carrying something quite bulky. "I just tips 'em into the hole, and the coffin is quite light after, so it's no trouble, though you are kind to ask."

"Very well, Mr. Berg. Do give my regards to your lovely wife."

"I will indeed, sir. And good day to you."

The cart sagged at one end as Mr. Berg presumably got onto the driver's bench seat, and Jack heard muttered clucking, the flick of a whip in the air, and the low grating of a metal gate being opened. The coffin almost jumped as the cart went in motion and Jack held his breath. With his eyes open, he could see bits of sunlight piercing through small spaces between the paint and the planks of wood, disappearing and appearing, as if the clouds were rolling in the blue sky above them.

The horse plodded slowly, iron shoes clanking on the road that led into town. Jack closed his eyes as he heard the gate move once again, the large sound of a key turning in a metal lock moving further behind him, and breathed slowly in and out and began to think, for the first time, that Nolly's mad plan might work.

It was even windier outside of the workhouse confines, and the air smelled damp and fresh where it leaked into the coffin. Jack thought he could hear birdsong, and the sounds of people talking. The cart rumbled across cobblestones, slowly, attracting, Jack presumed, no attention whatsoever, for who would want to have anything to do with a cart full of coffins on a beautiful Saturday afternoon? Nobody, that's who.

For a good ten minutes, the cart rolled into town, the smell of coal fires and dung heaps and the clattering sounds that Jack could not identify coming closer and closer. Jack was eased into quietness because this might actually work, and he'd kiss Nolly like he'd never kissed him before, and tell him how bloody clever he was, over and over, until it brought that smile to Nolly's face, the one Jack loved to see.

"Up, Dilly, up," said Mr. Berg, speaking to his horse. "Come on, here you go."

When the cart came to a gentle stop, Jack felt his eyes go wide, his heart racing as he waited for Nolly to call his name, for the signal that he should break out of the coffin before it was tipped over. But rather than hearing the quiet of a churchyard, Jack heard the rumble of a hand cart, two ladies talking about the spoilage of fish, a child's laugh.

This didn't sound like a churchyard at all. It sounded as though they were stopped along a street of some sort, in the middle of town. This wasn't going to work after all; Mr. Berg had been alerted to their presence somehow and was now getting off the cart to go fetch the authorities, and he and Nolly would be taken back to the workhouse in short order, and then Work-master Chalenheim would—

The wheels of the cart squeaked a bit, as if the horse was shifting herself, and then Jack felt a dash of fresh air hit him in the face, and the light splashing down as the lid was lifted. Only instead of Mr. Berg or an angry constable, it was Nolly's face, the sunlight marking a crown of his hair as he looked at Jack and bent low as he held up the lid to Jack's coffin.

"Slip out, there's a good lad, quick as you can."

Needing no prompting, Jack clambered over the edge of the coffin, holding himself low, slipping to the ground, his knees almost buckling beneath him as he looked about. The cart was stopped in a small alleyway off a main street, which explained the sharpness of the voices and sounds that he'd been hearing, for they'd echoed off the brick walls of the alley and into his ears.

With quick hands, Nolly put the lid of Jack's coffin, his former coffin, back down, then slithered off the cart and into Jack's arms. As they were hidden behind the back of the cart, absolutely nobody could see them, and he smiled at Nolly, his face almost breaking with pleasure.

"Oh, sweetheart," Jack said, clasping Nolly's shoulders. "You are somethin' else again. What a clever idea, what a bloody *clever* idea."

But Nolly was far too serious to enjoy the compliment, let alone, it seemed, to hear it. For he was pulling away, looking up the alley to the street where Jack could see the bare edge of what looked like a tavern sign.

"He's stopped off to have a pint, I reckon," said Jack, pointing at the sign.

"We need to get away, before he gets to the churchyard and notices the coffins are light, before anybody notices we're gone," said Nolly. He scanned Jack up and down, as though appraising him for market. "We need to get out of these clothes, we need—"

"The cart," said Jack. "That would get us a ways, if we took it."

"Loaded with coffins, drawn by an old mare, Jack? No, we need a horse to ride upon, and different clothes."

For a moment Jack didn't quite understand what Nolly was saying, unless he actually meant that they should *steal* a horse. But this he understood.

"Take off your jacket," said Jack, tugging. "The shirt an' trousers are ordinary enough but that jacket is a giveaway. Mine too." He showed Nolly what he meant, tracing the straight line of the collar of the jacket that was devoid of trim, marking it as a garment only a pauper would wear. "We'll get somethin' else as we go but for now, we're two lads walkin' through the village, lookin' for our master's horse."

"Just walking out in the open like that?" asked Nolly, and Jack understood that Nolly had imagined skulking about would be the order of the day. But if Nolly knew about coffins and such, well, Jack knew about hiding in plain sight.

"We're two lads walkin'," Jack said, more slowly now so Nolly, who was surely addled by his time in the coffin, could follow his train of thought. "It's market day that's windin' down, an' two lads walkin' through a village in their shirtsleeves on a warmish, windy day will attract exactly no attention. Whereas, two boys runnin' an' lookin' panicked will be remarked upon. D'you see? We're lookin' for the master's horse, I'm tellin' you, as he wants us to collect it."

He could tell the moment that this story made sense to Nolly, the idea of it, for his eyes brightened. "Was he having it shod, then?"

"No, he loaned it to a friend of his, so the friend would know of its speed. Now the master wants it back, but the friend has tried to keep it."

"We're very loyal," said Nolly, with some seriousness, "to be so careful of the beasts in the master's stable."

"That we are," said Jack.

He slipped his arm around Nolly's shoulders to lead him out of the alley. That way, they would be seen to be walking arm in arm like two lads on their half day, larking about, talking like mad, barely alert to their surroundings, for they were having such a festive time.

Nolly's neck was stiff beneath Jack's arm, his cheeks bright with a bit of flush that could only be panic, a signal that Nolly was about to bolt, as he had that day of the mangled pickpocketing job so long ago. Jack's heart was racing, though he did not want to admit it, so Jack threw himself into the moment and made himself smile broadly and laughed out loud.

"Oh, that's a good one," he said, chuckling. "Did you hear the one about the farmer's daughter?" He gripped Nolly by the neck and jostled him, as if encouraging him to see the humor in the joke. "Never mind, I've told that one a hundred times an' you never laugh!"

Which, as far as anybody else could see, was a very humorous notion, for Jack slapped his thigh and pulled Nolly along with him, following the curve of the pavement, avoiding the two women who were standing in front of a fishmonger's stall, wending his way around the child skipping rope. Minding the old woman as she tottered along with her cane.

"The master said we should find him up along here, didn't he?" Jack tipped his head at Nolly, scrunching his brow with some confusion.

"Up the way a bit," said Nolly. His voice was a bit sharp and clear, though he was doing his very best to be as Jack was, a lad going about his business in the village with no worry on his mind but the mere errand he'd been sent on. "At a tavern along the high street."

Jack kept them walking together, moving apace, but with a casual ease that would indicate to anybody who took the time to note their passage, that they knew what they were about. He kept his eyes peeled for the constable, noted the street that they were on was busy with shops with their doors open and their wares on display. Noted women in sturdy dresses and thick white aprons, and those women in fine bell skirts, followed by servants.

Mostly women shopped this street, then, so Jack kept them both moving to where the street slanted upward a bit and curved. Where the shops became more prosperous and, indicative of that, the folks in the street were doing less shopping than strolling, simply because they could. Showing off their clothes, their clean hands, their well-fed faces, their wealth, their riches.

He had to stop thinking that way, for it would show in his face, and make him notable. So he slipped his arm from around Nolly's neck, and jerked his chin to indicate that Nolly should walk behind him, now that the crowd was more busy. He kept them to the edge of the pavement, so that his betters could have the inside passage.

"Oh, come on, Tom," said Jack loudly. "We'll never be done at the rate you are going."

The false name threw Nolly, but to his credit, within an eye blink, he was shaking his head. "You're one to talk, uh, Bill, for wasn't it you who dawdled all morning?"

Several people let them pass, shaking their heads at the pair of them, two servant boys arguing over who was to blame for the delay. Jack knew that by the sun's setting, they wouldn't even remember Tom and Bill for the life of them.

When they finally reached the high street, Jack could see the church steeple to his left, and along the right, the shiny gleam of fresh painted plaster buildings that faced a large square. He led the way, striding along with supreme confidence, smiling at Nolly, waggling his eyebrows to get Nolly to smile back.

At the corner, Jack took a left, where the square widened out to display a string of fine buildings, a hotel, a tavern, and again, more shops, with the better sort milling about, as much considering whether or not to spend their golden coins as to be seen doing so. Toward the end of the row there were coaches lining the street, and a broad stable door, open wide to let the stable hands bring the horses in and out, to cool them after a ride, or tighten their saddles beforehand.

"You don't mean to take one from there?" asked Nolly. He was shrinking back from this, and Jack had to grab him by the arm to keep him from bolting.

"Not exactly the stable," said Jack. "But do you see there?" He pointed at one of the hotels. "A lad comes an' takes your horse. You assume it's going to the stable where you can collect it after your hour spent poncin' about an' showin' off. We'll be one of those lads."

"I see what you mean now," said Nolly. He swallowed, then said, "It needs to be me. I'll be the one to act as stable lad, for I'm the one they would not suspect."

Jack had to agree, as Nolly's handsome face and fair hair were fairly much a guarantee that nobody would think he was about to steal a horse. And, as well, he felt a rush of admiration at Nolly's being so brave. The least Jack could do was help him.

"I'll go to the far end," said Jack. "And you lead the horse there, and from then, we ride out of town."

With a nod, Nolly marched forward, shrugging his shoulders

to make them loose as he went up to the hotel with the gold-gilt sign and stood out front, waiting, half in the street. From where Jack stood, he could see Nolly was doing a valiant job to appear as though he wasn't about to piss himself, though he had to be terrified of what he was about to do.

Presently, a man in a silk top hat came riding up. Nolly reached out and said something to him, and the man nodded and dismounted. Handing Nolly the reins of his sleek brown horse, he also handed Nolly a coin.

They exchanged words Jack could only imagine were about where the horse could be collected after the man's business in the hotel. Then, with a nod, Nolly gathered the horse's reins and began to lead him up the street, past the stables, going very slowly and methodically, until he disappeared around the corner.

Jack could barely contain himself at how neatly this had been done. Nobody would be the least bit suspicious to see Nolly with his beautiful face leading such a lovely horse as if he'd known the beast all of his life, as if it were his very own.

It was all Jack could do not to run up the street to follow him, though he did hurry, and turned the corner to see Nolly checking the horse's saddle girth, brushing its neck. And then he turned to see Jack there.

"I've ridden before," said Jack. "But only once or twice, and never on a horse like this one."

"You will ride in front," said Nolly and, with ease, he led the horse, turning it around so the beast's near side was facing uphill. "I will sit behind you, and wrap my arms around you, and steer."

Nolly said this so softly that Jack knew he was thinking that Jack still needed rescuing, as if there were any chance of Chalenheim getting to him. Jack half-wanted to beg him to stop, for it was making his throat feel thick that Nolly would be so protective of him, so gentle. He would break apart if it continued, he knew that he would.

"Come on, Jack. I'll give you a leg up."

As Jack put his foot into Nolly's cupped hands, it was like

that time at the river, in the rain, when they'd been covered in mud and dripping wet, about to be taken back to the workhouse for what awaited them there. This time, Nolly's hands were steady and mostly clean, and he nodded at Jack, and lifted him up to where Jack could swing his leg over the saddle.

The saddle was fine and slippery, well oiled and cared for, and Jack almost went off the other side. But Nolly was putting his foot in the stirrup now, and Jack reached down to help pull him up because Nolly was looking quite white about the face, the full weight of what they were doing, now that they were doing it, hitting him.

He thought for a moment that Nolly would back down from this, and tell Jack to ride off on his own. This Jack would not do, not simply because he couldn't ride, but because he would not leave Nolly behind.

He was about to say so, when Nolly shook himself and put weight on the stirrup and used Jack's arm to slip into the saddle behind Jack. His hips pressed close to Jack's thighs as he settled his feet in both stirrups, the warmth of his groin cozily close to Jack's backside.

Nolly put his arms around Jack, as promised, and arranged the reins in his hands to his liking. Then he squeezed with his thighs, clucked to the horse, who began to walk. From this far up, the ground almost seemed to bend away before Jack closed his eyes,and leaned back to tuck himself against Nolly.

❧ 23 ❧

TRAVELING ON HORSEBACK
WITH JACK

The road from Axminster led up away from the village before flattening out to go between open fields. Although the traffic was spare, with only a farmer and his wagon, a dogcart with two ladies driving themselves, and a trio of gentlemen on horseback, all headed into the village, Jack's skin began to prickle before too long had passed.

He found himself trying to look over his shoulder, but was only twisting in Nolly's arms and unsettling the horse. He also could see Nolly looked as though he was preparing himself for the hangman's noose, for that was the punishment for the theft of a horse. Naturally, Nolly would want to take full blame, as if his loftier notions of obedience and suchlike made him the responsible party, though Jack knew he was not.

"What is it, Jack?" Nolly shifted his weight behind Jack, and Jack turned back around to face forward, in spite of the fact that they were so high up, and the horse's gait seemed to pitch him about every other moment.

"Should we, perhaps, dear Nolly, take a lesser road?" Jack tried to keep his voice calm, but they were so out in the open. Yes, the sun was shining, the wind stirring the clumps of winter-dead grass, the green shoots springing up along the roadside, and this was all very lovely, but they were currently the only thing on the road, and quite remarkable, on account of the fine brown horse that they rode.

"Do you think so, Jack? Why-ever so?"

He heard the tremor in Nolly's voice, and realized Nolly's thighs were bunched up tightly beneath his, and that Nolly's arms, as they held the reins, were as stiff as they ever could be, and that while Nolly was perfectly capable of doing what he was doing, it was taking its toll.

It had only been about an hour of them solemnly riding along, doing their best not to attract attention, but Jack imagined that Mr. Berg had just about finished his pint and dumped the coffins. To his amazement, there would only have been two bodies in one coffin, and the other two coffins would have been very light on account of they were empty.

It might have been amusing to have hidden in the shrubbery to watch this discovery, but they were better off away. For Mr. Berg to return to the workhouse to bring the horrible news would only take a short jaunt in the cart, now empty of its burdens, and his frantic announcement would raise such a stir, and Workmaster Chalenheim would surely be at the forefront of any search.

With a shudder, Jack nodded, grasping the pommel in front of him between his legs.

"Perhaps we should get a bit of a move on. Can you make it go faster?"

Nolly tightened the reins and clicked to the horse, but Jack was not prepared for the surge of muscle beneath him, the press of Nolly along his back, and the way the air grew sharp as the horse began to canter. He could not admit that he felt a bit sick, his legs dangling uselessly, the metal of the stirrup banging into his ankles. He wanted to grab Nolly's hands and tell him to stop so Jack could get off before he fell off.

"Jack," said Nolly above the sound of the wind whistling in Jack's ears. "Tuck your legs up. Press in with your knees."

Jack tried his best, he really did, but the horse kept moving, the tips of its mane flicking the back of Jack's hands, and he just kept slipping back and forth on the saddle. His legs wobbled about as Nolly pulled the horse to slow down, leaning back, the reins dropping on the horse's neck as it stopped.

The air felt warm around Jack's ears, the air in his chest sharp, and he felt Nolly petting his arm.

"Don't be afraid, Jack," said Nolly, very softly. "I won't let you fall."

"It's not that," said Jack, even though it was. He waved his hand over the horse's neck as the beast reached back to nuzzle his leg. "There's all this space, an' I can't look without fear of tumblin' to the ground."

"All right," said Nolly, without hesitation. "We'll do it a different way."

Without another word, Nolly slid off the horse. Jack saw him wincing as his feet touched the ground, and wondered how this was going to work. But Nolly knew what to do. He motioned for Jack to slide backwards in the saddle and led the horse along the road for a bit till he found a stone mile marker. He used this to stand on, hefting himself up to slip into the saddle in front of Jack.

Immediately this felt better, for even if Jack couldn't see where he was going, he could wrap his arms around Nolly's waist, smell his scent, and dangle his legs behind Nolly's without hitting the stirrups. He reached out to pat Nolly on the thigh and sighed.

"This is better," he said. "Not going to fall off now."

Nolly turned and gave Jack a little smile and drew up the reins again.

"Hang on," he said. "We'll get some distance between us and him, and soon we'll be very far from anybody who might recognize us."

When the horse began to move faster, its long legs sprightly beneath them, Jack was ready. He held onto Nolly, and fixed his front to Nolly's back, so that when Nolly leaned forward and the horse began to run, Jack went with him, keeping his balance by echoing what Nolly was doing. He'd never been on a horse this fast, so high up off the ground, the air sharp and streaked around him, the speed of it making his heart race.

But it was only a short while before Nolly leaned back, pulling the horse to slow to a walk, now upright, his back as stiff as a board.

"What are we doing?" asked Jack. "Is everything all right?"

"We need to let him walk," said Nolly. "We need to let him breathe."

Jack nodded; Nolly must know about these sorts of things, then.

The road dipped down into a wooded copse that was springing to green, the tips of each branch full of curled leaves that had not quite stretched out, the drops of a recent rain leaving round tiny balls of silver on each end, sparkling in the sunshine. It felt better to be amidst the trees like this, not so exposed to anybody else who might be on the road, even if the shade was chilly without their jackets.

OLIVER WOULD HAVE PREFERRED TO HAVE SAT BEHIND, WITH Jack in front of him so he could press his chest to Jack's back, and wrap his arms around Jack's waist to hold the reins. To feel the weight of Jack's thighs upon his. To be able to tuck his chin against Jack's shoulder, look down at Jack's hands cupped around his own, and truly know that Jack was safe. Far away from Chalenheim's dark urges, and out from behind the workhouse walls, within which they had been trapped, unable to escape Chalenheim's whims, the cruelty of the attendants, the slow killing machine that was the workhouse system.

When he'd been young, the workhouse had been his world, with every movement, every thought structured to a rigidness that killed all the kindness out of it. Upon going back to the workhouse, he'd succumbed to that pattern all over again, going under without even the merest struggle, simply because that cruelty, that blindness to humanity, had felt so familiar somehow, and it had been easier to follow along than to do anything else.

But something had happened to him in Axminster Workhouse, the possibility of which had never before occurred to him, the realization that he could determine his own fate, and not just speak up for himself, but for others, less able than he. Had he been able to rescue all of the paupers from the tight grip of the workhouse, he would have, first among them Finley, who would have bloomed without those walls around him, but who now was destined to waste away, a pale and frightful ghost of himself until the day the angels came for him. Like Martin—

At least Oliver had been able to get Jack out of there, and they were well away, on horseback together, with Jack clinging on behind him, his body tense, his thighs cupping up beneath Oliver's thighs, his arms almost biting into Oliver's waist.

That Jack was uncomfortable on horseback was almost painfully clear. Jack was pressed so close to Oliver that his welts felt itchy and sore, and each movement of the horse, up and down, caused those points to press against the saddle, or against Jack, or the sides of the horse, until Oliver had to bite the inside of his cheek to keep from complaining out loud.

He did not want Jack to feel bad that he was clinging so close. Besides, if Oliver could feel him, then he was safe, safe and alive, and kissing the back of Oliver's neck and singing his praises, which, though Oliver could barely admit it to himself, warmed his heart and soothed his aching backside.

"Nolly," said Jack, "You're the cleverest thing, the cleverest fuckin' thing I ever did see."

"I just wanted you out of there," said Oliver as he kept a close eye on the coach and four horses coming toward them, trotting fast, too fast to be anybody but a well-to-do gentleman or lady ensconced within, without any need to consider the wear and tear on the horses, the coach wheels, or even the coachman. "I should have figured it out sooner than I did."

"You figured it out faster than I would," said Jack. "I thought about that story, time to time, but not in the way you did. It's like we was them, ain't it?"

Jack sounded rather too jolly about being considered either Edmond Dantes or the Abbot, but Oliver understood what he meant. They weren't those characters, but they'd drawn on that story and, in effect, brought it a bit to life. Which was rather like the moment when they'd been carrying coal out of the coal store in the cellar, and the light from the candle-lantern had struck Jack in such a way that he had looked like a smuggler, a daring one, a dashing one, just like something out of a book.

It was only too bad that Oliver was now aware of the true evil contained beneath the surface of some men, and while he might have been more content not to know it, there was no turning back now. Only he didn't know whether or not reading would have its same charms, having gotten a good bit of what he might once have called adventure at him. But these were gloomy thoughts for a rainy-bright afternoon, with a good steed beneath them and a road to something new ahead of them. Jack was safe, and he was safe, and together they might find somewhere good to go.

"I might, you know," said Oliver, as he guided the horse to go along the edge of the dirt road so a slow, lumbering wagon could get between them and a pair of gentlemen on spotted gray horses. "I might write and find a way to get Finley a place where he could learn a trade, and become an apprentice, and where someone would feed him."

In the back of his mind, he was thinking of Mrs. Pierson, who might take one look at Finley and do right by him. Though, considering her reaction to Martin's death, and her fury at Oliver's attack on Mr. McCready, any request from Oliver would be promptly tossed on the fire. There'd be no favors coming from her. But perhaps he could find another household to take Finley in.

"'Tis foolishness, Nolly," said Jack, leaning forward to lay his chin upon Oliver's shoulder. "But then, you know that."

"Yes," said Oliver, clucking to the horse to pick up its pace. "I can't save the world, I know that now."

"Well," said Jack. He reached forward to pat Oliver's thigh, as if wanting to signal that he meant nothing dismissive by his remark. "If you took Finley out, you'd have to find a place for his wee friend, his bedmate, or perhaps the lad that sat next to him in the oakum-pickin' room. An' what about the one that was always behind Finley in line, the ginger-haired one—can you save them all, Nolly? No, you can't."

Like a swamp tide, grief engulfed Oliver, bringing up rage and the futility of it all. For what chance did Finley have, or other boys like him? And what about boys in workhouses, or coal cellars, or dingy shops where nobody cared for them? Where there was nobody gave them decent shoes to wear, or stockings without holes, or a hot breakfast in the morning before they went about their back-breaking labor, working for absolutely nothing but the right to exist.

"Nolly, you all right? I can feel your sides gettin' all stroppy." With his hand still on Oliver's thigh, Jack petted him gently, up and down, and Oliver determined that the horse moved quickly enough so nobody on the road would notice, for he could not bear to have Jack stop.

"It's just—" began Oliver.

The fist in his throat expanded, and his eyes were wet and hot, and he could not bear to speak it aloud, the futility of it, the indifference that became cruelty the longer it went on. Jack moved about in the saddle, trying to look at Oliver and comfort him and, in another moment, Jack would find himself unbalanced, tumbling from the saddle into the road. So Oliver squeezed with his thighs, and urged the horse to a faster pace so Jack would have to stay put, and just hold on tightly to Oliver's middle. So that Oliver could take a deep breath and, lifting one hand away from the reins and Jack's hand, scrub at his eyes with his fingers.

"Nolly, sweetheart—"

There was no hiding anything from Jack, then, and for a moment, Oliver didn't, just bowed his head and let the horse guide itself down the road. Perhaps, after seeing the workhouse from the inside, Jack might understand a little better how Oliver felt about it. Jack didn't say anything, but held on tightly just the same, moving against Oliver's back as the horse plodded beneath them.

After a time, Oliver took up the reins and opened his eyes, and tried to focus on the dappled sunlight coming through the leaves that dripped with crystal rain. On the wind that whisked through the tops of the trees, the smell of damp earth, the low, loam-rot of winter-dead leaves, and of Jack behind him as they made their way out of Axminster Parish.

THE WEATHER HELD, IT BEING A HARDY SPRING DAY, THE SORT that Jack remembered, with the brisk wind high in the trees, but enough sunshine to warm him. It would have to be a good deal warmer for the sun to warm him all the way to the bone, but he was content to be where he was, on horseback, his arms wrapped around Nolly's waist, the horse plodding along the wooded road, and their destination, as yet, ahead of them.

The middle of Nolly's back, his shirt at least, smelled like harsh soap, and beneath that, a bit of sweat. Jack laid his cheek between Nolly's shoulder blades and held himself there, breathing in long, slow breaths. But it occurred to him, as they went along, the clop of the horse's hooves on the dirt road, the various spring birds calling out to each other in the pale green woods, that they were going somewhere. Headed in some direction. Otherwise, they were only wandering when they should have a plan. A plan would be better.

"Nolly," he said, his cheek still pressed to Nolly's back. "Where are we goin'?"

He felt the shift in the body that he held, a tightening that told him Nolly was drawing in a breath, as if preparing himself to answer, preparing himself to convince, as Nolly had a way of doing when he thought he was right.

"Nolly?"

"Oh," said Nolly, and Jack drew back to see Nolly looking up at the trees, as if his answer was there. "I thought we might head up to—"

"Not Hale," said Jack. "I don't want to go there, you know that. I don't care what's there."

Under his breath, Nolly huffed.

"Wouldn't you want to see your family? Meet your mother and father?"

For a good long while, as the horse ambled and the wind scattered fallen leaves and the loamy smell of the woods rose in the flicker of afternoon heat, Jack considered this.

To Nolly, the letter from the parson in Barnet had been an answer to the puzzle he wanted to solve, about Jack, about where he'd come from. Even faced with evidence to the contrary, that of Jack telling Nolly *no* in no uncertain terms, Nolly felt it was important. That Jack actually had a mother and a father and a sister was almost too much for Nolly to resist, though why his own aunt and uncle and nephews weren't enough for him was a mystery.

"Don't care about them, I told you that. You're awful interested in somethin' that's got nowt to do with you."

The moment Jack said it, he wished that he hadn't, for

Nolly's whole body tightened up, only Jack didn't know why it was the wrong thing to say. He felt Nolly leaning back, his elbows drawing close to his sides as he soothed the horse to a halt. For a moment, while the wind whisked around them, and the smell of damp rose and fell, Nolly looked down at his hands, curled around the reins.

"I mean," said Jack, "it ain't important. That family don't matter to me. I gots you, an' that's all I need." He gave Nolly's belly a squeeze, then straightened up to hook his chin over Nolly's shoulder. He could see the faint scowl on Nolly's face as Nolly thought it through, but Jack didn't care about the family in Hale, and Nolly needed to believe that.

"I thought you were going to die—"

"Oh, that again. I ain't never goin' to die, Nolly, you know that, so just leave off goin' on about it, will you?" Pulling Nolly to him, he gave him a kiss on the cheek with a loud smacking noise that should have been very amusing but only made Nolly dip his head the other way. "Besides, we may as well be headin' to Chertsey to see your people, an' never mind goin' to see mine."

"We can't go see Aunt Rose and Uncle Harry," said Nolly. He urged the horse to starting again with a shift of his hips forward and a few clucks to the horse under his breath.

"And why is that, when they're perfectly good relatives to have?"

"You know very well why."

"Then," said Jack. "'Tis the same for me, for I daren't track my bad manners an' rude upbringin' an' my criminal ways into my own mother's house, now, can I?" He gave Nolly a squeeze, feeling very satisfied with himself that he'd produced such a clever response to Nolly's argument.

The road was rising a bit, and Nolly had to lean forward in the saddle. He reached down to curve his arm around Jack's arm and held it tight against his belly. Then, as the road leveled out, he pulled Jack's hand up and dipped his head to kiss Jack's palm. And all this without a word.

Jack was about to ask when Nolly nodded once or twice as if his mind was made up.

"Then I will make you a proposition," said Nolly. "For you are right, it wouldn't be fair to go to just one family. We should see both. We'll go visit your people, and then, afterwards, we will visit mine."

The deal was not perfect, at least the way Nolly laid it out, for it still meant going to Hale. But since Nolly was so keen on family ties, it would probably not be long after their arrival in Hale that he would want to be continuing on to Chertsey. In that way, the visit to Hale would be short and quick, and Jack determined he could manage that much.

"Agreed," he said, kissing the back of Nolly's neck.

"All this kissing," said Nolly in a way that was obviously meant to be cross, but came out soft as Nolly reached back, as if he meant to pat Jack on the cheek, so Jack helped him, and cupped Nolly's palm to his face, and kissed the middle of it.

"I'd kiss you even more," said Jack, breathing across the back of Nolly's neck as he said it. "But I'm half starved an' we're on the back of a horse an' not far enough away from the workhouse for my likin'."

"Shall we canter till we're through the woods?"

"Don't mind it," said Jack, as he looped his arms around Nolly's middle and scooted his hips forward until he was plastered behind Nolly. It would be a pity and a waste if he were to fall and crack his head open, just as they were putting the workhouse behind them.

THEY HAD BEEN ON HORSEBACK FOR ALL OF THE AFTERNOON, plodding along a dirt track that widened in some places and narrowed in others, but that always followed the course of the bottom of a slight valley. The sun was cutting through the trees, low at their backs.

They had been alone on the road for enough time that Oliver thought they might be becoming a bit conspicuous. Enough so that had anybody reported a missing horse, or had inquired after two boys wearing workhouse-brown trousers, the two of them would be directly remembered and commented upon. Besides, his legs were sore along the insides, and his ankles were raw where the stockings had torn through. His arms ached from holding the reins, and Jack, still hanging on behind him, could not be faring much better.

"Jack," said Oliver.

He did not want to act as though he were directing their course; that they were headed to Hale was enough for him. Still, they needed to get off the horse and find another way to their destination. Horse thieves, as everyone knew, weren't even given a trial, but were sent straight to the hangman's noose.

Jack made a sound that seemed affirmation and question all at once, and Oliver felt Jack's lips kiss the back of his neck. He let that happen for a moment, enjoying the shiver it sent up his spine before he reached back to cup the back of Jack's head to caress him and draw his fingers through Jack's hair. He took his hand away with a slow pet and curled his fingers around the reins.

"Do you reckon we might want to shed the horse and go onward by foot? We're the only ones on the road, and I'm fearful we'll be more noticeable now." He meant to go on, wanting to stem the rush of feeling a fool for being so hesitant, when surely Jack would scoff at him and state that they need not concern themselves with that. But as often happened, Jack surprised him.

"That's good thinkin', that is. Can't feel my legs anyhow, an' we need to find someplace to rest."

For how long that rest would be or what they might do for their supper, Jack didn't say. Oliver lifted his head to look down the road, and noticed the wood-and-stone fence. There was the same type of fence on either side of the road, as if a well-to-do country gentleman owned the farm all around and pleased himself by marking his territory with a certain type of fence. Up ahead, beyond the slight turn in the road, was a grouping of buildings that looked like a farmhouse and barn, as well as a fine stable, and a paddock where several sleek horses were cropping at the new spring grass.

"Yes," said Jack, and Oliver nodded, and urged the horse to go up the slight bank to where there was a gate to the field.

"We should," Oliver said, pulling the horse to a halt, "put this one in the paddock with the others. He probably won't be noticed till morning."

"What about the saddle and that?" asked Jack. "We can't carry it, not even for a little while. If we try to sell it, someone'll notice."

"We could put it on the fence, along with the bridle and blanket," said Oliver, looking at the well-cared-for horses, the new roofs, the cleanly stacked stones. "As a payment, perhaps."

"Who knows if they'll be honest enough to report an extra horse, eh?"

Jack laughed low in his throat, and of course, he would imagine that the farmer would keep the horse, and was perhaps counting on it. Oliver did not naysay him, for by the time the horse was discovered, they would be well away from there, and it wouldn't matter, anyway. The horse would have a good feed before being taken back to the stable in Axminster, at any rate.

He guided the horse up to the paddock gate and pulled it gently to a halt with the reins. Its ears were perked upright upon seeing its fellows cropping green grass at their leisure, and Oliver knew the beast had to be thirsty as well as hungry.

"Jack, will you dismount, or do you want me to first?" For knowing how unaccustomed Jack was to riding, getting off the horse would not be as straightforward for Jack as it was for Oliver.

"I can do it," said Jack, somewhat boldly, as if saying it in so stout a manner might make it so.

Oliver took his foot out of the stirrup for Jack to use. He

could feel Jack shifting his weight in the saddle, and the clonk of the stirrup against his heel as Jack tried to put his booted foot into it. In the end, Jack hung onto Oliver's waist and the edge of the saddle and slithered to the ground. Where he promptly crumpled into a heap, rubbing his legs, looking up at Oliver with a wide-eyed, astonished expression.

"My legs, damn it, they're all wobbly."

Not laughing at this, Oliver nodded.

"It's normal the first time you ride for that to happen. I've not been on horseback myself for a while, so—"

To demonstrate that it might be the same for anybody, Oliver used the stirrup and swung his leg over the saddle to get down. The moment his foot landed on solid ground, the whole of his leg bowed beneath his weight and he had to hold onto the saddle to remain upright. This struggle he did not take pains to hide, and turned to look at Jack.

Jack, still on the ground, had circled his arms around his bent knees and was watching Oliver's actions with much appreciation. Open mouthed, and staring, and not bothering to hide his delight.

"You've got the finest backside in all the home counties, you do," said Jack.

This was Jack, this was how he was, saying it as he saw it, and all in delight over watching Oliver dismount. As if the past week had never happened, and Chalenheim merely a bad dream from long ago. Though, as Oliver tied the horse's reins to the post to unsaddle it, he thought he saw a flicker of something in Jack's eyes.

The flicker told Oliver, in a way he heard deep within his heart, that Jack wanted Oliver to see him this way, as brave and unaffected by the workhouse, because he was the Artful Dodger, and only cared about what he wanted to care about. Well, Oliver would let him go on acting that way, being that way, even to the point where Jack might stare at his backside if it pleased him. For if that made Jack more at ease with what had happened, and what had almost happened, then Oliver would not stand in his way.

"I'll unsaddle this horse as quick as I can, and what do you reckon we should do after that?" For he did not want to make decisions the way that he had when he and Jack had first set out from London, with him determining the way that both of them should go.

"Well," said Jack. He ran a finger beneath the neckline of his collarless shirt, which let Oliver see the line of demarcation where the collar of his brown woolen jacket had left its rough mark. "I reckon we should get somethin' to cover up with, rather than continue to walk around half naked, an' then find a place to sleep. That's all I want to do right now."

They might be near a small village, or they might be miles out from anywhere. From the road where they were, as Oliver began unbuckling the saddle's girth, the farmhouse looked tidy and well-run; thus there would be no chance there of hiding out or stealing clothes.

He dragged the saddle from the horse, who gave a gusty sigh of relief. He placed the saddle on the round-pole fence, and then the saddle blanket on top of that. At the very last, he untied the horse and led the beast through the gate that Jack had gotten up to unlatch.

With a fond pat, Oliver undid the buckles on the bridle and slid the gear from the horse's head, and gave the horse a nudge with his hand, signaling that it was free to go eat and rest and be with its fellows. This it was happy to do, trotting off with a well-mannered gait, nickering to the other horses before stopping abruptly to drop its head and begin eating the sweet, spring-green grass.

When Oliver came out of the field, Jack re-latched the gate and after Oliver had hung the bridle from the post, for a moment they stood on the bank that slanted up from the road to the fence.

"Shall we walk along an' see what we come to?" asked Jack.

To this, Oliver nodded, for each step took them farther and farther away from Axminster, and closer to Hale, where they might find Jack's family. At which time Oliver would consider that he'd done right by Jack, who deserved nothing less than the utmost happiness to be found within a family's embrace.

TAKING MILK AT SUNSET

While they walked, the wind began to whip through the trees, though the dusty road straightened out and brought itself right up to a three-way corner. And there, as there might be at any respectable crossroads, was a tavern, whose sign indicated that it was the Eagle. The trees had been cleared around it, and the half-timber beams looked fresh alongside the stucco, with the low, gray stone wall around it.

The whole of the town had a tidy air, a place that Oliver would have liked to enter to take some rest, and perhaps get something to eat for him and for Jack. He had a penny the man with the horse had given him, but that wouldn't buy them much, besides which their disreputable state alone would bar their entry. Also, they were still too close to Axminster, and as long as the sun lit the sky, he wanted to be moving in the direction that would take him and Jack far, far away so Chalenheim could never find them.

"Clothesline," said Jack, giving Oliver's sleeve a tug. "Right there, just waitin' for us."

Of course, it could not be so that someone had hung out their laundry in the hopes that Oliver and Jack would soon be walking past and divest them of some of their clothes. Nor could it be that anybody would have hung out their laundry when it had rained and would rain again. But it just might be that some articles had been hung out some days ago, had gotten rained on, and had been left behind in the hopes they would eventually dry.

"Jacket for you," said Jack as he began walking along the stone fence line to where the laundry line was attached at one end to a shed.

"Jacket for *you*," said Oliver firmly. He could see that the other suitable garment, among the towels and single bed sheet, was a farmer's smock, all yellowed with age and quilted in that old-fashioned way that would look amazingly foolish when anybody but an elderly farmer put it on. So Oliver determined to take that for himself, and would insist upon it. "I'll wear the smock."

Thus he hurried to overtake Jack, and grabbed the smock from the line and put it on himself, all without waiting for Jack, and hardly thinking at all about the fact that he was stealing, outright, and had done so before Jack had even pulled the jacket from the line.

The jacket was a dusty black that had aged badly in the sun and from the hard labor of the person who had worn it, which had faded the cloth to dullness beneath the arms and along the neckline. But it fit Jack, at least mostly, and Jack pulled his arms around himself after he'd put it on, shivering into it, making himself fit into it in a way that hurt Oliver to watch.

"When we get somewhere," said Oliver. "When we gain some lucre, however filthy it might be, then we shall buy you something better to wear, something that fits, and that will keep you warm."

"You keep me warm, Nolly," said Jack.

He was looking down at where he couldn't quite button the front of his jacket, as if this thought, this expression, were so much a part of him it did not even need consideration before it was out of his mouth. Oliver wanted Jack to look at him so he could express how this made him feel when, of a sudden, Jack drew the edges of the jacket together, and shuddered, his fingers splaying over the black cloth as if it were his only protection.

"Jack," said Oliver, moving close, reaching out to touch Jack, gently, on the arm. "We'll get away, we will. We've come about ten miles on horseback, I should think, and should be well out of his reach. We'll keep going till nightfall and then get some rest. They won't know which way we went, or where to start looking. Or, perhaps, they've not even noticed we're gone yet."

"'Tis past suppertime at the workhouse," said Jack. "They know."

"Well, perhaps they do," said Oliver, determined to keep Jack's spirits up as well as his own. "But they can't search in all directions at once. Most likely they'll think we returned to Lyme and go that way."

"I miss Lyme," said Jack, looking up as he reached out to straighten the collar on Oliver's smock. "Never thought I'd say that, but I do."

"It was lovely," said Oliver, tipping his head to one side so Jack could run his fingers along the inside of the neckline of the smock to smooth it. "Except for Mrs. Heyland. I shall never forgive her for the way she treated you."

"Poor woman," said Jack, with a sudden spark of humor in his eyes. "But if it hadn't been for her—"

Oliver cut him off by turning away. He owed Mrs. Heyland a debt he would never be able to repay. Her sense of Christian duty had benefited them both, even if it was, toward Jack at least, begrudgingly given. In the end, she'd had Jack arrested, though, and for that, the scales balanced out. Then there was Dr. McMurtry, to whom was owed money. And then there was Mr. Thurly—

"Nolly," said Jack, following after him. "You must not carry all the troubles of the world upon your shoulders. Let them go, or tell me of them and I will help you."

Shaking his head, Oliver paused to let Jack catch up to him, and determined that his own state, pensive over the ill treatment of some and the kindness of others, was not as important, would *never* be as important, as the consideration of what might benefit Jack. Jack was putting up a good front, and it was Oliver's duty to be with him in that. So he tugged on Jack's lapel, the sunburnt black cloth fading to thinness beneath his fingers, and nodded.

"Shall we walk a little way until we get tired? Surely, we can stop for the night, somewhere, at least."

"Under one of your hedgerows?" asked Jack, laughing open mouthed at the tease. For there weren't any hedgerows along the road where they were walking, just bare fields on one side, plowed with black, turned-under earth, and a copse of trees on the other, catching the wind and shedding drops of rain to plop on the dusty road. "That'd be a trick."

"Indeed it would," said Oliver, finding the joke in it at last, for after what they'd been through, they deserved something more comfortable than the hard, damp ground for a bed.

They walked along for a while, as Oliver counted his own breaths, and steadied his nerves by the even sound of Jack's breaths matching his own. He liked the way their footsteps were in tandem, the way their shoulders bumped against each other as they walked so close together, as if there wasn't the width of the entire road on either side of them. But after what they'd been through, what they'd just escaped from, he couldn't bear to be far from Jack and imagined, by Jack's closeness, that Jack felt the same.

He caught Jack looking behind him. For all he seemed at ease, or perhaps wanted Oliver to think that he was, he was not. Oliver looked behind him to see what Jack was seeing, but there was nothing. Only the tavern disappearing behind a slight bend, the trees dancing lightly in the wind, the smell of rain coming as the clouds formed above the tree line.

"Should we keep walking a main road like this?" asked Oliver. "Likely a road past a tavern will have a coach or a cart or whatnot?"

"What about that turn there?" asked Jack, as if his ability to think ahead was miles beyond Oliver's, and he'd already figured it out.

Up along the road, where the dirt road cut through the trees, was a turning to the right, and the growth had not quite covered the sign. It was windy enough to carry a ball of dust over the next hill, and it was probably better to walk along the smaller road than the larger one. If anybody was following them, and they had certainly been noticed missing by now, it was best to go the obscure way, even if it did mean sleeping under a hedge, if they could even find one.

"Yes," said Oliver, with a calmness he did not feel. "You're right, we should turn off this main road."

It seemed so straightforward to do this once they got to the turning, and Oliver remembered from his walk from Harding-stone that he'd followed the way-signs to London and had never considered that going right or left unexpectedly, once in a while, would have covered his tracks far better. It was a miracle nobody had caught up with him before he'd reached the City. And now that he had Jack, Jack who had a nimble mind and was always three steps ahead of Oliver, they would fare better and be more inconspicuous, their travels less traceable.

WEARING THE JACKET, A RUSTY, FADED OBJECT THAT WAS probably worn to feed the pigs or some such, Jack nevertheless felt a little warmer. A little safer, as well, now that he was no longer naked to the breeze, which had grown chilly in the tunnel the road made through the trees, tipped with spring green that trickled down, from time to time, cold dashes of water when the wind hit the branches.

Though he was truly doing his best to keep up with Nolly, who had once walked seventy miles to London on his wee legs when he was only nine years old and looked to be continuing that tradition, as one should do when one was running away from a workhouse, Jack was lagging behind. It was not on purpose, and he was glad of it that Nolly seemed truly aware, this time, of what might befall them if they were caught, and was doing everything within his power to not get them caught. They were not safe, but they were *enough* safe so that a pause in their hightailing it out of whatever parish that controlled the workhouse might not be beyond reason.

They could huddle beneath one of those hedgerows that grew alongside the fields beyond the trees, as young men might when they are on the run. Then he could wrap his arms around Nolly, and breathe his breath, and get him to stop glaring and marching, and also so he could tell Jack that he was all right.

Not that Jack would stop worrying, as there was too much Nolly wasn't saying about what he'd found out about the fact that, in spite of his rose-colored view of the world, there were men like Chalenheim, and there were lads like Jack, upon whom such men preyed. Almost not one word had Nolly said about any of it, except to assert, and to make true that assertion, that Chalenheim would never again lay so much as a finger upon Jack, so long as Nolly had anything to say about it.

The road wound like a dull, brown ribbon through the trees, the direction of which might take them to a village or a fork, at which point they'd have to determine to go right or left. Though Jack had a general sense they were headed north, he could not be certain at what length they might arrive at their destination, nor how they would manage to eat along the way.

That is, unless they came to a village, whereupon Jack might use the talent of his fingers to acquire some funds. Then they could eat, get better clothes, and find a coach to take them where they needed to go. Though it was not at all certain, Jack might place odds in his own favor that Nolly would make not a single objection to Jack picking pockets this time around. Nor would he be as shocked by it once it happened. Of that particular change in Nolly's nature, Jack could not be certain whether or not he was glad.

He bestirred himself to catch up, to be able to walk by Nolly's side. When he did, he found that Nolly was looking along the road, and Jack refocused his attention there. Up ahead there was a slight dip in the road and, after that, a wide space, wherein collected a huddle of buildings built in the old style with gray stone and thatched roofs, and there was a village green upon which several cows strayed.

A stone well stood alongside the green, and across from it, shining somewhat new against the faded buildings, was a squat little building with a newly painted sign indicating a coach stop. Which then explained the tidiness of the road, in spite of the fact that no one had passed them either walking or riding, for several miles. The little village was along a mail coach route, somewhat infrequently visited, but enough so the fact of it kept the citizens employed, however marginally.

They walked along the main street and, on the other side of the street, Jack saw a few faces within the bull's-eye windows, but since they were not the mail coach, no one came out to greet them. Which was all to the better; there would be no picking of pockets in so small a hamlet, not unless Jack wanted them to get arrested on the spot.

He was about to ask Nolly why they were walking a little slower, a fact about which he was not intending to complain, but merely to inquire, when Nolly nudged him and pointed to the last house on the right. It was a pretty cottage, with new thatch and a door that had been lime-washed into a sparkling white, perhaps only days ago, as its brightness attested. Beyond the cottage was a shed, a miniature of the house against which it abutted, with a pair of green-painted half doors swung wide so the interior of the stable might sweeten in the spring air.

Nolly walked right up to it, and before Jack could ask what the hell he was doing, he saw a man in a cottager's smock, his legs fastened with cross-ties to keep his gaiters in place. The man wore a slouched hat that was meant to protect him from rain in the field, but in the finer weather, it sat back on his head. He was just inside the doorway, on a three-legged stool, milking a cow.

There was a slight pause as the man seemed to notice their presence, though his hands stilled on the cow's udders for a fraction of a second. Then he continued as if they weren't there, the *silz silz* sound of the milk hitting the metal pail, and suddenly all the spit in Jack's mouth raced to water it as his stomach became unsettled. Oh, he'd been hungry for ages, now, but, really, his whole body seemed to know that now it might be fed.

"If you be wantin' some milk, you need t'be asking' for it, eh, or you don't get none. Nicely now, for I cannot abide rude beggars."

Nolly's mouth, which had been opening to inquire politely, Jack assumed, on the availability of spare milk, snapped shut. Jack was fairly certain it was the word *beggar* that had thrown Nolly off. For what other lad would work so hard for a bit of bread in order to avoid being associated with somebody so low? To be considered such a one would be beneath Nolly's dignity, and never mind that he might go hungry for it.

But Jack was not above it, not if it meant bringing a shine to those blue eyes, and feeding his own poor stomach, which was quite howling at him by now.

"Say, mister," said Jack in his brightest voice, swallowing the moisture in his mouth. "Have you got any milk to spare? We find ourselves a bit far from town, an' have nowt to eat, since we've no coin, an' so thought we might ask."

If Jack had had a cap, he would have doffed it. As he did not, he touched his forelock and ducked his head, and gave Nolly a look that said he was to do the same. 'Twas only a game, and easy to play, if you knew the rules. Nolly obliged Jack with a quick echo of Jack's motions, and though the man wasn't looking at them, he nodded his head.

"Let me finish up, an' there'll be plenty of cream to go 'round."

The farmer, with sturdy, roughened hands that looked as though they'd milked plenty of cows, tugged on the cow's teats, stripping the last of the milk out of her. Then he stood up and gave her several solid pats, pulling the bucket out of the way as he reached for something on a shelf inside the door. It turned out to be a round blue and white china bowl, chipped in places along the edge, meaning that the bowl was no longer part of a fine service, but was intended, perhaps, to feed the barn cats, if there were any.

The man put the bowl on the stool, and poured out a portion of milk from the pail. Then he handed the bowl to Nolly, who took it with both hands.

But Nolly did not drink. Instead, after a moment's pause, he turned and handed the bowl to Jack. Who had to take it or the milk would be spilled, though he wasn't quite sure what he was to do with it, and for a moment, both of their pairs of hands held the bowl.

"You must drink first, Jack," said Nolly, in a calm, measured way, though his face was quite drawn. Jack saw him try to swallow, as if his mouth, like Jack's, was full of a sudden and inexplicable moisture.

"No, Nolly, you take it. He gave the bowl to you."

"You must drink first, Jack," said Nolly. "Or else if I do, I'm liable to drink the whole bowl, for I am too hungry to share."

This was a backhanded compliment by any means, to Jack, and a criticism about himself that Nolly should not have felt compelled to make. Whether or not it was true, the truth of Nolly's stubbornness was a certain thing, so Jack took the bowl from Nolly, tipped it to his lips and, standing in the open doorway of a crofter's barn, drank the milk.

It was warm, straight from the cow's body, the cream floating over his teeth and right into his stomach in a delightful swirl, sweet and thick. He took several large swallows, feeling rather greedy himself, then looked at the level of milk in the bowl, wiping his mouth with the back of his jacket sleeve as he did it.

"That looks about right," he said, trying to hand the bowl to Nolly.

But Nolly shook his head.

"One more swallow," he said. "Then it will be about right."

As to what the farmer was making of all this, Jack did not know, and it probably didn't matter that he didn't care. He could feel the energy from the milk racing through him, and took one last big swallow to make Nolly feel that it would be a fair share, then handed the bowl to Nolly with some insistence.

This time, Nolly took the bowl and, putting his mouth across from where Jack's had been, just to the right of the largest chip, tipped the bowl up and drank from it. For a moment, all Jack could see was the painted swirls of the bowl and the grime across the bottom and across Nolly's fingers where they gripped the bowl tightly. And the spare little trickle of milk that slipped down Nolly's chin before he swallowed huge in his throat and dropped the bowl from his mouth.

If there had been no farmer to observe him, Jack suspected Nolly might have been inclined to circle his tongue around the inside of the bowl, and wouldn't that have been a sight to see. Still and all, they'd gotten something in their bellies, and Jack figured he could now walk until they reached a village or town without falling over with exhaustion or hunger. He anticipated that they'd give the farmer an appropriately hearty thanks and be on their way, but the farmer surprised him.

"You'll have another serving, I think," said the farmer. "For the sake of the Christ child, so hold the bowl out."

The farmer poured milk from the pail and into the bowl that Nolly held. This second helping was on account of Nolly's face, beautiful in spite of the hollows under his eyes, the way his cheekbones were sharp beneath his skin, the way his hair was growing out from its unbecoming crop in sweet waves.

Or, perhaps, it was just Nolly, and the way he was, with his unselfish gesture when he was first given the bowl. Christians, such as the farmer, certainly did set a store by self-sacrifice though, as Jack was certain, the farmer could have made it clear from the very beginning of their encounter that there would be two bowls on offer, and not made Nolly go through all that sacrificing.

The farmer nodded at Nolly that he was to drink first, for which Jack was glad, for along the surface of the bowl of milk was where the cream was, and if you opened your mouth wide enough, it would slide right in. Jack was glad to see Nolly was doing this and licked his own lips in anticipation for the second half of the bowl.

Which, soon enough, was handed to him, and Jack polished the rest of the milk off with a smack of his lips and a small burp he took no pains to hide. Nor did the farmer seem to take offense, because he took the bowl back and set it once again on the shelf.

"Which way you headed, then, lads? To town, I expect."

"Yes," said Jack, for he could see that Nolly was still mulling over the taste of the milk in his mouth and could not be bothered to speak just then. "Something a bit bigger than this, where we might find work." As to what kind of work, he did not say, because it was nothing the farmer needed to know, however kind he'd been to them.

"You're not but several hours walk from Taunton," said the farmer. "If you follow this road, through to the next village and just keep walkin', you can't miss it."

"Where are we now?" asked Nolly, finding his voice at last. "What is the name of this village?"

"This here be Coombesbury," said the farmer. "An' then you go through Buckland St. Mary, and then there's woods, and then there's Taunton."

It sounded straightforward enough, and Jack would be glad to be within the surrounds of a real town, even if it wasn't London.

"Thank you, mister," Jack said, touching his forelock again for good measure. "We'll be on our way, then, seein' as how you've been so good to us, we won't want to keep you from the rest of your chores."

~

THE SKY WAS MADE DARK BY CLOUDS GATHERING ALONG THE tree line, all the branches and green-leaved ends making a great whisking sound, battering against each other as the rain started to fall. They'd passed through the tiny village of Buckland St. Mary with its low stone walls lining the road, and the gray-stone church being the tallest building upon the horizon, hurrying without stopping, as if they were two country lads on an urgent errand.

Oliver had seen some men, dressed in workmen's clothes, standing in front of a low-roofed building that might have been a tavern. He'd felt them looking him and Jack over, but did not pause, not to exchange greetings nor ask for directions. If they were local lads, as they wanted to be seen as, then asking directions was a sure way to be remembered, and it was very important that they not be remembered.

Jack stayed close at his side the entire stretch of what passed as a high street, and when they were on the other side, they kept walking, in case someone was watching.

"Nolly, it's goin' to rain."

"Yes, I am aware of that," said Oliver. He wanted to point out the hedgerows that had appeared on a road heading out of the village, but they'd kept walking so now the hedge was behind them. Along the right was the church, and the graveyard, all green and mossy with the headstones all yawing to one side as if the wind had, over time, pushed them over. "Shall we keep taking this road, or—"

"Out of the village," said Jack. "The sooner the better, to my way of thinkin'."

The road Jack gestured toward with a slight motion of his hand at his hip was narrowed by stone walls on either side, but up ahead, there was a curve to the road where the stone wall dropped away along one side, and the trees again started.

Oliver did not know why this village had unsettled him and the stop at Coombesbury had not, but the change was apparent. Perhaps it was the turn of the sky towards nighttime, or his exhaustion in spite of the milk in his belly. They'd ridden on horseback, and walked, and must have come almost fifteen miles. They needed to stop and rest if they could but find some type of shelter to keep off the rain.

"Jack," said Oliver, not wanting to make decisions for them both.

"We'll find a barn," said Jack, as if he'd heard Oliver's suggestion and agreed with it completely. "Look, up there, what's that?"

As the road rose before them and the light began to slink away, Oliver could see there was another gathering of buildings, a large, stone-walled crofter's cottage, and some outbuildings that could be small barns or storage sheds. With the wind came the scent of wet hay, and animal dung, and the undercurrent of oil that might have been rubbed into a harness to keep the leather supple.

"We'll go along here," said Jack.

He led the way off the road to a narrow path went led at an angle between the buildings, and curved around to a large stone barn that sat in a little hollow, with its doors facing where the sun would rise in the morning. The doors were shut, but that was nothing to Jack, who marched right up to them and jiggled the handle to open it.

"Country folk," he said by way of explanation.

Oliver could not fault him for this, being derisive of the country habit of leaving doors unlocked, because it would benefit them. He hurried to Jack's side and slipped through the open doorway, waiting in the near darkness as Jack pulled the door shut behind them.

It took only a moment before the gray light slipping through the narrow rim of the door was enough to see by. It was a small barn, with several cows chomping through their suppers along one side, and perhaps equipment was stored along the other wall, where Jack was pulling him.

"Ladder," said Jack. "Let's climb up."

Oliver let Jack go first, somewhat undone by the quickness with which Jack had found the ladder, but when they got to the top, he knew where they were. It was a storage loft for straw that was used as bedding for the animals below. The straw was from last year, by the scent of it, somewhat moldy and old, but it was dry. They were under the barn's solid slate roof as it began to rain, but they were not out in the weather. They were inside, where they could form nests in the hay.

Oliver could almost see Jack's outline where he was crouched beneath the slanted roof, and hear the *shush-shush* sound of him pulling hay into a pile. Oliver went to him and hunkered low on his heels to help, patting the hay into a bed-shaped lump and pulling the smock over his head to lay it at one end.

"That'll be our pillow," he said, tucking bits of hay beneath it to make it round-sided.

"You're my pillow," said Jack, not unexpectedly, for he seemed to prefer it when Oliver had the pillow, and he had Oliver.

Obliging Jack in this, Oliver laid himself down and pulled Jack to him, shivering a bit now that he was still, all his muscles screaming at that stillness while his stomach rumbled around as if looking for something to eat. Jack lay down, but did not relax, even when he tucked his head against Oliver's shoulder. Breathing in the dusty, hay-scented air, Oliver waited a moment, thinking now that they had gotten away, now that they had stopped, finally, to rest, that Jack might tell him the parts of his story that he'd not shared before.

"Jack?" asked Oliver, low, so as not to disturb the darkness around them.

"No, Nolly," said Jack, and he seemed to quiver in Oliver's arms, enough to drive a sense of alarm that Oliver half sat up, and tried to focus in the dark so he could see what was the matter.

"What do you mean, no?" he asked.

"Don't want to talk about it," said Jack, and Oliver could feel him try to still himself.

"But—"

Jack cut Oliver off by squeezing him hard about the waist, startling him into quiet.

"Not just this moment, will you *please*—"

But Jack could not continue. His words came out broken, and Oliver felt the sense of anger all over again, at the workhouse that had held them, and the system that allowed someone like Chalenheim to—but it wasn't about his anger, it was about what Jack needed just now. And that was for Oliver to not ask questions that Jack obviously did not want to answer.

Jack was now curled up, his knees digging into Oliver's side, as if he'd curled in upon himself, wanting to make himself as small as possible, even in the dark corner of a barn where no one would even think to look for them. Shaking in reaction, now that the walking had stopped, and his attention to their surroundings was cut off by rain at nightfall. Oliver's questions would only serve to remind him how close he had been to succumbing to Chalenheim's base desires.

"We're well hidden, thanks to you," said Oliver now, as if he had no curiosity about Jack's past whatsoever. He tucked Jack's shoulders closer to him and petted the curve of Jack's backside with his other hand. Jack was curled so closely that Oliver could reach all parts of him, and he did so, casually, slowly, touching Jack everywhere to let him know he was not alone in the dark.

"It's raining. They won't search through a rainy night. Tomorrow's a Sunday besides, so they won't be able to hire any good Christians to search for us, and they won't know which way that we went to begin with. So it's just you and I now, me and thee, on our adventure, headed north."

He stopped to swallow, as he felt his own chest hitch with a sense of panic that their direction and final destination held no certainty, only the unknown, unframed family that Jack had left so long ago behind him. So he changed his tack, taking a deep, even breath to sound as calm as he could while he continued to draw his hand along Jack's side, his legs, to smooth back the tangle of his hair from his face.

"Do you reckon," Oliver began, "that once we get to a larger village, that we might—that is, *you* might, practice your skill so that we could get something to eat? For I'm terribly hungry, Jack, and, as you know, food coming from your handiwork always tastes better to me."

Slowly, as if he might be imagining it, he felt Jack nod, Jack's chin brushing against his breastbone. He wanted Jack to relax a little, to know Oliver was not going to force from him information he was not yet willing to share. That much he had learned, that Jack would share when he was able, thus forcing him to do so, especially in the current circumstances, in spite of the fact that they were quite, quite alone, would be the worst of cruelty. It might even be that Jack would never tell him the whole of it and, if so, Oliver would content himself with that.

"I would particularly enjoy the opportunity to have a good wash, you know, with soap and hot water, such as I like to do. Then we could have a good, hot meal, you and I. Nothing fancy, mind, though I wouldn't mind a bit of good, fried potato, and a slice of meat pie, and a pint of beer and, of course, apple tart with pouring custard. And what about you?"

Not pausing to wait for Jack's answer, Oliver pressed his cheek to the top of Jack's head, and breathed slowly in and out while he talked of mundane things. "Oh, you'd very much enjoy a beefsteak, I should think, all fried in grease, and some thick soup, made with cream, with sweet carrot and spring peas in it. You can have some of my meat pie, if you like, and—"

He felt Jack move against him, felt the clonk of Jack's boot against his ankle, as if Jack felt safe enough to stretch out a bit, which would be much more comfortable for him than sleeping all rolled up like a pill bug. Oliver pretended he didn't notice and continued on, his stomach growling like a wild thing, and Jack's joining in every once in a while.

"Do you think if we started with veal in cream, that we'd have enough room for the pie *and* the beefsteak? Well, I'd much rather just have two servings of something sweet, perhaps treacle tart or a nice slice of cider cake."

Jack mumbled something against his shoulder, which Oliver felt as warmth along his collarbone. He did not let on that he was relieved Jack was joining the conversation; his only desire was that Jack not feel as if Oliver was doing anything to try and trick him into revealing himself too much.

"What is it, Jack? Should you care to add to the menu?"

"Eel," said Jack. "Eel stew, your favorite." The words were muffled by Oliver's shirt, and Oliver was glad the darkness hid his smile as he felt the relief surge through him. He was not used to Jack needing such coddling, but he was glad to have been able to give it, and even more so relieved that Jack seemed more like himself.

"I do believe," said Oliver with a very gentle nod so his chin would not bang against Jack's head, but rather caress it, "that I would be sorely tempted to eat eel stew, provided there was a good amount of broth, which I would eat instead of the eel. Tempted, I say, but I am well able to resist such a temptation, and would ask the serving girl to bring me something else instead."

Jack's breath rumbled in his throat, as if he were almost laughing at Oliver's refusal to eat eel in spite of his hunger. At which point Oliver took a deep breath and felt himself relax, in spite of the fact that the straw was poking at everywhere on his body, his hips felt stiff in the stillness, and the welts there pounded along long, cane-shaped lines.

It hurt to lie on his back, but he'd rather that than disturb Jack.

"But truly," Oliver continued. "I'd give you the veal in cream, and the beefsteak, and the meat pie, if I can just have dessert, about five different kinds, all lined up, one after the other, all crusted with sugar and slathered with butter-cream. What do you say to that?"

"You c'n have whatever you like, my dear Nolly," said Jack. "But you should have a little bit of something else first so you don't get a bellyache, for then you would have to stay in bed all day, and then what would we do?"

"We'd stay in bed all day," said Oliver, quite promptly. "And I'd need you at my side to ring the bell for the servants to bring me some soothing tea, and you some bread and butter and coffee."

He did not know why he said that last group of items, for it was a meal eaten on the street that rather belonged in London, when the weather was cold and the sky filled with snow. As it had been, when Oliver had worked at the haberdashery and Jack had seemed to lurk around every corner, as if just waiting for Oliver to show up so he could taunt and tease him. When everything had seemed rather more straightforward than it had been of late.

But perhaps Jack understood, for he stretched out fully now, and pressed the length of himself along Oliver's side. As Oliver's bruises protested, Jack's body added warmth to his own and made him sigh. Jack's arm was looped over his middle, making him feel snug in the scratchy hay and dusty darkness.

"I shall have the servants bring you whatever you wish, Nolly," said Jack, softly but clearly. "But I will admit I'm now hungrier than I was before with all of your talk about beefsteak an' the grease to fry it in."

Which meant that Oliver had gotten Jack's preferences correctly considered, and he would make sure that Jack had plenty of whatever it was that he would want after he'd consumed that first beefsteak. And this, rather than merely letting Jack dote on Oliver's needs, as had happened in the past.

"I'm sorry, Jack," said Oliver, meaning it. "But all I can think about is food." This was not quite the truth, of course, and Oliver considered that Jack probably knew this, and knew the reason why. "Food, and hot water and soap, and clean sheets, and perhaps—"

"Perhaps what?"

"Perhaps a good book to read, and a fire to sit beside. Is that too much to want, do you think?"

"No," said Jack. "'Tis only what you've ever wanted, an' there ain't no harm in it."

All at once, Oliver felt better, for if Jack approved of this little story in Oliver's head, then perhaps he would want to be a part of it. And continue on being a part of it, even though working in a shop and wearing a white apron to please their customers was not quite what Jack would consider his preference of lifestyle.

But then, Oliver was thinking too far ahead, as he often did. Were he to speak any of this aloud to Jack, Jack would remonstrate him to leave tomorrow's troubles to tomorrow. Because Jack was right, as he always was, about these things. Oliver needed to keep his focus on the near future, of how they would find their way to Hale, and how they would get money so they could eat along their journey so that when they met Jack's family they would not arrive as starving wrecks upon their doorstep, and—

"Nolly," said Jack, yawning in the darkness.

"Yes, Jack?" asked Oliver.

"Only do stop thinkin'. I can hear your mind goin' on an' on till it's makin' me dizzy. So stop, will you, an' let a fellow get some rest?"

"Yes, Jack," said Oliver as somberly as he was able, though he was smiling as he pressed a kiss to the top of Jack's head. He waited a moment, as Jack's breathing slowed down, and Jack's head became heavier upon his shoulder. Then, very quietly, he said, "I love you, Jack."

He thought he felt Jack go still, just for a moment, then felt Jack's arm tighten about his middle, and the warmth of Jack's mouth as he turned his head to press a kiss upon Oliver's neck. Then he sank back into stillness, his breath evening out, until, when he was sure that Jack was quite asleep, Oliver let himself fall asleep, also.

❦ 25 ❦

THE RING OF BELLS

The rain had stopped sometime in the middle of the night, though Oliver, as he awoke just before dawn, could hear the sound of water, as if the roof were leaking from a slipped tile, or a misplaced slat of wood. But the overarching sound was that of birdsong, full-throated beyond the chinks in the stone walls of the barn, and Oliver could picture them, swaying on the tall grasses, larks, and curlews, and perhaps a thrush or two.

They were deep in the country, so of course there would be birds, and perhaps a bright brook where the ducklings might swim, and he felt a wash of loss over that childhood time he'd had in the Maylie household. When his only duty had been to carry notes between Aunt Rose and Uncle Harry, and his reward had been sweet things to eat and, perhaps, a new book on flowers, or geography.

He'd recognized that those traits, of reading, and studying, and being good, had been what was desirable then, and he'd been happy to do it. But what he mourned for was the fact that it had been so short-lived, and had been ripped away so quickly.

He couldn't imagine Jack wanting to go with him to that kind of life, so sedate and still, in addition to which, Jack had obliged him to going to visit his own family first. Where Oliver was sure, quite sure, that Jack's mother and father and sister would love Jack as Oliver did and would want him to stay with them, and be their son, and a brother, again. And if that was the way it was to be, well, then—

"You sleep serious," said Jack, mumbling into Oliver's smock. "An' you wake the same. What I tell you afore? Let tomorrow's—"

"—troubles belong to tomorrow, yes, Jack, I remember," said Oliver.

But it was hard not to imagine how it might go and, when Jack did decide to stay with his family, which surely he would, whether at the same time they would want Oliver to go back to where he came from. Which meant Oliver would be proceeding to Chertsey on his own, which was too bad, for he was sure that Aunt Rose would have cared for Jack the moment she saw him.

With a sudden movement, Jack hauled himself on top of Oliver, laying upon him with the length of his body, boots banging Oliver's ankles, knees digging into Oliver's thighs, their hips aligned. Jack's hands cupped around Oliver's head, with Jack's thumb making a soft sweep across Oliver's mouth.

Oliver's breath was snatched from him, his whole body shivering with pleasure at the thought that Jack might kiss him now. And, given that, Jack might be up for talking about the part of his past that had been so dark he'd never summoned the desire to share it with Oliver.

"For fuck's sake," said Jack, his head falling forward till his forehead rested on Oliver's breastbone. "I see that look in your eyes, an' it won't do. I'll tell you when I'm ready to talk about it an' not afore that. Understand?"

Realizing he'd done once more what he swore to himself he wouldn't do, Oliver nodded. He'd let his mind go in motion and, as always, settling on what he wanted, and not what Jack needed. Which was, for the present, that Oliver not badger him about it, about anything. Jack had agreed that they would travel to Hale, which should be enough for Oliver, and indeed it was.

"I'm sorry, Jack," said Oliver, lifting his chin in the hope Jack's kiss would still be forthcoming. "I only mean to help."

"Of course you do," said Jack. He lifted his head and looked down at Oliver with half-lidded eyes. "An' you be wantin' a kiss as well, I see."

Oliver nodded, for of course this was true.

"You c'n always kiss me anytime you please, y'know," said Jack.

This was certainly true, but perhaps the habit of being easy with Jack, of touching him gently or pulling him close, had been lost in the span of days that they'd been trapped in the workhouse. It was up to him now to relearn those traits and impulses that Jack had so kindly guided him into knowing. How it felt, the difference between giving a kiss and taking one.

Besides, he had Jack on top of him, and though they were both hungry, and Oliver felt as if he'd slept not at all, he sensed that Jack's skin was warm beneath his shirt. And, as Jack stirred on top of him, the length of his cock pressed into Oliver's, not quite hard as when filled with passion, but not quite relaxed either. Which meant that if Jack could be at such ease, then Oliver could, too.

"I could never be as brave as you, Jack," said Oliver. He drew his hands from Jack's and tucked his hands behind Jack's head, cupping with easy fingers in case Jack wanted to draw back, and pulled him in close for a kiss.

Just as Jack's lips brushed Oliver's, Oliver felt a puff of air, as if Jack were about to laugh. Letting Jack pause, Oliver looked up at him.

"Now that's a bloody lie, an' you know it."

Jack kissed him then, open mouthed, as if bestirred by Oliver's simple confession, even if he felt it untrue. The taste of Jack's mouth was thick with sleep, and Oliver sank into the comfortable sense of the familiar, of a mouth he knew, of lips that caressed his, of Jack's hands coming to circle around his shoulders.

Pulling back, Jack whispered against Oliver's mouth, "You are brave as a lion, an' you always have been."

Just then, from below, came a hideous pounding, and the floorboards beneath them shook with it.

"What is going on up there? Who is up there? Come down at once! Have you been stealing my eggs?"

Had Oliver known there were eggs to steal, he still would not have taken them. At least not for himself, for he could not abide the taste of raw eggs, having tried it once at Uncle Harry's urging. He'd vomited the entire egg up in a moment and had no wish to try it again. But for Jack, who probably did not mind the taste of raw egg, Oliver would have stolen for him an entire dozen.

"Come down at once, I say! Or I will come up there with my pitchfork and spear you through!"

Jack's eyes were wide as he looked at Oliver and, Jack being on top of him, it had the feeling of being caught red-handed, in a position so compromising there was nothing either of them could have said to explain it away. All at once Oliver wanted to shove Jack from him, as the most sensible thing to do, but he felt the heat of irritation, for how dare anybody make him want to think that way about Jack? About who they were together?

"Come down from there, or I shall call the constable!"

That the closest constable was likely to be a good twenty-minute walk away did not matter, for there were probably strapping farm lads about who might lend a hand, so they needed to climb out of the loft and face their aggressor before anything more dire happened.

"I'll go first," said Oliver.

As Jack shook his head, as if to dissuade him, Oliver shifted his whole body so Jack was forced to roll off of him, but away from the ladder. Oliver gave Jack's shoulders a squeeze, pulled on the smock, and got up on his hands and knees and climbed down the ladder.

There, at the bottom, dressed in a smock similar to Oliver's, was an angry farm crofter, red-faced and wielding a pitchfork with the pointed end in Oliver's direction. Oliver could hear Jack scrambling down the ladder as well, but when the farmer jerked the pitchfork too close, Oliver reached behind him to grab Jack's arm to make sure Jack stayed behind him.

"We ain't done nothin' mister," said Jack, in careful tones over Oliver's shoulder, as if that would be enough to settle the situation.

"I should say you have," said the farmer, insistent, his eyes narrowing. "Coming into my barn as if you was invited, messing up my straw."

"It was last year's straw, sir," said Oliver. "And we've hurt nothing, and caused harm to nobody by sleeping in it."

"I shall be the judge of that," said the farmer, though it was beyond Oliver how he could be unless he climbed up into the loft himself.

"We mean to be on our way," said Oliver, taking a step back, bumping into Jack with his boot heels.

To their right was the open barn door, through which was the racing spring sunshine and the farmyard and, beyond that, the tree line and the road headed north.

He did not know exactly where the road would lead, but anywhere was better than where they were. He did not know how to convey, exactly, what he thought they should do, but if Jack could use Oliver as his shield, and make a break for it—but when the farmer made another stab at Oliver with the pitchfork, Jack did not run, but pulled Oliver back, and then ran, dragging Oliver behind him, his hand like iron on Oliver's forearm.

They ran together in the damp morning air, kicking up bits of muddy earth from beneath their boots, tearing around the corner of the stone wall to pound up the dirt road until they were beneath a stretch of trees. Oliver's lungs were burning, his thighs shaking as he pulled Jack to a halt. He had to bend over with his hands on his knees to catch his breath, not knowing when he'd been so winded after so short an exertion, but Jack was the same.

The workhouse had drained their strength, making it a miracle of sorts that they'd gotten away from the farmer at all. Who, on a good breakfast of sausage and eggs, could have surely outmaneuvered them if he'd been able.

"That was stupid," Jack said, straightening up, his hand on his stomach. "An' completely foolish of you to do what you did."

His face was a washed-out white, gray beneath his eyes, his lips pale. He couldn't quite look at Oliver, and Oliver realized in that short moment, when they'd seemed trapped, how scared Jack had been. If Jack was cross with him, it was because of that and nothing more.

"Well," said Oliver, brushing his hands across the knees of his trousers as he straightened up and moved closer to Jack. "With regard to you, I lose all common sense."

Which, in and of itself, might not make sense to Jack, so Oliver lifted his hand to push Jack's hair back from his forehead. Only Jack jerked back so Oliver couldn't touch him, and then winced, as if sorry for it.

With Jack still not looking at him, Oliver tried another way, by moving close enough so their shoulders touched, and he could brush up against Jack as a fond hunting dog might, looking for affection without demanding it.

Though Jack seemed to want to tighten and pull away, he was trembling with the effort of standing still, so Oliver remained that way, motionless, with only his shoulder touching Jack's, until the trembling softened, and Jack's chin sank to his chest.

"So scared, Nolly," said Jack. "So scared." His voice was whisper-thin and pained Oliver's heart to hear it.

Oliver wished he could ever be as brave as Jack to admit such a thing, for Jack always was this way, straightforward with himself, at least when in Oliver's company. To repay this bravery, the cause for which did not need explaining, Oliver turned his wrist so his fingers could link with Jack's, and they could clasp hands as they stood in the middle of the road, with Oliver looking at anything but Jack.

Instead, he looked at the light coming through the branches, the way the wind whipped through the tops of the trees, sensed the way the air still smelled like rain, and waited until Jack could settle himself, until he felt at ease to squeeze Oliver's hand back, and let go a little. Though not all the way, as was Jack's way.

"Shall we walk a bit?" asked Oliver, as he had the previous night, when speaking of innocuous things had seemed the better thing to do for Jack, rather than insisting that Jack explain whatever was the matter with him. He started to walk and tugged on Jack's hand for him to come with him. "Though, if you do happen to see a coffee busker, or a vendor of meat pies, or whelks, even—"

"How the fuck can you eat whelks when you don't like eel?" asked Jack, falling into step beside him. His voice was a bit uneven, but he seemed to want this, the distraction of walking, of casual conversation of what they might eat at their next meal, rather than anything serious and so, for the nonce, Oliver would keep his peace.

"As it happens," said Oliver, conversationally, as if this were often a topic of discussion between them, "while whelks might be overcooked and a bit chewy, they taste of the butter-broth they were cooked in, while eels taste like something that's been cooked in stale brine, which I cannot abide."

"Did you vomit, then, Nolly?" asked Jack. "The last time you had eel?"

"Indeed I did," said Oliver, with no shame whatsoever, for if that's what Jack wanted to distract himself from overly charged feelings about which neither of them could presently do anything, then Oliver would describe every item that had caused him to be sick, and every dish that had given him pains upon being forced to eat it. He would expose himself in such broad terms that Jack could tease him about it from now until eternity, which was fine by Oliver, if that was what Jack needed to feel less exposed himself.

"An' before that?" asked Jack.

Oliver felt that Jack was looking at him and, when he turned his head to see, was welcomed by the sight of Jack half-blinking at him, the way a cat might, contented on its sunny windowsill, and Oliver knew that he was doing it right, in taking care of Jack this way.

"If you must know," said Oliver, pretending to be affronted that Jack would ask so personal a question. "There was a string of very delicious tarts that came out of Aunt Rose's kitchen, and I spent a great deal of time in the privy, in the heat of the afternoon, mind you, after partaking of them before we discovered that Cook had determined we were all ill, and put castor oil in the tarts. However, unaware of this, Aunt Rose allowed me to have an entire tart to myself, which, being made of pear, and having such a horrible association, I can no longer abide."

Jack snorted, though what seemed to be his attempt at delicate restraint became untethered, and Oliver was very glad to feel Jack's forehead bump against his shoulder, as if he were asking Oliver to join in the absolutely grand joke of the very proper Oliver Twist stuck in a privy with his trousers and smalls down about his ankles, wracked with ill bowels for hours and therefore ever after unable to enjoy a pear tart. This Oliver did with a small smile, restraining himself from reaching out to touch Jack, or sling his arm around Jack's shoulders, just yet.

"Though I do still enjoy a pear in its natural state, I just can't abide them in tarts anymore, even with cinnamon and sugar."

"What a tender stomach you have," said Jack, as he himself slung his arm around Oliver's shoulders, and reached to gently pat Oliver's belly, which felt very hollow beneath Jack's slight touch.

"Delicate as bone china," said Oliver, pretending to be prim about it. "Though when Mr. Grimwig would say that, it was with much less grace."

"Fuckin' bastard," said Jack.

Jack pulled his arm away, but stayed close to Oliver as they walked along the dirt road, and Oliver considered that it was interesting to think now of Mr. Grimwig without the fierce, overriding anger surrounding any interactions he'd shared with the man.

It was as if having someone finally see the situation as he saw it helped remove him from any immediate feeling about it. Which was Jack's way of being kind. As was, *perhaps,* what Oliver had been doing, when he'd realized that talking about anything but what had bestirred Jack so uncomfortably was a way of rescuing Jack, as much as standing between Jack and a pitchfork-armored farmer intent upon eviscerating them had been.

That Oliver was not normally comfortable talking about himself so casually to others, preferring to not expose his more intimate thoughts and tender feelings, with Jack it was different. For if Jack tended to tease, and had done upon many an occasion, when Oliver was being so very serious or perhaps glum, too glum for Jack's liking, the teasing had never been with any real cruelty, and so, it seemed, as was the real revelation dawning upon him, that for Jack, to do the same in return was a way of taking care of him.

This was something to be remembered and acted upon, that while Oliver could shield Jack from those who might hurt him physically, as had happened, he might also create a shield of words, for Jack to use for himself when his skin might feel raw from a memory so strongly felt that his whole body trembled from it, even if he did not feel emboldened to share the memory with Oliver.

"Don't think about him n'more, Nolly," said Jack, swinging his arm down so that it might brush against Oliver's. "But do tell me of aught else you cannot abide, for I shall be sure to order them for you when we next come to some place where we might get a bite to eat."

Never more sure Jack would never do any such thing, Oliver realized that he himself had fallen silent, when it was his duty, his responsibility, even, to chatter away like a magpie, however foreign it might feel for him to do so. But for Jack, he would talk all the way to the next village, as well as beyond, if need be.

"As it happens," said Oliver, mentally lining up any number of innocuous topics that he might expand upon. "One spring in Chertsey, there had a blight among the field peas that had gone unnoticed, as the marks along the pods were pale and yellow rather than being bold, black spots, as might warn Cook that they would be unsuitable to eat."

"Blast Cook anyhow," said Jack, shaking his head, as if despairing over Cook's habit of attempting to poison the family.

"Yes," said Oliver, shaking his head as if saddened by the thought of such trust misused so casually. "After the entire family was fraught with a mild malaise, Cook was dismissed. Afterward, we got another cook, who has such a tender hand with pastries that she works for my aunt and uncle still."

"Did you suffer much, Nolly?" asked Jack. Which was, of course, Oliver's cue to describe in some detail his illness and the repercussions of it.

"Since I never did care for peas overly well, I'd not taken more than a spoonful. Since my aunt had not had peas at all, she was at my bedside, as well as my uncle's, with ginger tea, and a cool cloth for my head. In retrospect, I do think she enjoyed the drama of nursing me when there was no real danger to be found, but rather, an excuse for me to lie in bed and be tended to, while she could be—" Oliver paused, as he'd never considered the incident the way he was thinking of it now, "—that she could be brave and calm and cure me through her attentiveness."

"Ginger tea?" asked Jack. "What's that, then?"

"Oh," said Oliver, for a moment startled before he realized that of course Jack would have had no experience with the dosage of such a thing as might be afforded by folk living in more civilized circumstances. Or with someone who might have considered such a thing useful for a small boy with a bellyache, even though Fagin was usually more attentive to his lads. "My aunt made it from ginger, sliced in hot water and steeped and, of course, to which was added several spoonfuls of honey." At Jack's confused look, he added, "It's very good for the stomach, if one has had, say, one too many slices of cake, or—"

"Rotten peas," suggested Jack.

"Yes, rotten peas, or, well, pear tarts soaked in castor oil, though I do not remember anybody having the least bit of sympathy for me after having had an entire tart to myself."

"Should have gotten ginger tea, anyhow," said Jack, as if trying this idea on for size. "For how is a small, wee thing, such as you were, supposed to stop himself?"

"Discipline against eating sweet things has never been my strong suit," said Oliver, half-chiding himself, even as it felt somewhat new to be admitting this aloud.

But Jack didn't seem to be the least bit surprised by this information and, by his expression, much calmer than it had been some moments before, he seemed unconcerned that Oliver's sweet tooth had oft run rampant, in spite of himself, but rather was more disturbed by the fact that the caring adults around him had been unmoved by his plight.

"Shall I make you some?" asked Oliver, now, for thinking of that time, and his aunt so soon to be visited, was a bit more than he could consider just then.

"But I'm not ill," said Jack.

"It's very good at any hour," said Oliver. "For even if the tea is cool, if there is enough honey, it tastes a bit like a summer day looks, you know, that bright bit of blue sky beyond the trees, with a breeze coming through to keep it from being too hot."

"A summer day?" asked Jack, suddenly stopping in the middle of the road, his hand on Oliver's arm to stop him as well. "What need have I of ginger tea when you are my summer day?"

When Oliver stopped and allowed himself to look directly at Jack, he could see, as if with new eyes, how Jack now looked. That the gray circles had gone from beneath his eyes, and the whiteness from his face, even the faint quiver of his shoulders, had settled into easiness, as if the walk in the country beneath the green trees with all of Oliver's words, his chatter so earnestly given, had wrought in Jack exactly the change he would have wanted it to.

It was as if, somehow, he had been the master of his intentions, of knowing that rather than anything he normally would have done, that the casualness of his own behavior had helped Jack to master himself. And now, for his reward, was Jack, coming close and cupping Oliver's head, his fingers tender along the back of Oliver's neck. The look in his eyes, the praise in his smile, made Oliver feel warmed through, and humbled by this, albeit unspoken, praise, he dipped his head, as if Jack had discovered within him some nefarious scheme.

But Jack must not have considered it so, for he alighted upon Oliver's mouth a tender kiss, once and then twice, his thumb hovering over Oliver's cheek, a sweep of skin on skin that was a kiss in and of itself. Oliver closed his eyes, thinking to seal this moment in his heart however long he lived, that he had come upon this moment where he felt utterly worthy of Jack's complete affection.

Drawing back, his hands still on Oliver's face, Jack smiled in his way, his mouth curled upward, his sharp teeth showing.

"Shall we continue to walk a bit more?" asked Jack, patting Oliver's cheek gently, as if completely unaware, as he perhaps was, or perhaps was not, of how affected Oliver had been by that simple kiss. "We are sure to come to a village eventually, where I promise to pick pockets from only the richest, sourest gentleman you can point out to me. An' then I'll get you somethin' to eat, food from my handiwork an' that." Jack waved his other hand in the air, as if dismissing Oliver's previous statement with apparently no care whatsoever.

That was Jack teasing him, filling the air with words so that anything engendered within his skin, or expressed through his hands, might be shielded so as not to overtake him completely. And while normally Oliver would have let Jack's announcement stay where it had landed, he now knew what Jack needed in return.

"But be sure to make it someone rude," said Oliver, clasping Jack's hand to his face for a moment before turning to walk again, knowing that when Jack stepped into pace beside him and they began going along the road once more that he was doing it exactly right. "Or someone unkind, with an overbearing air, at the very least, and a cross way with his servants. D'you think you can manage, Jack, or do you need me to walk up and tap the particular person on the shoulder so you will know which one is the mark?"

"Teach me how to suck eggs, will you?" asked Jack.

He clapped Oliver on the shoulder with an open-mouthed laugh, and together they walked in the fine spring day beneath a copse of trees for a good many minutes, shielded by the rolling sunlight among the clouds. They walked along a hedgerow that bordered a newly plowed field, the rich, dark furrows sending up a good scent, full of energy and the brightness to come when the plants would push up through the soil and turn their faces to the sun.

THERE WAS NEVER A CHANCE OF THEM NOT HAVING TO DO this, though Jack admitted this only to himself, and thought Nolly had believed the same. But to pick pockets in the market square next to the church that now was filling with milling parishioners just leaving the sermon was to bring the concept into a terrible and clear light.

As he stood with Nolly at the far edge of the square, leaning against the brickwork of a venerable building that currently housed a fashionable milliner, they absorbed the sunlight streaming through the clouds, the precursor of warmer days, and Jack considered what he might say. Not to convince Nolly, for Nolly had already agreed, but to tender his guilt about it; the hunger in their bellies wasn't enough, it seemed, so Jack needed something more.

"We'll spend it wisely, you know," he said, tipping his head so he could gaze upon the way the sun gilded Nolly's hair, and cast roses in his cheek, and made his eyes bright.

"Of course we will," said Nolly, a response not to what Jack had just said, but to what he meant.

There was no way around this plan, unless they wanted to snatch food out of the very mouths of the parishioners who had brought baskets and were sitting on the stone benches on the edge of the churchyard and the far end of the square to partake of a little refreshment in the open air, while the day was fine.

Jack couldn't blame them, for he liked to eat a bit of grub in the out-of-doors as well. But there were too many of them who might get in the way, if Jack were to retreat with one of their new loaves of bread freshly cut, or boiled eggs, with a bit of salt and pepper, wrapped in a twist of paper, to dip the bitten egg into. No, it would have to be cash that he took from a thick wallet, from the sort of gentleman who would not miss its contents so very much.

"What about that one over there?" asked Jack, keeping his voice casual, as if he was asking this merely for theoretical reasons. The gentleman in question had on a fine wool coat, deep brown with bright gold buttons and a silky top hat. "He would do, I'd say."

"What about his friend?" asked Nolly, and he too sounded as if he were trying to keep his statement casual, as if this singling out of a mark would affect himself not at all. "The coat's newer, and his gloves are silk. He's got not a speck of mud on his boots, for all the square is so damp."

Nodding, Jack agreed. The friend was a little older with a

bushy, graying beard, but stoutly built, as if he'd never missed a meal in his entire life. To add to this, Jack watched as the man took off his gloves and snapped his fingers, and a serving girl, carrying a hamper way too big for her to be carrying, hurried forward to present it.

Orders were given as to which bench the repast might be taken to and laid out, and the girl struggled with the hamper and began to set out the food. Not simple fare, as the bowls were good china, and the napkins snowy white.

"What do you need me to do?" asked Nolly.

His heart wasn't in it. Jack knew that it wasn't, but that's just how Nolly was. He would help Jack because he said he would, and though he might not like that part, Jack would wager that the resultant meal that would follow might help him forget his distaste.

"It's a handoff job," said Jack, steepling his fingers together and stretching his hands out in front of his body to ease the tendons in each finger, in his wrists. "I get in close, ever so casual like, and you're right behind me so you stumble on me. I'm cross, so I shout at you."

"Won't this attract attention?" asked Nolly in a small voice.

"It will indeed, my smart lad." Jack rubbed his hands together. "They're lookin' at me shoutin', and not at you, stuffin' the wallet I've just given you down your trousers."

Nolly was silent for a moment, chewing on his lower lip as the fingers of one hand worried the ragged edge of his farmer's smock. He looked sweet in it, though Jack knew quite clearly that he'd get, at the very least, a cuff to the back of his head if he mentioned that fact out loud, just now. Later, he would be able to tease, but not just now.

The contemplation that now harnessed Nolly's gaze to the man in the fine wool coat and all the food from an enormous hamper at his disposal went on for another good minute until Jack considered that he might have to voice out loud the very good reasons as to why picking pockets was their only option.

They needed cash, and they needed it fast, both to eat before they fell over in a faint, right in front of all those good, church-going folk, and also to get tickets on a coach heading north in short order.

These were solid, without-argument reasons, and Nolly needed to understand that. It wasn't on a whim they were doing this, rather it was for their own survival.

Just as Jack figured he'd have to start all over again, Nolly looked at Jack.

"This is like the last time, when you made as though I'd just stepped on your feet, right?"

"Right," said Jack. "I'm just goin' about my business, an' you're a clumsy country lad walkin' about an' gawpin' at the fine folk in their Sunday best." He put his hand on Nolly's arm as gently as he could, as he wanted Nolly to know that this was a simple thing they were doing. Nobody would be hurt by it.

"There you go, sweetheart. Walk to that end, an' when you see me gettin' near the gentleman in question, come across the square, like you're goin' to the church. When I bump into you, an' you feel my hand down your trousers at all, don't think it's for affection, for this is strictly business. Got it?"

As Jack was glad to see, Nolly, trying to hide a smile and fail-ing, obeyed orders and proceeded across to the far end of the square. When he was just about there, Jack began to walk forward, ambling, tugging on his jacket lapels as if he'd not a care to worry him, and on this fine day, so much to distract him, the fine weather and the fine folk.

He pursed his lips as if he were whistling, all very casual. He even moved out of the way as two little girls, dressed in fashion-able flowered frocks and curved straw bonnets, wanted to skip where he was walking. Well, that was nothing to Jack. He continued on his way, sensing Nolly coming closer out of the corner of his eye, right up to the moment where Jack was quite close to the gentleman.

Nolly was one, perhaps two, feet away, and Jack turned left

while his right hand reached out to gently reach inside the gentleman's suitcoat. At that very moment, Nolly bumped into him from behind, and Jack rotated quickly to the right as he reached under Nolly's smock and briskly shoved the wallet in. He could only hope that Nolly had the sense to push out his belly to keep the wallet at his waist, rather than let it spill down his legs, for it was quite a thick wallet, and Jack was sure he'd heard coins jingling as well as bills rustling.

"I say," said Jack, in his best imitation of how a young, well-brought-up gentleman might speak who has just had his toes trod upon, and is not quite sure how much fault to find with the culprit. "You should watch where you're goin'!"

"Yes, indeed," said the gentleman whose pocket Jack had just picked. "I saw the whole thing. This bumpkin plowed directly into you, not looking where he was going, the fool."

"Terribly sorry," said Nolly. He even ducked his head and scratched in front of his ear, as if quite perplexed and astonished to find himself where he was. "I'll be going on my way now. Terribly sorry, terribly sorry."

Then, with a heavy-footed gait, Nolly turned around and went back across the square, as if he felt foolish to have caused so much trouble, his head hanging down, one arm limp at his side as he walked. The other arm, Jack was glad to see, was plastered over his middle as if he had a stomach ache. A stomach ache of fine leather and gold coin, that is. Fagin would have been quite proud of the two of them, picking pockets in unknown territory amidst a gathering of yokels who had no idea what had just happened.

"He's a simpleton," said some woman from behind the gentleman. "Bless him, poor thing."

"I was wrong to be so cross, then," said Jack, rather stoutly. "I'll go and make sure he gets home all right."

In the face of the general good nature of the crowd that had gathered all around, Jack gave a small bow and hurried across the square after the retreating back of the beautiful simpleton who'd done such a good job with the handoff. Jack knew he was going to have to come up with rather a special treat for his brave and beloved Nolly. After they were both rested and fed, that is.

He caught up with Nolly inside of a moment, and put his arm around Nolly's shoulder, broadly so the crowd could see him do this. He guided his brave boy up through the archway that led into a warren of streets beyond the square, the shops tidy with clean front steps, the streets narrower than London's, but with the gutter running down the center from the recent rains, the cobbles repaired and swept.

It was a prosperous little town, then, for all Jack had never heard of it before. But then, he'd only ever been in London and Australia, so who could fault him for not knowing? Nobody, that's who.

"Walk a bit slower, Nolly," said Jack. He leaned close, not releasing Nolly's shoulders as two of the town's fine gentlemen passed them in the street, headed toward the square, no doubt, where the day's strolling and watching and being watched were taking place. "Too fast gets you noticed right about now."

"It's slipping, Jack," said Nolly. His arm tightened about his own waist, his fist clenching as if he truly had a bellyache and was trying to soothe it. There was a white ring around his mouth and the tender skin beneath his eyes was dappled with sweat. "How much further do I need to carry it before I hand it over to you?"

Quickly, Jack looked up the street. Nolly was barely hanging onto the wallet as well as to his own nerves.

"Just along there. Just to the alley."

Before they got to the alley, a gathering of well-to-do folk came down the street, with servants following carrying hampers and umbrellas and blankets, each one of them in haste to get to the square.

Jack watched where they'd come from and drew a mental map in his head. It was Sunday, so the shops were closed, but the rich folk seemed to be coming from the high part of town, down the slope to the square, as if they were deigning to gather around a country churchyard and an empty market square, as if it were the fashionable thing to mingle with the common folk on the Lord's day.

It might be amusing to mull over how long that would be fashionable, once some fine lady put her slippered foot in a cow pat, but Jack needed to focus on what was at hand, his dear Nolly, all white with sweat, and looking sideways at Jack, as if expecting the hangman's noose at any moment.

But perhaps it wasn't that bad, for just at the mouth of the alley, Nolly bent and pulled out the wallet to hand it over to Jack. This, in broad view of the street, though he did try to turn himself sideways to hide what his hands were doing.

"It was slipping, Jack," Nolly said. "Right down my leg, and I couldn't hold it up any longer."

There was some saucy joke Jack could make about this, but Nolly had the expression of someone who expected to be roundly scolded and given a good drubbing. But it wasn't Nolly's fault. If ever Jack had thought it, as he thought it now, with a face like that, and a temperament so fiery beneath the quiet surface, Nolly was made for the big shill, not this street-level stuff.

Hopefully it would not come to that, for as Jack slipped into the alley with Nolly right behind him, he held up the wallet and unfolded it. It was stuffed nearly full with bills, and there was a folded-over leather flap at the end that jingled with many coins, big and small.

"Oh, Jack."

Jack looked up at Nolly, who blinked at him, a little open mouthed at the prospect of having so much money to hand all at once. And, Jack suspected, of being relieved of having to hold the wallet.

"How will we—" began Nolly.

"I'll keep it so it's all together, in my shoes, some in pockets. If I had a hat, I'd tuck some bills folded inside my hatband. We throw the wallet away, though; it's a gentleman's wallet, and too good for the likes of us. D'you see?"

Jack went about doing this, checking his pockets for holes before putting a folded note around three or four coins to keep them from rattling too much, then he added the same assortment in each of his stockings, and then in Nolly's pockets and stockings. He didn't mention how Nolly had lost their money on the hill going into Lyme, but that had not been Nolly's fault. With all he'd had to worry about, and carry Jack besides, well, Jack still wasn't sure how he'd done it. Besides, they had money now, didn't they.

Nolly, after handing over the penny the man had given him for stealing his horse, stood very still for all of this, watching Jack as he went about his business of tucking the money away. He bit his lip as Jack tugged on his trouser waist to straighten it; the trousers were so loose that Jack could feel Nolly's hip bones beneath his shirt.

"Can we get something to eat now, Jack?"

The voice came out so softly that Jack looked up with one last tug on Nolly's smock. Did Nolly think Jack meant to make him *wait* to eat? Not for anything would Jack do that.

"Of course we can, sweetheart," he said, patting Nolly's cheek and, on the last pat, cupped his hand there to soothe that frown. "That's what we did this for, to eat an' to drink an' get a dry place to rest so as we won't get poked with a pitchfork in the mornin'."

"Do you think he's following us?" Nolly scrubbed at his mouth, but it was a feint to bring his own hand to curve it around Jack's, his fingers warm on the back of Jack's hand.

His eyes upon Jack were serious as he leaned his face into Jack's palm, his eyes falling closed for a moment as he did this. Then, as if comforted, he opened his eyes and straightened his shoulders. With one last stroke to Jack's hand, he let go, and Jack's hand fell to his side.

"Perhaps he might be," said Jack, wanting to be honest in

this. "But I've been checkin' behind us an' I ain't seen no one that I recognize. That don't mean he ain't lookin', mind, just that he don't know which way we was headed."

With a nod, Nolly turned to look up the street. "I imagine we shouldn't be standing in the street such as we are, in case that fine gentleman determines that his wallet is missing."

"Right you are," said Jack. "I reckon we should head toward the high street. Find a tavern, an' get some food. Some sleep." For while a belly full of fresh milk was good to fall asleep on, it had been well worn off by a long walk through the woods and along streets, all the while checking over the shoulder for someone who might or might not be following them. "We'll order one of everythin' they have an' a room with thick blankets, an—"

He stopped there. He was so hungry, his belly was eating itself away, and while curling up in the dark with Nolly at his side sounded very good indeed, he couldn't manage much else, though he wanted to.

"And then you'll kiss me goodnight, won't you, Jack?"

"An' hold you in my arms," said Jack in return. That he could manage forever, if Nolly would let him. "Now, c'mon, we've got to keep movin' as it looks like more rain."

He caught Nolly's sleeve in his fingers and tugged on it. Nolly turned with him and, in the growing onslaught of rain, they went up the street.

AFTER NAVIGATING ALONG SEVERAL TWISTY COBBLESTONE streets, where the brick houses seemed to close in overhead, almost enough to shield them from the rain, they came upon a sturdy tavern of stuccoed-over brick at a wide, three-way corner. The tavern had a green-painted door and windows, and a broad green sign with gold lettering that proudly announced that it was the Ring of Bells.

Against the soaking dampness of the street, it was such a cheerful-looking tavern, with its hatch-crossed windows through which warm lantern-light poured, that Oliver stopped full on. Jack nearly trod on his heels, sputtering a bit at Oliver's clumsiness, though not scolding him for it, rather only looking at Oliver to provide an explanation.

"We might stay here," said Oliver, raising his eyebrows to emphasize what a good idea this was.

"You must be tired," said Jack, by way of agreement.

"As are you," said Oliver. He lifted his chin, refusing to allow, for one moment, that Jack would not get his fair share of caring and attention.

It was still new, this ferocity, but it was energizing nonetheless, because for all his prior attempts at it, he had at last stumbled upon how it might actually be done. How it *needed* to be done, even, how Oliver might demonstrate the way Jack made him feel, deep within him, where any words he might have to describe such a feeling would never venture for fear of being swallowed whole and, besides, being only a paltry representation of the actuality of it.

"We'll get a meal, shall we? And a room, and rest without fear of being woken up by any farmer, armed with pitchfork or otherwise."

"And we'll order for you peas an' eel," said Jack. "With a pear tart for after."

"The way to my heart, Jack," said Oliver, pretending to be quite affronted by this, "is not to order me any of those items, as well you know."

"So you want me to know the way to your heart, then?" Jack asked, rain dripping from his forelock and into his eyes, steady and constant while the streets poured with rain water, the future an uncertain destination and, all at once, this from Jack seemed too much to bear.

"You know that I do," said Oliver, in spite of his discomfort at being so unused to having it already known.

That it was so readily apparent made him want to turn away and pretend he'd not said it, even though he knew Jack would take what he'd said and accept it for what it was, just like he might cup his hands around a gently feathered bird so as not to harm it. In spite of his trepidation, Oliver met Jack's gaze as steadily as he could, blinking against the heat in his eyes, not pretending, even for a moment, that it was the rain that bothered him.

"Can we just go in, Jack?"

"Yes," said Jack, as calmly as if the moment were quite ordinary. "Yes, we can."

With permission thus given, Oliver stepped up and pushed open the thick, green-painted door, and entered the tavern. Jack was close on his heels, as he often was, with his warm breath upon the back of Oliver's neck, and the nearness of his presence giving Oliver the courage to tend to both of their needs, in spite of a sudden feeling that he was adrift in the world where nothing was familiar and never would be again.

"Can I help you, sirs?" asked a gentleman, coming up to them, his small belly capped by an apron tied with a string, once snowy white, but which, at this time of day, had some grease stains that spoke of customers hurriedly taken care of. For it was true that if the tavern had seemed welcoming to Oliver, a stranger in town, then it was to the village locals a common place they knew well and frequented often, for there was barely a spot at any table that was not occupied. "Supper? Room? Quick now, haven't got hours to wait while you dally."

"We'd like supper, please," said Oliver. "At a table near the fire. And a room, for we've been walking a long way today."

"Fancy you, then, wanting a table near the fire." There was a strange curl to the man's words, the way they bobbed up and down as if he were close to singing a song. He was mocking them, as well, for wanting so genteel a thing as a good seat such as that.

"Anywhere out of the rain will do," said Oliver, amending his request. "It's just that my friend was quite chilled by the rain, we got caught in it, and, uh, his jacket, too thin, you see—"

"Yes, yes," said the man, waving the rest of this away as too troublesome for his attention. "Got seats at a table, along the wall there. You see? Go and sit; the girl will come by when she's able."

It was, it seemed, no easier than ever it had been to spin false tales about who they were and what they were about. But Oliver felt Jack clap a hand on his shoulder, and the gentle push that served to direct him.

They moved among the crowd of tables, coats draped along the backs of chairs, the occasional cane or walking stick, the general air of dampness being slowly warmed by the enormous fire lit in the fireplace along one wall. It was a fireplace they would not be sitting near, but the warmth of the fire seemed to have spread itself just about everywhere, so perhaps it might not be so bad, after all.

"Do you want to sit facing that way?" asked Oliver, gesturing to the chair facing outward, for he knew Jack would want to sit across from him so he could see Oliver and the door and most of the room, all at once, even if that same arrangement would leave Oliver with only the view of the wall, a bit of window, and Jack. Which, given so many unhappy alternatives, was the best view Oliver could ever wish for.

"If it's all right," said Jack, with his hand already on the chair.

"Of course," said Oliver.

He sat down, his legs meeting the edge of the chair in a way that made him hide a wince, but a rush of warmth and stillness overcame him after being in motion for so long. His stomach, as well, seemed to sit up and take notice of its surroundings, for Oliver was quite sure he could smell something being roasted on a spit in the kitchen, and the crisp, wheat-smell of newly brewed beer.

Jack, having sat down, tipped his chin upward at some unseen person behind Oliver, and rubbed his hands together.

"Here she comes, so what will you have? Some of everythin'?" Jack's eyes were wide as he looked at Oliver, as if tempted to order that very thing so the table would groan with food, and Jack could sit back and watch Oliver eat, having provided the repast with his very own handiwork.

"Something hot," said Oliver, thinking he might even be able to stomach eel stew. "Something with—" He stopped as the serving girl came to their table, busty and young, her hair tumbling out of its lace-edged cap. "Something with potatoes."

He gestured in the air, unable to articulate how exactly they might be prepared, but he could always eat potatoes any way that anybody served them to him and, besides, as he was starving so it really made no difference.

"What's good here?" asked Jack looking up at the serving girl, seeming as confident as he ever had been, which made Oliver smile.

"Well," said the girl, her voice lilting up and down the way the man's had as she coquetted a bit with her eyelashes at Oliver. "We've got a very good beef stew, with new spring potatoes and fresh carrots from the garden. We're all out of the roast chicken, mind, but the cook's got a right crafty hand with the sausage, which he cooks in cider, very good, that, and greens and cheese, if you like, but that's extra."

"We'll have all of it," said Jack, startling Oliver out of the dreamy state into which he had fallen, with the warmth of the room soaking into him and the detailed recital of what food was on offer. "We'll share," Jack said now, looking at Oliver. "You shall start with the stew an' I the sausage, an' then we'll switch. Unless," said Jack, looking up at the serving girl, "unless that isn't done here?"

"You may please yourself, sir," said she, with her hands on her hips, looking somewhat bemused, though most of her smile was sent Oliver's way. "Since you're hungry, would you like something sweet as well? Better say so now, lest we run out. We got seed cake and sponge with treacle and that's it."

"Both, if you would, kind miss," said Jack. He attempted to charm her with a wink, though she only had eyes for Oliver, even though Oliver knew he was dripping with rain. Still, they both were, and Oliver was wearing the most disreputable outfit, for Jack, even in the faded, streaked black jacket, looked a good deal more presentable than himself at the moment.

Oliver didn't protest as the serving girl sashayed off to get their food, nor at the amount that Jack had ordered, for he knew in normal circumstances it wouldn't have seemed so much, but in his hungry state, all this comfort and warmth and food and convivial though damp company, all to be had and theirs for the taking, on account of the money in Jack's pockets, was beginning to overwhelm him.

Though Jack might have noticed that the serving girl had practically ignored him, he did not comment upon it, but only put his elbows on the table top and curled his back to sag his weight upon his hands, his head resting on his fists beneath his chin. Rain from his hair dripped on the table, leaving long circles that, if left to dry, would surely mar the surface.

Oliver, who very much might have once taken Jack to task for such casual rudeness, instead leaned against the wall, and propped his own chin up with one elbow on the table, and sagged a bit himself. He was simply too tired to do otherwise. As well, the tavern room seemed busy enough that they did not stand out overly much, as everyone seemed to be attending to their own suppers of generous portions and crisp draughts of beer drunk from shiny, tin pots.

"We forgot to order beer," said Oliver, his mouth feeling dry, his throat parched, at the thought of it.

"She'll bring it, never fear," said Jack, shaking his head and sighing. Unconcerned, because of course, Jack knew how things worked, ever in the wide, wide world, even in places where he'd never been.

In the flickering light from the candle sconces and the ruddy glow that the wide hearth spread out over the patrons, it was good to just sit there and let the wall support him, and the table, and the chair, and let his mind whirl on about nothing. Not on their close call that morning, nor on the miles that they had walked, nor on the fate that surely would have claimed Jack had Chalenheim had his way, or the despair Oliver did not have to feel upon finding out about the whole truth of it, as he surely would have, come the morning after. Or would he have?

There was, it seemed, a great deal that Jack had kept to himself, in spite of him calling Oliver out on this very practice. Though it was not lying not to tell, it was unlike Jack to behave in this manner. Though, with all the evidence available to him, Oliver supposed that this instance, this *particular* instance, was an isolated island Jack had been loath to depart from, or to alert Oliver to the location of.

Before Oliver could determine how to start that difficult conversation, the serving girl came over to them with a large tray that she held deftly tucked against her hip, laden with the food they'd ordered. She also had two pints of beer clutched in one fist. These she placed upon the table, somewhat in the center, along with the food and, delightfully, she placed on the table a small plate of roughly sliced bread and a bowl of sweet butter.

"Thank you, miss," said Jack for the both of them, for Oliver's mouth was watering too wildly for him to speak. Jack handed her a shilling, which she took with a nod and a quickly curled fist, and sauntered off, weaving among the seated crowd, the tray banging against her side.

"Stew or sausage?" asked Jack as he pushed the plate of bread toward Oliver, though he had to have been just as hungry himself.

With a short breath of exasperation, Oliver pushed the plate of bread back to the middle of the table.

"Stew," said Oliver, for he had seen Jack's eyes flick toward the sausage, which was swimming in pale gravy that smelled of sweet cider, with mashed parsnips fried with bacon and onion tucked neatly in the curve of the sausage.

The plate of sausage was what Jack wanted, so Oliver pulled the stew toward his side of the table. He was careful not to slop any of it over, for the bowl was also as full as the plate. The stew was a dark broth with bits of beef and pale potato and golden carrot bobbing along the surface, which, to Oliver's pleasure, had pale circles along the top where bits of butter had just melted.

Oliver picked up his spoon, completely forgetting that the serving girl had not brought them napkins, when Jack tapped the edge of the bowl of stew with his fork.

Oliver looked up at him, startled, as if Jack had been about to forbid him eating just yet, and how on earth was he to manage that?

"Slowly, mind," said Jack. "Wouldn't want you sick all over the floor an' hatin' beef stew from this day hence."

With a quick nod meant to impart full agreement, Oliver took a small spoonful of just the broth, brought it to his mouth, and let the broth just sit there upon his tongue, with warmth and salt and the taste of beef and onion, and sighed and then swallowed it.

"Good, yes?" asked Jack.

Nodding, Oliver gestured with his spoon that Jack was to proceed with his meal and not wait upon ceremony. This Jack did, and Oliver as well, and between the two of them, they passed a good many minutes without speaking. They ate as slowly as they might until their stomachs became used to the feeling of being full, and the desperate feeling of rabid hunger became only a ghost of itself.

Oliver knew he could probably put away a few more bowls of stew, as well as all of Jack's sausage and parsnips, but Jack was so contentedly attending to his plate, curled over the table, in fact, his face very close so his fork didn't have so far to go between plate and mouth, that Oliver determined he would pretend to forget they had agreed to share and switch plates. Besides, between large swallows of cool beer, the stew was very good, so he would be satisfied with that.

When he was almost finished with the stew, Oliver reached for the bread and used his spoon, since he had no knife, to spread the butter upon it. In the warmth of the room, it went on easily, and he was about to use it to dunk into his bowl when Jack looked up at him.

"Forgot that we were meant to share," said Jack, his mouth half full of food. But while he might look somewhat comical, pausing half-chew, his expression, with his eyes drooping at the corners, was despondent that he'd denied Oliver his fair share.

"'Tis of no matter," said Oliver, handing over one half of the prepared slice of bread that he'd torn in two so Jack could more easily dunk it in the broth of the stew, which Oliver pushed across the table. "There's still a bite for me to try it."

With a nod, Jack prepared a forkful of the last slice of sausage, against which, using his knife, he tucked a small mound of fried parsnip, and this he handed over to Oliver. Jack didn't bother to disguise what he was doing, for it was terrible manners to share this way, though the tavern room as a whole seemed unconcerned except with their own suppers, and what was upon their plates.

Oliver took the fork from Jack's hand and ate the sausage and parsnip in one huge mouthful, raising his eyebrows at the taste, the crisp, fried edges, the sweetness of the parsnip. With a coarseness that might have put any sailor to shame, with only a few chews, he swallowed it down and belched into the back of his hand.

Jack polished off the last of the stew, scraping along the bottom of the bowl with the slice of bread, and then, at the last, using his thumb, as he was wont to do, to catch the last drops, as if theirs was a world with no manners and no expectation of them, in spite of the public setting.

"Here she comes," said Jack, somewhat unexpectedly, and the serving girl was at their table, putting two plates and two forks down with a plonk, hurrying off before they could thank her. "Timin', eh?"

"Yes, indeed," said Oliver, though his gaze was taken in by the treacle sponge, which had so much dark syrup that it was oozing off of the plate and onto the table. Over the syrup was spread a layer of yellow custard that, with the warmth of the sponge, was circling into the treacle. The seed cake, in comparison, looked a bit dry and dull, and wanted sweet tea to make it palatable, though there was none to be had.

"Only do go on," said Jack, pulling the seed cake toward himself. "All this self-denial is making me itch. For the love of God, Nolly, just enjoy it."

This Oliver did, digging his fork into the soaked cake with no hesitation whatsoever, without even a modicum of restraint, and ate the entire thing within only a few breaths between huge bites. Then, his belly full, he attended to his pint of beer, quite forgotten until that moment, when he could sink back in his chair. His shoulders began to relax as his smock began to dry upon him, and he could watch Jack slowly make his way through the seed cake, nodding and licking his lips as if it weren't so dry and ordinary as it looked.

"It's quite rich, this," said Jack. "Can taste the butter."

For a sad, private moment, Oliver regretted taking the treacle sponge, and wondered if it would be too greedy by far to ask that Jack order another serving so Oliver could try the seed cake. At which point, Jack held out a forkful of the cake, and nodded that Oliver should take it and without question, which Oliver did. The cake was rich on his tongue, butter surrounding the bitterness of the seed, which was sweetened by the crisp flakes of sugar along the top of the cake.

"That's very good," said Oliver, handing the fork back. He was quite full now and satisfied with his choice of sweet desserts, though he was glad to know for certain that the seed cake was indeed quite tasty, for Jack deserved something nice to eat as well as Oliver did.

Presently Jack finished his cake and, without having been asked for it, the serving girl brought over two more pint pots of beer, and held out her hand for the payment. This Jack handed to her, doling out coins until she nodded, and curled her fingers once more over her palm before slipping the money into her apron pocket.

With her hand on her hip, and a jaunty tilt to her chin, she looked down at Oliver.

"Did you want a room, then? Master said you did."

Though she was paying attention only to Oliver, as if he were the only one at the table, her service had been quick and efficient, so he nodded at her.

"Yes, thank you. Will you give us the key or do we—"

"Go up to the counter by the stair when you're ready. You'll have to share a mattress on the floor, as we're quite booked up tonight, though Master said you looked in need of a dry place to sleep."

A mattress on the floor in a room they had to share did not seem the most amiable of arrangements. Not only did it sound uncomfortable, they would lack privacy, which Oliver felt in need of, as he planned to draw Jack's story out of him, if only to understand better what Jack had been through, and how Oliver might be kinder to him now, in future, always. If Jack would let him.

"Yes," said Oliver now, nodding at her.

He wanted her to go away so, contented and full, he could settle back into his chair as he drank his beer in the warm, convivial room, and look at Jack, doing the same, and know that they had come together to a place where they might be happy, free from the strife that seemed to follow Oliver's every footstep. And Jack's as well, though Oliver had not known it till they'd been in the workhouse.

"Washbasin's by the kitchen, if you've a mind," she said with a little crinkled expression to her mouth, as if she was displeased by Oliver's lack of attentiveness to her round bosom and saucy ways.

Oliver gestured at Jack, thinking to mention that he might

give her another shilling for her troubles, but before he needed to speak it, Jack was handing over the coin, pressing it into her palm with both of his hands, like a handshake, looking up into her eyes beneath the edge of her cap, smiling, as if announcing he was the one she should have been flirting with, only now it was too late, *but here's a shilling for you, just the same.*

Oliver dipped his head to smile, knowing now that if they wanted to flirt, those serving girls, they inevitably got it wrong, for Jack was the one that could make an interaction amusing, leaving both parties feeling pleased with themselves without offering offense. Whereas Oliver never had any idea the flirtation was happening until it was over and the serving girl was disappointed with him for his lack of response. Perhaps he might learn from Jack how to be more easy in this, to make those moments a little smoother, and though perhaps that might make the exchange of goods and money more frivolous, it certainly never seemed to hurt anybody. Quite the contrary, in fact.

When she went away, Jack took a large swallow of his beer, putting the pint pot down on the table as his throat worked. He settled back in his chair, sitting upright at last, as if the food and drink had restored him enough to do this. Oliver felt the same, and took a drink of his beer also, finishing off the first pint before taking up the second, the tin pot feeling cool and silky beneath his fingers.

As he drank the first sharp taste of country beer, he looked up at Jack and realized Jack was looking at him with somewhat hard eyes, as if considering whether or not to point out that Oliver had dribbled beer on his smock. But Oliver had not, even if his smock was streaked with dried rain and glittering with bits of straw that he'd not been able to remove.

"What is it, Jack?" he asked, licking his bottom lip to taste the foam there.

"Here we are, then," said Jack, shrugging. His jacket tightened across his shoulders in a way that reminded Oliver of the moment at the barn, when Jack had seemed to want to pull his jacket close and disappear within it. "Ask away, then. You might as well, since I see it in your eyes that's what you want."

"I have been patient and kept my peace," said Oliver, knowing that he had, but he also knew Jack was not angry with him, only wary that the story would be too difficult to tell.

Jack had been barely able to speak of it in the workhouse. Now, though, the warm room and good food, not to mention the second pint of beer Jack had already worked his way halfway through, was having its effect upon him. "It's not for any prurient interests, I assure you."

"You an' your bloody fancy words," said Jack, which took Oliver directly back to the time Jack had shouted amidst the snowdrifts in the park, so angry his eyes were cold, and his words snapped from between his teeth as if he were biting them. Then Jack shook his head, taking a breath, and opened his mouth to loosen his jaw. "Never mind. Ask away, an' I'll do my best. But this is it, mind you. I'll tell you an' then we walk away from ever talking about it again, right?"

Oliver nodded, then pushed his pint of beer away with his fingers, across the tabletop, as he felt he might have more need of it later, rather than just now.

"Tell me what happened in Port Jackson," Oliver said, and when Jack opened his mouth to begin, Oliver put up his hand, palm out, and continued. "Tell me what happened in Port Jackson as to allow a man such as Chalenheim, upon even so brief an acquaintance, to know that *you* would know what he wanted and be willing, albeit reluctantly, to give it to him."

"You been practicin' that question all day, Nolly?"

Jack's face was white, as white as it had been at the barn, or in the room at the workhouse, where the grates had never fully been blackened nor filled with lumps of coal. Then he blinked and took his gaze away from Oliver, as if to hide from his sight.

That reaction, as Oliver could see, as he could not have seen before, even in Lyme, only meant Jack was fearful, perhaps of Oliver's impending reaction. And though Oliver might have assured him that all would be well, if Jack would only tell him what happened, he began to feel that apprehension which so firmly kept Jack from speaking.

"Perhaps I have," said Oliver, admitting it, though there was nothing further from the truth. "As I wanted to say it rightly, to ask it rightly."

This mien of honesty, however false it might have been, seemed to settle Jack, for he nodded into his beer before taking another swallow. Oliver watched him as gently as he could, and waited.

The question had been asked because Jack had offered him the opportunity. Besides, there was nothing for it but that Jack would speak now, or they would continue on with this between them, for Oliver did not think he could ever forget the look on Jack's face, the defeated slump of his shoulders, when Oliver had walked in to interrupt the interaction between Jack and Chalenheim.

"It began," said Jack, pausing for a moment to run his tongue over his teeth, as if tasting the strangeness of words spoken out loud to another person. "It began when I was sent from the farm to the garrison fort."

"Sent from the farm?" asked Oliver, interrupting, though he'd promised himself that he would not. "Where Kayema was? How could you leave her?"

"I did not—*leave* her," said Jack.

All of a sudden, he seemed unable to speak, his eyes narrow and gazing into some distant place that had nothing in common with the warm tavern, or the table with its half-drunk pots of beer, or even Oliver himself. Though Oliver felt cold all over, and wanted, desperately, to ask that Jack stop telling his story, he knew it would be better if the words were out of Jack and into the air, where Oliver could help him carry them. So he kept silent and still, fingers clutching the curved handle of his pint pot.

"The farmer," said Jack, "had huntin' hounds that he used to keep the kangaroos from eatin' the garden, you see." Here Jack spared Oliver a glance, as if to share with him how ordinary this fact was. "They needed to be fed, those hounds, an' so the farmer took up his machete an' selected some blacks to be cut up for food for the dogs. We were in the cow shed, Kayema an' I, an' she was taken from me an' hacked into pieces an' there was nothin' I could do about it. Someone held me back from stoppin' him, an' when it was over, I didn't know anythin', just curled up in the hay an' slept an' slept until someone else came an' took me to the garrison, where—"

"Where the marine was." Horror at the image Jack created with his words seared Oliver to the bone. "Where he could control you."

Jack nodded, a single jerk of his chin that seemed to cut through Oliver's skin, right to his heart. He felt the pain of the memory reflected in Jack's face, the tight line of his mouth, the quick blinking of his eyes, as if he were desperate to hold back any reaction to his own story. Because, as someone, perhaps the marine, might have told him, enough time would have passed to cover over the memory, and that his duty was merely to forget.

But Oliver knew differently. Some pain lingered like a deep line across the soul, drawing attention to itself from the first moment of its occurrence, never ceasing, never stopping. Oh, you could ignore it, if you tried, and were dutiful in your prayers, and believed when you were told to just move on that you could just forget. But the way Jack had talked about Kayema, even in the most casual of ways, told Oliver that Jack had not moved on from missing her, and never would.

"Before I met him, he'd come on a ship bringin' convicts," said Jack, plowing through with such defiance, his teeth grit together, those gray circles beneath his eyes once more. "He'd arrived on the *North Briton* in '42, as part of the 99th Regiment, who were a bunch of bastards—well, anyway, what with one thing an' another, the lieutenant was in need of a boy to polish his boots, a manservant of sorts, an' there being absolutely no power on earth that could make me go back to the farm, the dust would always be red-wet to me, y'see, that I took him up on his offer."

"So you went with him willingly," said Oliver, though he could see how it might have gone. That Jack, undone, reeling from the loss of his friend, had taken up the first hand of kindness offered to him, no matter the strings that might have been attached to that hand.

"Well, a little willin'," said Jack with a shrug that was obviously meant to be casual, dismissive even, but Oliver felt he could see right through the gesture.

"You were willing to let him hurt you."

"No, I was willin' so he *wouldn't* hurt me."

"But he was not kind," said Oliver, surmising the truth. "And he did hurt you."

"Yes, well," said Jack, drawing his hand up to his face where he pressed his palm into his forehead, as if to drive the thoughts away. "But he was the best I could do, seein' as how there were bigger cocks an' rougher hands aboundin'."

Into the moment of stillness following Jack's words, his story of what had happened to him, summed up in a few tersely spoken sentences, Oliver could think of nothing that he might do or say to make Jack feel any better. Let alone to erase what had happened to him, to somehow have been there when Jack had picked that particular pocket and stopped Jack—but Oliver had thought this before, had wished it before, that he could have prevented all of this from happening, only there was no way he could have saved Jack from any of it. This knowledge, permanently in place, painfully twisting in his belly, became a reality.

That the world was indifferent to the suffering of those among the lower orders, the paupers and the pickpockets alike, had been pointed out to him more than once, by Jack himself, in fact. But that did not make it any more palatable or defensible, even while it smacked of blind cruelty that had been the boundary lines of so much of Oliver's own life, which, actually, paled in comparison to what Jack had been through. Though to speak this out loud felt as if it would only diminish what Jack had suffered, and had just shared with Oliver.

"What is his name, this lieutenant?" Oliver asked this, even though he had not intended to, the words grinding themselves out of his mouth as if some insistent, rather indifferent part of his mind wanted to know, and this in spite of his better intentions.

"Oh no," said Jack, with a small laugh and a flush to his cheek that surprised Oliver. "You have enough blood on your hands on my behalf, an' besides—" Jack paused to take a long swallow of beer that must have felt cool upon his throat. Oliver did like-wise, closing his eyes for a moment over the taste of the beer, and regret at the loss of having been complacently in the dark before. About this. About Jack.

"Besides," said Jack, pushing his hair, now dried, back from his forehead. "He's stuck in Port Jackson an' he ain't never comin' home."

"Then," said Oliver, hating himself for the sigh of relief that filled him, that Jack had so easily changed the subject. "How on earth did you come back to London? Transportation is forever, Jack, everybody knows that."

"Amusin' story, that," said Jack, laughing silently and open-mouthed, in that way Oliver was coming to learn that the humor Jack expressed sometimes tasted dark and bitter, but that he would share it anyway in the hopes that someone else, Oliver perhaps, might derive some pleasure from it. "His fiancée, with thousands of pounds to her name, was to arrive come mid-winter on the *Sally Ann,* an' of course, he was desperate she shouldn't find out 'bout me an' him."

"Would you have told her?" asked Oliver, thinking he might already know the answer to that question.

"In a heartbeat, my dear Nolly."

"So how does that explain—"

"He got me an A.P., paid for with her money, no less." Jack

seemed to find this part of the story amusing, for he tipped back his head and gave a low chuckle aimed at the ceiling. Then he looked at Oliver, as if expecting him to join in.

"An A.P.," said Jack slowly, as if in deference to Oliver's apparent idiocy, "is an absolute pardon, records erased, transport home. The whole of it was paid for, d'you see the irony in this, with *her* money."

"But you paid for it with your—"

Quite insistently Oliver wanted to point out to Jack that he had paid for passage home with his own skin, when it occurred to him that he might finally comprehend what Jack had told him in Lyme. That having intimate relations was a gift, always a gift, and that it should never be used as trade for anything else.

At the time, that had seemed a rather highbrow notion, something to be found in a book, rather than from the mouth of a street thief. Only now Oliver knew exactly and precisely how Jack had come by this knowledge. How he'd divined it, all on his own, without book learning or having had a somber, more experienced mind to explain it to him. The learning of it, first hand, had cost him dearly, just the same.

"Got you stumped, eh?" said Jack, with some kindness in his eyes.

"Yes," said Oliver, the single word almost too much for him to utter.

"Well, now you know," said Jack, drinking the last of his beer to set the now-empty pint pot on the table with a sharp tap. "The whole horrible truth of it, only there's nothin' nobody can do about it, 'cept to move on, as it's all behind me anyhow."

There was beer left undrunk on the table in front of Oliver, but he knew he could not abide even another swallow of it, with his belly churning about, his heart littered with this new darkness.

While he was entirely willing to carry that for Jack, he felt as if he'd been injected with glass shards, all over, and if he moved so much as an inch, he would be sliced to ribbons. But he stood up anyway and went over to where Jack was sitting.

"Eh?" asked Jack, as calmly as if this were any other day and Oliver had just walked over to his chair. Jack looked up at him now with some surprise, as if he'd not just gotten done telling the story that would break even the hardest of hearts, and which had just shattered Oliver's into tiny, painful fragments.

"Let's go to bed," said Oliver. He placed his hand on Jack's arm, praying with everything he had that Jack wouldn't pull away from him as he had at the barn.

But Jack did not. Instead, he flitted his eyelashes at Oliver and gave him a saucy grin, as if Oliver's suggestion was full of the most rapacious promiscuity that had ever been offered.

"Bed, is it?"

"I need to—" began Oliver, ignoring Jack's attempt at levity, and stumbling over the words. "That is, I want to—"

He stopped again, feeling the heat in his eyes, the dampness there, as if he couldn't decide whether he wanted to scream or cry.

"I cannot be brave in front of this room and you at the same time. I only want to lie down with you, and hold you close and say sweet things to you while I stroke your hair, in the way that you like, that I never told you that I knew about, until you fall asleep. And while you sleep, I will stay awake, on guard, and let you know I will never, never let anything bad happen to you while you are in my care, for you *are* in my care, Jack, though I feel as if I had failed you—"

To his horror, a pair of enormous, hot tears raced down Oliver's face and landed on Jack's sleeve, to be absorbed by the streaky, uncomfortable-looking, black cloth.

But instead of continuing on with a cocky grin and a devil-may-care indifference to the propriety of pretending everything was all right, Jack's eyes grew bright and wet, and he stood up next to Oliver and touched his cheek.

"It happened long ago, it seems, sometimes," said Jack, but

solemnly, carefully, as if he were acknowledging Oliver's pain, as well as his own, and nodded. "We'll get the key, then, an' get you your wash, an' just turn in early, an' hope them fellows not sleepin' on a mattress on the floor won't come stompin' in like a bunch of sailors."

"This far inland," said Oliver, swiping his face free of tears to be in keeping with Jack's attempt at making everything feel more normal, "they're more likely to be miners."

"Miners have boots as well, 'tis true," said Jack, by way of agreement.

He left another shilling on the table, and pulled Oliver with him among the tables to the entryway, where, quite numb from all feeling, Oliver used the lukewarm water in the basin. He did not bother with the soap, as there seemed to be none, merely rinsed his face and rubbed his hands together.

Jack was standing by with a thin towel. It was already streaked and damp in places, but Oliver used it anyway, then held it out to Jack, his eyebrows rising with the unspoken question.

"If it were hot water with rose-scented soap," said Jack, looking down his nose at Oliver, "then I'd be lavin' my hands an' face this moment, but this basin has been used by such common folk that I am appalled, completely an' utterly *appalled*—"

"Yes, all right," said Oliver, taking the joke with good humor, smiling in spite of himself. "I'm a bit fussy, and it's not the best wash I've ever had, I'll admit, but it's better than nothing." Which, for him, to make such an observation instead of the complaint, felt a long way from his days at the townhouse.

"You fellows need a key?"

The question came from behind them, and they both turned in tandem. Oliver did not scrub at his eyes again as he wanted to, because to do so would attract more attention than he could bear, just then. But Jack nodded and held out his hand, gave the man in the white apron some money to cover the costs of what was sure to be the most paltry of accommodations, and jerked his head sideways that Oliver was to follow him up the stairs.

This tavern, unlike the Three Cripples, had stairs that were painted white, with a colored wool runner down the middle, in that ubiquitous way middle-class houses always had, in an effort to seem more genteel than could really be afforded. But it added a nice touch to the simple white walls. And yes, he was grateful that they were beneath a roof, and had been well fed, and would sleep without the rain on their faces, or a pitchfork in their bellies come the morning.

The key jingled in Jack's hand as he tested the door with the appropriate number on it, and opened the door to a long, narrow room that had a single candle burning in it, as if the maid had just gone from preparing the blankets on the mattress on the floor. The actual bed in the bedstead was quite wide, as might be appropriate for the rougher sort of traveler who would be accustomed to sharing a bed for the night with perfect strangers.

As for him and Jack, the mattress on the floor did not look all that wide, but it seemed plump, especially with the two round pillows and the white pillow slips tucked over the white sheet and dark gray blanket. That they'd gotten this far into freedom was a miracle, and the bed, however plain and on-the-floor it was, would do them quite nicely for one night.

"Will you sleep on the side furthest from the other bed, Jack?" Oliver asked this quite casually, feeling rather than seeing Jack's shoulders stiffen up when they entered the room.

It would not be, of course, that any of the men who would also be sleeping in the room with them would actually take it upon themselves to demand sexual favors from anybody, but it made sense now, why Jack would, unconsciously or not, be tense with anxiety. It did not matter that it wouldn't happen, Jack was ready for it just the same. Though considering that, how Jack had managed a single moment of sleep at all in the workhouse was its own sort of miracle. The toll on Jack must have been extreme, only he'd never said a word.

"If you please," said Oliver, pulling the smock over his head to lay it on the floorboards beside the bed-mattress, "I'd rather sleep on the outside, for I know I shall toss and turn. And if you're against the wall, I know I shall have more room, which I *must* have, to get a good night's sleep."

Jack ducked his chin then, as if wanting to hide a laugh that would surely be a signal that Jack knew exactly what Oliver was up to.

Then Jack didn't hide it. He lifted his head and, holding his mouth in a rather stiff line, as if trying to keep it from wobbling, and in a very soft, sad voice said, "What a love you are, to carry on so. I hadn't known, really didn't know, whether or not you would—"

"Did you think I would despise you, Jack?"

Oliver swallowed over the fist in his throat and, with a determined tightness in his jaw, moved forward to take the black jacket off Jack, and to kneel at his feet to undo the laces on his boots, though Jack was perfectly capable on his own. He undressed Jack to the point where Jack was only wearing his shirt and trousers, with everything else neatly lined up along the short bit of wall at the end of the mattress.

He pulled back the covers so Jack might crawl into bed a bit easier. Then he took off his own boots and stockings, pulled his shirt out from his trousers, and tried not to rub his sore backside, to draw any of Jack's attention to it, and slithered into bed beside Jack.

There, he turned his back to the single candle, and tucked his hands beneath one of the pillows, and sighed as his neck relaxed upon it, and his head sank into its downy depths. To his surprise, the pillow was stuffed with goose feathers, every single one, with not a strand of straw to be found.

Jack, in an echoing position, tucked himself into the shadow that Oliver's body cast in the candlelight, and looked up at him somewhat expectantly. It could not be, of course, that Jack wanted more conversation about Port Jackson, so it only took Oliver a moment to remember what he'd told Jack he wanted to do.

"Is it easier now, me knowing?" asked Oliver as he reached up to cup the back of Jack's head, and twine his fingers in Jack's hair, to draw his fingers along those dark strands, over and over, quite slowly, as Jack half-closed his eyes and nodded his assent.

"I'm quite tired," said Jack, his mouth barely moving over the words. "But I don't know why."

"Then you fall asleep, and I'll stay awake for a bit, doing this, like you like it."

Oliver kept stroking through Jack's hair, though his arm felt exhausted within moments, for it wouldn't do to simply give up doing something Jack wanted and liked, especially when Oliver had been pretending, like the selfish thing he was, as if he had no idea about it.

"Are you warm enough?" he asked now, dipping his head to kiss Jack on the forehead. "Let me know if you are not, and I will fetch a blanket for you for your own use."

"You're enough blanket f'me," said Jack, and he reached up to clasp the hand that Oliver was using to stroke through Jack's hair, and held it still for a moment, as if he wanted Oliver to stop. "Only with your arms around me, both of 'em."

"Yes," said Oliver and,hearing the door opening behind him and the clomp of three pairs of boots and the easy-going, robust chatter of three strangers as they entered the room, he shifted close and took Jack in his arms so Jack might nuzzle into Oliver's shoulder, and wrap his arms around Oliver's waist.

Oliver was fairly certain the men would be too busy with their own undressing and arrangements of who would sleep where in the bed, and who would get stuck in the middle, that they would take no notice of the young gentlemen apparently already asleep on the mattress in the corner of the room. And indeed they did not.

Jack sighed and turned his head to kiss Oliver anywhere that it might land, which was on Oliver's collarbone as it happened, and Oliver lifted a hand to tuck the sheet back from Jack's face so he might breathe easier in the night.

He stayed pressed close to Jack, and held him gently, and whispered in the dark when the candle was snuffed out, how much he loved Jack, and what they would have for breakfast, and what time the coach headed north might leave town. And again, how much he loved Jack, until he was quite out of words, and the warmth of Jack's body so close to his own, their toes tangled beneath the weight of the blankets, made him feel sleepy and calm and, in spite of being on the floor in a new tavern with three strangers in the room, quite sleepy and safe.

Besides, anybody who might want Jack, would have to go through him, and that would cause such a foolish individual to lose not only eyes but limbs and the whole of his heart, which Oliver would tear out of his body with his bare hands, with his teeth, even.

"Nolly," said Jack, his voice low and sleepy. "Only do stop, will you now? Stop, stop, stop."

"Yes, Jack," said Oliver, smiling as he pressed his cheek against the top of Jack's head by way of an apology, and matched his breath to Jack's and finally fell asleep.

❧ 26 ❧

BECOMING POSH GENTLEMEN

When Oliver opened his eyes, sunlight was streaming into the room, a bold yellow slant that lit up the wall next to the mattress on the floor.

Jack was curled in his arms, and Oliver was exactly where he'd fallen asleep last night, with the bedclothes tucked up over his shoulders. And though he felt comfortable and warm, he turned in the bed, letting Jack go, and looked up to see one of the men from the night before.

The man was standing there in his rough wool coat, though unbuttoned, and his heavy hobnail boots, dressed to go out. He used one of the boots to kick the edge of the mattress.

"Sun's up, youngin'," said the man in that up-and-down accent the locals seemed to have. "Time for you an' your friend to get up as well, as you shouldn't miss breakfast."

Voiceless, Oliver nodded, wondering what the man saw, or how he might interpret it as he looked down at them, with Jack so close to Oliver. Would they be taken for two young men sleeping close for warmth? Or would it be seen as something else?

"Thank you," said Oliver. He shook off his concern about this as the man stomped out of the room and closed the door behind him. The smell of piss in a used chamber pot layered throughout the room, and beyond the window, the sun was golden-bright, though Oliver didn't think that would last long.

"Jack," he said. He bent his head and kissed Jack's temple, stirring the dark, witch-wild hair to tuck it behind Jack's ear. "Can you get up now? They have breakfast downstairs."

Mumbling, Jack opened his eyes. His mouth had a downward pull, as if he regretted everything he'd told Oliver the night before. Had the sharing of a memory so painful been Oliver's, he would have drunk his way through a dozen bottles of gin and then thrown himself in the Thames with a stone tied around his neck.

Everything Jack had ever told him, the pieces of it, jagged-edged and confusing, now came together like a child's picture puzzle. It was easy to see the whole of it if you knew what it was meant to be. Boys did get buggered every day, innocent native black girls were butchered on a whim, and young convicts had their innocence traded to provide shelter.

Jack's ready humor, his insistence in seeing everything through the lens of a joke, was his way of not looking at that puzzle, not the whole of it, anyway. For it was an overwhelmingly bleak picture, and while Oliver was honored to have it in his hands now, he resented each and every person who had done this to Jack. Even Fagin had had a hand in it, sending Jack out to work in the streets on a day when, really, Jack had been too distracted by his worries about Oliver and should have been given the afternoon off.

Oliver was interrupted in this swirl of thoughts as Jack seemed to be mumbling, so Oliver put his concerns aside, and shifted down so he could wake Jack up properly with a kiss on his sleep-dry mouth, and on his nose, and his forehead. Until Jack, with a slight smile curving his mouth, pretended Oliver was a small room fly that needed to be brushed away. But then he ducked his head beneath Oliver's chin and kissed his neck.

"Is it mornin'?"

"Yes, it is. Shall we get up?"

He was looking forward to the day, in spite of everything, for now he knew what Jack hadn't been telling him, whereas Jack had known all about Oliver from the very first, so he felt as if they were on more equal footing. That Jack trusted him more, that they fit together better.

They had money, now, and time, and if the weather didn't hold, well, at least they had this moment, with the gold and white patterns on the walls, the soft ribbons of gray light that Oliver realized were clouds pushing past the windows. It would rain later, but later was later, and besides, Oliver was hungry, and knew Jack had to be as well.

"I'll get your clothes. Here." Oliver sat up, pulling the bedclothes back, letting the cool air of the room swirl around his neck as he ran his fingers along his lower eyelashes to remove the sleep dust.

"Cold," said Jack.

"Yes, I know; wait a moment."

Oliver made himself get out of the bed, putting the covers back a little ways to keep Jack warm, and stood up with his bare feet on the floor boards, trying to focus on which pile was Jack's. It was the one on the left, with the black jacket on top.

Oliver was coming to despise the black jacket, for it was ugly and didn't suit Jack at all, and represented, somehow, all the bad things that had happened to Jack, all the discomfort and the cold and the hunger.

He needed to find a way to get rid of that jacket, and the rest of the clothes as well, and acquire some clothes instead that would not only suit Jack better, but that would be comfortable and warm, rather than scratchy and thin. But for now, he grabbed Jack's pile and went over to sit on the edge of the mattress, his legs half on the wooden floor, and tried to encourage Jack to get up.

"Here," he said. "I have your trousers and stockings, will you—"

"What the bloody fuck," said Jack. He pushed himself up on one arm, and glared at the sun, and the room in general, and wiped his mouth with his palm. "You're always so fuckin' cheery in the mornin', but why?"

Though Jack was still waking up, and couldn't properly see him, Oliver shook his head and shrugged his shoulders, and held out Jack's trousers once more.

"Food awaits us, Jack," said Oliver, giving the trousers a shake.

Then he realized that forcing the issue wasn't going to hurry Jack along any faster, and stood up to put his own trousers and stockings on, then sat down to lace up his boots. Whereupon he felt Jack, having pushed aside the covers at last, laying back to pull on his trousers without actually leaving the bed. He smiled, and reached for Jack's boots to straighten the laces and to drag the jacket on the bed behind him.

When he stood up, he pulled on his smock, which now, having dried all the way while folded, had a musty smell and black lines along one side. It looked as though he'd used it to roll in a dust heap, or perhaps to polish the silver, but there was nothing for it but to wear it, until they could find something better.

This seemed to work, as Jack was tugging his boots on, and had scooted to the edge of the mattress to tighten the laces, then stood up and let Oliver help him with his jacket. With a grunt, Jack nodded at Oliver and found the key in his pocket. He held it out so Oliver could lock the door behind them, and Jack could stay as much asleep as possible until they got down the stairs, and went to the dining room, and Oliver led the way to the table they'd had from the night before.

There was no fire in the fireplace, no candles lit, but with the sunlight, through the parted curtains, cropping through the racing clouds, the room was cheery and bright. As soon as they sat down, a serving girl, a different one from the night before, but still perky and smiling, put two bowls and two spoons on the table, and ladled out huge servings of porridge into their bowls.

"Fixings and treacle are on the table," she said. "I'll be by with your tea."

Without a word, and without waiting to be polite about it, Oliver pulled both bowls toward him and scooped up flakes of butter to layer over the surface of the porridge. Then he poured out the treacle, which, instead of being dark and smelling musty as it had in the workhouse, drizzled itself out, a thin, bright, golden stream, as though it had been spun from a weaver's wheel.

Jack watched him with quiet eyes, and did not protest when Oliver, having found the pitcher of cream, poured some of that on top of the porridge as well.

"There," said Oliver. He pushed a thusly prepared bowl toward Jack, who sat, still half-asleep with his spoon in his fist, as if he were about to start banging on the table. "It doesn't look as though there's bacon or anything, but this should do us, right? Eat, Jack, you must eat."

Soundlessly nodding, Jack curled himself over his bowl and began to shovel the porridge into his mouth, swallowing without tasting, it seemed, until the third bite, when his eyebrows lifted and he shared a half-smile with Oliver.

"You know what you're about with food, don't you," Jack said, licking his lips, which were glistening with butter.

"That I do," said Oliver. "I like breakfast best of all the meals, I think."

Then he began to eat his own porridge, savoring the thick, creamy taste of it, and did not let himself think of all the paupers in the Axminster workhouse who would have sold their souls to be where he was right now.

If he let himself dwell on that place, on that time, he would have turned over the table with a roar and demanded to everyone he saw that they join him in marching down to Axminster to set all the paupers free. Which would have gotten no response except for nasty looks, and wasted a good breakfast. And, besides, he had his own troubles, and Jack's, to take care of, at least for now.

The serving girl came over with two mugs and a pot of tea and, with a slight *tsk tsk* sound, took the cream pitcher away and brought it back full. Oliver thought about assuring her that she'd not neglected to fill it in the first place, but rather that Oliver was a pig about cream. But his mouth was too full of sweet porridge and, as well, he rather liked the way Jack cocked a knowing eyebrow at him, at the secret they shared. Jack would not sell him out to the serving girl, not for all the money in the world, and certainly not over a pitcher of cream.

"Shall we ask if there's bacon?" asked Oliver, around a sip of the hot, sweet tea.

His mouth full, Jack nodded his assent.

"Good, then, I shall ask," said Oliver. He waved his hand at her when she passed by, and his mouth watered at the thought of it.

BY THE TIME THEY WERE DONE WITH BREAKFAST AND HAD paid their bill, when they stepped out of the door, the sun was gone and it began to rain upon their heads, as if from a bucket. Jack nudged Oliver to go up a narrow passage, which felt as if they were going between two banks of bricks, so close were the buildings, where the water sheeted off the roofline into silver puddles down the middle of the street.

The passage emptied out to a regular street, with carts and horses and foot traffic making, as even Oliver could see, a wonderful sort of living camouflage, for if they traveled the same speed as everyone else, they wouldn't stand out, in spite of Jack's faded and stained jacket and in spite of Oliver's yellowed linen smock, which was only good for milking cows, and even then only if he'd been an old man in his nineties.

Or, at least, he hoped. Jack was doing his best, as Oliver could see, to appear as carefree as ever he might have been in London, on his own territory, rather than being in a strange town with its industrial brick and old castle walls half falling to pieces. Jack had his hands in his pockets, sauntering along as if nothing were amiss, but Oliver was close enough to see the fists Jack had made of his hands, and the way he pressed them to his thighs as if to hold them from quivering.

In another minute, Jack was likely to start whistling to show Oliver, along with everybody in town, just how concerned he was not. But they were not as unremarked upon as Jack might have hoped, for their garments and dirty faces made them stand out, in spite of the money Jack had stuffed in every available pocket and corner of their clothes. Someone was bound to mark their passage and, should anybody come following from Axminster workhouse, they would have a tale to tell.

As they walked, Oliver remembered the white-painted building along the street they had traversed the day before. It had been quite distinctive, with half a ground floor beneath street level and a stairway of sturdy red brick leading up to the door on the first floor. The sign above had indicated it was a used clothing shop, with garments to hire or sell, and that a tailor was on the premises for any alterations needed.

"Jack," said Oliver. He made himself bold enough to sling his arm around Jack's shoulders so that they might appear the errand boys Jack had described them as before. Turning Jack in a firm-handed manner, he walked Jack back along that same street so he could look at the building in question, and then waited while the idea occurred to Jack as well.

"We shouldn't keep going on the way that we are, looking as we do," said Oliver. "Not if—"

"There's somethin' else we could be wearin'," said Jack, finishing the thought for him.

Nodding, Oliver led the way up the stairs, determined, as ever he might be, to remove from Jack any traces that would remind him of Axminster, like the black and dour jacket he was wearing, or the grime along the back of his neck, or his exhaustion from having quickly walked the many miles from Buckland St. Mary's and told Oliver all of his secrets. Oliver knew he needed clothes for himself as well. He would not deny that fact, but he would see Jack comfortable first, and thus intended, pulled Jack up the stairs, and entered the shop.

It was like many a used clothing store, with racks for jackets, and frock coats, and shelves of hats, some looking new and sleek, others looking tattered and not much good for more than collecting dust. There were some dresses, and lady's bonnets, as well, but fewer of these, as it seemed the shop was not oriented toward the fairer sex, but rather to the working man who might like a bit of polish to his outfit.

The wood paneling behind the racks and shelves was clean and free of dust, and the floor beneath their feet had been recently swept. Oliver nodded his approval just as a thin-looking man with spectacles and a white apron, a cloth tape around his neck, came up to them.

"Might I help you?" he asked, looking at them somewhat askance, as anyone might to see them so roughly attired and in such a place, dripping on his clean floor.

"Yes, thank you," said Oliver, taking the lead, thinking that Jack would not mind. "We've just come to town, and our luggage has, apparently, taken a quite different coach than the one we were on."

"Oh?" asked the clerk with some indifference. "Which coach did you come on, then? There's none I know of that would lose anybody's luggage."

"Um—" Oliver wiped the rain from his forehead with the back of his linen sleeve. "It was—uh—"

"Why, it was the Comet, sir," said Jack, as if astounded that the clerk didn't already know. "We've taken it before, but when we discovered our luggage was missing, we had to alight the carriage at once to do somethin' about it."

"There isn't any coach called the Comet going through Taunton," said the clerk. He was looking about him as if prepared to call on a fellow clerk for assistance in throwing them out. And if they couldn't convince the clerk they were on the level, then they wouldn't be able to pass muster with anybody else, either.

"It made a special stop," said Jack, nodding assuredly, though the clerk didn't look the least bit assured.

"Mr. Weston's the coach driver," said Oliver, doing his best to appear suspicious that the clerk was not already well acquainted with the driver though, in his heart, Oliver knew he would never be as good at playacting as Jack was. But it was then Jack reached into his pocket and pulled out two of the five-pound notes, and unfolded them in his hand, as if considering the amount.

"This is all we have for our travels, you see," said Jack, shaking his head in consideration. "But my friend here says your shop looks top rate, so perhaps you could assist us?"

But the money had already spoken the words for him, as the clerk's expression, the whole line of his body, changed. He nodded his head respectfully and gestured them over to the rack of frock coats and jackets and suit coats. Jack gave Oliver a quick wink and, as he looked at the assemblage of clothes, he reached out his hand to touch a fine wool frock coat of dark sky blue.

"I'd see you in brown or green, my dear," said Jack to Oliver as if he talked to him this way every day. "But this would suit you so much better, especially after we get our luggage back."

Not to be outdone, Oliver marched over the rack himself, and began touching the jackets and pushing them to one side when the texture didn't suit him. "And for you, this dark blue one, what do you think?"

Jack just smiled and gave one of those silent laughs that he did, which told Oliver he was relaxing, being indoors and out of the rain, and distracted by the thought of a new suit of clothes.

"Sir," said Oliver, thinking that perhaps he knew a bit more about how to legally procure garments than Jack did. "Might you take these jackets and pull up some trousers and waistcoats and stockings. And do you have shirts? Yes, some shirts, and then cravats, an arrangement of cravats. We'll pick those out ourselves. But what we really need, while we're waiting, is a place to wash. Do you think you could accommodate us?"

The clerk showed them to a basin, where there was an actual bar of soap. Oliver washed his hands and face and bade Jack to do the same, and when they were done, they went back to the front of the shop, where the clerk was waiting.

"If sirs would care to try these, there is a screen you might use, and we can tailor for fit, if that is desirable."

With some gladness, Oliver walked behind the screen, carrying the pile that had been presented to him, and stripped off the smock, the pauper-brown trousers, the stockings with holes in them, and the undergarment that the blood from his cuts had stained dark red-brown and would never come out, and put on the newer clothes.

They were soft and clean, the stockings snug around his calves, the buff trousers more closely cut than any he'd owned before. The shirt was of silky, white cotton, the jacket of such soft, sky-blue wool when he put it on that he stroked his arms over and over before he realized that there was a dull-patterned gray waistcoat still left in the pile.

So he took the jacket off and put on the waistcoat, and though the color might have seemed unobtrusive to his unpracticed eye, the cloth was luxurious when he petted his chest and stomach to smooth the lines. Putting the jacket on once more, he stepped out from behind the screen where, open-mouthed, he saw Jack standing there, looking like a stranger, but with Jack's eyes.

The clerk had picked out for Jack blue trousers that were so dark they might have been black, and a dark blue jacket with a richly striped blue and white waistcoat. The shirt had a high

collar, a bit old-fashioned perhaps, but it looked nice on Jack.
The only thing missing was a cravat.

"Do you have," said Oliver, looking at the clerk, "any red
cravats?"

"Indeed, sir," said the clerk, and he gestured to a tray of a
rainbow of cravats, all silky, and bright, or somber and soft.
Oliver ran his hands over them until he pulled out a red one that
reminded him of the scarf they'd once owned.

"Come here, Jack," Oliver said, ignoring Jack's raised
eyebrows of amusement at Oliver's bossy tone.

He ignored, too, Jack's outright stare, his open-eyed appreciation of Oliver in the sky-blue jacket. Oliver knew he looked
very well, but he wanted Jack to look better. So he slung the
cravat around Jack's neck, on the outside of the collar, and lifted
his chin to indicate that Jack should do the same.

Jack, for once obedient and not teasing, lifted his chin to let
Oliver arrange the cravat as he pleased. Oliver twisted the silk into
a shape that was not too serious, a bow with trailing ends that he
tucked into the top of Jack's waistcoat, and petted till it smoothed.

"There you are, my bright bird," said Oliver.

"Your *what?*" asked Jack.

In that moment, Oliver knew he was caught out. His face felt
warm as he gave the red cravat a last pat and stepped back to
admire his handiwork, and the clerk's selection, as if he was not
the least bit undone by having his opinion so known. Not to
Jack, not after their talk the night before.

"You are my bright bird," said Oliver, looking directly at Jack,
not wanting to pretend about this, wanting Jack to truly know.
"For that is how I thought of you, in London, in the snow. You
were so recently come from antipodean climes that your skin
was golden, and your waistcoat—the blue one you wore—was so
bright in contrast to the darkness of winter. It was a treat for my
eyes to see you that way, a spark of color amongst all that dreary
fog and coal dust, wearing your plumage with your head held

high, and I shall always see you that way, my dear Jack. For you are the brightness of my life."

Oliver's throat closed up, and his eyes filled with tears, for he was not used to speaking thus, or to seeing how the expression in Jack's eyes became full of wonderment, or the way his mouth softened, and a sharp blush colored his cheeks. But he did not look away, and though Oliver could see Jack was looking for some saucy reply, he knew also that Jack could find none.

Instead Jack, swallowing hard, turned to the box of cravats and picked out a bright green one, which somehow matched the color of Jack's eyes and, waving the clerk away, came up to Oliver and began the business of tying it around Oliver's collar.

They were quite close now, he and Jack. He could smell the tea on Jack's breath, the scent of soap on the skin below his jawline, feel the nearness of him, as if the steadiness of Jack's heart were enfolding them both, leaving him knowing that the love in Jack's eyes was the only thing he would ever need.

"You look well, Nolly," said Jack, his voice gruff as he arranged Oliver's cravat to his liking.

"And you also," said Oliver, in kind. He looked down as Jack reached out to touch one of the bright buttons on Oliver's jacket.

"These are silver, eh?" asked Jack.

"No, sir," said the clerk, who had been watching them but, with his measuring tape still around his neck, he seemed unaffected by the intimacy between the two now-very-well-dressed gentlemen in his shop. "They are but tin, but well polished to shine. Do the garments suit, then, sirs? And the top hats?"

He pointed to the dark, shiny well-brushed hats he'd set out that were obviously used, but that would serve to mark the change in both Oliver and Jack's statuses: that of young men rather than runaway orphans.

"Yes, they do," said Jack and then, as he was the master of their money, he pulled out the fold of bills he'd shown the clerk before. "Would you be so kind as to tote up the bill? We've a need to catch a coach going north and must be on our way."

"Very good, sir, one moment." The clerk took out a small tablet and, with the stub of lead, wrote down the figures and, nodding, appeared to add them in his head. He showed the amount written down to Jack, and then said, "You'll be wanting to go past the Ring of Bells, just down the street, to the St. James, the coaching inn."

"Thank you," said Jack, handing over the pound notes with all the grace of a young man well used to being waited on and attended to, though Oliver knew he was not. "There's somethin' extra in there as well, for you are to keep the change."

Taking up their hats, they barely put them on before tipping them to the clerk as they exited into the rain that had turned into an on-and-off sprinkle that dampened their spirits not at all. Oliver wanted to race down the street shouting, but stayed by Jack's side, ignoring the stare from the man in a shop doorway as they strode past, or the smile of appreciation from serving girl at the Ring of Bells, the one from that very morning, who bowed them a curtsey as if she didn't recognize them at all.

Presently, as the rain let up, for good, it was hoped, they walked along the busy street, past the church to a wide, four-way corner, upon which near end was the coaching inn, the St. James. It was already a busy place, with a private coach and six just leaving, and a gathering of folk dressed for travel in front of the door.

Oliver started to push his way through the crowd, with Jack close behind, except that the folk stepped back, as if making way for them, as if seeing them as the clerk did: two well-to-do young men who, somehow, deserved the privilege of not having waited in line.

Normally Oliver might have balked at taking advantage of this, but they did need to be moving north and out of the reach of the authority of the Axminster workhouse. Thus emboldened, he walked up to the man in the apron who held a slate and a slate pencil, and who was selling tickets for the next coach out of town, headed north.

"Do you have two seats available on any coach heading toward Liverpool?" Oliver asked this with the security of knowing they could pay whatever the fare was, and have money left over for lodgings and food along the way, and he was never so glad as to have a street thief as his closest companion.

"Indeed, I do, sir," said the clerk, looking him up and down. "But they come at a dear price, for they are inside, both facing forward."

"We'll take them," said Oliver.

He gestured that Jack should hand over the money and take the tickets, which made the clerk's opinion of him, perhaps, raise another notch or two, based on Oliver's casual attitude about spending money.

Jack took the slips of paper and grinned at Oliver, enjoying the game they were playing, which, of that moment, seemed to be more real than playacting, for they did have money, and family connections, alive or dead, and were traveling with some urgency and had the money to pay for the haste.

They did not have to wait long, which was a good thing, as the stares of the crowd were becoming a little overbearing, and the coach pulled up, the horses' hooves sparking on the cobblestones. Handing their tickets to the driver, they clambered inside the coach, where Oliver admired the freshly scrubbed interior, with the new hay in piles at their feet, the clean and sparkling windows. The top of the coach lurched a bit as the outside passengers got on.

"Will you be all right on the coach ride, Jack?" asked Oliver. For while he would not mind nursing Jack if he was ill, he would prefer that Jack felt perfectly well, well enough to enjoy himself.

"Ain't got no headache this time," said Jack, looking as though he were considering whether or not to protest Oliver's worried attention about this matter. "I'll be fine."

With a snap and a whistle, the coach jerked into motion,

throwing them both against the leather-padded seats, but it was an entirely different feeling than the coach ride from when they left London. The rain-dappled air smelled sweet, and their bellies were full, and they weren't on the run from the hangman's noose. It was an altogether different day.

Oliver smiled and turned to Jack to get him to join in with this feeling of pleasure, which Jack did, an easy hand on Oliver's thigh, and a quick kiss that nobody standing on the street could have possibly seen. But it was inside of ten minutes that the coach, having neared the edge of town, came to a quick stop and the coach door opened.

Oliver's heart sped up, but it turned out that the coach had stopped to let in an elderly woman with a wicker basket. She was dressed in pale, lace-flounced skirts. Hands pushed her up the short stair and into the coach, those hands supporting her well-rounded backside. An elderly gentleman waited with his foot on the step as he watched her with careful eyes.

The woman looked at the backward-facing bench, which was somewhat more narrow than the forward-facing one and, preparing to sit down, gave both Oliver and Jack a kindly smile.

In that instant, Oliver shot to his feet, for he could never resist the rush of affection he felt whenever he saw an older woman in an old-fashioned pelerine such as Mrs. Bedwin used to wear.

"Grandmother," he said, ignoring Jack's look of astonishment. "Would you care to have the facing seat, for Jack and I could share the backward-facing one with room to spare."

"What is he saying?" called the old gentleman, his foot still on the coach step and his hand on the door. "What are you doing, dear? Just sit down so the coach can keep its schedule."

"These young gentlemen," said the woman, turning slowly to her husband. "They wish to give us their seats."

"Yes, yes," said Jack. He jumped to his feet. "We would like to do exactly that," he said, and he took off his top hat and graced her with a courtly bow that actually made her cheeks rosy, and her smile more genuine.

"We're taking the seats, dear," she said to her husband, and Oliver and Jack quickly moved to the backward-facing seats as the husband clambered in, his lined face wrinkling with confusion.

"Have they been flirting with you, dear?" asked the husband, eyeing the two young gentlemen who were so firmly ensconced in their seats that they could not be moved.

"Only in the mildest of ways," said the old woman.

She sat down and spread her lace skirts that even Oliver recognized as being so hopelessly out of fashion that they belonged to a previous century. But they suited her somehow, pale and lilac and just a bit fussy. Her husband, as well, looked decked out as if for a private ball, with his long lace cravat and the tri-cornered hat that he politely took off and placed on his knee.

Following suit, Oliver took off his top hat and gave Jack a gentle elbow to do the same, just as the driver snapped his whip and the coach banged into action, which caused the passengers to jostle about until the road leveled out and the speed rocked the coach back and forth with a gentle, even sway. They all looked at each other for a moment, strangers on a coach who, while not entirely known to each other, would nevertheless, over a course of hours, become more intimately acquainted than perhaps they might have wished.

In that silent moment, the old woman untied the ribbons on her curved straw bonnet, and handed it to her husband, who held it in his hand, dangled by the laces that he held with his fingers. The bonnet bobbed against his stockinged leg, echoing the motion of the moving coach.

Smoothing the loose strands back into her arrangement of gray hair, the old woman lifted her wicker basket onto her lap, and opened the lid to peer at the contents. Then she smiled at Oliver and Jack.

"There's so much food in here," she said, shaking her head. "I'd hate to see it go to waste, wouldn't you, dear?"

The husband nodded, rubbing the length of the ribbon with his thumb, as if deep in thought about something else entirely.

"Does anyone care for some pear tart? For I have some here that Cook made just this morning, though I do believe she might have put too much sugar on top, just simply too much."

Jack made a sound in his throat, and when Oliver looked over, Jack looked as though he were attempting to swallow his own tongue rather than laugh out loud, which the woman might take as an insult. Though it was funny, considering the treat she was offering to share.

"Is there aught amiss with your friend, dear?" asked the old woman, looking at Jack somewhat askance.

"No, grandmother," said Oliver, and since he felt like smiling, he did, and watched the woman's reaction, her raised brows, the appreciative curve of her mouth. "He and I were just talking of pear tarts last evening, and how much they are my favorite."

"That and apple tart," said Jack, swallowing and wiping his mouth with the back of his hand. "Though," he added, "my friend here has a mouth full of sweet teeth, and if it has sugar on it and some sort of cream to go with, then he would eat it all without pause or breath, makin' me ever despair of his manners."

"Well," said the woman, as if considering this. "I do have pear tart, prepared way too sweet, mind you, and a quarter of cheese, and some apples, and some pork pie. My dear husband does not like pork pie, so it shall go to waste unless there is some young man who prefers savory to sweet."

Without waiting for their answers, the woman handed out napkins and broke apart the tart, giving each of her male companions a section of it. These they placed on their knees with the napkins beneath, and watched as she handed slices of pork pie to Jack. Then, putting the basket on the floor between her skirted feet, she took out a small paring knife and began to cut off slices of apple and cheese for herself, popping them in her mouth, as if she were at a picnic on a blanket in the grass.

"Well, do go on, the food isn't going to eat itself," she said, chewing and looking at them with bright eyes.

It was only then Oliver realized, as he bit into the pear tart, that his previous daydream, which had been conjured up in his formerly less-experienced imagination, had just come true. He and Jack, well dressed and contented to have interior seats on a well-appointed coach, were sharing a picnic meal from a wicker basket with an elderly couple to whom they had done a favor, which in return had earned them open-armed goodwill, and something delicious to eat, besides.

"How is the tart, Nolly?" asked Jack, his sharp teeth biting into the pork pie with some relish.

"It is excellent," said Oliver, smiling around the bite he'd just taken, at the world in general, and at the flake of sugar melting on his tongue, and the way the butterfat from the pastry was coating his mouth.

"As it should be," said the old woman. "I pay Cook a great deal too much for her to not have the coolest of hands with all pastry, and a smart way to know when the pear is cooked just enough, but not too much, lest it get mushy in the tart. Do you know what I mean, young man? I should say that you do, the way you are looking at me. Don't bother to answer. It's rude if your mouth is full, as you know, but the pear, had it been cooked one second longer, would have ruined the entire tart, isn't that right, dear?"

"Yes, dear," said the old man, but it seemed he only pretended to be dour and disinterested, for as he bit into his serving of tart, he sighed with pleasure and nudged her skirts with his knee.

She gave him the corner of her smile as she chewed and ate and watched the young men whose forward-facing seat she and her husband were now occupying, as if she were concerned lest the tart not be enough.

"I do have rock candy and peppermint circles, if anyone is interested in those." She nodded at her husband. "You should have something else in your stomach first so you don't become ill."

"That was only the one time, dear," said the old man, chewing and swallowing his pear tart with some concentration. "Must you always bring it up when we travel by coach?"

"Yes, I must, dear," she said in return, making the teasing about the illness seem like an old habit.

Oliver scooted back so the backs of his knees met the edge of the bench seat and his back was supported by the padded leather. He tapped Jack's boot with the edge of his own and smiled around the sugar that clung to his own lips.

"Peppermint is good, I hear," said Oliver, looking at Jack, saying it in a way that would be appropriate for the general company, "if one has a sour stomach, or when the rocking of the coach becomes too much."

As if understanding, somehow, that Jack was the one who might need the peppermint at some point, the woman bent to pull out a folded paper, which she handed to Jack.

"Then you shall have all of it you like, young man, and we'll prop the window open, unless it rains, to keep the fresh air on you. Fresh air is always best for someone who is sensitive to travel."

There was nothing that Jack could do but take the packet of peppermint, though his face was colored with bright circles of red, and Oliver felt sorry, though only for a moment, about teasing him.

"Thank you," said Jack, as he tucked the candy in his pocket.

Oliver gave him a nudge with his shoulder to let him know it was all right. He wanted to ask Jack if the pork pie was as tasty as it looked, but Jack became too focused upon it, and wouldn't want to be interrupted, as Oliver would not, so he contented himself with swallowing large mouthfuls of tart and licking the crystals of sugar from his lips, which, in spite of it being quite rude, was looked on with approval by all of his fellow passengers.

The coach, perhaps knowing of Jack's delicate stomach when it came to this sort of travel, rocked only gently, with a slight sway to the side, perhaps, once in a while, but never was there a jar, or jerked motion, or a scrambled turn around a corner that would have sent them all tumbling from their seats. Just a gentle rock, as if they were in a child's cradle.

Oliver, finished with his tart, held out his hand for some candy, and was given a piece of each. He put the rock candy in his mouth first and, holding the peppermint circle in his hand, turned it over and over, while his eyes closed over the sweetness of the candy, and his tongue concentrated on smoothing out the square edges.

He rested his head against the padded seat and let himself drift off. He deserved this treat, this goodness, and Jack did as well, but that didn't mean Oliver couldn't also take a little nap, which he did, his mouth full of sugar, his belly contented, and his truest companion close at his side.

THE SWAN IN WINTERBOURNE

The coach rattled along the macadamed road, but Jack did not feel jarred, even though he was growing weary of constantly being on the move. The coach slowed, and Jack looked out to see the approach of a small village, with the church spires through the trees and the smell of manure. Beyond that was the scent of coal smoke, though the dark pall of fog was whipped away in the wind that had brought rain on and off all the afternoon.

When the coach stopped, the old man and old woman cheerfully got off. Jack woke Nolly up to say farewell to their traveling companions and felt, only a little sadly, the break of the cocoon that had surrounded them because it meant the coach was empty now and he and Nolly could slide across to the bench seat facing forward for the remainder of their journey, as long as it lasted.

As he settled with his back against the curved seat, his neck supported properly now by the leather-covered cushion, he held out his arm for Nolly to tuck himself into, which Nolly did with a sigh.

"Is this the village where we'll stop?" asked Nolly.

"I believe it is," said Jack. "The Chamberlains said they were gettin' off at Winterbourne, same as we, but them at the George and Dragon an' us at the Swan."

Jack watched as Nolly sat back as well and took his arm down. The curve of the cushion meant he didn't have to cradle Nolly against him, though it had been nice for a moment.

Nolly rubbed his thumb across one of the silver buttons of his blue jacket before pulling it to rights. The jacket was quite fitted, and when they'd gotten out to stretch their legs during the change of horses, it had drawn eyes to Nolly, with his straight back, his tapered waist, and those long legs in buff trousers. But it was the perfect disguise, for who would suspect they were on the run from a workhouse?

If Chalenheim ever made it this far and sought to inquire after them, he would get exactly the wrong answer. *Two boys in workhouse brown? No sir, they never came through here.* Chalenheim could look and look, but he'd never find them.

"We'll get our own room tonight," said Nolly. He looked down as though addressing his fine leather boots, coal black and polished to shine.

"That we shall," said Jack, "for I believe the bank will bear it."

Nolly smiled at his boots, then sat upright to appraise Jack with a glance of his eyes, as if in anticipation of a fine dinner and a night to themselves.

Jack, of course, could never be certain what Nolly was thinking, and they'd not had the privacy that day of talking about any of it, at least they'd talked about some of it the night before. Enough to ease Nolly's mind, though Jack suspected that Nolly suspected there was more to know, more to tell.

But not just yet. Nolly liked to mull things over and over before putting them away, only to mull them over again later.

Jack determined to find some books for the next part of their journey, for if they sat inside, even facing backwards, Nolly could read, and would not have hours to spend mulling, for it only seemed to unsettle him. As for Jack himself, he knew if he tried to read facing backwards, he would vomit all over everybody, so it was a chance best not to be tested.

When the carriage stopped, and the driver announced they'd arrived at the Swan, Jack and Nolly got out. Jack took the time before the horses raced off to tip the driver and touch the brim of his hat. This the driver thanked him for with a return tip of his hat to Jack and Nolly. Then he cracked his long whip, and the coach shot off, sparks flying from horseshoes digging into the cobblestones, mud from the ruts spraying up.

Jack had just enough time to step out of the way himself, but Nolly did not, and a streak of brown slashed the front of his fine blue jacket.

This was not a disaster in Jack's mind, for they had enough coin to replace their entire wardrobe three times over, but for Nolly, it was. Dripping, he turned to Jack, trying to flick off the damp mud, but failing, a furrow appearing between his brows, his mouth turned down in dismay. Their perfect afternoon was ruined, in Nolly's eyes, and Jack could see it.

From the doorway of the Swan, the proprietress came out, wiping her hands on her thick white apron, her sturdy shoes clopping on the stones. She held her hands out to Nolly, as if she could fix him with a single touch.

"Are you all right, young master?" she asked. "'Twas terrible careless of the driver to splash you so."

Nolly turned to her, his head tilted back, looking down at her as he might to any servant.

Jack fully expected Nolly might take advantage of the fact that he looked like a fine young gentleman and exercise his temper, as Jack had seen young gentlemen do. As Nolly, perhaps, deserved to be able to do, after all they'd been through. But Jack should have known better.

"He didn't know I was still so close," said Nolly. "It's not his fault I was gawping at your beautiful inn."

Jack felt himself start in surprise, but held it in check. The inn was much like all the others along the road that day, with cream-colored plaster and a tidy roof of dark slate, a sign hanging out front noting the name of the inn, which, in this case, was a portrait of a swan's head. And though this inn had two stories at one end, and a one-storied tap room at the other, there was not much else to set it apart for Nolly to say such a thing.

But then Jack saw it: along the wall under the eave was a painting of an entire swan with the head bowed towards its body, a bit of grass in its mouth. The painting was done with a skillful hand, with blue touches around the edges to suggest water, and it gave the otherwise common inn a touch of grace.

"We've been on the road a while, missus," Jack said to build on this story, however unconsciously it might have been started by Nolly. "An' we've not seen such a pretty decoration all day."

The woman preened a bit and gave them a small curtsey. "You're kind to say so, gentlemen. Now, I'm Betsy and this is the Swan, and will you be needing a room for the night? And a meal? We serve only the very best."

As to whether that meant only the best food was served, or that the inn catered to only the best sort of person, Jack did not stop to determine. For there was already a gleam in Nolly's eye, in spite of his stained jacket, and Jack couldn't resist the situation: the woman would be good to them, on account of the accident and Nolly's praise of her inn and, besides, they could afford the very best.

"Indeed," said Jack as he took off his hat to her. "We'd like a room, if you have one, a private room, for my friend here snores an' I would not want to subject your other guests to it."

"I do not snore!" said Nolly, affronted, though perhaps a bit overly so, for effect. If they were two workhouse boys on the run, they would not, at the same time, be standing so publicly in the forecourt of an inn, arguing whether or not Nolly snored. "Well, maybe a little, so a private room would be best."

"I do have one," said Miss Betsy with another curtsy. "It has a little fireplace, and a nice coal fire we can put in there for you.

'Tis a bit extra, but it includes hot water brought up, if you young gentlemen should care to wash before supper? As well, I could take the young man's coat, and see to it that it's cleaned and brushed by tomorrow morning, if the young gentleman would like that."

"Yes, thank you, ma'am," said Nolly, all purity and manners.

"Come along in, then," said Miss Betsy. "We'll get you squared away with a room, and I'll take that coat."

They followed her into the inn, going across the threshold, ducking their heads beneath the low, time-darkened lintel as they stepped into a passage. There were stairs leading up from behind a counter, and a doorway through which Jack could see tables and chairs, a small spark of a fire, and he could hear pots and pans banging, could smell something salty cooking.

She stopped and held out her hands, and Nolly doffed his coat, turning the stain up so it could plainly be seen, and the mud wouldn't get pushed into the wool.

"Sarah!" Miss Betsy called, and presently a young maidservant, also in a thick white apron and cloth cap tied around her hair, came up.

"Yes, miss?"

"Take this jacket, It's the young gentleman's. The coachman's been careless, for you can see the stain there. Give it a good brushing, and get all the mud out, mind."

"Yes, miss," said Sarah and, with a swirl of her dark skirts, turned down the passage from whence the good smell of cooking came.

"We'll sign you in, and send you up, for there's nothing more wearying than being on the road all day."

She stepped behind the counter and drew out a large ledger and, for a moment, there was hesitation.

Jack's handwriting was perfectly fine, that is, if he wasn't pretending to be a fine young gentleman who probably had hours of tutors behind him sculpting his signature. So he gestured to Nolly, who stepped up, dipped the pen in the ink pot, and signed both of their names with all the right curlicues and swirls as befitted their apparent station. Then he wiped the nib on the blotter and set the pen in the tray.

"Here's your key, gentlemen," Miss Betsy said, as she pulled a brass key from the drawer. After glancing at the registry book, she nodded at them. "Supper is in about an hour, so when you come down the stairs, you just go along here, and Sarah will get you a seat. By the fire, do you think? We do build it up, come supper, but not too much, as when the room fills with customers, it can get quite close."

"That'll be fine, Miss Betsy," said Nolly, and Jack could see that the day was brightening up again for his best beloved. A chance to wash, and a fine supper on the way? Jack reasoned that since the ground floor was as clean and well-looked after as the outside of the inn, the rooms above would be immaculate. He'd be on the lookout to catch Nolly if he swooned at the sight of it.

Hiding his smile, Jack took the key, feeling the heft of it in his hand. It was a good solid key for a good solid lock, and Jack's shoulders relaxed.

They'd have time, and they'd have warmth and full bellies, and the privacy they'd not known for a good long while. He'd be able to touch his beautiful boy, and take his time, let Nolly take his time, and they could be together as they were meant to be.

"You're the last room on the left, in the corner,. The water should be up in a moment. Now, I must oversee the cook, but do let me know if there's aught you need."

With that, she turned down the passage, leaving Jack to gesture that Nolly was to go first, leaving Jack able to watch his backside as Nolly mounted the stairs. It perhaps was not quite fair that Jack was taking advantage like this, but he felt so keenly the pleasure rolling about inside of him, that they'd gotten this far, that they were about to eat, that he'd have Nolly to himself, that he could not quite help it.

Besides, when Nolly looked over his shoulder to make sure Jack was right behind him on the narrow, white-painted stairs, he gave Jack a little grin, and a bit of a blink that looked like a wink, and Jack knew he was forgiven for having lascivious thoughts.

The hallway was whitewashed with pale blue, and the dark paneled wood floor had a strip of gray carpet running the whole length of it, all the way to the white-framed window at the end. There were three doors on either side and, as Nolly led them along, Jack listened for rats and sniffed for damp, and couldn't find either. As he nodded to himself, he put the key in Nolly's hand so Nolly might have the honor.

Nolly turned to him as he took the key. "Thank you, Jack," he said.

"Top of the line, this is," said Jack, though he'd not yet seen the room.

Concentrating, Nolly turned the key in the lock, which was silent, and nothing rattled. The dark green door opened onto a cozy room, and though the ceiling slanted slightly, on account of the roof, it stopped way above the window that overlooked the roof of the other side of the inn.

To the right was a washstand in the corner and next to that was a small fireplace. The grate had been recently cleaned and blackened, as though ready for a fire. The edge of the mantle was set with white tile, each piece displaying pictures of ships or ponds with grass growing or, of course, swans, all delicately painted in blue with a fine-edged brush.

There was a table in front of the window with two chairs and a small dresser tucked in the other corner. On the left was a high bed, high enough to need a stool to climb into it, with four thick carved posters and a snowy white comforter that Jack had no doubt was filled with clean eiderdown. Across the bottom of the bed, folded lengthwise, was a soft, green-wool blanket.

At all this, Jack just had to stop and stare, for he'd never seen such a fine room, except to steal from it, and never to stay in.

"They'll never find us here," said Jack, shaking his head as Nolly closed the door behind them and turned the latch.

"They'd never think to *look* for us here," said Nolly with some awe in his voice. "Did Miss Betsy say that hot water was coming, or that we had to ask for it?"

Naturally, that was the first thought to cross Nolly's mind, but Jack didn't care. He swept off his hat and crossed to the table so he could look out of the window while he took his jacket off. He shook it and put it on the back of the chair and gestured to Nolly.

"The window-glass is spotless, so why don't you come here, and sit down and look out of it, and I'll go make sure of the water."

As if dazed, Nolly let himself be led to the chair, let Jack urge him to sit in it, and Jack watched him closely while he did it.

Nolly deserved to be in rooms like this, and if Jack was at his side, so much the better. What Nolly did not deserve was to sit down with a wince, as if it pained him to do so.

Jack suspected the wince was not because the ride in the coach that day had caused him pain, nor even the walking the days before. It was bloody Chalenheim and his bloody fucking *cane*—

"You don't have to do that, Jack," said Nolly, looking up at him. "I'm quite capable of going down myself, as you're not my servant."

"I know it," said Jack, holding out his hand to stop Nolly from getting up. "I know it. But, bein' me, I'd like a look around the place, get my bearin's in case we need to make a hasty exit. D'you see?"

It was a good enough lie because it was partly truth. Jack did need to get his bearings, but he also wanted to make sure there was enough hot water for Nolly. A single jug wouldn't do, and Jack didn't want to have Nolly have to wait if they needed to call for another.

"I'll be back directly, Nolly, an' you're not to worry. Just sit an' look beautiful, as you always do."

Nolly snorted at him, but sat back obediently in the chair

and looked out the window as the blue sky churned to gray and it started to rain.

Jack ran down the stairs and encountered Miss Betsy at the door to the dining room just as she was finishing up a conversation with a round woman in a stained apron, presumably the cook.

"Yes, sir," she said, turning to him as she wiped her hands on her apron. "Is there aught amiss?"

"No, missus," said Jack. "But if your maidservant is bringing up one jug of water, could she just as well bring up two? My friend an' travel companion is so very fastidious, you see, an' cannot relax enough to eat when there's dirt on his hands." Though this was a lie; Jack had seen Nolly eat old crumbly bread with bits of smashed bone beneath his fingernails.

"Indeed sir, I'll send Sarah up this very minute with two jugs."

"An' if it's possible—" Jack paused, scratching the back of his head. He did not quite know how to put it.

"Yes, young master?" Miss Betsy eyed him with the patience of a woman experienced in dealing with all matter of travelers.

"My friend, dear Mr. Twist—well, he had a bad fall in the yard after church yesterday. An' what with him, as you might say, sittin' on it, all day, I was wonderin' if you had somethin'—"

"Some balm, perhaps, young master?"

Jack nodded. He didn't quite like the taste of being called *young master* every other minute, as he imagined Nolly might, though it was a pleasure to have his needs so catered to.

"Yes, somethin' like that, to soothe his poor, sore, um, skin. It'll make him ever so much more amiable to more travel by coach. All that sittin'. D'you see?" Even he knew that in mixed company it would be bad form to explain it any more clearly than that.

"Indeed I do," she said. "We have some that we make for the maidservants to keep their hands soft so they don't snag the sheets, and it eases soreness as well. I'll fetch some for you directly."

She left him standing in the passage, and he wasn't quite sure if he should wait or go up, not having much experience with people running and fetching and carrying for him in this way. But by the time Sarah appeared with two full jugs of hot water in her hand, Miss Betsy was back, holding out a small tin pot with a lid with a wee golden bee painted on it. She handed it to him and closed his fingers over it.

"We're to make more when the weather clears, so this is from last season, and I won't charge you for it. Not when you're taking such good care of your friend."

"Thank you, missus," said Jack.

He put the pot of balm in his pocket, reeling a little from the unexpected kindness. But perhaps it was the coat that made her treat him so, for if he'd been in his old jacket, wearing his bright blue waistcoat, sporting beer stains on his trousers, smelling like the Three Cripples, she'd not have been so welcoming. And never mind what her behavior might have been had they stumbled into the Swan dressed in pauper brown. Best not to test that particular idea, however, for it would only lead to trouble. It was the coat that had done it, and Nolly's pretty face, and his small predicament of a mud stain on his jacket.

"He'll be very glad in the mornin', I should think," said Jack. "After I put this on him."

As Jack reflected how that sounded, Miss Betsy curtseyed at him, and Sarah waited on him to lead him up the stairs. He thought about taking one of the jugs from her, for they were quite large, but considered it might be more remarkable, and thus, more memorable, if he did so, so he did not.

Instead, he followed her up the stairs and down the hallway, then slipped past her to knock on the door so Nolly wouldn't be startled by the maidservant barging in. Not that she could have opened the door with her two hands full, but he wanted to be sure.

But, somewhat predictably, the door was unlocked, as if Nolly had gotten distracted by the window and forgot to latch it after Jack. He was standing at the window with the blanket around his shoulders, watching the rain come down the window in big gray streaks.

As Nolly turned to look at who had come through the door, Sarah gave a little gasp, and Jack couldn't blame her. The light from the window set off the angles of Nolly's face in clear relief, making his jaw handsome, and lit his eyes quite blue. The green-wool blanket dropped from his shoulders as he drew it away from his body, perhaps not wanting to be seen by a servant in such a relaxed state. He took it and folded it in his arms and went over to the bed to lay it down, breaking the spell of his beauty.

"Is that the water? Two jugs? Thank you, Jack."

Sarah struggled over to the washstand between the window and the fireplace, putting one jug in the bowl, and the other carefully on the floor, next to the wall. Nolly looked as though he wanted to help her as Jack had wanted to, but it was not the way things were done. Maidservants carried water, and young gentlemen used the water, after which, the maidservant would carry the water away again.

"Thank you, Sarah," said Jack. "Can I give you a penny? Would your mistress let you keep it?"

"Yes, sir, thank you, sir," said Sarah. She took the penny, clasping it in her palm as she bobbed a curtsey. When the door closed behind her, Jack latched it and turned to gesture to the washstand.

"Now you can wash," he said, as pleased as if the entire idea was his very own. "An' there's no need to rush through. I'll sit over here an' watch."

Which was not exactly the right thing to say, for as Jack had been speaking, Nolly had been striding toward the washstand, but then he stopped.

Such rough talk was the way men in taverns talked when they

were trying to woo a whore for which they had plenty of money to pay for. It was not for his Nolly, though who, while he had seen so much of the world lately, did not deserve to be talked to in such a way.

"Never mind me," said Jack, and he walked across the floor as quickly as he could, to where Nolly was, by the edge of the table, clasped Nolly's face in both of his hands, and kissed him soundly on the mouth. "'Twas not the way I meant that to come out. Only that I'm so glad, so very glad, to be here with you. I could watch you wash your hands all day long an' never need another thing."

That hadn't come out exactly right either, but Nolly put a hand on Jack's wrist, and kissed him back.

"It's just that it's not quite dark, yet." Nolly rubbed his thumb over the bone in Jack's wrist, and Jack could feel the faint tremor of his touch. But Nolly wasn't running, hadn't backed up, or told Jack, in so many words, to shove off.

"It's not now," Jack agreed. "We've a supper to eat first, an' then it will be dark later, so I'm only watchin' for now. Only a little."

There was no such thing as a *little watching*, but either Jack was here while Nolly washed up, or Jack went downstairs to wait in the tap room, or at the supper table, which was just being set for them.

But after what they'd been through together, and Nolly was still so private about his person? It was perplexing to try and think around it, though Jack knew he would go downstairs if Nolly wanted it. *Still*.

Something shifted in Nolly's face, as if he'd been thinking it over and determined how it would go. He stuck out his chin a little bit and took his hand away from Jack's wrist to gesture at the chair.

"You can see better if you sit there," said Nolly, blushing pink like a rose. Then he rubbed at his nose with the back of his hand, and Jack realized how nervous he was, how hard he was trying to act as if it were not so.

"All right, then," said Jack.

He undid his red silk cravat, and let the ends dangle as he unbuttoned his vest. Rubbing the palms across the silky brocade, he pulled out a chair and sat down. Unlike the chairs at the Three Cripples, or the benches at the workhouse, or pretty much anywhere he'd ever planted himself, this chair, for all it was wooden, was comfortable. It was wide enough so he didn't feel as though he was going to fall off, and long enough so that the edge of it wasn't biting into his thighs, but instead met the crook of his knee as if it had been designed for him.

"Say what, now?" asked Jack, shifting a bit.

"What is it?" asked Nolly as he doffed his waistcoat and put it on the back of the other chair.

"Just comfortable for once, is all. Now, go on, you. I'll wash up after."

Nolly proceeded to undo his green cravat, unbuttoned his collar from his shirt, and laid both on the top of his gray waist-coat. Then he rolled up his shirtsleeves, carefully making long folds to preserve the linen rather than the hasty wrinkles Jack would have made.

As solemn as a monk at his prayers, he unbuttoned the top buttons of his shirt, and lifted the jug to pour the hot water into the bowl. He put both of his hands in the bowl, to the point where the water almost overflowed onto the finely polished wood floor.

For a moment, he merely stood there, as if absorbing the heat of the water and the smell of the soap on its little shelf. And perhaps he was merely enjoying the moment, that they had come this far and that Nolly, at last, could wash his hands before he ate his supper.

Jack didn't say a word.

Lathering up the soap, just a bit, Nolly washed his hands, and his forearms, gently along his scar, then his face, wiping the soap away after. He was about to wash the back of his neck, Jack saw him lift up the flannel cloth to do it, when he stopped and put the cloth back down. Looking somewhere at the wall in a state that was most puzzling, Nolly suddenly undid the rest of the buttons on his shirt and slipped it off.

Being Nolly, he didn't let the garment fall to the floor, but instead laid it upon the back of the chair with his other clothes and, still not looking at Jack, turned to the washbasin to pick up the flannel cloth to wash the back of his neck.

Jack stood up, fury rushing through him, heat boiling behind his eyes as he strode over to Nolly to still the hand that held the washcloth.

"This why you changed behind the screen at the shop, I take it."

"You must have known," said Nolly, tucking his chin down to look at where Jack's hand was gripping his, water dripping from the cloth onto the shining wooden floor in round, silver circles.

"Figured it," said Jack, "know it now, though, don't I."

And indeed he did know, now. That the bruises covered Nolly in black and green ladders, from his shoulder blades to past the waistband of his trousers. Which hung on his hips, being a tad too big for him, revealing the layer of undergarment that was tied with a string and fastened with two buttons.

As Jack moved closer, he put his hand on Nolly's waist and felt the heat there, dipped his fingers and felt the welts from the cane. Nolly drew in his breath and instantly, Jack pulled his hand away.

"You play it so close to the vest, Nolly," said Jack, his anger roiling around inside of him with nowhere to go. "You never said nothin', never complained once."

"There was no point," said Nolly, and his whole body stiffened as though he wanted to move away, only Jack couldn't let him go. "We had to escape. That was the important thing. Now we're here, and it'll get better. A thrashing never lasts long if you just leave it alone."

"I counted more than one thrashing, Nolly, so give yourself some credit, an' take down them trousers."

Startled, Nolly looked at him, his eyes going wide, then narrowing, and Jack knew what that was about.

"Not for that, my foolish lad. I got you somethin' to help. Here." Jack reached into his pocket, pulled out the pot of balm, and balanced it on his palm. "Told her you'd fallen after church, an' did she have somethin' an' this is what she gave me. Guaranteed to soothe all ills, so just unbutton, will you, an' give me that flannel. The way you been sittin', I just know, well, cane cuts skin, don't it. So."

For a moment it seemed as if Nolly had not heard him or, if he had, was not inclined to be obliging. There was nothing in the entire world that would make Jack force Nolly, so if Nolly shook his head, then Jack would have to spend the entire evening knowing Nolly was in pain and was stubborn enough to do it and, perhaps, cruel enough to make Jack have to stand by and do nothing about it.

But then Nolly shrugged his shoulders and, taking a quick breath, undid the buttons on his trousers, and the string and buttons on his fine underdrawers, and let them fall away from his waist, just to his hips, until he was halfway to standing in a state of nature in front of Jack.

The bruises were bad, especially along the curve of the top of Nolly's backside, welted black, turning to green, and hot when Jack put his fingers gently to them. But they would, as Nolly said, heal.

It was the cuts from the cane that looked the worst, six long purple slashes that had quickly bled and dried into vicious stripes. Those stripes curved across and up his right hip to his waist because Chalenheim was a right-handed bastard and hadn't pulled back on one single blow.

Nolly would have to take his trousers all the way off for Jack to do any proper nursing, and the way his whole body twitched let Jack know that Nolly had just had the same thought. And this, in daylight, however late and going toward evening, was something Nolly simply could not do.

Jack got up and grabbed the green-wool blanket and threw it over Nolly's shoulders like a cloak. Then he pulled the chair over, settled it at Nolly's side, and tugged, very gently, on Nolly's trousers, pulling them all the way down to his knees, until Nolly had to let go to clutch at the blanket.

It was perhaps for the best that Nolly was so shy, because it meant that this sight was only for Jack's eyes, and he could admire the length of Nolly's thighs, the skin along his waist, the dark gold hair between his legs, though he did not stare or make crude remarks.

Instead, he put the tin of balm on the washstand so Nolly would have something to look at while Jack took the cloth and dipped it in the water, which was cooling from its earlier warmth. He rubbed a bit of soap on it, and then, as gently as he could, he cleaned the blood from Nolly's skin, listening to Nolly's hitched breath as he began.

The flannel cloth would snag a little, of course, but Jack went along carefully, making sure the cuts along Nolly's bottom were clean, and thinking that he might leave a sacrifice to whatever deity Nolly wanted him to if the cuts would heal cleanly, and that the backside he so admired even when it was not on view, would not scar.

Scars faded, Jack knew, if they weren't too deep. Besides, there were already scars from a cane, faded white against his flesh, as if from long ago, from before they'd met, and Jack couldn't help but run his thumb along one of them, where the white line cut exactly across both buttocks.

"Who did this?" asked Jack, his voice rough.

Nolly turned his head slightly, as if thinking about it.

"That," he said, his voice coming out like an apology. "It was Mr. Bumble. I'd asked for more, you see, at the workhouse, and they didn't quite like that, so he beat me, and then locked me in the refractory room. I called it the dark room, on account of it was so dark, and—"

"And you only little," said Jack, understanding a great deal more now about Nolly's dislike for the dark, and for pain, and for shame. And going hungry.

He leaned forward, shifting his weight, thinking of Nolly sitting all day in a rattling coach, and not complaining, not even once. He kissed the hollow behind Nolly's hip, with care and very softly so Nolly wouldn't think he was going to do anything else. Still, Nolly twitched, and Jack petted the spot.

"Should have stopped to take care of you sooner. I'm sorry, sweetheart."

"There wasn't time, Jack, and I only started to feel it when we sat still."

"Or moved or walked or bent or *rode*," said Jack, almost sputtering the words with his exasperation. "Bloody fuckin' hell, you galloped that horse!"

"'Twas only a canter, Jack," said Nolly with an unaccustomed meekness. "We had to get away as quickly as we could, for I couldn't let him get at you. I couldn't."

And that, simply, was that. It was Nolly, galloping off into his hero-colored idea of what a friend would do for a friend. Of what he was willing to do for Jack.

Jack felt cross with himself for wanting Nolly to say how he felt about Jack out loud and while sober, instead of being contented with what was right in front of his eyes, this very day. Jack's throat grew thick, and his eyes prickled with heat, and he had to blink very fast and swallow. And swallow again, before he could draw breath to speak.

"Can you take the lid off an' hand that pot to me?"

Now obedient, Nolly did as he was told, and Jack caught his gaze as he took the pot from Nolly's hand.

In those blue eyes was a darkness, as if Nolly feared Jack wouldn't understand why he'd done what he done. But Jack did, though there were no words that would properly explain what it meant to him. So he hefted the pot in his hands, and drew his thumb into the balm, and began putting it on Nolly's skin, following the lines of the cuts from the cane and, ever so softly, spreading the balm out to cover the bruises, until Nolly's skin began to smell quite sweet.

"'Tis made of honey," Jack said, lifting his fingers to his nose to inhale the scent. "An' some kind of flower, I don't know. But now you do smell as sweet as a poesy, so no arguin' with me, y'hear?" Jack traced the longest welt, the one that went from the top of Nolly's right hip, all the way down to his left thigh, easing the balm in while he cleared his throat. "An' don't hide your pain from me like that again, for I won't have it. I won't have you—not even a *single*—you so much as get a splinter, an' I want to know about it, understand? Nolly?"

"Yes, Jack," said Nolly in a very soft voice, as if he were fearful of upsetting Jack even further.

Jack looked up at him, considering his task to be just about finished. Nolly's face was flushed, but it wasn't with shame, for he held his blanket about his shoulders with easy hands.

Perhaps it was that nobody had ever fussed over Nolly like this, at least not in a long time, and it made Jack feel hot all over, all over again. He had to take a breath to quiet himself and, besides, he was here now to take care of Nolly when he needed it, whether that meant cleaning his wounds, or giving him a stern talking to when he did something foolish like putting himself in danger, or—

The breath that Jack didn't know he was still holding whooshed out of him. He clucked at Nolly, as though he were a spooked horse, and pulled up his underdrawers and trousers, all in one go, and turned Nolly toward him so he could do up the string and the buttons.

"How many, d'you reckon?" Jack asked, busy with the string, looping it around his thumb to make a small bow. "Buttons, I mean."

Nolly looked down at himself, at Jack's hands, and seemed to consider this.

"Ten, including the underdrawers," he said in a level voice, as if this had been their conversation all along. "Unless the tailor has determined to play a game with us and has sewn one somewhere that can't be seen."

"Perhaps he has," said Jack, in kind as he clasped Nolly's hips in his hands and stroked the curve of Nolly's hip bones beneath his thumbs. He looked up at Nolly and felt badly that he'd had to put him through any of this, of baring himself to the skin, and having Jack find out something he'd wanted to keep secret. "At least," said Jack, clearing his throat, "your trousers won't fall off during supper."

"That they won't," said Nolly and, with a small smile, he bent forward, holding the green-wool blanket on his shoulders with one hand, much like a young prince might hold his cloak, and gave Jack a kiss.

"Now you," he said. "Now it's your turn to wash and my turn to watch."

❧ 28 ❧

JACK IS CARED FOR

Though Jack was a bit startled by Nolly's suggestion, he nodded, and began to take off his brocade vest, untied his cravat the rest of the way, and undid the buttons to detach his collar. These he grandly handed to Nolly to fold or toss on the bed, as he saw fit, and unbuttoned his shirt to shed it in the same way. Then, with much splashing, he lathered up and washed his face and hands at the basin, smirking because Nolly's gaze was very attentive as he watched from the window where he'd propped himself.

It was a good thing Nolly was not sitting, as standing would help the balm ease his aches and, besides, it put them eye to eye so Jack could make faces at Nolly to show he didn't care that the water was getting on the floor and that he was wasting half the water in the basin whilst mucking about. It was for a lark anyway, to please Nolly by doing this simple thing that only half a year ago would have had him balking and backing away.

"You've got a few bruises yourself, Jack," said Nolly. "What are they from?"

Of course, Nolly would ask.

"From gettin' knocked about, but it's nothing that I regard," said Jack, confident that he could distract Nolly by soaping up

437

his hand and circling his thumb and forefinger to blow bubbles through.

This lasted for about a moment, until Nolly's attention was drawn elsewhere, to Jack's waist. At which point Nolly pushed himself off from his lean against the window frame and came over to where Jack was.

His green-wool blanket hung from his shoulders, a hooded cape that he clenched together with one hand, while the other reached out to Jack, one finger extended to trace the line along the front of Jack's waist.

"I thought it was a stain," said Nolly. "Perhaps from badly dyed workhouse cloth, but it's not. Is it, Jack."

Water dripped from Jack's hand against his neck where he held the flannel cloth, the soap drying along his chin beginning to itch. He looked down to where Nolly was touching him, and the contrast was clear. Nolly had bruises all up and down him, and Jack only this one, really. A thick black line that showed just above his trouser waist like spilled ink. It was from where Chalenheim had abused him, and Jack jerked away, not wanting Nolly to touch him there.

"Then there's this."

Nolly looked at Jack as he traced the line of rash beneath Jack's left arm. The rash extended down his left thigh as well, as Nolly knew, having been there when Mr. Bassler had scrubbed at it with his brush.

It had itched off and on during their stay at Axminster but, with more pressing concerns, Jack had been able to ignore it. Especially since it might go away when the weather got warm. Or it might not. Either way, it wasn't something Nolly should have to worry about, given the marks on his skin that Jack had just tended to.

"'Tis nowt to concern yourself about, my dear Nolly," said Jack, keeping his voice light as he reached down to move Nolly's hand away.

"I should say it is," said Nolly sternly. "I remember from seeing it in Lyme, but it's not gotten any better."

He let the blanket fall from his shoulders and caught it with his free hand. He tossed the blanket over on the bed all anyhow, while Jack's eyebrows rose in his forehead that Nolly was now standing there, dressed only in his trousers and stockings, as if completely unconcerned about being nearly naked. "Since you're mine to care for."

Jack's breath shuddered in his chest, for the light in Nolly's eyes was pure and clear, his gaze steady, and Jack knew that look. It happened when Nolly made up his mind, after which point, there was no power on earth that could get Jack to deny him.

"If you would, please," said Nolly. "Unbutton your trousers. Or, let me."

Wiping the water away from his neck, Jack put the flannel cloth back in the basin, making the water splash over the rim. Then he lifted his arms and pulled them back to signal his willingness for whatever Nolly had in mind. Which, given the hour, was likely to be fairly straightforward and, given Nolly's expression, would consist of the same type of care Jack had just dispensed.

"Will you catch a chill if I take these off?" asked Nolly, undoing the buttons on his trousers, one by one. Ten in all, if their mutual count had been right.

Jack shook his head, his arms still in the air.

His belly was sensitive to Nolly's gentle fingers as they undid the string to his underdrawers and then the two buttons, hidden by a tab that held the waistband smooth. Nolly tugged on Jack's garments to pull them down past his hips, and then all the way to the floor.

Seeing as how Jack still had his boots and stockings on, he felt slightly foolish with his trousers crumpled about his ankles. That is, until he felt Nolly's hands upon him, petting the skin around the rash on his ribs, along his thigh. Nolly was looking at Jack all

439

over, as if he searched for other ills the world had done to Jack, as if he meant to soothe them and then, when he was finished, he would march out that door and find whoever had done them.

That's what his expression said, and again it was as if the words Jack had proclaimed he wanted to hear had no weight, not against the intent of Nolly's hands, the firm line of his mouth that announced to Jack that he was quite angry about it, that someone had hurt Nolly's bright bird.

"My turn, I think," said Nolly as he knelt down in front of Jack.

Jack could see the goose pimples on Nolly's shoulders from the chill in the air as the rain began to smack against the windowpanes. Nolly reached for the washcloth, soaped it up, and gently washed the long red blotches of Jack's rash, stirring Jack so he finally felt he must remind Nolly where they had come from.

"When they disinfected us, when we came back to England," Jack said, his voice coming out rough. "They tossed us over with powder, some kind of lime, an' it burned a bit, but there was no water to wash with, an' so. Well. It burned a bit."

Nodding, Nolly continued to wash Jack's side and thigh. The water trickled down, and the rash itched, but was soothed shortly after when Nolly took fresh water and rinsed off the soap. Very quickly he took the balm and, with the edge of his smallest finger, applied it to Jack's skin, all the while on his knees in front of Jack, shivering in the chill air.

Jack could not let him go on very much longer like this. It would have to be much warmer for either of them to loll about naked, which he hoped they could, one day. But today was not that day, as it was growing darker and raining harder now, and he did not want his Nolly to catch cold.

"That feeling better?" asked Nolly.

"'Tis," said Jack, somewhat short as he brought his arms down. "But you should put a shirt on, else you'll catch your death."

"You wanted my shirt off," said Nolly, pressing the balm into Jack's thigh with his four fingers. "Now you want it on, so which is it?"

He was only pretending to be gruff about it, Jack could tell. The privacy of the room and the growing gloom were making him saucy.

"On," said Jack. "An' we should hurry, for I can smell roastin' meat, an' my stomach cannot take much more without eatin'. You're distractin' me from eatin'. Besides, crouchin' like that can't be good for your backside."

"It's not exactly," said Nolly, straightening up. He went over to the chair and pulled out his shirt to put it on. "But it does feel better, as will you, if you just take care, Jack. You must have cool water on your skin, and the balm afterward, and I'll help you with it each day until it gets better."

That sounded just fine to Jack, for he'd have an excuse to have those hands upon him so very often, each day, in fact. He knew he could bear anything as long as he knew that was coming.

Nolly knelt down in front of him again on the carpet that covered the floorboards. His white shirt that brushed his knees almost glowed against his skin in the gry light from the window.

Jack could stare at this sight all day, the top of Nolly's golden head and just a bit of his chin. That chin jutted out with determination as his hand reached out to touch the bruise on Jack's groin, the long, black mark from Chalenheim's hand, the one that still hurt and felt tender, even beneath Nolly's gentle fingers.

"There's nowt you can do for that, Nolly," said Jack, his voice gruff. "'Tis a bruise only, an', as you say, they go away if you leave them."

"This one will leave sooner than that," said Nolly, not looking up, though his hand stilled, his fingers creating a little circle on Jack's skin around the top of the bruise. "For I cannot abide it, and it must go."

Nolly did not use the cloth on the bruise, though Jack had

thought he might have, given Nolly's love of soap and water. Instead, he leaned close, so close Jack could feel Nolly's breath stirring in his private hair. Then, ever so gently pushing that hair aside, Nolly placed his mouth upon the bruise and kissed it, with his lips sweet and soft, all up and down the length of the bruise. Kissing the hurt away, quietly. Slowly.

No inch of that bruise was left untreated by that beautiful mouth, and Jack felt all of his blood rushing to his groin. It could not be helped, not with that kind of treatment. The strongest man on earth could not have withstood the effects of that mouth upon him.

Jack reached down with one hand and pressed on the other side of his groin, along his hip, in an effort to bestill himself, for it was not his intention to force Nolly's hand in this, or his mouth, either, even though Nolly was right there, and Jack was plenty willing to let him do it.

Then, of a sudden, Nolly's hand was upon Jack's hand and, looking up at Jack from his kneeling position, he pushed the hand away. There was such an expression in his eyes that Jack almost staggered back, had he not been aware he would have tripped over himself had he tried to move at all, what with his trousers still around his ankles.

He opened his mouth to apologize for his unruly cock, or to make a joke of it at least, because he did not want Nolly to feel he must attend to it, that he should feel no obligation at all as regards to Jack's cock. Jack would take care of it himself so they could get dressed and go to supper.

At the same time, there was a secret ripple up his spine in the hopes that Nolly *might*, because his mouth was so close. It was right there, even as Nolly drew back and considered what was before him.

"Close your eyes," said Nolly in that low voice that he had sometimes, that Jack noted he had sometimes, when he was, perhaps, feeling something intently inside of him.

Obediently, Jack closed his eyes and reached out to put his

palm flat against the wall. And felt in that moment, as Nolly put the circle of his mouth around Jack's cock, that he had no weight. That he could not feel his feet, or his arms, or his head, or any part of himself, save that part that Nolly touched.

At first, Nolly suckled gently around the head of Jack's cock, his mouth slick and tight, as if unsure of what he was doing. But then Jack felt Nolly swallow, felt him pause, as if considering the taste.

Then Nolly's hand was on the base of Jack's cock, holding it firm as he sucked and slicked the length of it with the moisture from his mouth. Jack shuddered with the pleasure of it, his head going back as he pressed against the wall for balance, his eyes still closed, as he had been bidden.

In all the days of his life, while he might have imagined this moment, he had not considered that such a thing would actually occur. With both of them pretty well considerably naked, Nolly in his trousers and untucked shirt, on his knees in front of Jack, favoring Jack with the pressure of his mouth, his hand, with his tongue along the bottom of Jack's cock, and the small shift of sound, of skin on skin. Nolly sucking while his grip eased and tightened, as if he'd been doing this to Jack for years now, instead of only a little while.

Jack's whole spine began to spin, his body feeling as though it were going around, as if he were about to fall, and he had to open his eyes to regain his balance, for his hand against the wall was doing him no good at all.

He beheld that sight of Nolly on his knees, his eyes shut in concentration, one hand braced on Jack's waist, that Jack had not felt there at all, but could now feel keenly. The warmth of Nolly's skin, the faint pressure, the smell of the honey-scented balm, all rose around Jack, going straight into every fiber of him, pushed there by the sucking of Nolly's mouth, his lips a pressure-ring, his throat swallowing—

Jack felt his whole body jerk as he came, shuddering into Nolly's mouth. He was unable to stop it, or to warn Nolly, as he'd wanted to do, as Jack did not want to make Nolly choke so he wouldn't hate to do this to Jack again sometime, if he wanted.

But Nolly was leaning forward, going into it, his mouth tight as he gripped Jack's cock, his fingers slipping down to dig into Jack's thigh. The pressure would not leave bruises, but it might as well have left a brand, for this moment Jack would remember for as long as he lived: Nolly sucking on his cock, his head so close to Jack that the sweet curls on Nolly's head, light gold and dark gold, mixed with the darker tight strands of Jack's private hair until they blended into one.

Jack closed his eyes, quickly, to capture that in his mind; forever and forever, he would remember this moment.

Nolly's throat swallowed, and his hand gentled Jack's cock, petting lighter and lighter as the skin grew sensitive, with little jerks that startled Jack, but oh, so sweetly. When Nolly finally took his mouth off Jack, his hands remained on Jack, one on his thigh, the other on his hip. Jack opened his eyes and looked down.

"You opened your eyes," said Nolly, seemingly so rattled that his voice came out rough. He brushed his hands down both of Jack's thighs now, and began to pull up Jack's underdrawers for him, settling the waist of the garment into place first, doing up the buttons and the string before pulling up the trousers to begin on the many buttons.

"That I did," said Jack, and he could offer no apology for it whatsoever. "I could not help it, for you were there, an' I found you beautiful."

Now discomfited, Nolly blinked. Jack reached down to take his hands and pull him to standing. With his thumb, Jack wiped a bit of moisture from the corner of Nolly's mouth, smiling as Nolly followed after with a scrub of the heel of his hand, scowling. Or trying to scowl, as if he was not sure why he'd done that, or what the reckoning might be.

Jack hurried to assure him that it was not so. He circled his arms about Nolly's waist, feeling the fine linen of Nolly's shirt crumple beneath his hands, and pulled Nolly to him, ever so gently, and buried his forehead in the hollow of Nolly's neck.

"I love you more each day, my dear Nolly," said Jack, low against Nolly's skin. "More each day."

He felt Nolly's body tense, and it hurt Jack's heart that Nolly could not simply believe this, or accept it if he did believe it. And when was the last time anybody had told Nolly something like that? It had been Jack, which determined that Jack didn't say it often enough, which he should do, every moment he could until Nolly believed him.

When Nolly wrapped his arms around Jack's body, pulling Jack close to him in return, Jack sighed, and felt Nolly echo that sigh.

"I keep thinking—" Nolly began, and when he stopped, Jack pulled back, out of Nolly's arms so he could see Nolly's expression in the last of the fading daylight. He cupped Nolly's face in his hands.

"Thinkin' what?"

"That I'm dreaming. That this is a dream, and we shall both wake up and find ourselves back in the workhouse."

The way he said it told Jack that the workhouse was not just a bad thought, or some dour consequence to mischief. Rather, for Nolly, it was a nightmare, the worst nightmare that his entire being could conceive of. It was up to Jack to make sure that the nightmare never happened. Not ever. Not again.

"But we're not, you an' me," said Jack, giving Nolly's mouth the lightest of kisses, for his stomach was rumbling and Jack was sure that the dark, growling sound he could hear was Nolly's stomach fighting with itself. "We're here, right now, at this moment. We'll care for each other, you an' I, an' I swear upon my life that you will never spend a single day doubtin' that."

He kissed Nolly again, then tugged on the tails of Nolly's shirt, for the room was quite chilly now. Besides, Nolly looked far too somber for Jack's liking, but that was Nolly because the world was a serious place for him. It was Jack's job to demonstrate how much this wasn't so. At least not always.

"Shall you get dressed, then? Shall I help you? Come, let me get you ready to go down to supper, an' I know I'm not your manservant, but this is what we do for each other. You just did up my buttons, an' now I'll tuck in your shirt, all right an' proper. 'Tis fair that way, ain't it? Ain't it, my dear Nolly?"

As if he'd been tensing for a blow of some kind, Nolly let out a breath, then took another deeper one. He reached up to give the back of Jack's neck a squeeze, his hand running across Jack's scalp, his fingers carding through Jack's hair. The way that Jack liked it, though he'd never told Nolly, for it made all of his skin tingle with pleasure, that simple touch.

Then Nolly bent to grab his collar and cravat from the chair, and Jack took his time tucking in Nolly's shirt, till Nolly rolled his eyes as he tried to do the top of his shirt at the same time, and then Jack pushed his hands away, to finish up tying Nolly's cravat.

"We're goin' to starve by the time you set yourself to rights," said Jack, half scolding, half laughing.

"Then we shall be bones in this room," said Nolly with some seriousness, though Jack could hear the laugh in his voice. "Merely bones, you and I, with our clothes half on, and our skeleton hands reaching for the door."

Jack snorted through his nose as he reached for Nolly's fine, gray waistcoat, putting his arms around Nolly so he could put it on. As Jack did up the waistcoat's buttons, Nolly kissed Jack on the forehead, though, in the near dark, it was more of a bump than a kiss, but Jack knew what Nolly meant it for.

"I'll leave my jacket off," said Jack, feeling noble about it. "As you won't have yours."

"You're most kind, Jack," said Nolly now, and Jack could see the outline of him, now all tidy and trim. "But I would be pleased to dine with you in any mode of dress, be it fine or coarse."

Jack ducked his head, though he didn't want to hide his smile at this, did not mean to, but Nolly's words, as they sometimes did, when they came, overwhelmed him.

He felt Nolly's hands at his neck, doing up the collar and buttons with deft hands, tying the cravat to just the right snugness, and no more than that. As if Nolly had been doing it for him a good long while, doing it for Jack, not because Jack couldn't do a reasonable job himself, but because he wanted Jack to look his best. Which, as Nolly gave Jack's belly a pat, Jack knew he now did. He could mix with the most properest of folk because Nolly had deemed it to be so.

"To supper, then?" asked Jack, looking about for the key.

It was on the table and Nolly handed it to him. Jack undid the latch and swung the door open to the slightly cooler air of the hallway. He gave a little bow that Nolly should go first, and so Jack could lock the door behind them. For though anybody could steal whatever they had, as Jack could always pick pockets to get them more, he did not want anybody to go in without his leave. It was their room, their secret place that no one should disrupt.

"To supper," said Nolly. He put his hand on Jack's arm as Jack put the key in his pocket. "I'm starving, Jack."

"I have no doubt you are," said Jack. "For I am as well. Let's go down then, an' tell Sarah an' Miss Betsy to serve us enough for ten men, shall we?"

"Yes," said Nolly and with a smile, he kissed Jack on the cheek. "And don't forget something sweet for after."

That Jack would not do, would never do, should all the tortures of hell rain down upon his head.

❧ 29 ❧

SUPPER AT THE SWAN AND WHAT
HAPPENED AFTER

A fter Miss Betsy had shown them to their table, a round,
well-polished table that sat in a cozy spot adjacent to
the small, coal fire, and Oliver had made sure Jack had
the seat he preferred, that being his back to the wall, able to
keep his eyes on Oliver and the entire room, as well as the
doorway to the front entryway, Oliver allowed himself to sit
back in his chair and relax.

He could even enjoy, now, the gleam in Jack's eye, and the
memory of his whole body shaking with pleasure beneath Oliver's hands, and the round surprise of his eyes when Oliver had
taken Jack in his mouth. Jack's mouth had fallen open, for a
moment, without any words, but in spite of which he'd managed
afterward to express his gratitude just the same.

Then Jack had told him that he loved him. As he had before
and would, no doubt tell him again. And while Oliver was
envious at Jack's ease in saying it, it never failed to stir within
him a kind of joy that built upon itself and never quite seemed to
fade, even when it had been a while since Jack had said it last.

Fairly soon, a male servant dressed in black trousers and a
spotless white apron and shirt, came over to them and gave them
a little bow. All at once, Oliver knew this was quite a posh place,

for there was no flirting in the man's behavior, no rush in his attitude. He was there to wait upon them, as long as it might take.

"May I tell you what's good on the menu?" asked the waiter.

"You may," said Jack, rather boldly and with a broad smile, as if he were a yokel, newly come from the country and unaccustomed to such grandness. "But I can smell the kitchen from here, an' am sure anythin' would make a tasty meal for my friend an' I here."

For a moment, Oliver wanted to wince because that was not the way one behaved in fine establishments with male waiters. But he had a feeling Jack was making a game of it for his own amusement, and said nothing. To his surprise, the waiter smiled in a genuine way, accepting Jack's enthusiasm rather than being dismissive of it.

"You are quite right, young master," said the waiter with another bow. "But if I might suggest a serving of carved roast, the fried cod, with the bones trimmed, of course, and perhaps some sliced pork? We cook it in cider; it's very good in these parts."

"All of that," said Jack, cupping his hands together as if gathering up the food himself. "Enough for two hungry fellows, some of each?"

"And bread and butter and perhaps some boiled potato?"

"Yes," said Jack, and Oliver felt his stomach agree with everything Jack was saying.

"We have some wine you might enjoy, red or white. It's from Spain, so it's not very fancy, as you might get in Bath or the City, but it is quite good, in a country way. And then, for dessert, we have plum tart with cream, pieplant in crust, blancmange with spring strawberries and, of course, the cheese plate. We had some apple tart, but I believe Cook is saving it."

As for Oliver, he would like any of those, anything with cream and sugar would do him fine, but he imagined he'd quite like to see the expression on Jack's face when a bite of blancmange melted on his tongue for the very first time. So, being generous with himself, as well as with Jack, Oliver took his turn.

"I do believe that we'd like a serving of plum tart, and could we get two of the blancmange? For I adore it and will not want to share, and Jack here has never had it and deserves an entire serving."

"Very good, young sir," said the waiter with an appreciative expression on his face that told Oliver their choices had been approved of, and though Oliver had not before thought he'd need a stranger's positive regard for his choice of supper dishes, he found he quite liked getting that nod of approval.

Fairly soon, before Oliver could do more than unfold his napkin in his lap and nod at Jack to do the same in such a place, though normally he would not, another waiter, dressed the same, though somewhat younger, as though he were only in training, came by.

He brought a plate of sliced bread and the ubiquitous dish of sweet butter and, as well, a decanter of each red and white wine, all carried on a wooden tray that he balanced not on his hip but rather over his head. This he lowered to the edge of the table, transferring the contents to just the right spot exactly between the two of them, with the butter as close to Jack as it was to Oliver.

"Will you try the red or the white, sirs?" This was asked in somewhat formal tones, in an accent that sounded as if the young man had come from someplace other than Winterbourne or Taunton or anywhere in the West Country.

Jack looked at Oliver as though he wanted to shrug and Oliver went ahead and shrugged, anyway. There was no point in pretending either of them knew anything about wine, for the waiter in his starched white apron would have been trained far beyond them being able to tell a story about it, that they favored this wine over that. They'd have been unmasked inside of a very quick moment.

"Normally," said Oliver, very formally so the waiter wouldn't think he was a complete fool, "I drink beer and gin."

"Very good, sir," said the young waiter with all of the dignity of his station. "I'd be very contented to bring you some of either, but perhaps, first, you might like to taste the red, which goes very well with beef, or the white, for the fish."

The waiter motioned to the table, and Oliver felt his face starting to grow heated at the thought that he would not know what the waiter was pointing at or understand why it was important. Jack, as well, looked a tad overwhelmed, his eyebrows going up a fraction as he too looked at the table.

Well, there was an assemblage of glasses, and Oliver had a memory, somewhat faint at this point, of him and Uncle Brownlow at a fine restaurant in London, near Hyde Park. There had been much cutlery and glasses and plates, though after they'd made their choices, half of that had been taken away, and the table had been transformed from a confusing menagerie into merely a supper table, albeit a rather elegant supper table, having had a white tablecloth laid beneath it.

"Shall you try some of each, sirs?" suggested the waiter, perhaps not being unaccustomed to tavern diners being in a bit over their heads. "'Tis quite a good way to make your decision."

"Yes, thank you," said Oliver.

He leaned back a bit to give the waiter room to pour the white wine into two wine glasses and the red in two other wine glasses. At the waiter's nod, though with some trepidation, Oliver tried the white and found it bitter, then tried the red, and found it bitter as well, although after, both wines seemed to smooth out in his mouth, with the red having the feel of warm butter in the back of his throat.

"Oh," said Oliver.

"You see?" said the waiter, quite pleased with himself. He held the tray in front of him, as though it was his reward for introducing Oliver to something new, for in that restaurant with Uncle Brownlow, Oliver's wine, of whatever type it had been, had been diluted with water far enough to barely taste like anything.

"Yes, I do," said Oliver, nodding at Jack that he should try now as well. "Would it be polite if I only had red wine? Red wine with everything? I prefer it to the white."

"Excellent choice, sir," said the waiter, nodding in agreement. He filled Oliver's glass with more red wine and lifted the remainder of the glass of white, as if this were the very action he would have recommended. Though Oliver thought, as he waited for Jack to have a taste, that the waiter would have been as polite regardless which wine Oliver had selected.

Jack took a taste of the red wine. He made a face, but Oliver waited until the feel of butter had touched the back of his throat, and watched Jack's eyebrows fly up.

"Red for me as well, I reckon," said Jack, lifting up his wine glass for more of the red wine.

The waiter obliged him by pouring him a full glassful. He then took the other white wine glass and moved away, and it was as if he'd never been there, as if the glasses of red wine and the plate of sliced bread and bowl of sweet butter had appeared by unseen hands.

"Oh, my, this is a bit posh, eh?" Jack looked across the table of finery, and, finally copying Oliver's motion, whipped out the folded napkin and draped it across his lap. Oliver had the feeling Jack was doing this for his benefit, so he kissed Jack with his eyes and nodded.

"Posh by my reckoning as well," said Oliver, in agreement and amazement. All taverns seemed the same from the outside, though this one had had a beautiful, graceful swan on the outside, so perhaps that was the key. Fancy out, then fancy in.

Contentedly, he buttered his bread, showing Jack, with a flick of his wrist, which knife to use, and how to lay the sliced bread on the small plate next to the big one.

If Jack followed Oliver's suit, then that would be well, or if he did not, then that would also be well. Though Oliver imagined in a place such as this that Jack would take some pains to color his actions and his words so as not to seem remarkable, to seem, as it were, like anybody else, even if he was, to Oliver, unique in all the world.

This Jack did, using the right knife and plate, echoing his motions to Oliver's, down to taking only a small bite of bread and butter, and following it up with a polite sip of wine, though his mien of elegance was broken when he almost moaned out loud at the combination.

"This what them Frenchies been keepin' from us all this while? Drat those bastards, this is good, I'd say, too good not to share."

"And the Spaniards," said Oliver, in mock consternation. "It's their wine, this time, after all."

"An' the Spaniards," Jack said, agreeing, then bit with sharp teeth into a much bigger chunk of bread. "Blasted Spaniards," said Jack, as he chewed with his mouth open, though perhaps only to make Oliver laugh at his antics rather than actually forgetting his manners in such a nice tavern.

Oliver obliged him, smiling from behind his wine glass before taking a nice, long sip of it, along with another bite of bread and butter, but delicately, to show Jack what a cretin he was.

Before they were properly finished with all of the bread, the meal arrived, carried by two waiters this time, each with a round wooden tray. They filled the table with the china serving dishes for the beef, and the galvanized tin one for the fish, and the pork in a crockery pot, with the cider juices still bubbling hot. Alongside this was a large bowl of potatoes and, after refilling their glasses, the waiters went away, leaving the table groaning with food, and Oliver's mouth watering at the anticipation of eating every bite of it.

In mutual silence, they did just that, sharing the plates between them, offering up bites of cod or beef that were particularly good to make sure that the other one had tasted it. They made gestures of knives and forks and brief clinks of their wine glasses together to celebrate the meal, though Oliver felt a bit foolish at not knowing what toast to make.

They ate the beef, and the pork, and the fish and, with bellies full, agreeably allowed the first waiter, looking as starched as he ever had, to take away the empty plates and dishes and bring them their three desserts.

Oliver pushed the plate of plum tart away and rather, with a gesture with his dessert fork, urged Jack to try the blancmange first before he sullied his tongue with anything so common as a baked plum, no matter how sweetened with sugar it might be.

"Only do try it first, Jack," said Oliver, somewhat urgently as he saw Jack plaintively watch Oliver's brisk dismissal of the plum tart. "For I want to see your face when you taste it."

This Jack did, his salad fork sliding through the jelly-like cream. He stuffed his mouth with it, unabashedly, allowed the treat to sit on his tongue just so Oliver could watch him do it. And the results were good, so very good, for Jack's face rather melted, all the tension gone away, as if he were a small child having been given his first taste of something so sweet and smooth that its match could never be found.

"Do you like it?"

"Nolly, you wretch, have you been keepin' this from me?"

"Yes," said Oliver, quite firm in his manner, though between large bites of his own blancmange. "I've been hiding it all this while, in London, on the road to Lyme, and in the workhouse. Quite the trouble I had with that, I can tell you, with all those paupers wanting their share of it—" Suddenly the joke tasted flat and harsh in his mouth and he stumbled to a stop. He sighed, shrugging his apology, fiddling with his napkin in his lap. "I can never do it, Jack, the way you do."

"The way I do what?"

"Turn an ordinary comment into something wry and amusing, as you can, the way you can, at the drop of a hat. I envy that talent, for I find I am not the most entertaining of company."

"Bollocks to that," said Jack loudly. He raised his glass of mostly drunk red wine and, with much aplomb, and with a complete disregard that he might be overheard, he said, "To the sweetest fellow, my golden-haired boy, for I am only amusing in your eyes, you know."

With that, he polished off the red wine and, with a slight burp, set the glass down and scrubbed at his mouth with the napkin to then crumple it up in a ball to leave it on top of his plate. Oliver did not let himself say anything, though he sensed that with the end of the meal, and Jack's gesture, the evening had taken a slight turn, and was about to go somewhere for which Oliver was not quite prepared.

"I can see it in your eyes, just now, that you're thinkin' 'bout it." Jack leaned back, scraping the legs of the chair along the floorboards so he could slouch and stretch out his legs beneath the table.

"Thinking about what, Jack?" asked Oliver.

He wiped his mouth with some care, and folded the napkin in the proper manner, showing Jack how it was done in case Jack ever might want to copy him when they were at a different restaurant, in a different town. Or perhaps he was affronted by Jack's manners of a sudden, on account of the wine, or the lateness of the hour, or the way Jack was looking at him, intent and still.

"Thinkin' about fuckin' me, Nolly? I mean, you do want to, after learnin' how long I been at it?"

For a moment, startled by this statement, Oliver felt his face grow warm, the skin along his elegant collar damp and hot. He wanted very badly to give Jack the scolding he so obviously was asking for, for ruining a perfectly good evening with such a crass and callous statement.

Then he saw the tightness of the skin beneath Jack's eyes, and the way he turned his head as if waiting for a blow, as he had in the workhouse. As if he now deserved Oliver's ire, and had brought it forward with his behavior to have it out now, rather than having to wait for what he obviously thought he had coming to him. Oliver's derision, perhaps, or his refusal, or a loud, raucous quarrel right there in the tavern room, with everyone listening and watching.

"I might have been thinking about it," said Oliver, low, and with such calm tones as he could muster, considering his temper had risen quite quickly just then. But he quelled it, swallowing the taste of wine in his throat without taking any more and wished he had some nice, cool water to aid him. "But not in the way you are suggesting. I have no wish to cause you pain, and when we are together—"

Oliver paused to lean forward, to explain in as earnest and truthful a manner as he might, to erase that expression from Jack's face so he would never again have to think of Jack thinking such dark and derisive thoughts about himself.

"When we are alone and together," he clarified this with a slow nod. "When I have pressed myself upon you, you do not like it. You do *not* like it, and I imagine that is how it would go, this intimacy, and so—"

In a thousand lifetimes, Oliver could not have imagined having such a conversation with anybody, let alone with Jack, in this fine restaurant, in a town he'd never before even known the name of. He stopped altogether to give Jack a chance to deride him if he might, or laugh out loud or dismiss Oliver's considerations as being foolish as well as completely unnecessary.

But Jack did none of these things. He only sat and listened, his body, in its long sprawl, seemingly relaxed, his head tipped to one side, his eyes on the middle distance of the tabletop, listening, as if to every word Oliver was saying.

Then, in the silence, Jack smiled, as if to himself at an oft-told joke.

"You can't even say it, can you. Fuckin'. Buggerin'."

"No, I cannot, Jack, truly. I want to share this with you, but I don't know anything, and I don't want to hurt you."

"But if *you* do it," said Jack, looking up at Oliver now, his green eyes bright, some glimmer of hope there that Oliver was unable to understand. "Then you can erase him from me."

"I would," said Oliver, quite plainly. "And I will, with all my heart, but if I were to hurt you with my fumbling inexperience, then I would never forgive myself."

"You could never do that, Nolly," said Jack. He sat up in his chair as if coming to a decision, but first he looked at Oliver, as if seeing him for the first time. "You have always treated me as if I were something rare an' fine."

"I have not," said Oliver, feeling the heat rise in his voice.

Jack merely laughed at this, a soft, low sound that surrounded Oliver as a caress from Jack's hand might, and he knew he was forgiven and that Jack would—

"You'll teach me, then, Jack, won't you?" asked Oliver. "Teach me what you like, when it's nice, the way it's supposed to be."

"Teach you to say the words, as well," said Jack, nodding. "You must learn to say the words, Nolly, to me, at least, with whom you'll be havin' it. Doin' it. Whatever it is. Will you promise to try an' say it?"

"In private, Jack," said Oliver, feeling quite stern about it and overly confused at the quick turns of Jack's behavior, though he supposed it was just as difficult for Jack after Port Jackson and the workhouse combined. "In private," he said again, for he would brook no refusal on the matter.

"I am forever your servant," said Jack.

He said this with such solemn tones that Oliver wanted to chide him. Only he saw the glint in Jack's eyes, and realized Jack was teasing him, as he always did, to drown the seriousness of Oliver's world and layer it with the more jaunty humor of his own.

The slight curve of a smile across Jack's lips as he gestured for the waiter to bring them their bill was what did him in. Oliver could never resist that smile, in all of its guises, just as he could never resist Jack himself, whether serene or rambunctious. He hoped that he would, in time, be able to express his feelings at any given moment, when Jack staggered beneath his own dark past, or when the difficulties that currently, most assuredly, awaited them along the road they would travel together.

"I'm just goin' to pay him, whatever the amount," said Jack, as if they'd been sharing another altogether different conversation. About the spending of money not rightfully their own and what a supper in a tavern in a small town should cost.

Oliver considered it would be quite a lot, an appallingly shocking amount. He nodded that Jack would be the only one to lay eyes upon the bill and pay it, for otherwise it might send Oliver into a miserly fit about it. And he did not want that, not that evening. Not when they had their lovely private room, with the soft blanket and comforter, awaiting them.

FROM WHERE OLIVER STOOD, POISED AT THE WASHBASIN, attempting with cold fingers to undo the buttons on his collar, the bed seemed enormous, looming. There was one candle on the mantle, and it gleamed in the corner of Oliver's eye, though he could clearly sense Jack standing in the shadow of the window curtain, waiting for Oliver. Waiting, it seemed, for Oliver, as Jack might put it, to finish mucking about and get on with it, his undressing and fussing and stalling so they could—

Oliver's shoulders slumped, and he tore at the buttons to get them to release the collar's hold on his neck, suddenly too tight, as if it were cutting off his breath.

"Could we just pretend," Oliver said, a taste of desperation in his mouth that he not ruin this for Jack, or shake himself to pieces with nerves. "Pretend we're only going to do what we've done before. I could manage better, if I thought that."

"Of course, Nolly," said Jack, as he might have done had it been the middle of the day, and them miles from the portending gloom of the private room that Oliver had entered quite willingly only moments before. "It'll be as easy as ever it has been.

I'll go slow, an' you can stop me whenever you like. At any moment, just say it, say *No, Jack*, an' I'll stop. With all my heart, I promise that to you."

As it was clear to Oliver that *no* might have been a word Jack had said often to the marine, but with no result, Oliver had to unclench his fists and take a slow breath, as casually as if he were only frustrated with his cuff buttons.

At which point Jack, who no doubt knew exactly what was going through Oliver's mind, stepped into the circle of the candlelight and began assisting Oliver. With the buttons of his shirt, the tabs on his trousers, the laces on his boots, which, finely polished, gleamed low and black and fine even in the darkness by the door where Jack put them, along with the clothes, still warm from Oliver's body, which he folded neatly on the small dresser by the window.

This left Oliver standing in only his shirt, though the rug was too thick and too softly woven to let even the slightest cold or damp come up through the floorboards, so his toes did not curl, nor did his teeth chatter with it. Especially not when he could watch the familiar and comforting sight of Jack disrobing in the most casual of ways, tossing his clothes about the room as always, with never a single consideration as to the confusion this would cause when he desired to dress in the morning.

"That's you, then," said Jack, now in only his shirt as Oliver was. Then, with a pat to the top of Oliver's partly bare chest, as casually as he might have done any other evening, he asked, "An' me as well, so which side do you want?"

For a moment, Oliver attempted to consider which side Jack might want, near the window or near the door, as both were equally close to the small, cheerful coal fire currently dancing orange and bright on the grate.

"No," said Jack, in a half-scold. "The door is locked and the windows also, for I checked. We're the safest as we've ever been, so we can both sleep with our eyes shut. I'm only askin' you, so you can sleep on the side you like. It's your right, ain't it?"

"Yes," said Oliver, his lips somewhat numb, though his blood felt as though it were racing through him, touching all the parts of him in anticipation he could not quite control, nor, as yet, enjoy.

"So," said Jack. He moved to the bed and pulled back the blanket and comforter and the snowy white sheet. "Climb in an' let's be havin' you."

"*Jack.*"

"Only messin' with you, Nolly, so you'll see it's meant to be a pleasant thing, that it's fine to smile, or to laugh, an' that it's only full of sweet kisses an' warm touches, at least—"

To Oliver's horror, Jack stuttered on his words, and his encouragement for Oliver's sake turned suddenly into a memory of something that was the exact opposite of what Jack obviously meant to share with him, here, in this room.

With a nod and a shaky indrawn breath, Oliver settled his shoulders and walked around to the other side of the bed, trying to consider whether he would prefer the candle be lit or out, but decided that it would be easier if the act they were about to partake did not occur in the dark. And, applying all of his courage, he drew back the bedclothes on his side.

"You are most kind, Jack," he said, climbing in, plumping the pillows behind him—at least three, to his count—and settled against them, pulling the bedclothes up to his hips before Jack could even blink. "Because, yes, this is my favorite side. Though, if it is yours as well, then you must tell me, and we'll trade off."

Silent for a moment, Jack nodded and clambered in to the bed, copying Oliver's movements and his position against plumped pillows, and smiled, as if unable to resist the wry thought that had crossed his mind.

"What is it?" asked Oliver.

"Here we are, then," said Jack with a laugh. "Now what shall we do first?"

A thousand thoughts flurried across Oliver's mind, and he jerked back, blinking, not wanting the decision to rest on him, at least not this time. Jack shook his head to show he'd been teasing as he reached for Oliver, and drew him into a kiss.

"It's all bollocks, anyway," said Jack, his mouth moving softly against Oliver's mouth. "All them rules an' cautions, it's all bollocks. I'll kiss you, an' you kiss me back. We start with that, an' go where we like. Or not, whichever seems best an' easy to you. Right?"

Oliver nodded, liking the feel of Jack's lips tickling his, as it made the room, the situation, the poshness of it all, feel not quite so strange.

"An' don't forget to say *no* to me, if you've a mind to."

Again Oliver nodded, somewhat confused now, with Jack moving closer, the warmth of his skin, his scent, crowding out the smell of burnt honey, the acid of the coal fire, for he did not know if Jack wanted him to say *no* now, or later or when—

"An' if you could," said Jack, drawing back. He looked directly at Oliver with all the seriousness he could muster, being dressed only in a shirt and with his hair all rumpled from disrobing, "Do me a favor."

"Yes, Jack, anything."

"Remember how you felt in Lyme, when you wanted to touch me, to give me somethin', an' this you did, an' I gave you somethin', an' it was good, yes? It made you feel easy after, with all them troubles you like to carry around as if you were bound by duty to do so. Well, they didn't matter anymore. D'you remember that feelin'?"

"I do."

"Then that's what we're headed for, an' not anythin' else. Except for our bloody shirts, which will get in the way, but we'll fling them on the floor, an' laugh 'cause it just doesn't matter, any of it, except for me an' thee an' where we are right now."

"Oh." Oliver said this with some seriousness, his hands clasped in his lap, as if he were about to start his evening prayers.

The feeling in his chest had lightened with Jack's words, the patience in his voice, the levelness of his expression, and his green eyes, so bright in the candlelight, the flicker of the fire's flames reflected there. All of this was for Oliver.

Jack was holding himself quite still, as if waiting for some signal from Oliver, some gesture, and it was selfish of Oliver to make him wait. The trepidation in his belly would fade, he knew, with Jack's soft kisses and the touch of his hands, a soft stroke to his neck. Oliver closed his eyes, as if he already felt Jack's kisses and touches, and then opened them to nod at Jack.

"The shirts, our shirts, should just come off now, I think, Jack," said Oliver. "For I feel as though my skin is on fire, and we're only just, you're just, well, you're right here, aren't you. So take off your shirt, if you would, and I'll take mine off so as to save us any later impatience and so we can now fully enjoy the pleasure of tossing them on the floor."

Without another word, Oliver reached over his head and, shimmying his hips to release the cloth from beneath him, he pulled on the back of his shirt. Slipping it down his arms, he flung it to the foot of the bed, and watched it flip over the edge to land where it might. But Jack was quicker than he, already bare to the skin, his chin dipped down to shade his smile, as if he feared Oliver might feel mocked by it and he did not want that just then.

Then, as if flinging himself across a wide, wide abyss, Oliver reached out and pulled Jack to him for a kiss. Which turned into many small kisses, upon any part of Jack such as he could reach, his face, his neck, everywhere. He could feel Jack smiling wide beneath those kisses, feel the softness of the sheets against his bare skin. And with a trust he would not have thought possible only moments ago, Oliver lay back and pulled Jack on top of him so he could feel the length of Jack's skin, the hard curve of his chest, the warmth of his belly.

Now there was the sharpness of Jack's hips, the scratch of his private hair, the pulsing tightness of Jack's cock, all at once. He shared those features of his own with Jack, for this they had done before, and it had been good, in a deep, quiet way, which ever before that moment, Oliver would not have thought possible. But all of that emboldened him to stroke the length of Jack's back and twine his fingers through Jack's hair, lavishing him with deep kisses.

He felt Jack's response, the returned caress, the weight of Jack upon him as familiar as breathing, though somewhat more charged. From within, from without, that charged feeling moved all the way through him till his own cock had hardened and was uncomfortable, pressed between their bellies as it was.

"Shall you turn over, Nolly?" asked Jack, his voice rough and low, a scarlet flush across his neck, his eyes as dark as a starless night.

Oliver looked up at Jack, feeling as solemn as though he were in church. He would not make Jack beg, not after everything, so with a nod and a last kiss upon Jack's trembling mouth, Oliver moved out of Jack's arms to turn on his stomach.

He propped his cheek upon folded arms, and was glad when Jack shoved the pillows out of the way, only to move one beneath Oliver's hips. Which made Oliver jerk with a start. Except then, Jack stroked him with long, slow pets along the length of his back, gentle across the welts and bruises that were still fading.

Oliver felt a light kiss upon each place that hurt, though Oliver did not understand why Jack's hands were slightly shaking where they touched Oliver. It was the best medicine, though, and he turned his neck to look over his shoulder to give that half-blink, a cat's kiss, to let Jack know that it was all right.

Still, he was startled when he felt Jack's kiss press upon the curve of his backside, quite low, near the place between his legs where he'd never had anybody kiss him, or touch him in that way. Jack's fingers were soft, but they moved between his buttocks, a long, slow caress that made Oliver want to jump away, and his shoulders twitched as he held himself still.

"Is that a *no*, Nolly?" asked Jack, whispering, his voice full of want and patience all at the same time. "Tell me true, an' I'll stop. Right this moment."

"It's a *yes*, Jack," said Oliver in kind. "But I'm quite tender there."

"Then I'll be gentle with you, my sweet, sweet, Nolly. So gentle."

Jack was, though Oliver could not quite contain his sharp, indrawn breath when he felt Jack's tongue lick between his buttocks, quickly, inching toward that pink, puckered skin that Oliver knew well and good was not meant for any of this. For this pleasure was quite hedonistic in the way it shuddered through his whole body from one simple, moist touch.

He took a breath and tucked his chin low and turned off his mind to any more words, any more thoughts of drawings of the human body that had never indicated this feeling was even possible, let alone desirable and delicious as it was. Jack's mouth was swirling over his anus, over and over and over, until Oliver was shivering, his legs spreading apart, all on their own, his body responding, a deep groan in his mouth, his forehead dripping with sweat even though Jack was doing everything—

It was as if his whole body was opening up, the petals of secrecy and shame unfolding, silk over skin, until he was wide open, in his heart, his head, clear of any doubts, as Jack's fingers traced the same line his tongue had followed. Oliver scrubbed his damp face on the pillowslip, and sighed as Jack's finger pushed into him.

"That still a *yes*, sweetheart?"

"Yes, Jack," said Oliver.

Or at least that's what he meant to say, though he rather considered the words came out more like a faraway cry of delight and surprise, all the stir of emotion within him that he could not articulate, but that, most probably, Jack heard as clearly as if Oliver had spoken it aloud. All of what he meant to say, one great oration of pleasure and surprise and the joy of abandoning anything else that was not him and Jack in this bed, in the night, right now, this moment, all of it was gone, swept completely away by the mere touch of a single one of Jack's fingers.

With each touch of Jack's hands, Jack made Oliver's skin dance; with more moist kisses, Jack made Oliver's thighs clench and unclench. The caress of his mouth was as assured and gentle, as though Oliver had been newly born, and he Jack's utmost responsibility.

This stirred Oliver to life, to liveliness, making his heart race, and his back, the curve of his hips, feel slick with sweat. His cock grew tight and blood-hot as Jack traced the curve between Oliver's buttocks and pushed into him with two fingers.

He was creating the space where his cock would later follow, but doing it with such care and deft slowness that Oliver felt his hips surge upward, and he let them. He wanted more of that, the pressure that Jack's fingers wrought, the slickness that Jack's mouth left behind, and was unabashed at the greediness he felt, that he'd been fighting so hard to resist right up to this moment.

He wanted to demand *more* out loud, but his mouth wouldn't work except to make voiceless, gasping sounds into the pillow until he curved his chin low and pushed the pillowslip aside to take a deep, clear breath.

"Jack," he said, finally able to articulate it, but only that one word, Jack's name, a burst of a prayer, reflecting the desire that fused through his brain and raced down his spine and made his toes curl with aching.

"Yes?" asked Jack, his fingers pausing, his mouth moving across Oliver's skin, somewhere, back there, at a spot that Oliver couldn't identify.

"What you're doing—" began Oliver.

"Yes?" asked Jack again with a tremor in his voice that seemed to mean he was afraid, terribly afraid, that Oliver was about to say *no*, and that he would have to stop.

But the thought of him being afraid because Oliver had denied him anything, nearly broke Oliver's heart in two, for he could not have Jack disappointed in any way, in any *thing*, not when Oliver was so willing to give it to him.

"What you're doing," said Oliver again. "Could you do it more, only—" His whole body flushed, for he could not toss off years and years of diffident politeness in only an evening. "Could you do it *more*, and—" He stopped, wanting to put it in just such a way that Jack would know, just *know*—

"Push in hard?" Oliver said, managing finally. "Could you do that and not laugh at me?"

"Oh, *fuck*," said Jack, and all at once, his fingers pulled out of Oliver.

Oliver felt Jack sit back on his heels, and he could not imagine that he'd distressed Jack or made him disgusted, because that's not the way Jack was about what they shared between them in bed.

"What is it, Jack?" Oliver asked. He pushed up on his elbows to turn and steal a glimpse of Jack, his chest sweating, and his face red with passion, hair dark-curled and damp across his forehead, his cock curling hard against his belly, his hands in fists upon his naked thighs.

"I haven't any grease or butter or anythin'—fuckin', stupid— I'll have to go downstairs an' ask."

"No," said Oliver, his mind strangely clear, for some reason. "There is the balm on the washstand. It is quite gentle and smells of honey. It would do, wouldn't it?"

With a curved smile, Jack lavished several kisses on Oliver's cheek and scruffed Oliver's hair before leaping off the bed, quite naked, all aroused and in a hurry, and Oliver understood then what Jack had meant. That this intimacy between them might be serious or easy or hurried or rough or soft, just as they pleased, agreed upon between them, spoken or unspoken.

As Jack grabbed the tin and clambered back on the bed, the weight of him kneeling beside Oliver's hip, Oliver let himself tumble hilariously to one side, right into Jack's knees, and pretended to flail for the stability of the bedpost.

"Oh, no," he wailed with mock seriousness. "The bed is tilting, it is *tilting*."

"It is not, you wretch," said Jack, in the most loving of tones.

As Oliver heard the metal lid of the balm being taken off and tossed on the floor any old how, he lowered his head once more to rest on his forearm and sighed. His whole body felt relaxed, the calmness of the sweat drying on his skin heating up again as Jack's fingers traced the curve of one buttock, as if Jack were letting him know where he was and what he was about.

Oliver felt his skin shiver, the energy within going up his spine so quickly the shock of it startled him, made him gasp. As Jack pushed a single finger inside of him, now slick with a bit of balm, Oliver opened his mouth. He would like to beg for what he wanted, beg out loud and for as long as it took, until Jack's gentleness, so much appreciated, was replaced with something more earnest, more insistent. More *Jack*.

"Could you, Jack, just, *please*—my heart is racing with the wanting of it, of you."

"More, then?" asked Jack, and his voice cracked in a way that made it seem as if his heart were pounding with gladness, and Oliver's heart pounded along with it.

"Yes, *yes*," said Oliver, hissing between his teeth, for so animal a feeling should involve words that were bitten, and bodies that moved, and gleamed with sweat, lit by candlelight, by ancient firelight, and if Jack did not do as he'd been asked, this *instant*—

"Easy now, I'll give you what you ask for, with all my heart, I give it."

And this Jack did, with a sweep of his tongue between Oliver's buttocks and his fingers, two of them now, pushing into Oliver, slick with the balm. The feeling was easy and sliding, and Oliver forwent all inhibition, surged up with his hands, and pushed back with his knees, because he'd damned if he would permit Jack to take any longer than he already had, to wait any longer—and shivering like a colt new-born, he grit his teeth, and dipped his chin nearly to his chest.

"You must do it Jack, do it now, and quickly and so *hard*—" For his body wanted it, had raced right past anything to stop that wanting, and he felt the growl rise up from his chest, almost crying with the frustration of it. "*Please*, Jack."

Jack obliged him. With a quick twist of his wrist, he withdrew his fingers and, snugging close behind, bent his knees between Oliver's spread thighs. He clasped Oliver's hips, damp fingers digging into the bone, snubbed his cock just against Oliver's anus and paused there.

"Let out a breath, Nolly," Jack said, sounding quite breathless himself. "Just do it. It'll be easier. I'll go hard, I promise, but for this first breach, you must relax."

Obedient, feeling the trust for Jack deep inside of him in spite of his angry wanting, Oliver took a breath, held it for a moment, and then let it out slowly. For his reward, he felt Jack's cock pushing into him, slowly, with caution and care, spreading him wide, with warmth and heat and pressure. Then, with a final, quick jut of Jack's hips, Oliver felt the scratch of Jack's private hair against the soft skin at the crease beneath his buttocks, felt Jack's heart pulsing through Jack's cock, which was now inside of him, a part of him.

Jack was connected to him so closely, skin to skin, that as Oliver's heart beat, it was in time with Jack's heart. They were joined, somehow, beyond the physical touch of their flesh, in some deeper way, of heartbeats and souls and the sweetness of Jack's smile and, all at once, Oliver wanted to cry.

"You must be rough now," said Oliver, his voice coming out clogged, as though he'd been screaming in the dark for hours. "You promised, you *must*—"

"*Take* you," said Jack with kisses to Oliver's spine. "That is how you say it. That I will take you, just like this." At these words, Jack shifted his hips, and moved a little way further in, an invasion that felt rough and right all at the same time. "D'you understand me, Nolly?" Jack asked this, sounding quite stern.

"You belong to me now, from this day forward. You are mine. *Mine.*"

"Jack," said Oliver, though he wanted no more words, wanted all of his thoughts to be gone, and Jack the only one who could remove them and fling them away where they need never bother him again. "You know I'm yours as I ever was. That's what you told me and I've remembered it ever since. So do *you* understand? I remember it always."

He felt Jack nod, just once, and then heard him take a sharp breath as his hands curled around Oliver's hips. His thighs pressed close to the back of Oliver's thighs where the sweat of their skin came together in one long slick, and they slid against each other as Jack pushed in and Oliver pushed back, his teeth grit, feeling the hammer of his heart.

Then Jack moved inside of him and shifted back, his cock moving across some spot, a wickedly sensitive spot, that made Oliver gasp. His mouth fell open, his eyes wide, though he was blind to the gentle light of the candle upon the pillowslip, and only saw it as a vibration, where all things narrowed down to that one spot.

Which, it seemed, Jack already knew all about, as his cock, pulsing and red hot like a brand, moved across it, over and over, a raw, scraping feeling across this oversensitive place, which climbed up to the edge of pain after each stroke, only to vibrate and move throughout his entire body, a liquid pleasure that wanted to drown him.

He was so willing until he realized he was grunting out loud with each curl of Jack's hips, the bang of his thighs, the meeting of skin, hard, almost to the bone, in a way that changed everything, just as it should. He knew this, knew all of it, without a single word forming in his head.

There existed only the strong, driving center of him that spread outward, hands and fingers and Jack's touches reaching every part of him, all at once. Then Jack's whole body jerked, and Oliver felt it, just for a brief instant, the hot spray of Jack's spend inside of his body.

His mouth opened with the shock of it, the very carnal bluntness of it, and he had to stifle a gasp as Jack shoved his hips forward, and reached around to grasp Oliver's very hard cock with the rough whole of his palm.

"Come on, now, Nolly," said Jack, gasping, his chest heaving against Oliver's back. "Rut into my hand now, just like that, like *that*—"

At this command, so given by Jack from his deepest heart, Oliver obeyed. He moved his hips forward and then back, learning the stretch of muscle at this unaccustomed curl, and the harsh pleasure of it. He learned the scrape where the edges of his cock caught on Jack's fingers, and the brief frustration that moved into the most sublime surge along his entire body that buckled into one tight knot that, as he felt his eyes roll back in his head, transferred every energy, every thought, into one long sigh.

Then he realized his whole body was pulsing through his cock, and felt Jack's fingers spreading, spreading, until he collapsed from within, the sigh from his mouth inarticulate and desperate. He turned his head, seeking Jack, blind from it, until he felt Jack pull from him and lay down on the bed so Oliver could collapse on top of him, and their mouths could meet and kiss and blend in a hot, wet, desperate collection of nerves easing down, while the sweat cooled on their bodies, the back of Oliver's neck, the line of Jack's chest.

"Lord Jesus," said Jack, his exhaled breath sounding anything but pious.

As Oliver tried to catch his breath, he realized he was leaking out the fluid heat of Jack's semen upon the sheets, and that his own sweat was cooling in a rather unappealing way. He felt loose, as if he had no control. He clenched up, but that felt sore, and was of no use anyway, because he was as messy as a small child who had soiled himself and, in spite of everything Jack had taught him, was trying to teach him, that Oliver so wanted to learn, he felt his face flush.

"Say, now," said Jack, ever attentive, looking at him. "What's this, then?" He traced his fingers along the curve of Oliver's cheek. Oliver restrained himself from pulling away, for Jack was being kind, had been kind, and did not deserve Oliver's refusal.

"The sheets," said Oliver, only able to manage that as an explanation, though surely Jack *knew* what he meant.

And Jack did, for he kissed Oliver without teasing him, and planted several kisses to the top of Oliver's head, and curled his arm around Oliver's shoulder in a friendly way, casually, as if nothing were amiss.

"The sheets have seen it afore, you know," said Jack. "This bed has seen it. These walls. The world, even. For we are not the only ones doin' this, this very night. An' the sheets will wash, for in such a place as this, don't you know they have the very best laundress money can buy? As for stains, she's seen 'em all, I guarantee it."

This made Oliver feel a little better. He liked it even more when Jack reached down to take an edge of sheet to wipe the moisture from between Oliver's thighs and drew up the white sheet to cover Oliver's shoulders as he grew cool, even in the warm room.

Thus covered, Oliver found himself yawning hugely, his mouth moist, as if he had been drooling in his sleep. He used that motion to spread an open-mouthed kiss over Jack's chest, taking a swipe with his tongue over Jack's nipple, just to see what it might be like. Jack's skin twitched beneath Oliver's mouth.

"Why am I so tired, Jack?" asked Oliver, for his eyes were falling closed as hard as he struggled to keep them open.

"That's what happens when the fuckin' is good," said Jack. "So never you mind it, just fall asleep, an' I'll get the candle when I feel like it. Or not." He seemed to chuckle under his breath and followed Oliver's example, a yawn pushing up his chest.

Oliver rolled toward him to circle Jack's waist with his entire arm, to bury his face against Jack's shoulder. And realized, with the part of him even slightly capable of articulating even the merest thought, that he'd been on top of Jack, wholly on top of him, even if only for the briefest of moments, and Jack had not minded.

Which was good, because it meant that Oliver could, in time, erase the effects the marine had left behind, and chase away the shadows of Chalenheim's threats. All with his own body, the whole of his skin, and his kisses, both of which he would most liberally and frequently apply to wherever upon Jack's body he could reach.

"Sleep now, Nolly," said Jack with long, slow strokes along Oliver's arm. "Sleep now, for I love you so, an' will watch over you—"

But the words cut off as the darkness rolled over him. Oliver felt his neck relax and his whole body float off so no part of him seemed to be touching anything else, save for the soft rise and fall of Jack's chest beneath his cheek.

❧ 30 ❧

DESTINATION: HALE

Though the morning was chill, the skies thick and gray with promised rain, they sat at a table by the fire and, contented, ate their breakfasts. Jack shoveled in the porridge, thick with cream and butter, at the same time as he gnawed a bit of sausage from the end of his fork. Nolly had better manners than Jack, of course, and held his spoon in a more genteel fashion, and swallowed each bite before he took another, though he ate rather more briskly than he had before they'd gone into Axminster.

It was as if the workhouse had awakened Nolly's fear of being hungry, and for that, Jack could not blame him. He'd been hungry himself before, of course, but it was with the knowledge that he would be fed enough, in due time to ease his hunger. In the workhouse, it was ever more of the same, just enough to whet the appetite without enough to quench it. And that was the cruelest thing of all.

"So, to Hale by coach, today?" asked Jack, more to distract himself than he really wanted the details of the day's plan. "There's no rush, as we have not actually announced our arrival."

"Announced our arrival?" asked Nolly, licking the traces of

butter from his lips. He sounded as if he could not quite believe what Jack had just said, and indeed he eyed Jack somewhat askance before looking away, his dark brows quirking together as he examined the remains of his meal, as if contemplating asking for another serving. More toast, perhaps, or sausage.

"It's what folks do, right? Sendin' the message ahead that they will arrive on thus an' such a day? You talked about it, in Lyme."

"Folks do, I expect," said Nolly after a moment of consideration, as if wondering if there was more cream to be had for his breakfast.

He looked somewhat more serious than he had a moment ago. Jack wanted that expression gone and, in its place, the somewhat more dreamy one that told Jack that Nolly was thinking about the night before. Of the sweet intimacy they'd shared beneath the sheets. Of how Nolly had cried out in the night as the pleasure had taken him, taken his whole body, in a way for which Jack could praise himself for quite some time. And would do, if Nolly would but look at him and smile to let Jack know that he remembered what they'd shared between them as well.

But perhaps Nolly was distracted about the niceties of forewarned arrivals, and the need for paper and pen, or perhaps it was something else, and indeed, Jack suspected that because of the daylight coming and going through the windowpanes of the dining room, Nolly would not allow himself to remember.

Which was a shame because it had been so lovely the night before, the two of them together. And just as lovely that very morning, when Nolly had woken Jack with small, soft kisses anywhere he could reach, and who had made Jack, wholly in a state of nature, stand by the washbasin so Nolly could draw a cool, damp cloth over Jack's rashes and apply a sheen of balm before allowing Jack to get dressed. Jack had made sure the tin of balm was in his trouser pocket, and hoped that they would have need of it again.

"Nolly," said Jack, not quite sure how to voice this little worry of his.

"Yes, Jack?"

Nolly looked up at him, his spoon resting on the edge of the china bowl, in which almost nothing remained of his breakfast porridge.

At least Jack had Nolly's attention, though still he could not determine how to put it. Not merely because there were other customers, even at this early hour, eating their breakfasts, threaded throughout the dining hall, and most of those were seated near the fireplace as Nolly and Jack were, but that it might startle Nolly into a severe state of quiet that would be difficult for Jack to work his way through.

He could only shrug his shoulders and shake his head, feeling his forehead scrunch up, though he tried to soothe this out, as he didn't want Nolly to grow concerned, to think there was anything wrong. Because there wasn't. It was only just—

"You're wrigglin' a bit there," said Jack. "It's natural to be sore your first time, but if I rushed you. If I *hurt* you—"

"I am a bit sore," said Nolly, dipping his chin down and looking up at Jack through his eyelashes, a sweet smile on his ashen-rose mouth, a slight blush coming to his cheeks, his gaze focused on the near empty cream pitcher in the middle of the table. "And you didn't hurt me, but I am undone and over-whelmed, but not the least bit regretful. Rather, I am grateful. Is that too common a word, Jack? It might be, for what I'm feeling. Only you might not know what I'm feeling because I am, well, I am not as adept as you, saying such things, either aloud or in my own head, but I feel them, I truly do. About you, Jack."

Nolly looked up at him with a flicker of eyelashes and a small, shy smile that took Jack's breath away with such consider-able swiftness that it took him a full moment to get it back.

At this request, Jack could only nod, and restrained himself from leaping outright from his chair to take Nolly in his arms and press their bodies close together so Nolly would know how much, simply how much, Jack adored him.

For saying it the way Nolly did, with words, and with feelings beneath those words, and the way Nolly leaned toward him as he said it, made him want to do more than this public place would allow. Would that it could be more than this, a world where Jack could kiss Nolly and stroke his cheek and gently run his thumb across Nolly's mouth to make him smile, both with the kiss and with the teasing.

"Why, yes," said Jack, with a cough he was sure did not quite cover his rush of feeling, at least not from Nolly, who was looking at him quite intently. "I should like that, very much. So perhaps we should take another coach today, only so far, and no further, and sleep in another inn along the way. For we are in no rush to arrive at our destination, seeing as how we have not, as yet, sent notice of our imminent arrival?"

The words felt twisted as Jack tried it on, the mannerisms and speech of those folks who had enough money to spend, and enough time to concern themselves with such niceties, as frivolous as they might seem.

"No rush, indeed," said Nolly, as if he understood Jack exactly and agreed with him completely. "A day's journey will be enough, I should think, for me and thee. For I cannot bear the thought of you catching a chill in the coach, should you go overly long in it, what with all this dreadful rain."

"Dreadful rain," echoed Jack, as it was all he could manage to say, though his mouth quirked up in a smile that, had anybody been looking, might have signaled the lascivious thoughts he simply could not keep from running all the way through him.

"Yes, it is dreadful," said Nolly. He scraped up the last of his porridge with his spoon and stuck the spoon upside down in his mouth to suck every morsel of porridge from it. He looked at Jack the whole while, his eyebrows quirking up, as if daring Jack to say anything about it. "Simply dreadful."

Jack almost choked, but he swallowed it and washed it down with the tea that had gone lukewarm in the cup. But the tea, while no longer hot, was still sweet and smooth on his tongue, and he smiled back at Nolly as he put it down.

"Well," said Jack, trying to collect his wits. "We should also inquire after pen an' paper so we can write the notice that we're comin'. D'you reckon?"

"Surely," said Nolly. He put his spoon in his bowl and licked his finger to swipe some of the porridge from the bowl's rim into his mouth. Then he wiped his mouth with the cloth napkin that had been in his lap the whole time, where likewise Jack's napkin had remained untouched on the table. "But not today, I should think. Presently, perhaps, but not today."

To this notion, Jack heartily agreed, and he stood up and nodded because Sarah was coming with Nolly's blue suit jacket, all brushed and cleaned from the mud the day before. But though they were to be well on their way when the coach came in a day or so, and even though the sun was not actually shining, and the dreadful rain would not stop coming, Jack knew he would have his dearest heart's desire at his side forever and forever.

~

WOULD YOU LIKE TO READ MORE ABOUT THE ROMANCE between Oliver and Jack? Pick up *Out in the World* today! (https://readerlinks.com/l/2237629)

~

WOULD YOU LIKE TO READ A COWBOY ROMANCE? CHECK OUT *The Foreman and the Drifter*, the first book in my Farthingdale Ranch series. (https://readerlinks.com/l/1703675)

~

WOULD YOU LIKE TO READ A TIME TRAVEL ROMANCE? CHECK out *Heroes for Ghosts*, the first book in my Love Across Time series. (https://readerlinks.com/l/1568447)

JACKIE'S NEWSLETTER

Would you like to sign up for my newsletter?

Subscribers are alway the first to hear about my new books. You'll get behind the scenes information, sales and cover reveal updates, and giveaways.

As my gift for signing up, you will receive two short stories, one sweet, and one steamy!

It's completely free to sign up and you will never be spammed by me; you can opt out easily at any time.

To sign up, visit the following URL:

https://www.subscribepage.com/JackieNorthNewsletter

facebook.com/jackienorthMM
twitter.com/JackieNorthMM
pinterest.com/jackienorthauthor
bookbub.com/profile/jackie-north
amazon.com/author/jackienorth
goodreads.com/Jackie_North
instagram.com/jackienorth_author

AUTHOR'S NOTES ABOUT THE STORY

My obsession, since the age of seven or so, has been with workhouses and I'm not sure why. I mean, you wouldn't ever want to end up there, as workhouses are always, nearly always, nasty, dark, and grim. And damp. And they don't feed you very much. You get one thin blanket, and maybe a pillow if you're lucky. Any yard where you might get some fresh air is covered with cinders or gravel or simply dirt.

Well, all of this has to do with the novel *Oliver Twist* by Charles Dickens, which has to do with orphans and pickpockets and the gritty, grimy world of workhouses and the muddy streets of Victorian London.

My obsession stems from my early exposure to that story when I saw the musical *Oliver!* once, long ago. Since then I've seen pretty much every version of this story, which I'm not ashamed to admit.

Over the years, my obsession about Oliver Twist turned into my desire to write more about him and his little life, and, indeed, perhaps sad to say, I wanted to get him back inside of a workhouse to see what made him tick. Putting him back there would show me how he survived it the first time, and whether he learned anything along the way. And maybe I just wanted to torture him a little bit, because I had a feeling that he would come out on top, in spite of me.

So I started writing my Oliver & Jack series with an eye towards that workhouse experience. Even as I wrote the first two books in that series, I was picking out workhouses and determining the best (that is to say worst) series of events ever to befall a parish boy.

First up, location. At the end of book two in the Oliver & Jack series, Oliver and Jack were in Lyme Regis, which is a nice place to be. So I had them arrested and thrown into the nearest workhouse, which just so happened to be located in Axminster. Isn't that a great name? It's got such a sharp-edged ring to it, don't you think?

I studied everything I could about Axminster Workhouse (which used to exist, back in the day), trying to determine what it might look like at ground level.

I discovered that it was what was known as a "square plan" workhouse, designed by Sam Kempthorn, and was meant to hold around 300 paupers.

I also studied interior floor plans, and imagined the color and texture of all the rooms.

Do you see the rabbit hole I went down? I was so deep in the weeds of details that won't make any difference to the reader or their enjoyment of the story. But to me, it's this type of obsession that tells me I'm writing about the right kind of thing, and telling the story that moves me. Which hopefully means that it will move the reader as well.

A LETTER FROM JACKIE

Hello, Reader!

Thank you for reading *In Axminster Workhouse,* the third book in my Oliver & Jack series.

If you enjoyed the book, I would love it if you would let your friends know so they can experience the romance between Oliver and Jack.

If you leave a review, I'd love to read it! You can send the URL to: Jackienorthauthor@gmail.com

Jackie

facebook.com/jackienorthMM

twitter.com/JackieNorthMM

instagram.com/jackienorth_author

pinterest.com/jackienorthauthor

bookbub.com/profile/jackie-north

amazon.com/author/jackienorth

goodreads.com/Jackie_North

ABOUT THE AUTHOR

Jackie North has written since grade school and spent years absorbing mainstream romances. Her dream was to write full time and put her English degree to good use.

As fate would have it, she discovered m/m romance and decided that men falling in love with other men was exactly what she wanted to write about.

Her characters are a bit flawed and broken. Some find themselves on the edge of society, and others are lost. All of them deserve a happily ever after, and she makes sure they get it!

She likes long walks on the beach, the smell of lavender and rainstorms, and enjoys sleeping in on snowy mornings.

In her heart, there is peace to be found everywhere, but since in the real world this isn't always true, Jackie writes for love.

Connect with Jackie:

https://www.jackienorth.com/
jackie@jackienorth.com